DANGER TIMES TWO
AN I CHING MYSTERY

Mickey Friedman

DEDICATION

To Robin and Will and my friends at Fuel Great Barrington who provided the espresso and the table and company that helped to make *Danger* possible. And to Bob and Toni Friedman, Rabbit the dog, and Danger the parrot, who inspired me in unique ways. And, of course, to the *I Ching*.

EPIGRAM

"By growing used to what is dangerous, a man can easily allow it to become part of him. He is familiar with it and grows used to evil. With this he has lost the right way, and misfortune is the natural result.

"Here every step, forward or backward, leads into danger. Escape is out of the question ... disagreeable as it may be to remain in such a situation, we must wait until a way out shows itself ..."

"K'an," the *I Ching*.

CONTENTS

PREFACE

I'm the least likely person to have written *Danger Times Two*. Cynical about the New Age, often skeptical and occasionally sarcastic, my first experience with the *I Ching* came many years ago when my girlfriend, a devotee who consulted the oracle about almost everything, insisted as a test of my love that I join in. With a slight sneer, I asked my question: "Why should I consult the *I Ching?*" I threw the coins and got "Ch'ien / The Creative."

I was convinced by the second line: "These unbroken lines stand for the primal power, which is light-giving, active, strong, and of the spirit." In the throes of what the *I Ching* calls "youthful folly," I was sure the book was telling me I was one of the chosen, exempt from the need to ask the oracle anything more. One of my *Danger Times Two* characters, Theresa, felt the need to confess our earliest skepticism.

My girlfriend quickly found someone who appreciated the book and her many charms more than I had. But unbeknownst to me, the oracle had hooked me. Several years later I found myself imagining a story: a woman with amnesia, and another woman who knew the *I Ching* and helped her. I tried telling their story off and on for twenty years.

Then a few years ago, something clicked. I made a deal. Every time it was appropriate, I as the character would actually consult the *I Ching*: Katie or Sarah or Frank asking the question. And all of us bound to accept the answer. There was only one occasion when I was so stumped by the offering that I tried to cheat. I threw the coins again and while the new answer seemed more convenient, the guilt got to me. I returned to the original answer and we all made our peace with it.

So this is a collaboration. Credit the better parts to the extraordinary authors of the *I Ching*, who defying time and space, capture truths as compelling today as they were then. Blame the mistakes on me, for my continuing inabilities to see everything there is to be seen in the *I Ching*. And please know that even more than Katie, I can't abide the accepted way to do things. So in my stubbornness and ignorance I have probably violated just about every convention that dictates how to properly consult and interpret the *I Ching*. I never had a Dr. Chau of my own, so these errors and omissions are all mine.

I have been extremely fortunate to have known several versions of Katie: bright, beautiful, and more sensitive than I to the deeper truths that lie beyond the rational. But this Katie is mine. As for my renditions of Detroit, Little Pointe, Brett, and Ripton: these are almost entirely invented places, inhabited by a cast of characters who dwell only in my imagination. And so any resemblance to real persons, living or dead, is purely coincidental.

I have been at this for many years and my fictions about Frank and his unfortunate Officer Related Shooting predate the real life horrors of Ferguson, Missouri and Staten Island, New York, the tragic and unnecessary deaths of Michael Brown and Eric Garner. It is even more difficult today than it was yesterday to consider the complex and explosive intersections of crime and race and policing. And so today I can only wonder if I would have written any of this any differently.

Along my winding way, the *I Ching* has proven to be always relevant and constantly provocative, and my respect for the oracle is profound. The one thing that is still true for me all these years later is my belief the oracle appreciates the fact that, given my many limitations, I'm doing my best to access its primal power.

Thanks to Antonia Small for permission to use her dragon poem from her "The Song Cycle." And finally my indebtedness to my favorite rendition of the *I Ching:* Richard Wilhelm and Cary F. Baynes, translators, *The I Ching, or Book of Changes,* third edition. Princeton University Press, Princeton, New Jersey, © 1950, 1967 Bollingen Foundation. Reprinted by permission of Princeton University Press.

Mickey Friedman, December 2014

ONE

She stood there, watching and waving as Frank and Danger drove off. So very grateful, but still overwhelmed. So much, too much, had happened in the last few months.

"If I knew then what I know now," she thought but didn't say. So very sad, because if she had known, two men she hardly knew might still be alive. And she might not have killed one of them.

She sighed and Katie reached over and silently took her hand.

*   *   *

Katie woke the next morning, alone again. She hadn't slept well, but then she hadn't had a good night's sleep in a while. She slipped into yesterday's crumpled jeans, then into the navy blue long-sleeved t-shirt Ralph had left. She could smell horses, hay, and sweat all mixed with hints of his pine-scented underarm deodorant.

She threw some cold water on her face and quickly brushed her teeth, ignoring the tangled mess that was her curly red hair. Then headed downstairs, her fifth day without a shower.

Rabbit, her husky, opened a sleepy eye just long enough to see if she was OK, then went back to his nap on the kitchen floor. He was still waiting for his energy to return, still waiting for the dull ache in his flank to fade. At least everything was a lot quieter without the noisy bird and his constantly restless human.

As she prepared some chamomile tea, sourdough toast and jam, Katie was acutely aware of the grief that enveloped her. The adrenaline and bravado that had sustained her this last week and a half were gone, and in their place a thick, almost impenetrable fog of despair.

Again and again, the critic that dwelled in the deeper, darker recesses wanted to know why this great gift of hers had failed to keep them safe? Why saving one person had meant losing another? Almost losing Rabbit, her best, most faithful friend.

Because what she did to help people, what she imagined, intuited, interpreted was so often unquantifiable. Intimations. Dreams. What, after all, was a vision worth? She knew this was an old and fruitless argument but that didn't still the critical voice. Yes, she had sensed danger, but she hadn't seen clearly enough how and when and where this danger might come. Or distinguished between a danger that was material, not metaphorical; a danger that brought more than momentary discomfort or defeat.

She felt the sun sneak its way past the white lace kitchen curtains, wondering whether the light had been there these last few days? Or had it been as gray outside as it was inside? Ordinarily, she cherished these Berkshire mornings. As the warmth began to chase away the night's nip in the air, and New England's odd idea of summer began to assert itself: too cold, too hot, then too cold again.

The tea cup in one hand, the toast in another, she went over to the table and sat down, across from where they had been sitting that day, wondering whether she would ever be able to sit at this table without seeing blood? The three coins, the yellow pad, the pencil and the *I Ching* were right where they had left them.

She knew she was stuck. So preoccupied with what she hadn't seen coming, she hadn't yet made sense of what had actually come. She could remember the three of them throwing the *I Ching* the night before Frank left for the city, but could recall almost nothing about the reading. Mostly she had been lost in a thick mix of exhaustion and survivor's guilt.

"What did I miss?" she asked, taking the three Peruvian coins, her cupped hands trembling.

The coins came spilling out. Two heads and a tail.

She asked the question again, and threw two tails and a head. Then two heads and a tail. And the same again. Then two tails and a head. And, finally, two heads and a tail. She drew the lines of her two hexagrams:

In the back of her well-used yellow copy of the *I Ching*, she found the hexagram "K'an / The Abysmal (Water)." The top three lines the same as the bottom three. "K'an" two times, a doubling doubled. Katie started to nod, remembering the teaching:

> In man's world, K'an represents the heart, the soul
> locked up within the body, the principle of light
> inclosed in the dark … The name of the
> hexagram, because the hexagram is doubled, has
> the additional meaning, 'repetition of danger.'

Danger once, danger twice. She smiled for a moment: an *I Ching* joke? Peril and the name of Frank's parrot, Danger. Quickly recalling that not so long ago "K'an" had been the answer to a question about the boat. Trying to remember that session, Katie was pretty sure she had acknowledged the risk that "K'an" foretold. But still when the most important moment had come, she had missed Danger squawking danger. And ignored Rabbit's nudge.

If there truly were discernible patterns to a life, her relationship with risk had probably begun with the life her parents chose. Carl and Theresa's heartfelt dedication to aid others. The jungles of El Salvador, Guatemala. The death squads and the friends dead. Carl's violent end.

When her father Carl died, Theresa, her mother, carried on with the work. With and for the poorest of the poor, Theresa created primitive day care centers and organized small worker-owned food and craft cooperatives.

Light and dark. Theresa's courage and the cancer that killed her. And their children. Brother Frank became a cop, trying to stop a bit of the bleeding, catching killers in the city, robbers, muggers. Then his shooting. Now this. Not one of them exempt.

Katie had tried her best to carve out a life on the outskirts, in the ether, unraveling dreams and divinations, for herself and more recently for others.

The others: Katie hadn't ever found an adequate way to refer to those who came to her for help. "Patient" seemed too medical; "client" too cold, too clinical, too business-like.

And this last time, forever and inextricably linked. Suffering together and apart the tragic results of not knowing; of not seeing how profoundly danger had woven itself in and amongst the very fibers of their shared experience; and of underestimating the power and persistence of the dark.

It wasn't Katie's style to deflect blame. There was William Burroughs' quote staring down at her from the refrigerator door.

And it was impossible to ignore those words of his she had used all too carelessly: "In the magical universe, there are no coincidences and there are no accidents. Nothing happens unless someone wills it to happen."

She wanted to rip the Burroughs' postcard off the door, but couldn't. As difficult as her failure was to accept right now, it was, she knew, something she had to come to terms with.

She closed her eyes, reminding herself to breathe again, one slow breath followed by another, in and out until she could feel some of the tension in her shoulders slip away. Eyes back open.

And to be fair, she reminded herself, there was much within "K'an" that was positive. Like all the teachings of the oracle, black and white, yin and yang, female and male, winter and summer:

> Through repetition of danger we grow accustomed to it. Water sets the example for the right conduct ... It flows on and on, and merely fills up all the places which it flows; it does not shrink from any dangerous spot nor from any plunge ... Thus likewise, if one is sincere when confronted with difficulties, the heart can penetrate the meaning of the situation. And once we have gained inner mastery of a problem, it will come about naturally that the action we take will succeed.

She had agreed to help, trusting her instincts, acting with sincerity, relying upon her understanding of the *I Ching*. Achieving in many ways success. And yet it was such a costly success.

She got up to replenish her tea and made another piece of toast. The sun was growing stronger. She closed her eyes; her face bathed in light.

Katie could feel Carl and Theresa here with her in the kitchen. Smiling in much the same way they smiled at her when they were alive and she was a girl, and she interrupted them, insisting they look at her latest painting. Proud, encouraging.

Carl and Theresa, and now Frank, knew more than most about right conduct, sincerity, danger, and the true cost of success. Katie closed the book. She would do her best to do better.

TWO
FOUR MONTHS EARLIER

José recognized her and her BMW the moment she drove up to the terminal. She was hard to forget: so very pretty, about five feet ten inches tall with not the fake blond hair but real, and bright blue green eyes with energy, sparkling, that reminded him of the cats-eye marbles he would play with during the dusty days of his Mexican childhood. Her body was strong and lean, unlike the puffy bodies of many wealthy American women.

José had seen her and the beautiful car several times before at the big house. She had always been so generous to Juan, his younger brother, giving him the gardening job even though he had no references in the States. Spending many hours working hard, kneeling beside Juan in the dirt with her colorful flowers.

He could see how confused she was, thinking she could leave the car there. Luckily, it was one of those times when they weren't so crazy busy at the airport. He asked his buddy Carlo to take over for him at the curbside baggage check-in.

Wondering whether he should call her house. But as he came over to the driver's side, he thought maybe that was a mistake. Because even though she had used much powder, he could still see the very bad bruises. Her hands were shaking and it was a miracle that she had been able to drive the car. She was wearing her fancy clothes but they were slightly off like she had dressed in a big hurry. The diamond ring was gone from her hand. He felt someone had tried to hurt her very much. And he was very scared for her.

She still hadn't said a word. He saw that panicked look in her eyes. He and Juan had much experience with running. Both in Mexico, where the armed gangs, or sometimes the greedy police beat you and took your money, and here in the United States. The first time making it from Oaxaca all the way across the border, only to be caught, their money lost to crooked coyotes, then back home again to save and start over.

He knew she would soon be found if she ran without thinking. He did not know who she was running from. But he remembered that Juan had never liked the man. Cold like the house, he said. Maybe "timador." In English, maybe con man. Hustler.

José had always hated bullies. The bullies who used their

physical strength and made others afraid, and the ones who used their mouths and money, the ones who did dishonest deals. He couldn't imagine hitting a woman that hard. So without hesitating, he made her get out and move to the passenger seat, and quickly drove them to Parking Lot B.

Still looking like she was far away. He hoped she understood he was helping, not hurting, because she didn't struggle; she didn't scream. She hadn't said a word and maybe he told her too many things too quickly.

"They can track your car. They can track your cards of credit. No planes. The bus. Many buses. Many cities. Más importante: no police and no hospitals who will call the police. Most important!" He reached for his wallet, for his cash, but she put her hand over his to stop him, and shook her head.

"Your purse, please," he asked. "I will take your cards and I will cut them up. You may not remember me, but I am Juan's brother. The one who takes care of your lawn and your flowers."

And she nodded, although José wasn't quite sure whether she understood what he was really saying. Then she reached in her bag and handed him her smaller black handbag. He quickly took the purse, moved aside several packs of hundred dollar bills, and took only what he thought could identify her. And her phone. He quickly wiped the steering wheel with his handkerchief.

"I will take you to the SMART bus, which takes you to the city." He kept talking as they walked. "On Howard Street, the big bus station. Ask for the buses. Your hair, change maybe to dark. Please take the first bus that goes far, far away. Many buses. Until you are safe. I am José Castillo. Thank you for your kindness to my brother. I wish I could help more but I have to work otherwise they will lose my job. This is the bus. Vaya con Dios, Señora."

*   *   *

She used the bottle she had just bought at the drugstore to turn her hair from blond to black. Sticking her head under the hand-dryer. Wiping the sink clean with paper towels from the dispenser. Checking again the bathroom mirror of the bus station, she saw the dark bruises on her face, and to hide them applied more powder until she looked almost like a ghost. Then went back out to the terminal.

She couldn't remember ever being in a place like this. So many people: mostly tired, mostly sad. The heavy women with several children tugging at them, shouting, crying. Men who stared at the floor, or into space, the random grumbles. So much noise, so many words she couldn't understand. Her head throbbing.

Had she always been this confused? Nervously pacing as different people knocked into her, rushing toward the little window as the ceiling announced: "The bus to Cleveland will be leaving in twenty minutes." Which somehow seemed a sign.

So she moved to the end of the line. While moments later, several older, slower folks crowded in behind her. She watched as one by one the people before her approached the window, giving money to the man behind the plastic. Then, offering money from her handbag, she too nodded when asked "Cleveland?"

Outside, she handed her ticket to the driver, and quickly found an empty seat in the back of the bus. Clutching her overnight bag and handbag to her chest, she placed her head against the window, and as the pain and exhaustion came, wave after wave, somehow she slept.

*   *   *

The process repeated itself. That voice reminding her: many buses. Cleveland to Des Moines; Des Moines to Pittsburgh; Pittsburgh to Washington; Washington to New York; New York to Hartford; and Hartford to Springfield. Hours, so many hours in these buses. By the time she made it to Springfield, Massachusetts, the pain in her head had moved to her shoulders and back.

More than anything, she was sick of the unrelenting sameness of the road, the dingy terminals, their dreadful rest rooms reeking of disinfectant, the ever-shifting array of unwashed seatmates, crying kids, the constant lack of space. Then on line for the Springfield to Albany bus, she heard an old man say "One for Brett," and she knew it was time to stop. Why not stop in Brett?

*   *   *

On the buses, she loved to sleep. She could sleep through the night and halfway into the day: a deep sleep, a hibernation. But that first night in Brett, sleep and her dreams brought no rest.

Everything was new in this place. A few blocks from the drug store where the bus let them out, and the place the old guy kindly drove her to when she stood there completely stuck. The second house on the left side of Oak Street, its yellow sign with black letters, "The Fosters: A Berkshire Bed & Breakfast" with Bea Foster who rented out rooms by the night, the week, the month, and sometimes even by the year.

Bea would remind her, and anybody else she could get to hear the story: "It could have been snowing that night, late April. It had the night before and it did the night after, four inches, then six, and there she was, mind you, 'the Lady' I called her, such a pretty woman, knocking on my door dressed for dinner with fancy folks.

"All she said was 'no hospital, no police,'" Bea continued. "Of course, she had tried to cover those terrible black and blue marks with lots of powder, but with my family history I know something about bruises. Being knocked about like my sister Enid. And let me tell you, the hospital called the police and the police never believed Enid. And Jim beat her some more. So I understood. Oh, and that bad dye job.

"She couldn't or wouldn't tell me her name or where she came from, or why she was here. Said she didn't know. No car, but considering the time she arrived, I figured she came in on the Springfield bus. She could have been a criminal but, you know, Enid was always a bit off, so I took a big chance and let her in.

"Her black wool coat probably cost more than I've spent on clothes in several years. But it was real dirty and stained. Ruined, if you ask me. She had this beautiful big silk scarf, dark blue, but the worse for wear the way she let it get crumpled, completely useless against the cold.

"And she had this soft black leather handbag with a little silver padlock, matching her snazzy overnight bag which she held onto like her life depended on it. Partial to black, with these low-heeled Italian pumps with a fancy bow and silver buckle. Ferragamo, it said on the inside, but you can tell they weren't made for whatever she did with them, because they were scuffed something terrible. The next morning, we threw most of that stuff out and I took her to the Outlet Village to buy some decent Brett clothes: jeans, sweaters, sweatshirts, sneakers, so she could be comfortable."

They were an odd pair, walking slowly from The Banana Republic to The Gap. Bea just about came up to the Lady's shoulder, and was twice as wide. She had an extensive collection of wraparound print dresses, each oddly similar yet just a slight bit different. There were various shades of pink and purple, blue and green. Each with large numbers of flowers, or birds, rolling pins, puppies or penguins barely containing her. This day she wore sunnyside yellow with its old postcards of the pyramids.

Bea's wide face was quick to frown, but even quicker to smile, and her always active coal black eyes seemed bigger, brighter, like pea coat buttons set against her very pale skin.

Unfortunately, Bea paid a price for her pallor and in a flash could turn red with embarrassment, or more permanently if she forgot her wide-brimmed hat, after just a few minutes in the sun. She used her orangey perfume much like she used her colorful muumuus: to amplify her presence in this often shaky world. To loudly announce to God that in spite of sixty tough years she still wasn't ready to surrender.

Bea loved to laugh but you could see in those big black eyes that she had endured more than her fair share of emotional wear and tear, of angst and anguish.

Back at Bea's, an hour later, with several shopping bags to unpack, her lodger seemed shrouded in sadness. For her, not knowing was the hardest part: not knowing why she was there with Bea or what she was supposed to be doing. Only softly sensing that something critically important was missing. But then growing tired again, so very weary. No name. No past.

She had found in the pouches of the overnight bag, in every pocket of her coat, and in her handbag, besides some make-up and a mostly empty bottle of Clairol Black, thick stacks of crisp new hundred dollar bills.

Which had come in handy and made this odd journey possible. All she had to do was hold out a bill. One did it most of the time. And she almost always got a lot of change. Then she could relax for a moment and smile.

She knew she had this smile because she had occasionally seen it in the reflection of the bus windows, or in the mirror in the morning. She thought that this was a hard-earned smile, coming from far away. She sometimes thought that this was a very pretty face, because of the way men always looked at her, though it seemed sad and worried to her.

The eyes reminded her of that magazine photo in Bea's upstairs bathroom, of the big bear standing in the zoo, with the forlorn brown eyes. Although her eyes weren't anything like brown, sometimes ocean green, sometimes sky blue, sometimes both. But the hair was a still a big mess. Hair, which Bea assured her, wasn't really her own anymore but could easily be fixed.

THREE

Peter Bishop was one of those guys who looked completely comfortable wearing the most expensive clothes. As if they were the natural extension of his skin. As nonchalant in his fifteen hundred dollar grey Armani suit as a local carpenter in his forty-dollar jeans. An inch under six feet, and slim with thick black hair, he reminded people of a younger, early forties, less-wired version of Peter Gallagher, that handsome television actor who used to be the father in the "O.C." and was now a CIA bigwig on "Covert Affairs."

Peter had spent the morning meeting with an expensive downtown real estate attorney he knew from poker at Arthur's. And the rest of the day at the MGM Grand Detroit in full view of several surveillance cameras watching sports at the bar. But he hardly noticed who won and who lost; worried that his brother Donnie would mess up.

He waited until after dinner to leave. The rough stuff was Donnie's department. Gambling, strategizing, convincing, maybe conniving, that was where he was best. And he knew he had a lot of that coming up.

The security gate closed behind him. He drove up the driveway and swung around to the front of his house to discover the first surprise of the evening: her car wasn't where she always parked it.

It wasn't like a lot of what Donnie did ever made sense, but they had gone over everything a dozen times. And they hadn't ever talked about Donnie taking her car.

The plan was for Donnie to park a block or so away, get there at least an hour before her, and be waiting inside. Peter knew that the Mexican had the day off, and that she wanted to get an early start on redesigning her gardens. He figured she'd do her usual ten-thirty to eleven-thirty at the exercise center at the country club, and would probably be back by noon

Now he would have to improvise and work the missing BMW into the robbery story. He certainly wouldn't have to lie about why the security system hadn't gone off, because everybody knew ninety-nine times out of a hundred she forgot to arm it when she left. Every time he reminded her, she made a point of telling him how annoying it was to have to punch the stupid passwords into

11

those little boxes just to get in and out of her own house. To hear the shrieking alarm when she made a mistake.

Peter went in to find the body. Though he would never admit it, he hated the house almost as much as she did. No soul or softness to it. Cold stone everywhere. Nowhere to relax. Its one advantage: it was bought and paid for, a gift from her mother. Who knew everything about cold. And it had quickly become the perfect way to make sure her wish to live in the lake house would never come true.

He saw blood on several of the marble steps, but didn't see her. He carefully made his way past the blood, wondering how the hell she had managed to make it back upstairs. Already rehearsing his call to the police.

He checked the second floor bedrooms and the large bathroom but still couldn't find her. He stopped to regroup, realizing he hadn't seen blood on the upper steps. And that he was much more nervous than he imagined he'd be. She had probably stumbled downstairs to the study, or the bathroom.

He made his way back down. There were traces of blood on the tile floor of the downstairs bathroom, though someone had managed to wipe most of it away with the several bloodstained towels he found stuffed into the hamper. And beneath them, at the bottom of the hamper, her crumpled peach colored blouse and black slacks stiff with her dark-stained blood.

He was trying to remember how many times he had told Donnie it had to look like a robbery gone cruel, and how they had to have the body waiting there for him to find. There, for the police, when they answered his call. The dead body he'd need to inherit all this as quickly as possible.

Wondering what could have happened? Wondering why Donnie would have taken the body with him? Or why the towels and her clothes were there? And her car gone? Realizing, of course, that everything had changed. No body, no phone call, no police, no land to develop, no money for Arthur. Not yet.

*   *   *

Donnie didn't understand why his brother was yelling. She had been there, lying there dead on the stairs. He hadn't touched the towels. And afterwards, he saw her car right there in front of the house. He had walked past it on his way out the gate.

The disappointment he was used to. Everyone knew that Petey was the smart one, the smartest one in the neighborhood. So smart and so successful that for most everyone else in the world he had turned into Peter. But because he was the stupid brother, whatever the mistake was, it had to be his fault. Still, he hated to hear the panic in Petey's voice.

He was still a bit foggy. Probably it was the ecstasy from the night before with Betsy. Maybe what was left of the ecstasy had affected his concentration. Made him soft. Though the extra coke in the morning should have taken care of that.

He remembered smashing her with the gun. He remembered her crumpling when he hit her, like one of those old-fashioned dolls, with a boom, banging her head on those marble stairs. That loud smack. So yeah, he hit her real hard, even with the gloves Petey insisted he wear so he wouldn't leave fingerprints. He could see a shit-load of blood. And she sure looked dead to him. Lying there completely still when he remembered to pull the diamond ring from her finger. Which took some time because it was on so tight.

So maybe once wasn't enough. He had thought about hitting her again. But she really hadn't moved at all. And it wasn't as easy as he thought. As easy as Petey had made it sound. A sweet face. So different from the usual morons he had beaten. There was that moment on the steps when he saw their boat, saw himself on it, and she was there, too, and the sun was out and she was smiling.

So yeah, he probably should have hit her again. But then he was hearing Petey in his mind: "Do the job quick and split. I can't have you getting caught." Taking care of people for Arthur and Little Francis, no one ever mentioned time. But today he knew he had to hurry. Petey must have said "Do it and split" a dozen times. Which is exactly what he did, leaving the house hours ago.

But somehow now Petey couldn't find her. Which made no sense. He tried to explain about the ecstasy but that just pissed Petey off even more.

"I'm going to need you to make this right, Donnie."

"I promise, Petey!"

*   *   *

15

If you looked very closely at the noses, the set of their jaws, and disregarded the way they dressed and held themselves, you could tell they were brothers. Even though Peter was dark-haired, perfectly manicured, and his teeth were professionally white, while Donnie had sandy hair and was a total slob.

When it came to brains, Peter was both street shrewd and book smart. As for Donnie, most everyone agreed with Sister Margaret, his third grade teacher. Having lost all patience with Donnie's inability to remember that it was the good Catholic Christopher Columbus who in 1492 sailed the ocean blue, Sister Margaret loudly announced to the entire class that he was "as dumb as the Detroit winter was dark."

Homework was only one of the many things Donnie managed to neglect. In the first years their mom was gone, his brother had bought Donnie's clothes, but these days almost none of his clothes fit. Not that Donnie noticed or cared. Peter shopped at the most fashionable men's stores, and for sixty dollars a pop had his hair trimmed every two weeks by Maurice. Donnie bought his jeans and shirts and socks and underwear on sale at whichever discount store he was closest to, without ever trying anything on. And every four months Donnie had Ken chop his hair off for twelve bucks and a three dollar tip.

Donnie was a big guy, not so much big as in tall, two inches shorter than Peter, but big as in wide, running back thick, thanks to years of body building.

As far as he knew, Donnie had never, ever lied to him, and Peter tended always to give him the benefit of the doubt. Believing once more that Donnie really, truly thought he had done the job.

So how, both brothers were wondering, had she managed to make it out of the house. And how, after that blow to the head, was she able to drive her car away and disappear?

So near and so far. From all the years he had spent at the poker table, he knew the cards were always what the cards were. If she was alive and gone, then she, too, had managed to pull a last ace on him and win the hand. For the moment, at least.

It was hard not to obsess about all the years he spent on this, the transformation from Petey to Peter, and the long haul from his dirty Detroit streets to Lakewood Drive. All that time in the local library, the books, school, the university. And yet, now that he had tried to have her killed, it was weird to remember that he was quite fond of her. Maybe, sometimes, even loved her. Of course, he would have loved her more if she had had different parents. If he could have given up the hate that drove him. But then he would still be Petey. And he would never have done all that Peter did to make possible this life with her.

If she was dead, somehow Donnie had to find her dead body. If she was alive, somehow Donnie had to kill her. Again, but better this time.

*   *   *

Then, when Rebecca Sylvan called later that night looking for her, Peter remembered how often they had talked at the club about their dream vacations. He found himself telling Becca that he had been able to swing a great deal at the very last minute for a first-class ticket to Delhi. The vacation Becca and all of her friends from yoga and stretch and spinning classes had heard her fantasize about: a glorious six month's worth of India, Nepal, Thailand, Vietnam and Cambodia, of beaches, temples, and backpacking to out-of-the-way villages, with no cell phone, no laptop, no email, no worries.

Becca was soon commiserating with him as he explained how some last minute consulting work had kept him home, but there was no way he'd keep her from her dream trip. With any luck, he'd finish his work early and catch up with her on the beach at Kovalum.

FOUR

"Will, my man," Donnie called out as he shut the door behind him. "What's up?"

"Will" was the only way anyone ever referred to Theodore William Scott. He ran Downtown Taxi in Detroit, one of Arthur's several operations. Will seemed to work a twelve-hour day, seven days a week. Except for the third week in October when he went with Arthur to the casino in the Bahamas to drink, whore, and gamble.

He had several girls answering the phones. But because his taxi cabs were busy delivering hookers, coke, heroin, speed, oxy and ecstasy to Arthur's many customers, they would only occasionally pick up real passengers.

Will was one of those exceptionally rare guys. No matter how much he ate or drank, or how little he exercised, Will never seemed to change with the years. Five feet six inches, he was rail thin, with not an ounce of excess fat. He had slightly drooping, unevenly set eyes, and always managed to have the same exact quarter-inch black-grey stubble. He'd hardly acknowledge your presence, and most times wouldn't answer your questions, offering instead an almost inaudible, noncommittal clearing of the throat. Most often he seemed sleepy. But that was deceptive.

Years ago, Petey, who was always reading and learning about things, said if you took Will and laid him flat on the floor, he looked just like a weasel. And once, a few years back, Donnie saw some crazy guy try to stiff Will two hundred bucks for an eighth of coke. Will went from looking half-dead to leaping over the counter. In a heartbeat, Will had a small gun pressed against the guy's ear.

"Weasels," Petey said. "They may look pathetic but they're smart, and they're killers."

Donnie put six hundreds on the counter. "I've got a little problem, Will. I'm going fucking nuts. I lost someone." Showing Will a slightly crumpled copy of a photo of a beautiful, exceptionally well-dressed blonde in her late-thirties receiving an award, a small slightly nervous smile on her face.

"Odds are she never made it from Little Pointe to downtown, but I'm trying to cover my bases. She drives a brand new silver BMW. The plate number's on the bottom of the photo. If you

16

could show it to the drivers and ask them to keep an eye out for her and the car that would be great."

Will, who had started his street life dealing Three Card Monte, made the hundreds disappear in a blink. "Humph," taking the photo to the copier. And picking his teeth as the copier spit out forty copies.

With another "humph" and a nod, which Donnie knew from experience meant Will would do his best.

Will was already back at his paperwork, and Donnie shut the door behind him.

He had said "fucking" again. At least Petey hadn't heard. Must have been a hundred times Petey had told him: "You can't keep saying 'fucking this' and 'fucking that.' Do me a favor, Donnie, at least try 'eff-ing?' For years I've been trying to teach you how to talk to normal people, and normal people hate the word 'fucking.' A guy like you can easily slide by with 'eff-ing.'"

As he walked away from Downtown Taxi, he was thinking that the real eff-ing problem here was that nobody he knew, except for Petey, even knew the kinds of rich people she hung out with. And so it was going to be eff-ing hard for him to track her down. But he would keep at it, because he knew he had fucked up big time. Thinking "eff-ing" was one thing, but "eff-ed" up sounded completely lame.

He felt real bad about letting Petey down. Petey had always looked after him. Even when he changed his name to Peter and went all-fancy on him, when he stopped working out, and took off to that big school and started talking all weird and correcting the way he talked. He would always owe his brother.

So he spread some more money around town. First, checking the hospitals. Then, he gave Dan Shine a grand to do a tour of Detroit's best places. Having been a detective downtown until the booze got him fired, Dan always needed money. But because he had a couple of good suits, his old contacts, and that cop air about him, people still answered his questions.

Dan spent time showing her picture at the hotels, to the doormen, the guys at the front desks, to the bellboys, and housekeeping staff. Anyone who might have seen her or heard anything about her. But he didn't learn a thing.

Then Dan drove out to her country club but no one had seen her the last few days. He told Donnie that everyone told him the same story: they had just heard from Rebecca Sylvan that she was finally taking that vacation she was always fantasizing about, traveling somewhere in India or maybe Thailand, they thought.

*   *   *

Peter's mind was racing. They still hadn't found her; and he hadn't heard a word from the cops or hospitals. If she was alive, he wasn't really a widower. And if she had crawled off to die somewhere else, until they found the body, it would be impossible to collect on the insurance policy or gain control of the estate, the vast land holdings of his dearly departed father-in-law.

He could remember spending an entire lunch with them at the country club listening to the old guy bullshitting about what he called the staggering loss of open space to development, the need to preserve the land, and the responsibility of the privileged to give back. Adding that as he faced his own mortality, he was beginning to understand how much it might mean to leave a legacy.

They had more land than you could imagine. But Peter cared most about the prime acres on Potter Road, the land bordering the lake. The land the family had owned for generations. The land he could get rich with. The same land he had trespassed upon, on the night that changed his life. The land he hated.

He had spent a year fine-tuning his plan. Ten luxury units on one-acre parcels. A gated, green community. Their own private dock. A shared park with a playground. With solar this and solar that. All he needed was the land, and, unfortunately, he now needed it a lot sooner than later. What before had been a dream to make a bundle, was now the only way out of his life-and-death mess. The only way to pay his debt and get Arthur off his back.

At least, he hadn't made the same mistake as his father. He was still here, still breathing, still in the game. And yet he had made a different mistake. He had lost at poker the honest way. And lost big.

He had been playing at Arthur's for more than fifteen years. He was a big enough winner to keep his father-in-law unsuspecting all these years; enough of a winner to keep his wife unworried and the bank account flush. And he had stashed a bunch of cash along the way. Unlike his father, he won because he used his mind, because he played the odds while others played a hunch.

Unfortunately, the night he lost was the night he broke his own rule, the night he chose to play with someone else's money. He had been reading the securities trader for hours. He had figured out when the guy was comfortable and when he was worried; when he had confidence in the cards and when he was just hoping he looked confident. Had he played too long? Maybe it was too late; maybe he was just too tired? Draw poker: his two pairs, kings and queens looked good.

When he raised twenty grand, the securities trader paused a little too long but stayed in. Then Peter ditched an eight and drew his third king. Maybe his kings full with queens looked too pretty. The guy took three cards, Peter accepting the fact he could have aces paired. But he was pretty sure Seymour across the table had just reluctantly folded an ace and maybe sixes or sevens.

The guy shuffled his cards. And this time when Peter bet everything he had, the securities trader did what he did all that night when he was faking: the eyes closed for just a millisecond. The tell. And then the guy raised him half a million with just a bit too much determination. Of course, there was the slight chance the guy had pulled the better boat, but based on what he saw in the guy's face, Peter felt especially good. Convinced he was reading him right. Any other time he would have known that as good as his boat looked, as good as his read, it just wasn't worth the gamble.

He had never welched. All it took was a look over to Arthur, and Arthur signaled the dealer who passed five hundred grand worth of chips over to him. And in it went.

Later, he asked the guy why he was so worried going in with the aces boat with the deuces. The winning hand. The hand that Peter lost a half mil on. The guy seemed a bit confused.

"There was always the very slim chance you had four of a kind or a straight flush, but that wasn't it. The truth is I wasn't thinking about your hand at all. Never really gave it a thought. I work for Lehman Brothers. How much do you know about sub-prime mortgages? One second I'm sitting here playing cards and all of a sudden it dawns on me that when I head into work this morning, I'm going to have to deal with the fact that I've lost my clients close to seventy-eight million … And that's a shitload more scary than your hand. I figured I'm already dead."

Now all Peter could think about was where the hell she had gone to? And would they find her in time?

FIVE

She sat on the front steps to Bea's porch and watched the clouds make a slow trek across the sky. Clouds were everywhere about her this morning, inside and out. Then her face fell down from the sky and she saw a delivery truck, moving slowly enough in traffic that she could hold in her mind the name she saw painted on its side panel.

"Sara," it said. "Sara Baker." "Sara" which she liked almost as much as "Pastry and Pie." A piece of cake, she thought to herself. Not quite sure why a smile was spreading across her face.

"You can call me Sara," she told Bea Foster a little later in the day. Adding "Baker" as an afterthought. About time, Bea thought. And that afternoon, when Bea left a note for her, she had added an "h." Fine, she thought: Bea probably knows best.

Cautiously, Sarah explored this place. Brett, Massachusetts, 01239, population 1,922, with its one big main road, which made it easy to navigate, and the many small streets jutting out on each side. Every day, a lot of walking, a lot of clouds in the sky above. Her favorite building was the Brett Free Library, up Main Street, sturdy but not scary. She could see it humming and watched the people enter; sometimes the schoolchildren hand in hand.

But she wasn't ready to go in. Imagining a counter, a question, an explanation required. For now, it was enough to sit on the bench outside. She tried to walk past it at least once a day before heading home.

Bea Foster's wasn't easy at suppertime: the young man, the old man, and Bea Foster, not only eating but talking. Mostly about the mill.

Some of the mill windows were broken, boarded up, but that didn't seem to stop the work. The young man worked the night shift several hours after supper. He didn't like the mill all that much but said again and again he was grateful for the work. The old man, Bea's slightly bent and grizzled father-in-law, talked about the mill of days gone by, his days, when there were three shifts not two, morning, late afternoon, and overnight, and close to two hundred worked there, and how he lost his youth and the tips of two fingers. Somehow complaining and bragging all at the same time.

The mill sat beside the gray river with the sign nailed to a nearby tree: a thick black line slashing diagonally through the image of a fish on a plate. "PCBs," the old man had explained, talking about when his father not only fished the river, but ate the river's fish and swam in it. The chemicals came from the GE. Upstream. From the General Electric transformer plant in Plattsford. "Nowadays, you eat the fish, you eat the PCBs. Cancer, they say. And the truth is I lost a bunch of friends to cancer. Who worked up there or lived near the plant."

The old man had put in fifty years and had fifty years of stories. But sooner rather than later, Bea Foster would end the conversation: "The mill, doesn't anybody talk about anything besides the mill? All Mr. Foster would talk about was the mill. I miss him sometimes, but I sure am glad he's not here to talk about the damn mill anymore."

The old man grunted. Sarah had nothing to say. Then she went to bed.

The next day, Bea took her to the bank to meet Carolyn, her best friend ever since grade school, the branch manager now. Saying Sarah, a second cousin on her mother's side, had lost her purse, her ID, and Carolyn, shaking her head at Bea as she had so many times before, opened an account for Sarah Baker with sixty of her hundred dollar bills, checking each one of them extra carefully, even though she knew from experience that Bea's instincts were pretty good.

Then Carolyn set up a safety deposit box for her, which Sarah used for most of the cash, and issued one of those plastic debit cards she could use instead of money. Bea celebrated by taking Sarah to Hair Haven to fix her nails and hair.

*   *   *

Brett had one of almost every fast food restaurant known to man. And maybe in reaction, Sarah was drawn to Dom's, the antithesis of Chicken City. Sometimes she'd stand so close to the door that people actually thought she was heading in, and they'd hold the door open for her. But she wasn't ready.

Dom's sits next to the mill, one of the cheapest yet best places to eat in Brett, a throwback to the days of the roadside diner. Joe Montano still cooks the homemade meals his father Dom taught him, each day two or three hot specials. And for eight dollars, Joe will give you a real turkey dinner with homemade mashed potatoes and stuffing, a small salad, two buttered slices of Vienna, and some halfway decent coffee. And no one ever wears a tie.

Dom's has seven tables and a counter with twelve stools, and if you try and eat at the usual mealtimes you often have to wait, which is why Dom himself early on decided to stay open twenty-four hours a day. And for thirty years Dom's never closed except for Christmas.

Brett has always been a rough and tumble working-class town, but with the cutbacks at the mill and the closing of the papermaking machine shop out on the highway, there's been less work, less money, more drinking and drugs, and more carousing. Finally, two years ago, Joe got so tired of throwing rowdy customers out the door every Saturday night, he decided to close from 6 PM Saturday till 6 AM Monday. His much appreciated day and a half of peace and quiet.

Sarah hoped she'd soon be feeling strong enough to go in and have breakfast.

SIX

Ralph was snoring gently. Katie thought about trying to roll him over onto his side, but before she knew it, she slipped from awake and slightly annoyed to asleep and dreaming.

She was inside a house she didn't recognize, looking back at the heavy, dark wooden door that had closed behind her. Moving in from the entryway, she turned and took a couple of steps to her right. There was a large window. She could see a garden, lush and green, several tall oak trees, a stone bench, and a fountain, water up into the air and splashing back down. There was a single squirrel scampering across the grounds. And she found herself wishing she could be that squirrel, outdoors and free.

She wasn't sure how she had gotten there, or what she was supposed to be doing. Only that she felt stuck, caught in an almost paralytic indecision. For a moment, her curiosity overcame her discomfort. So she turned and took a few more cautious steps inside.

She was in a grand room of stone, with a high cathedral-like ceiling. Remembering the Cloisters, the medieval museum Carl and Theresa had often taken them to on weekends, over the bridge from The Bronx into Manhattan, a trip back in time.

Somewhere, from further within, she heard what sounded like a man cursing, but couldn't see anyone. Uneasy, she moved back to the entryway. Prepared now to try and open the front door.

But she woke, heart pounding, eyes opening to the wood beams of her own bedroom. It was five-thirty in the morning. Even as the dream faded, she felt it mattered. A message? She could smell Rabbit, his thick fur suffused with the smoke of seasoned oak from the downstairs woodstove. All Siberian husky and half-human, he was there at the foot of the bed, staring into her eyes, worried. Ralph's soft but steady snores sounded like the tide.

She carefully eased herself out of bed, grabbed some clothes, and tiptoed out of the bedroom and downstairs, Rabbit a few steps behind.

Like old times, she and Rabbit in the early morning. She put some dry food in his dish, a bit of olive oil, and cracked an egg over it all. Then grabbed a homemade blueberry muffin for herself. A few minutes later, Rabbit licked the last of his breakfast from his lips. Rabbit knew all about Katie's nightmares, and hoping to help, slowly moved against her thigh, lifting his head slightly.

She scratched behind his ears, a smile spreading across his face.

Katie left a note for Ralph on the kitchen table: "Bad dreams, couldn't go back to sleep. I'm off to do some work at the bookstore."

*   *   *

In small towns, information spreads like the flu. Instead of coughs and sneezes, a word here, a whisper there, and it didn't take long before almost all of Ripton's six hundred and forty-two residents had learned that Katie Greenberg, that slightly odd woman with the red hair that goes every which way, the one who bought the old Leavitt place several years ago, who never wears a dress, well she has a certain kind of spooky insight and a strange book and some foreign coins.

For Katie, ever since that night many years ago when she was a girl, dreams were never just dreams. The night she saw a jungle and a small church and, most of all, the gunfire and the women and children screaming, trying to run. Sweating and trembling, waking Frank up at midnight: "I dreamt of Uncle Ignacio. I saw men and guns everywhere, and people falling. And then Ignacio lying still in the church, not moving."

"It's just a bad dream, Katie," Frank managed through several deep layers of sleepiness. "Theresa is waitressing at a wedding. A nightmare. Go back to sleep."

A couple of weeks later they learned that Carl, because he was expected the next morning in San Sebastian, an eight-hour drive on dreadful Guatemalan roads, had left the meeting an hour before the gunfire. But Ignacio, who Katie and Frank had met when he crashed on their couch during a trip to New York to raise money for his coffee cooperative, was trapped and died inside the church with his wife, Luisa, the sympathetic priest, and twenty other poor coffee growers. Carl later told them that the church had been raided by Army officers dressed in civilian clothes. They had blocked the exits and started shooting. Those who survived had thrown themselves out of windows and miraculously escaped into the jungle.

Frank, too, was used to nightmares. His dreams were almost

always bad dreams. He had been exhausted that night and had forgotten Katie's dream as soon as he had heard it.

But the night she saw the guns was the night Katie chose never to ignore her dreams. And since neither her parents nor her brother acknowledged her gift, Katie decided that this eccentricity, the vivid visions that sometimes came true, was one she wouldn't talk about with others.

There were the rich, intense night dreams, the complex yet convincing daydreams, then the occasional odd feelings she couldn't ignore, knowing that something wasn't quite right with what she was seeing, with what she was hearing.

In the Greenberg/Falco family, it was impossible to find the point where politics ended and the personal began. Carl and Theresa were parents so determined not to invoke traditional parental privilege, they insisted on being referred to by their first names.

Frank was three years older than Katie. And because Carl and Theresa early on opted for full disclosure, Frank had known more, seen more, and suffered more for knowing what was really going on with his parents. A reluctant participant, Frank had at least an idea if not exactly where but why Carl was so often gone, and understood if not appreciated that his parents' radical politics was primary.

He knew their phone was tapped, the mail often opened. He had been stopped several times by the guys Carl called "fibbies," the FBI. The only men wearing white shirts and ties on their blue collar streets, black shoes brightly burnished.

"We haven't seen your father in a while, Frank. That's your name, isn't it, Frank? Frank Greenberg, right? We're from the government and we'd like to talk to your father. Can you tell us where he is, Frank? It's important we talk to him today."

Frank knew as early as four that the proper answer was "I don't know" and often he really didn't know. But as a kid he was so very pissed to be put in this position, and it was so much easier to blame his father than the federal government.

Carl and Theresa inhabited a rare multi-racial, multi-cultural universe: black, brown, white, and in-between. Their friends were tenured professors and hospital orderlies. They believed the world could be a better place, and would be only if they did their part. But, as they explained once to young Frank on the eve of one of

Carl's month-long trips to Central America, it was because so many other people weren't yet ready to act that they and their friends were often compelled to do slightly more than their fair share. But hopefully that would change soon.

At various times, they worked as organizers for unions like Local 1199 of the Hospital Workers, then the American Federation of State, County, and Municipal Employees, then for several different charitable organizations working in Central and South America. Carl and Theresa were quick to insist that these were labors of love, and that they were missionaries on a mission from not-God, servants of a secular movement for social justice. And to supplement their meager incomes, Theresa would often work as a waitress.

With all of their increasingly dangerous work and their profound passion for political struggle, Carl and Theresa just plain forgot to give Frank a childhood. And Katie knew that Frank never quite forgave Carl for putting politics ahead of his kids.

Many a late night, as he made his way in his pajamas to the bathroom, Frank found Carl and Theresa and an ever-changing, collection of "brothers" and "sisters" arguing about pamphlets and picket lines, strikes and strategy in their tiny living room.

While Frank tried to give Carl and Theresa the benefit of the doubt, to a boy, then a young man, their politics seemed often to manifest as a constant and fevered commotion. He just wanted a father who wasn't always on his way somewhere else, to help someone else's kids.

It took a while, but Theresa was able in time to acknowledge the burden they unwittingly had placed on Frank, and she and Carl tried to spare Katie. As a consequence, she probably knew too little. With crayons and sparkles and string and dolls, Katie made a rich world for herself in that tiny three and a half room Bronx apartment. And in the summer, Katie sat daydreaming on the fire escape while Carl recovered from the extended trip he had taken to Chile, El Salvador, and Nicaragua, and he and Theresa mourned the death of friends. And there were too many deaths, as Latin America exploded.

Over the years, Frank built a life around his many grievances. In his naïveté, and/or his spite, at the age of thirteen with the bemused consent of his parents, Frank petitioned the court to change his name. He hoped that by substituting Theresa's maiden name, "Falco," for Carl's "Greenberg" he could change his life, slip from Carl's world to another, more normal universe. And the fact was, Frank often imagined himself more his mother's son than his father's. If Katie had inherited Carl's reddish brown hair and fair complexion, he was much more the Italian American, dark-haired, stocky and strong like Theresa. And if given the choice, Frank would eat pasta whenever he could.

Katie had no problem with her name, but she too often felt uncomfortable in the world she inhabited. Other people didn't have parents whose garbage was inspected, or were followed by federal agents. Other people knew, without the slightest doubt, that they were proud Americans: the best, the most accomplished, the most free people on Earth.

And, most important of all, none of their friends had a father whose politics had killed him.

It was, Katie could never forget, a cold December night. Carl had been gone several days. He was, they learned later, driving the well-known and wanted leaders of a Salvadoran peasant cooperative in a rented van from New York City to exile and sanctuary in Ottawa. They had stopped to spend the night at a cheap motel off the interstate by Watertown. And, as Carl was about to start driving at five the next morning, the van blew up, gone without a goodbye.

Even though the Salvadoran Army had told the family many times they would be killed for starting a movement to occupy the lands of the wealthy absentee landlords of the region, and even though several members of the Salvadoran Army and secret police were being trained at the School of the Americas here in the States, that such a complicated act of revenge had occurred within their jurisdiction was beyond the comprehension of the local police, who quickly ruled the deaths accidental.

And even for Frank and Katie, it was still easier these many years later not to imagine Carl's death a well-planned assassination.

Carl died while Katie was in high school, and Frank moved out the next year. He soon had his sixty college credits, passed his exams, and entered the Police Academy. Theresa acknowledged the irony of her son's decision but steadfastly continued to travel to Central and South America, helping women organize weaving and farming cooperatives, setting up small rural medical clinics.

After four years as an A student at City College, and a degree in

Art, Katie got a tiny two room apartment in the East Village, then bounced from job to job. She applied to, and got accepted with a full scholarship to the graduate program at the Rhode Island School of Design but chose instead to teach seventh and eighth grade in the South Bronx, wait tables on the weekend, and with the money she saved, went to see a therapist. She and Theresa would meet for dinner whenever her mother was in town.

One evening, Katie stopped at her local video store. She was moving from the latest releases, nothing really grabbing her attention, past Science Fiction to Adventure, when her eye caught "The Call of the Wild," a proud Alaskan husky on the cover, ears at attention stretching up above the title. As she moved away and toward "Raiders of the Lost Ark," she thought she heard a husky howl. Quickly looking back to the dog on the cover, then over to the check-out counter, to other customers, all clearly oblivious. She shook her head, as if to banish a lone, foolish, if highly convincing hallucination. When, a few seconds later, she heard a second howl, she quickly decided that a movie wasn't the greatest idea.

Outside, catching her breath, she looked up and across the street, and although it had been there a year, Katie for the very first time saw the bright turquoise neon sign in the second floor window above the flower shop: "Dr. Chau: Learning to Read The Book of Changes." Through the window Katie could see a Chinese man moving gracefully back and forth, talking energetically to what she imagined was a roomful of attentive disciples.

It took a week of wondering before she ventured up. Then she spent the next two years, twice a week, studying the *I Ching*. And while it quickly became apparent to Dr. Chau that he now had a very special, if too often silent student, Katie kept Dr. Chau and her classes to herself.

Then when Dr. Chau was invited to lead a week-long workshop at Kripalu, the spiritual healing center in the Berkshire mountains of Western Massachusetts, Katie was chosen to serve as his assistant.

"I am picking you because you do not follow instructions. By the time most students learn the rules, the rules they learn are already dead and frozen. Yours is a living, ever-changing gift. Please pack more clothes than you think you'll need," he told her.

And when the workshop was done, and Katie reluctantly told Dr. Chau she'd be staying in the country, Dr. Chau smiled and said,

"You're welcome, and better suited to the country. You and your dog."

Katie knew there was no point telling Dr. Chau she didn't have a dog.

Theresa had long sensed her daughter's dissatisfaction with the city, but Frank was shocked to discover she was moving to Massachusetts.

It took only a short-term stay renting a small room in a large house off Route 7 in Sheffield before her dog found her. Thanks to a Range Rover driven by two New York City corporate attorneys determined to become Vermont country farmers, and a fortuitous flat tire. As the lawyers struggled with their spare, and as Katie came to offer help, two proud husky parents and their seven husky puppies took advantage of an open door to spill onto Katie's front lawn. Six puppies tangling with each other while the seventh, the only brown-eyed boy of the bunch, plopped himself directly in front of her, eyes locked onto hers, claiming Katie for his own. Twenty minutes and twenty-five dollars later, the Range Rover headed north with only six husky puppies. Looking more like a bunny than a dog at nine weeks, Katie called him Rabbit.

Then, a few months later, with the help of Tom and Susie at GB Properties and her share of Carl's life insurance policy and the money she had saved in the city, Katie found her fixer-up dream farmhouse on a dirt road in nearby Ripton.

Despite Dr. Chau's consistent encouragement, Katie wasn't completely comfortable with her ability to do what he had referred to as "guessing right almost all the time" with her *I Ching* readings. And she certainly didn't advertise this skill. What Dr. Chau insisted was her impressive and unique gift was still an intensely private matter for Katie. But things began to change with the Ripton Women's Group.

Though the 1960s was but a vague and distant memory, there were several small congregations of Berkshire women who found it helpful to meet twice a month to talk about their lives without the distracting presence of men. Carl and Theresa's affinity for groups and organizations and endless meetings had paradoxically engendered a predisposition toward solitude in both their children, and Katie much preferred a quiet night at home baking bread with Rabbit to sharing a living room with discussion-hungry friends.

But then, without warning, Lizbeth Spencer and Deborah

McAfee decided to move to Sedona, Arizona to open Greater Vibrations, their combined yoga studio and organic frozen yogurt store. All of a sudden, the Ripton Women's Group found itself two short. And, not surprisingly, Bette Montgomery, the gentlewoman farmer and Katie's neighbor from up-the-road, was tasked with recruiting replacements.

Bette was renowned for her open-hearted yet fierce persuasiveness and Katie, drawn by a mixture of curiosity and the hard-earned acknowledgment that Bette would never come to accept a no, quickly found herself relenting. The newest member of the Ripton Women's Group, Katie was soon bringing her homemade bread to the homes of their rotating hostesses.

Despite her introversion, her magnified modesty, and the fact that she was more than ten years their junior, Katie's secret life slowly revealed itself as she grew more comfortable with her women friends. Several months later, Katie introduced the group to the *I Ching*.

While what was said in the Ripton Women's Group was considered to be confidential with a capital C, there were some things so interesting they couldn't be contained, especially when it came to Emily, the most exuberant of members. Ms. Emily Foster-Blodgett-Gorman-Turner, married and divorced three times, was all these mistakes later especially delighted to be an active member of the RWG. Devoted to the proposition that love was ever-present, everywhere, and a firm believer in the restorative powers of daily sex, Emily was constantly in relationship flux, and always enthused by the insights and wisdom the others bestowed upon her.

Hers was a small slip, born of concern for her favorite cousin, Cyrus Foster, who had just come home from work to find his wife and all her clothes and all their cash gone. Emily, without thinking, blurted out: "Cousin Cyrus, you have to ask Katie Greenberg to tell you what's going on. She's got this Chinese book. They know everything. I mean it. And Katie sees things."

The next afternoon as Katie was about to do what she did most days of the week without much thought, which was to pick up her mail from her box at the Ripton Post Office, she saw Cyrus Foster uncharacteristically waving at her.

It hadn't taken Katie long to learn that if you required any help whatsoever to send mail off to the rest of the world, or just as importantly to receive your mail from wherever it came, you enthusiastically acknowledged and appreciated the powers of Cyrus Foster, Ripton's postmaster. Cyrus had been the steward of the mail for close to twenty years. He lived and breathed correspondence, somehow managing to keep track each day of who had been in to empty his box and who was AWOL.

If you unexpectedly disappeared from view without telling Cyrus you'd be gone, he'd delegate some nearby neighbor to check on you. If you told him in advance you needed to leave town for an extended period, he'd fiercely guard and protect your mail, and it would all be there, awaiting your return, in chronological order wrapped in neat rubber-banded packets.

A man of few words, all Cyrus said as she approached the window was "I need you." At which point, without knowing it, Cyrus became the first person who officially came to Katie for help. And, in the process, changing her life in a profound way.

That night, Katie learned that Cyrus wanted to understand why his wife up and left him, where she might have gone, and if she was OK? And because he needed to know all that, he first needed to know what the heck Emily was talking about: what this book and this seeing stuff was all about, and if and how the heck it worked?

Which required Katie to put into words something about herself she had previously regarded as inexpressible: "Now I'm not saying I really understand all this but I spent an awful lot of time living in my own universe, doing what some people call daydreaming. But it moved beyond that, and well it's not that I've ever been able to do something as grand as that, but I imagine it's like hearing some music in your head that's never been heard before, or designing a building that's never been built. I began to see things I'm pretty sure I hadn't seen before. Things that may have happened, or maybe were about to happen.

"I don't understand time or space, or black holes or quarks. I still don't understand how my TV works. When people talk about infinity I just don't get it. Most of the time it was OK with me that I didn't understand how or why or even what exactly was happening to me, and what I saw.

"But there were also times, especially in the beginning when I completely freaked out. Luckily, I began to study the *I Ching*. It's called *The Book of Changes*. It's a very old Chinese book that people for generations consulted when they had a problem or were facing a difficult decision. In those early days, they used the stalks from a flowering yarrow plant to consult the oracle. Nowadays, because it's a lot more convenient, people throw three coins.

"You ask a question that can't be answered with a simple yes or no. You throw three coins six different times, and depending on the number of heads and tails you get, you draw two hexagrams with six lines. Then you're offered a story or stories about your problem, possible answers for your question. I trained with a very smart man who knew many of the mysteries of the *I Ching* and who was kind enough to teach me some of what he had learned.

"For me, working with the *I Ching* created a sense of safety, a way to add my intuitions and my dreams to some ancient wisdom. It wasn't just me and my slightly weird visions anymore; now it was me and some very old and very smart Chinese friends."

Cyrus sat there for what seemed like an awfully long time without saying a word, then nodded a couple of times. "I think Emily is right. I'm not sure I understand a lot of this. But I think you can help. Considering that I love my work and when I'm not working, I love to fish, I'm thinking I should never have married a woman fifteen years younger, and certainly not Mary Lou Sweeney's girl, Charity. Especially considering that she hates to work and hates to fish and doesn't have a charitable bone in her body."

After several sessions throwing the coins with Katie, Cyrus dreamt that his wife and Everett Abbott, the trust fund nutritionist from Alton, MA, were driving together in Everett's fancy Lexus with his twin twelve year old boys, stuck in a major traffic jam, the boys whining that even though the sun was always shining, they hated Orlando, Florida and wanted to live in the Berkshires with their mother, Sonia, who threw pots and taught modern dance.

Of course, he thought: Charity and Everett together made perfect sense, remembering all the time and money that she, actually he, had spent on emergency appointments, day and night, as Everett spent half a decade unsuccessfully treating her migraine headaches with kale extract and acupressure.

Now that he had assured himself that she hadn't been kidnapped, but was a willing participant in her own disappearance, Cyrus could acknowledge how grateful he was that her very best and very British friend Harper had convinced Charity to consult Everett Abbott in the first place. Cyrus could still remember the night he and Charity and Harper and her boyfriend Otis had dinner at the overpriced Prima, spending thirty bucks on some glorified spaghetti.

"Everett Abbott is the most successful holistic practitioner in the South Berkshires," Harper Remington-Smyth had insisted over three tiny farm to table squash ravioli. And, of course, everything sounded just a bit more convincing with her accent: "Only Everett Abbott can really see what's happening with the heart-head nexus. It's the kind of deep connection that always seems to elude traditional Western practitioners. Everett's got magic hands. He gets right in and re-positions your polarities."

"God works in mysterious ways," Cyrus reminded himself as he thanked Katie, so very thrilled to learn that Abbott had taken Charity, her migraines, her polarities, and all that kale extract with him to Florida. Knowing now he was forever cured of Charity Sweeny Foster.

And from then on, Cyrus took every opportunity to tell everyone in Ripton: "Katie Greenberg helped me an awful lot and I don't give a hoot what anybody says about her New Age voodoo, I'm very grateful."

SEVEN

So it wasn't surprising that Cyrus suggested to Margaret Dennard that she talk to Katie when Douglas, her husband of forty-eight years, died suddenly of a stroke while working on Anne O'Toole's VW Passat. The last thing Douglas had said to Margaret when he left that morning to go to his auto repair shop was: "By the way, I finally did it. I'll tell you more tonight."

That they never had that tonight haunted Margaret. And even though she had long ago stopped listening to much of what Douglas said, this one unfinished conversation seemed to overshadow everything he had successfully shared with her.

Katie silently cursed Cyrus for the recommendation. Because Margaret so often drove her batty, and there wasn't much she could do to help. She couldn't see anything other than Margaret's severe impatience, disappointment, and pain, because that was all Margaret brought her. It took Katie several sessions to convince Margaret that together they could retrieve some sense of what Douglas had in mind, but only if Margaret could see him as he once was: real and three dimensional. To move past the feeling that overwhelmed all others, that Douglas had somehow cheated her.

Fortunately, Katie had her own memories of Douglas to bring to the process: the several times he had patiently mended Hermione, her ailing Volvo, holding on to an almost extinct, old-fashioned commitment to hard work and fair prices, the small-town mechanic as family physician, including driving out without hesitation one frigid, ice-encrusted morning when Hermione refused to start.

Finally, she was able to convince Margaret to throw the coins, and to ask the oracle the most obvious of questions: "What did Douglas want to tell me?" And even then Margaret tossed the coins with annoyance. She threw "Lü / Treading" changing into "Chia Jên / The Family."

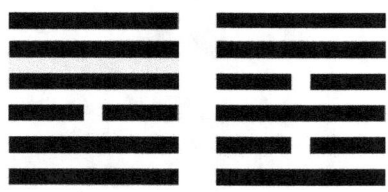

Slowly Katie read aloud from "Lü:"

> The name of the hexagram means on the one
> hand the right way of conducting oneself ... the
> difference between high and low, upon which
> composure, correct social conduct, depends ...

> That which is stronger and that which is weakest
> are close together. The weak follows behind the
> strong and worries it. The strong, however,
> acquiesces and does not hurt the weak, because
> the contact is in good humor and harmless.

Katie paused, realizing the next passage could as easily be meant
for her as for Margaret:

> In terms of a human situation, one is handling
> wild, intractable people. In such a case one's
> purpose will be achieved if one behaves with
> decorum. Pleasant manners succeed even with
> irritable people.

It was one of those moments, the two of them staring, each
convinced the other was the problem. Then realizing what was
happening, slightly embarrassed, they shared rueful smiles.

A few moments later Katie read aloud from "Chia Jên,"
the second hexagram:

> This hexagram represents the laws obtaining
> within the family ... The strong line in the fifth
> place represents the husband, the yielding second
> line, the wife.

Margaret looked at Katie then started to laugh, "Men, right?"

Katie smiled: "Two thousand-year-old Chinese men. Sometimes
I change 'men' to 'women' in my mind. And this passage helps:

> THE FAMILY. The perseverance of the woman
> furthers.

The foundation of the family is the relationship between husband and wife. The tie that holds the family together is the loyalty and perseverance of the wife.

As Katie continued to read about the "natural affection" of the family, she could see Margaret soften:

... one's words must have power, and that they can have only if they are based on something real.

Katie paused, then looked to Margaret: "You know, for me, everything about Douglas was real." Then she read some more:

It is upon the woman of the house that the well-being of the family depends. Well-being prevails when expenditures and income are soundly balanced. This leads to great good fortune. In the sphere of public life, this line refers to the faithful steward whose measures further the general welfare.

Margaret nodded: "Damn straight. At least they appreciate I worked forty years as a registered nurse up at the hospital. A lot of men, Chinese or otherwise, wouldn't even have noticed. Do you know I met him the day he came to the Emergency Room? Before he took over the station in Ripton, working for the Chevy dealer in Barrington. Horsing around, wasn't more than twenty-one at the time and he got his hand caught in the lift. As I was bandaging him up, he asked me out. Those days going to the roller rink was a big deal." Smiling as she remembered.

"I guess more than anything I'm just so disappointed. He promised this would be his last year with the cars. And we'd finally take some time to go travel ..."

Katie turned back to the *I Ching*:

He does nothing to make himself feared; on the contrary, the whole family can trust him, because love governs their intercourse. His character of itself exercises the right influence.

Katie remembered the last time she had seen Douglas, smiling as he made change for Scooter Winston. She had stopped to ask him to order new tires for Hermione. And once more Douglas was there, clear in her mind:

> His work commands respect.
> In the end, good fortune comes.

The feeling she had grew stronger. Trust. Work. Good fortune. Where so much of this happened, day after day. The garage. And Margaret so very reluctantly agreed to meet Katie at Douglas' shop, the one place she hadn't allowed herself to be.

The service station had been closed ever since the ambulance had taken Douglas away, and it was hard for Margaret to even turn the key. Inside, there was dust and more dust and Margaret almost faltered. But there on the blackboard was Douglas' list of things to do:

1) A. O'Toole VW Passat brakes

2) 4 tires for Katie Greenberg: 195/60R15

3) Don Pearson Replace Battery, check rattle front end and Grease Job

4) More Greece – Troy's Travel, confirm September 17th to November 3rd trip to Greek Islands with Margaret

Which was where Margaret's eyes stopped, not really seeing what came next. She started to weep, imagining herself and Douglas sitting at a seaside café on Corfu, watching as the small fishing boats came in with the day's catch.

Two months later, Margaret was having lunch at Dom's in Brett when she overheard her waitress, Deb, telling another customer that her missing dog still hadn't returned. She scribbled Katie's number on a napkin and wrote in large letters: "Deb, call this woman."

EIGHT

Deb had come to Brett via the Massachusetts Turnpike. On her way to a Bruce Springsteen concert in Saratoga, New York, when the car lights on her ancient and ailing Ford Taurus started to fade. Then the radio went, the generator shot. It was one in the morning. The state trooper who found her fifteen minutes later had dispatch call Brett Citgo, just a few miles up ahead, and fifteen minutes after that Jack Spencer came with his tow truck.

Jack was thirty-five, carrying about twenty more pounds than he ought to be for his five feet ten inch frame. For pretty much every day of his life these days he wore dark blue work pants and a blue work shirt with the Brett Citgo patch.

For the entirety of their youthful relationship, Jack's sweetie, Diane, said she wanted to wait, then slept with him the night before she moved with her Air Force father to North Dakota never to return. Years later, Jack was still reluctant to love.

Deb was twenty-five, and had lost count of her men. It was mostly an embarrassing haze. She had wavy black hair that spilled down her back. She was about five feet eight inches tall and at different points in her life had taken karate, then kung fu, and taught Pilates in the local health club. She was in great shape. Her dark eyebrows matched her hair and her fire engine red fingernail polish matched her lipstick. It was hard for Jack not to stare. Especially at the thin silver ring that pierced her right nostril. And the fierce eagle tattoo on her right bicep, as alive and electric as the charge coming from her dark eyes.

But there wasn't any way Jack was going to get his hands on a generator till later in the morning, and she declined a ride to any of the nearby motels, deciding she'd rather save the money and wait at the station. Jack often spent weekday nights alone with the cars and trucks and all his tools working through to the morning, still amazed he owned his own place after the years he spent learning the trade working for Douglas Dennard in Ripton.

Deb made him nervous. And because he couldn't figure out what more he could possibly say to her, he went back to tackle Fire Chief Jenkins' 1949 Cadillac on the lift in Bay Two.

Deb sat in the front room, staring at the calendar, out the window to the gas pumps and sparse traffic, then back to the little yellow fuse boxes stacked high in their own special display case. Then she returned to the calendar, trying to make some sense out of the names and the times Jack had scrawled in pen and pencil: his own chaotic appointment book. The minute hand trudged its way around the dial. Finally, bored out of her mind, she cracked and went into the garage where Jack was doing his best with the Chief's points and plugs.

"Excuse me," she said and Jack, jerking up reflexively, almost destroyed his head on the Caddy's substantial hood, dropping his gauge down past the motor.

"Whoops … I'm sorry," she continued, "but there's got to be a place around here to get some coffee and look at something besides fuse boxes … "

Jack fought the pain, which radiated down his spine, and still silent, bent unsteadily to recover his gauge. But as much as he wished her away, she wasn't going anywhere. She stood there expectantly. And because there really wasn't anywhere for Jack to hide, he reluctantly ended up driving her the mile and a half up Main Street to Dom's, the only place in town that was still open.

Over coffee and even more coffee, Deb talked about self-defense, tattooing, and her mother who died last year and the lousy father she wished were dead, about her fear of spiders and love of stray cats, and Jack found his sense of shock and surprise slipping into awe and adoration.

As for Deb, nobody had ever listened to her quite the way Jack did, and somehow going to see Bruce & the E Street Band, or getting back to Springfield Tech for her cosmetology courses no longer seemed important. She charmed Joe Montano as thoroughly as she had Jack. And with time out to marry Jack and have the kids, and without the nose ring, Deb had been waitressing at Dom's ever since.

Deb was working the Tuesday lunch when Sarah finally came in. Deb had been taught in her very first classes that "customer-contact" lay at the heart of successful cosmetology, then was trained in advanced diner skills by Joe's most experienced "girls." So she did her best to draw Sarah out. That first day Deb wasn't even sure Sarah had heard her "how long have you been in town?" Sarah's eyes moved a bit, then it seemed like she went blank.

She was a very attractive woman, Deb thought, and would be even more so if there was some spark to her. Her distinctive greenish blue eyes had great depth to them, and could easily be highlighted. Deb put her close to forty. By the end of week one, Sarah had graduated to "coffee and a roll, one butter please," no hello, no goodbye, just a concentrated sitting there, sipping and staring for several hours on end.

It was Joe who filled in some of the blanks: that she was boarding over on Oak Street at the Fosters, that Bea had said Sarah had walked in off the street with hardly any luggage. Seemed nice enough, quite polite. "But then," Joe added "Bea has had a soft spot for strays since her daughter Lucie drowned twenty years ago in that boating accident with the Benedict boy out on Peck's Pond."

Soon after, Sarah started speaking, or rather asking, then taking her turn with the newspaper. It wasn't quite the normal way of talking at first, but slowed-down, a bit tentative, more like she was remembering along the way. Not that that was so unusual, for as Joe told Deb early on, there were an awful lot of eccentric people in town. "Odd," he said, "was something just about everyone in Brett was used to, especially because these days you had to add the dumped-heres to the born-heres."

The local variety was bred over time: a product of the stress of millwork, some remarkably bad choices when it came to picking mates, too much alcohol, crack, oxy, or amphetamines, and the insidious side-effects of the grab-bag of potent contaminates used by the GE and Brett's several small industries.

Then, ever since the state legislature, in the name of community care, let the mental patients out of Brookmead State Hospital, the out-of-town strange were added to Brett's homegrown mix.

Now there were a half-dozen group homes in Brett run by the mental health people, who tirelessly tried to reassure the neighbors that their tenants weren't really dangerous, only different. And, by and large, that seemed true. They certainly proved less dangerous than Rob Butler, the constantly delinquent son of the local cop, Sergeant/Shift Commander John Butler.

Add them all up, Joe suggested, and there were so many strange birds walking around Brett that Sarah hardly seemed to stick out.

Except for Bea Foster and her borders, Deb was the first person Sarah talked to, and Sarah thought of Deb as her first real friend in Brett. Deb made Dom's possible for Sarah. Deb always said hello, making sure the counter was clean as she asked about her health, and told her stories about the kids and Jack and cosmetology, always smiling. Deb went out of her way to tell Sarah about all the specials of the day, and once even steered her away from the corned beef, "just a little too stringy this time," she said.

It was to Deb that Sarah first talked about the clouds and not knowing, then about the young man and the old man and dinnertime. Deb was very busy, rushing from one customer to another, but she never forgot what Sarah had said. Even though she was gone many minutes at a time for eggs over easy or burgers, sandwiches and salads, Deb always picked up the conversation right where they left off. And no matter how little Sarah had to eat, she always left Deb a five-dollar tip.

Then, one afternoon when Sarah was taking a walk, had actually stopped, transfixed in front of the MagicMart, the big discount store next to the supermarket, wanting to go in but frozen by the thought of too many things and too many people, there was Deb with her two kids: "Sarah, I don't think you know Rachel and Jack-Junior. Say hi, Rachel. You too, Jack-Junior.

"This is Sarah!" with hardly a breath lost, "my friend from Dom's. I swear these kids go through clothes like black flies through our lousy screen door. Every day off, it's shop, shop, and shop some more," then grabbing her arm.

"C'mon Sarah, you can help us." All of this before Sarah had time enough to think, time enough to be swamped by the fear of it. And so there they were in the middle of MagicMart, a contemporary Emerald City, trinket-full and fluorescent, a constant twinkling.

A voice came from the ceiling, much clearer than the bus terminal but without its power over Sarah: "Attention shoppers! We have a MagicMart special in Ladies Underwear. Go, go, go to aisle seven. For the next ten minutes, all bras are twenty percent off our usual low, low prices. Just the MagicMart way of saying 'thank you.'"

Imagining a new toy, the wanting powerful enough to take his thumb out of his mouth, Jack-Junior began to yank Deb with both his arms.

"I want a toy, Mom. If I ate my peas, you said I could," his voice getting higher. Deb was tilting like a ship in a storm when Rachel started in: "Me, too, Mom. I ate my peas. I want Barbie." "The Hulk, Mom," Jack-Junior reminded her. "I want the Hulk!"

Deb looked at Sarah, shook her head, then turned the cart back toward aisle eight and ToyLand. The kids screamed, victorious. "Kids," and Deb turned back to Sarah, "you have any?"

Sarah looked down at Rachel and Jack-Junior to remind herself, but couldn't find the answer in their smug faces. "Kids? I don't know."

"I've got two. They're on sale. Just the Deb Spencer way of saying thank you!"

Sarah smiled.

Then, after picking toys for the kids, they headed for the lunch counter.

Later, after the kids were stuffed with grilled cheese and cokes and fries, Deb turned her attention back to Sarah:

"I have an idea for you. I waited a while to mention it because some people are very suspicious about this sort of thing. They think it's just a waste of time or, even worse, throwing your money away, like she's a fake or fraud. But I'm going to tell you anyway because I went to her and you wouldn't believe what Katie did for us."

Jack-Junior grabbed Rachel's new Barbie and she started crying. Deb's hand was out in a flash, swiping Barbie from Jack-Junior's hand and returning it to Rachel in a heartbeat, then back for a quick shake of the boy.

"Jack-Junior, you bother your sister one more time and I'll flush Hulk down the toilet. You know me, Jack-Junior, I do what I say. And I could care less about his super powers. I always eat my peas, so right now I'm Super-Mom and you and the Hulk don't want to mess with me." And, without missing a beat, she turned back to Sarah.

"A few years ago, Tippy, our crazy dog, decided to jump out of the open window of our parked car in Plattsford, probably because we were taking too long to visit Jack's sister. Tippy's a pure-bred Samoyed, and she's convinced she's a doggie version of a real-life princess. As far as she's concerned, she can do whatever she wants. By the time we got back to the car, she was gone. Jack and I drove all over the neighborhood looking for her and I was pregnant with Jack-Junior, and Rachel was completely upset. We were all pretty crazy.

"Anyway I heard about Katie from Margaret Dennard, one of my customers at Dom's. And Jack used to work for her husband in

Ripton. She said Katie was a kind of psychic who helped people find things and figure things out. So I brought her a picture of Tippy, and Katie looked at it for a couple of minutes, then closed her eyes. Here she is quiet as a mouse, and I'm getting worried that she's probably charging me by the minute, when she opened her eyes and smiled. 'I'd like you to throw these three coins,' she said. 'This may seem a little strange to you, but I want you to think of Tippy and ask the oracle where she is.'

"I couldn't help myself and started to laugh. 'My husband loves tie-rods, transmissions, and wrenches,' I told her. 'When I said I was coming to ask you about Tippy, he did this thing with his eyes that he always does. He looks at me like even though he still thinks I'm adorable, he's imagining that I've been hijacked by aliens. So just in case he asks what happened this morning, how about for this first time I ask you where Tippy is, and then you can ask this oracle of yours?'

"Katie started to laugh. 'That works for me,' she said. 'You know, sometimes I wish I could focus on nuts and bolts, things I can hold in my hands. Like the boxes with toy Legos or furniture you have to assemble with the diagrams showing how one part screws into another. Somehow whenever I try to do something like that, I lose my concentration. I start daydreaming, and my mind moves elsewhere. And then I end up with three extra screws, and the desk is shorter on one side than the other, or the toy castle tips over and breaks apart.'

"Then Katie picked up the coins and handed them to me and with a big smile she looked up to the ceiling and asked: 'Where is Tippy?'

"So I threw the coins and watched her make a bunch of lines. Then she checked this book of hers. I must have been in some kind of state because I can't really remember most of what the book said, but I remember Katie talking about thunder, a horse and wagon, and a robber who wasn't really a robber.

"Anyway, Katie said she thought because of the horse and wagon that it was likely that Tippy was staying in a barn, and that whoever was there, wasn't taking her from me, but understood that Tippy was lost and wanted to go home, and was just taking care of her in the meantime.

"Katie said that maybe the storm in the story meant there was a weathervane atop the barn. There was something about bloody tears, which Katie thought could be about Tippy's sadness, but possibly a clue that the barn was red. Then Katie said if she had to guess, her guess was that the barn was at a farm just a bit outside Plattsford. Off to the West.

"She said, 'Don't give up, Deb. Focus on the line "all things breathe again." Which is why I feel that Tippy is waiting for you.' And then she was done.

"I sat there for a minute, thinking about how I could find that barn and, to be honest, wondering whether any of this could be true. But, you know, all of a sudden somewhere inside I knew I trusted Katie, and began to trust that Tippy was still alive. And I knew Tippy would never stop looking for me because that dog thinks she's my mother or that maybe I'm her mother or something deep like that, and then I remembered I hadn't paid her, so I went for my purse and Katie smiled at me and said: 'When you find your dog you can come back and give me twenty dollars.'

"The next morning I left Rachel with Jack's sister. I figured I'd drive the back roads of Plattsford. I saw a bunch of farms but nothing like what Katie described. When I called to tell him what I was doing, Jack probably thought the aliens were leading me on a wild goose chase, and after a while I was thinking maybe he was right.

"Then I headed out of town toward New York State and a few miles out, there it was. The barn. Big and red. Up on top was a bent and twisted weathervane. There was nobody around. I got out of the car. Walked around and maybe this sounds crazy but I could feel Tippy's presence there. I whistled and called but she didn't come so I figured that she must have taken off again. Tippy's a scrounger. Here in Brett, if she ever gets out, I just take a drive down to Chicken City and I'll find her in back by the big dumpster.

"So I said to myself: 'OK, it's early morning, and considering it's time for breakfast, where would Tippy go?' Then I remembered Friendly's, the burger and ice cream place on the corner of Simpson and Route 20. I decided to take the back way from the barn towards Plattsford, and in about three minutes there was Tippy on the side on the road headed toward Friendly's. She had lost her collar.

I was barely out of the car before Tippy was on me, yipping and yapping, jumping up and down, beside herself with joy. Like she had just made it to Doggie Heaven. And I was crying too.

"I insisted Katie take thirty bucks. You think about it, Sarah. Katie's got a lovely small house over in Ripton. I'll take you there."

NINE

In Donnie's world, everybody did coke. Coke didn't care if you washed dishes, washed dogs, or currency. Donnie liked to joke that one minute he was in the basement with the superintendent, and the next in the penthouse with the super-dupers.

The great thing about coke was that you started out wanting it then ended up needing it. For Donnie, even more so for his boss Arthur, the recession-depression was bullshit. Everybody loved coke. Everybody bought coke. If they couldn't afford what it cost, they stole enough to cover it.

And because of that, Donnie was always a popular guy. So it was no surprise that when the word finally trickled down to the street that it was Donnie, not really Dan Shine or Will, who was interested in finding the beautiful blond lady, then the calls started pouring in. From a whole bunch of folks hoping that with some info they'd get a serious discount or even better, a free ride.

All of a sudden, she'd been seen just about everywhere: in Big Pointe, Little Pointe, Highview, Templeton, on into the city. Doormen, limo drivers, waiters and waitresses placed her at the best hotels, the snazziest restaurants, even local pizza places.

And because everybody wanted what Donnie had, in their need or desire they often ignored the fact that he was growing more desperate to find her. And even in normal times, he was a little bit lacking in the empathy department.

Daniel Ruiz made a modest living as a paparazzi snapping photographs of the rich and famous whenever they found themselves anywhere near Detroit. The last few years he had snagged Madonna and Bon Jovi and Tim McGraw round about town when they were playing the Palace at Auburn Hills, and Clint Eastwood when he was filming "Gran Torino." Daniel had gotten used to coke helping him stay alert past midnight. He told Donnie over the phone he was sure he had seen the blonde lady just the other night slip into the side VIP entrance to take in a Pistons' game at the Palace.

And so Donnie met him at the bar at Big Pink. Daniel told his story, showed him a shot of the back of a blonde head in the midst of a crowd, and said he thought the information was worth an eighth of an ounce. Unfortunately for Daniel, Donnie called Petey.

Donnie had to hear Petey lose it: "Donnie, she hates basketball. The only way you'd get her to a basketball game was if her dead father and mother were playing for the Pistons."

Whereupon, Donnie's fist landed an almost lethal shot to Daniel's gut, and he crumpled to the floor. And so the word went out that Donnie really needed to find this lady.

Luckily, an hour later, Will called: "Lot B. Parking. Coleman Young."

Donnie's "I owe you big time, Will" was heard by no one, because Will had already hung up.

Donnie took Petey's spare key and got a ride to the airport. He quickly found her car, but it was empty. So while he was out there, thinking two birds with one stone, Donnie dropped in on Denise, his friendly coke-adoring Blue Sky junior executive, who checked her computer system but couldn't find a departure for her anywhere out of Coleman Young. Progress. He had her car but there was still no knowing where she might have gone.

*   *   *

Known to all his fellow street people for his mismatched shoes, filthy straw porkpie hat, and sunglasses as black as his skin, Harvey Bapson, the small-time, down and out junkie hustler, almost hadn't made it. Overdosing yet again on some too-strong smack, this time in the men's room at the bus station. Found by Dippy Don, his ashen without-a-hat white alcoholic partner, in what turned out to be the nick of time. Dippy stopped just long enough to empty Harvey's pockets before he called the ambulance. Then the hospital and a couple of hours of sleep.

And it was a day after, when back on the street, seemingly none the worse for wear, that Harvey learned about Donnie's offer of a hundred bucks for info about a blond lady. Shuffling over to Downtown Taxi to check the photo, and seeing that it was, in fact, the same blond lady who had come into his bus station with the powder-covered black and blue face. The lady who after twenty minutes or so came out of the ladies room with hair that was now black, not blond.

Harvey had zoned in on her again on the ticket line, seeing the spiffy shoes, hoping to hit her up for a buck or two. When the shakes came, and he could barely talk. But just before hurrying back to the head for a shot, heard her ask for a ticket to Cleveland. And even Donnie, once Harvey caught up with him, agreed the tip was worth one-fifty.

Donnie couldn't wait to tell Petey. Who, it turned out for the first time in a while, seemed better. This was his third bit of good news, because even though Arthur was growing impatient, he was willing to give Petey a short extension on the debt. And, still hopeful he could swing a deal to develop the land, Petey was going to meet with some Detroit money folks tomorrow.

Now this break, and thinking about Cleveland, Petey remembered meeting her cousin Elizabeth who lived there with her dentist husband. In fact, he told Donnie, she had asked him a couple of times to go with her to Cleveland, to take a break from Little Pointe, to visit the Cleveland Museum of Art. None of which they ever got around to doing. So it was worth a trip just in case, and if she was in Cleveland, Elizabeth's home and the museum were the places to check.

Thinking this was something he ought to keep from Arthur, Donnie took from his clean collection a Smith and Wesson .38 Bodyguard he could ditch if he had to. Petey rented him a Mercedes Benz, then entered the addresses of the dentist and the museum into the GPS, and Donnie began the one hundred seventy mile journey from Detroit to Cleveland.

Petey had told him many times about all the trips he had taken to different Caribbean islands in the wintertime, to places like Paris and Rome and London and the Swiss Alps in summer. But Donnie could care less. He loved Detroit, the streets and neighborhoods. He liked most of all the places he knew best: the two or three coffee shops, depending on where Arthur sent him that day, where they knew exactly what he wanted: a fried egg and bacon sandwich on an onion roll with extra cheddar cheese and ketchup. The egg over medium-easy, so with the first bite the yolk burst over the bacon, with enough melted cheese to smother not only the egg and bacon, but the top and bottom sides of the roll. And all of the short order cooks understood how much Donnie hated undercooked bacon.

There were the local bars who gave him the good stuff; and, of course, Charlie's and Big Pink, his favorite strip joints. Anywhere else was pushing it. Not knowing where things were, like the bathroom or the best parking, was very stressful. He hated having to explain himself: like the roll, never a bagel, no toast; or the kind of woman he liked: an inch maybe two shorter than him, blond, and thin like the magazine models and not too big on top.

He spent the night in an Econo Lodge a bit outside of the city and made it to the dentist's house by five-thirty the next morning. Parts of Shaker Heights looked like Petey's new neighborhood: big beautiful houses with gates and lots of lawns and gardens. His rented Mercedes was indistinguishable from the rest of the fancy cars.

The short slightly balding dentist left first around seven-thirty in an immaculate black BMW sports coupe; and his wife and their daughter, he wasn't great about kids but she was maybe thirteen or fourteen, drove out about a quarter to eight in their green Range Rover. Creepy how the mother and daughter seemed to be dressed the same way, both of them trying to look seventeen.

He followed them slowly along a zigzagging several mile drive through well cared for tree-lined streets, ending up at the entrance to a posh private school, Guilford Country Day. It took her about ten minutes to chat with the other parents and drop the kid off. Then, instead of heading back home, she drove off in the opposite direction.

He followed her to an outdoor café at a quaint little shopping center, and watched as she rose to her tiptoes to passionately embrace a tall, well-dressed, lawyer-looking guy with a phony tan and big brown briefcase. When it became clear that Elizabeth had other things on her mind besides going home, Donnie figured this might be his best chance to check for any signs of her cousin.

The GPS guided him flawlessly back to her house. Reminding him a bit of Trixie, the hot young stripper from Charlie's with her blonde wig and hint of a Southern accent, a left here, a right there. Unfortunately, the rental car aroma of the Benz was nothing like the lovely lilac perfume that helped to make Trixie's lap dances something special.

Donnie had learned to pick locks when he was eleven. There were a couple of break-in gangs based in the neighborhood, and they could always use a kid with steady hands and quick feet in case something went wrong. The gangs figured if the cops nabbed a kid with lock picks he could always pretend he found them, or if caught in the act, the worst he might get was some time in juvie.

Donnie was a hundred times better at locks than he was at math or social studies, and he was one of the few kids who managed never to get caught. These days, working for Arthur, he sometimes had to make use of those old skills.

The dentist, like a lot of rich folks, thought it was enough to tack a couple of phony security signs near his doors, rather than spend the serious money a really good system cost. It took Donnie only a minute to make it past the back door and inside. Then a quick stop at the refrigerator for a swig of milk and a chunk of cheddar.

He went through the dining room, checked the pantry, the living room, even the basement but found no sign of her.

Donnie had to fight the temptation to camp out in the TV room where the dentist had installed a sixty inch plasma and a bunch of high-end speakers. He could easily spend an hour or two on the big soft leather couch.

Then upstairs to the master bedroom, the kid's bedroom, and guest room. Nothing. Even checked the medicine cabinets for her prescriptions, stopping to snatch some Valium and Percocet.

He was bummed that he hadn't found her. Luckily, he was already out of there and across the street when the dentist's wife pulled up to the driveway, still glowing.

GPS Trixie took him to East Boulevard and the Museum. He and museums had nothing in common. He knew squat about art and had vague memories of a single school trip to the Detroit Historical Museum, remembering mostly the spitball battle they had on the bus ride over. Then something about the Ojibwa Indians who used to live in the neighborhood.

Donnie left his piece under the front seat, and took the long walk to the entrance. He hated buildings like this with their fancy entrances and weird modern arty sculptures that didn't look like anything. Because he just didn't get it. And things only got worse with the overweight armed guard in the lobby who kept eyeballing him as he made his way to the ticket counter.

There was an old guy sitting behind the counter, with his black uniform jacket, and white nametag with the dark blue letters: Ken Graham. Trying surreptitiously to boost the volume on his hearing aid as Donnie approached. Doing his best to pretend how happy he was to have Donnie visit his museum, all the while trying hard not to let on that he once made eighteen dollars an hour working in a unionized machine shop. Preparing himself for the required rap:

"So glad to see you, sir. Here's your ticket. In case you have to leave for a bit, please hold onto it. The ticket is good all day long. I've got a map here showing our exhibitions. And you might be interested to know there's a new show of European Impressionists on the second floor."

Donnie moved a bit to the right to shield them from the guard, whose suspicious eyes were still glommed onto him. Almost as if the guard was worried that Donnie might at any minute start slaughtering every art lover in sight.

Donnie very carefully slipped a folded fifty toward Ken: "I have a feeling the tips aren't great in a place like this. Ken, I'm looking for my cousin who's one of those art appreciation types. We had a plan to meet here a couple of days ago but I got held up. You know if she's been here?"

In the four months he'd been doing this, nobody had ever asked him about anything except where the art and the bathrooms were, but Ken took another look down at the fifty and quickly decided that answering questions was exactly why they hired him. He pocketed the cash and Donnie smiled, taking the photo out and holding it so no one beside Ken could see it.

"Have you seen her?"

Ken put on the reading glasses that were hanging around his neck, then leaned in a bit to get a closer look. "She's an attractive woman. But can't say that I've seen her." Ken hesitated, worried that maybe he wasn't giving the guy his money's worth, not sure what fifty bucks bought when it came to information. Deciding to continue on, and adding a chuckle: "Mister, I've got a pretty good eye for the women and, please don't tell my wife, but I do look. It's not like I've got anything else to do. So I'm pretty sure I would have noticed a really attractive lady like your cousin."

Donnie wasn't happy. "She loves this kind of place. You must have seen her before. How about you do me a big favor, Ken, and take another extra careful look?"

Ken could see past Donnie's shoulder that Morris, the guard, was getting antsy, staring, wondering why he was spending this much time with a single customer, and a scruffy one at that. "Hey man, Morris over there is getting restless … and I really need this job. How about I try one more time?"

Donnie slipped the photo back his way and Ken took another long look. "Sorry, friend. I can pretty much guarantee I haven't seen her. You know, seeing how she likes museums, maybe she meant the Museum of Natural History. They've got a seventy-foot long dinosaur, a diplo-haplo-something-or-other. I took Oscar, my grandson. Big teeth. Big mistake. My daughter's still angry. Kid had nightmares for a week. A lot of folks go there. But no, I don't remember seeing her."

Donnie was pissed. Pissed at Ken. Pissed at Petey. Pissed at her for not being dead and making him go to a museum. And pissed at himself for wasting his time. Ken could see the guy was getting angry. He could give the money back but didn't want to. He could already imagine a bacon cheeseburger and a whole bunch of beers at The Dugout. And so he found himself hoping that Morris would finally get his ass in gear and come on over to the counter.

But Donnie, like in one of those holy shit, smack yourself in the head moments, all of a sudden knew where he should have gone in the first place. He was done with the museum and done with Ken. He pocketed the picture: "Well, Ken, thanks for nothing. I think I'll pass on that haplo thing."

And Donnie hurried to the door, fighting the urge to pop the fat guard just once in the Adam's apple so he could watch him fall.

*   *   *

With directions from a guy selling pretzels and the help of a little more coke, Donnie made it from the Museum to the bus terminal. Where he immediately felt better, taking a seat to scope things out. Everyone dressed pretty much like him. Most of the ladies carried their belongings in those cheap plastic shopping bags; some of them juggling a couple of squirmy kids. Lots of them looking real tired.

You had your usual collection of mumbo-jumbo mutterers, and the folks who no longer had jobs, or worse, no homes to go to, plus all the travelers who could only dream of traveling by plane. And none of them acting like they were better than he was.

No need for fifties here. Donnie took his time moving slowly through the terminal, photo in hand, offering a five to anyone who seemed to react to her picture. A lot of headshakes; a few grumbles.

Until the very large black woman. Barely contained by her orange plastic chair, with a pink rain hat that had seen better days several years ago, and two double-bagged brown paper shopping bags wedged fiercely between her knees, her own personal safe, she was talking to herself in a rapid-fire private patois. It took a while to make her way back from the Jamaican village where she grew up to the land of Donnie, offering a loose denture smile. Beginning to focus on the photo he held out for her, then bobbing a bit, patting the empty chair to her left: "Here, boy. Here!"

Donnie sat beside her, slightly overwhelmed by the smell of marijuana, onions, sweat, lousy red wine, and cheap women's perfume that seemed to surround her like her own private swarm of bees.

"Burger lady, here, nice lady. Burger lady, one burger, two, for me, for you." Then pointing to the photo. "I said Burger lady, nice lady. Hair black, lady blue. But burger for me; burger for you."

Donnie gave her a five, then thinking about it, gave her another: "Where did burger lady go? Do you know where she went?"

The woman checked to see if anyone was watching, then quickly stuffed the two bills under her extra, extra large tattered gray knit sweater into what Donnie hoped was a bra. "Here," she said, pointing first to the chair, "then there," pointing to the ticket booth at the other end of the terminal.

"Burger lady; nice lady," quickly lapsing into a low recurring chant, rocking back and forth, "been here going there, been here going there," with a bit of a reggae lilt, oblivious to anyone and anything, falling into the beat. But Donnie had the feeling she was what his mother used to call "a smart cookie," and knew more than she was saying. So he took a stroll to the lunch counter, ordered a couple of burgers and two cokes. When they were ready, he walked back to the bench, and sat beside her. As she looked his way, Donnie smiled then said:

"Burger guy; nice guy. Burger for me, burger for you" as he handed her a burger, then the soda.

"Burger guy," she repeated, laughing only long enough to steady herself and chomp down on her unexpected bounty. Eating it too quickly and gagging, then gulping down her soda.

When Donnie finished, he took out another five. "So when Burger lady was sitting here, right here, where did she say she was going? On the bus. What city, what town?"

She quickly snatched the bill from him, adding it to the others. Smiling as she took another sip: "Burger lady; nice lady."

"Where was she going?"

"A, B, C, D ... E, F, G ... H, I ... Burger lady she took a bus. A, B, C, D ... the D, D, D."

"Are you saying D?"

"Burger lady on the bus. The D, D, D ... Dubuque, Des Moines, Denver. The D, D, D. Burger lady; nice lady. Bye-bye. Bye-bye."

And then Donnie watched as her lights went off, from awake to gone in a moment. He walked to the men's room, into an empty stall, unscrewing the black cap, tapping some coke from the vial onto his left hand, a toot for each nostril. Energized, on a roll, feeling the coke as it made its way through his system. Back out with a new idea and headed to the ticket counter.

There was an old man in front of him, hands trembling, clutching some bills:

"I've got a hundred and forty-nine dollars and seventy-five cents. Gimme a ticket that gets me to California."

Donnie was surprised when the guy behind the counter didn't bat an eye. "Ernie, the answer hasn't changed since yesterday. I still need two hundred and fifteen dollars to get you to Los Angeles. We're getting close. You keep saving and we'll talk again soon."

Ernie wasn't surprised by the answer and moved off without a peep.

"Next!"

Donnie stepped up to the Plexiglas window. "I'm looking for some information, not really a ticket ..."

"That doesn't make you much different than Ernie over there."

"Well, this does," as Donnie moved close against the counter, slipping a fifty halfway under the slot of the plastic window through to the clerk. Donnie then held the picture up for him to see. "My friend took a bus. I'm not sure whether she went to Dubuque, Des Moines, or Denver. I'm hoping you sold her a ticket."

"Mister, I'm here eight hours out of twenty-four. I see hundreds of people. I remember Ernie because I see him every day. If I've seen her, or sold her a ticket, well, I don't remember. You can check with Betty or Clayton or Stu or Tim. They all worked recently at one of the windows. What I can give you for your money is a count of how many seats we recently sold to each of those cities."

Donnie nodded and the clerk covered the bill and swept it toward him. He was quickly clicking computer keys: "Cleveland to Des Moines, 32; Dubuque, 14; Denver, 28. It's sad but the truth is I don't see faces anymore, just the cash."

While it seemed like a good idea a few minutes ago, Donnie wasn't sure the information helped. So he headed to the lunch counter for additional gifts, then back to the bench to try the rocking lady one more time. It didn't take her long to smell the fries. And she slowly drifted back to life, her eyes opening wide enough to make sure this wasn't just another wine-induced dream.

He offered the fries, then another burger, one in each hand. She seemed temporarily paralyzed by the possibility she had to choose. Then greed and hunger prevailed and she grabbed both, alternating bites. Donnie waited until she was done.

He pointed to himself proudly: "Burger man; nice man."

But she was instantly annoyed, shaking her head violently and sharply correcting him: "Burger guy; nice guy!"

"Whoa ... Sorry, lady ... You're right. Burger guy; nice guy. Who needs some help. Remember 'Burger lady; nice lady ... and the D, D, D' ... So I need you to do a really big favor and help this Burger guy out. What do you think? Did Burger lady go to Dubuque, to Des Moines, or Denver?"

Then, remembering again, "Burger lady; nice lady," she smiled. Going back in time once more, gone again. Donnie was trying hard not to lose it. Knowing it wouldn't help to smack her around. Counting to ten under his breath. Then he tried again:

"So we have your D for Dubuque and there's D for Des Moines and a D for Denver."

Slowly she re-emerged, then started to rock again: "A, B, C, D ... E, F, G. And the D, D, D. Dubuque, Des Moines, Denver."

She steadied herself to look directly at him, and stuck out her hand, rubbing her fingertips together.

Donnie smiled back and found another five. But she shook her head, then shook it again. He added a ten, which she quickly snatched, and then with a wicked smile offered him "Des Moines."

TEN

For the second week in a row Ralph Parker was pissed to find himself alone with Rabbit in the early morning. Reading yet another note, this one explaining that Katie had had a difficult session the day before and needed to do some research at "Books, Books, & More Books." Ironically, it was the kind of matter of fact early morning goodbye note he had left on lots of kitchen tables, bedroom nightstands, taped to refrigerators, even placed atop some toilet tank covers.

As he drove off, disappointed again, he realized he had never before been on the receiving end of such ambivalence. Because so few women had been able to resist the sight of Ralph riding his horse in the annual I Love Ripton Day Parade, or nonchalantly drinking beer from the bottle in his tight jeans at many a Berkshire bar, women had always seemed simple and amenable.

For some women, it was the smell of his worn flannel shirts; for others, the sight of him with his close-cropped sandy brown hair, and magazine cover deep blue eyes. RP, as he was known about town, was six feet one and extraordinarily fit from hauling hay and building fences. Maybe he appeared icon-like, an afterimage from a fading age, a cowboy in a computer-ridden world. But whatever the hook, he couldn't help but provoke an enduring fantasy. And, as a result, he had left bits of broken hearts in almost every small town in Western Massachusetts.

Ralph's reputation for commitment-phobia had percolated to the deepest recesses of the sisterhood, yet somehow he failed to impress upon his latest, and there was up until Katie Greenberg always another and another latest, that acknowledging the desire for any kind of long-term relationship was the very kiss of death.

How was it they managed to believe they were immune? That no matter what they had heard from the grapevine, or closer to home, from their best girlfriends with whom Ralph had undoubtedly slept, that they were somehow so blessedly different? That they alone could, and would, melt the heart of a man every other woman had previously found impossible to melt?

Again and again, the story repeated itself. Every woman Ralph had known had fantasized about a future. Sooner or later, they couldn't help but talk about it. It began with the simple wish for a weekend trip together; some closet space at his place for her clothes; dinner with her married friends; or a joint gift for his cousin's new baby.

And just about every woman he had ever known had made it easy for him to drift away. Katie was the "just about."

So you can imagine how cataclysmic it felt to have the tables turned. To discover there was something terribly elusive about Katie. That even when he was there with her, in her own home, he kept expecting her to leave him. And that was often the case, because she relentlessly went about her business whether he was there or not, departing one room for another to cook or to read or to clean, to rake leaves in the front yard, or to spend time with Rabbit. Never imagining that leaving him behind to get on with what she wanted or needed to do, for reasons he couldn't quite understand and chose not to share, seemed each time to unnerve him.

Of course, insecurity was something Ralph absolutely refused to acknowledge. He had no experience of longing or failure to fall back upon. Because sooner or later, mostly sooner, he had left every woman he had been with. What made this relationship so mind-bogglingly different was that he actually accepted he was in a relationship with Katie. And yet, unexpectedly, with that came jealousy: he was jealous, even, of her dog. He'd never own up to it, but sometimes he was overcome with the sense that he would never, ever be as close to her as Rabbit was.

The truth, he only occasionally allowed himself to admit, was that he didn't really get her. Get, not only in the sense of have, but understand. Get what she did, or how she thought. The part-time bookstore job made sense, but then he wasn't much of a reader. The psychic stuff, well that was just about as far as you could get from planting feed corn and bailing hay and hanging out at bars. Because he had met almost all his women at bars, softball games, or the bowling alley. And he never would have met Katie that way. Everything about them was improbable.

It was the dog.

The Parker farm was eight crooked miles from Katie's house through the woods, but more like twelve by the road. One day, Rabbit appeared out of the blue, then came back to visit every few days for a month, resting an hour or two, friendly, never begging, then all of a sudden on his way again. One afternoon, he stayed late. Ralph was coming into Great Barrington to bowl, so he decided to take a short detour and, thanks to the dog-tag, drop Rabbit off c/o Katie Greenberg, 146 Long Pine Road, Ripton, MA, curious about the owner of this presumptuous dog. Rabbit had his head out the window of Ralph's pickup the whole way, ears slicked back, his smile widening the stronger the smells of home.

Rabbit leapt out the window as soon as they arrived, and Ralph closing the truck door behind him, took one step, two, three into the front yard, Katie coming toward him, eyes as direct as the dog, an unambiguous welcome. Unaccountably, his heart was sinking, stomach dropping, legs almost useless, voice gone somewhere else. Not that she was anything like magazine beautiful, quite different from the pictures of all those Playboy Playmates he had collected over his teenage years, red hair wild, blouse crinkled, dirt-stained jeans, her unadorned make-up-less face wide, with real shoulders, but somehow glowing, like those sunset nights atop Post Hill Road, the sun dying beyond the hill, that last glorious gasp of purple, orange and pink.

The guys from Campesi Plumbing wanted to kill him. Down only eight pins to Brett Citgo, he threw two gutter balls. Unheard of, Ralph, a terrific bowler, always great in the clutch for Team Campesi, distracted most of the evening, seeing himself standing awkwardly before Katie. As she came to him, hand out, thanking him. The scene came back to him twenty times that night, the day after, the day after that. He'd stop in the middle of whatever he was doing, and let out a deep moan, shake his head several times and blush. Remembering how truly lame he sounded: "Here's your mawg, d'am!" Because then he would remember how all of a sudden she was laughing. He didn't think dogs could laugh but even the dog was laughing. The laughter everywhere about him. And not remembering how a few minutes later he found himself, still blushing, driving to Great Barrington.

Then, of course, the very next morning running into Jack Spencer at Dom's, who insisted on buying him breakfast in front of thirty people, those two gutter balls clinching the league trophy for Brett Citgo. And then waiting for the dog to come back, just looking for a proper excuse to see her again. When luckily, Katie stopped by a week later with a peach pie and an invitation to supper.

And last night he couldn't help himself. He asked Katie

something he had never before asked a woman: "Why me?"

She never hesitated: "I like the you that you don't know."

Which, of course, didn't help at all. And he really wanted, probably needed her to explain but ...

She could see the question there, stuck in his head. And she certainly would have told him more. But she had learned how often offering unsolicited information backfired with men. It was hard enough for them to hear answers they asked for, let alone explanations unsought, unexpected, and most often unwelcome.

The answer was the way he was with Rabbit when he didn't realize she was watching, and, despite his reputation, the boyish uncertainty he couldn't hide when she sometimes grew impatient and helped him make love to her. That he was Ralph to her and never RP. So, she thought, maybe it was just as well he didn't ask.

What Ralph didn't understand was that Katie was one of those exceedingly rare beings who embraced the present. Didn't talk about it, but did it. Because, even when her parents were alive, and even with brother Frank lingering in the background, she early on realized she was on her own. First Carl, then Theresa was gone, while, more recently, Frank was emotionally AWOL. And so, when it came to Ralph, this romance worked for her now, and now was more than enough. Because for Katie there was no functioning tomorrow; and she inhabited no future.

So there developed this odd dynamic where Ralph sought reassurance by paradoxically telling himself that sooner or later Katie would turn out to be like all the rest, demanding more than he could deliver. But the fact was that Katie was merely amused by the slightly suspicious look in his eye, the consistent wariness. And, ironically, as the weeks became months, all of her completely unpredictable behavior spurred him to do something he had never done before, to actively pursue her, and to want more than she was giving.

Ralph, it turned out, was a lot smarter than most people knew, and understood intuitively that standard gift-giving would scarcely do in Katie's case. So, lo and behold, without ever asking for it, Katie brought out in him the solicitous lover that all the women who preceded her had so vehemently yearned for: with his hand-painted stones, the arrowheads, and the series of personal, even poetic, love notes he tied to Rabbit's collar.

The other thing he did, and this was something he had never

previously felt impelled to do, was to tell Katie how beautiful she was. But for reasons he never quite understood, this seemed to backfire. Sometimes, she'd even recoil. Other times, she tried her best, but failed to smile. And, occasionally, she offered an oddly off 'thank you.'

Sadly, the reality that these declarations scarcely made an impression on her, spurred him to tell her again and again. To convince her. And he really meant it. There was something so very distinctive, even exotic about her. Her curly red hair, anarchic and almost always uncared for. The lovely full figure hidden beneath the mismatched, loose-fitting, often masculine clothes. Never in stockings, and never ever in heels. Instead, a variety of scuffed and ugly hiking boots. And even though she owned a couple of dresses, they had slowly made their way to the furthest corner of the clothing closet, banished and forgotten. Yet, for Ralph, who was used to women who spent prodigious amounts of time making themselves look their best, this only served to make Katie more unique.

Katie, it turned out, didn't really believe him, or believe in her beauty, for that matter. Or, more exactly, doubted its relevance to her daily life. By any of the usual standards, Katie was quite convinced she didn't inhabit beauty-land. She knew her breasts were real and imperfect and smaller than Halle Berry's; she weighed considerably more than Keira Knightly; and she could never, even in her wildest imagination, summon up the unrelenting perkiness of Julia Roberts. And her freckles, though faint, seemed randomly and inconveniently placed.

For Katie, the word "beauty" engendered not smugness, not validation, not even a small satisfaction. If anything, it brought displeasure, yanking her back to a world she never wanted to inhabit. And, once again, at least for now, she had a feeling that this was just another conversation that Ralph wouldn't really get. If things ever got to the point where it was essential that Ralph understood her, well then she'd probably try harder.

ELEVEN

Sarah was hurrying through a plush white field, moving past hip-high small bars on her left, squinting, slightly blinded by an intense and sparkling sun. Hearing only a soft indistinguishable hum. Then, through the smoky white wisps, a dark shadow moving menacingly toward her, an inevitable collision. She watched helplessly as an upraised, threatening arm came crashing down.

She woke terrified, her body tight, cramped and clamped all the way from her lower back up to the top of her neck. The clock flashed two-fifteen. It was hard to get up, but she slowly swung her legs over the side of the bed. She found her robe and tiptoed to the bathroom. She washed her face once, twice, three times, then slowly dried herself. Before she had a chance to put the towel away, she started to tremble and sob.

And she thought about Deb's friend.

*   *   *

Katie had been up since six-thirty, the early morning crisp and crystalline. Taking advantage of the cool breeze to spend several hours turning over the garden, imagining another summer of her own fresh lettuce, tomatoes, broccoli, cucumbers, carrots and peas, spinach and, as always, much too much zucchini.

She made some fresh tea, and gathered some of the corn muffins she had made an hour earlier. Then quickly tidied the living room, and stoked the woodstove. She placed the teapot beside the muffins on the table then closed her eyes. She had choreographed several of these extended pauses to slow things down: before meals, before and after appointments, every couple of hours at the bookshop.

She had so much energy these days, so pleased with home, her small house surrounded by tall oaks on the edge of her two acre open field, enveloped by work she loved, shared with Rabbit, and yes, occasionally Ralph. Sometimes she had to pause, to remind herself to acknowledge her good fortune, for she was apt to spin right over it all, hardly appreciating, never stopping till sleep.

Just a soft and quiet breathing in and out was enough. And now she thought about Deb who was bringing a friend. Deb made her smile, so full of life, zany and unpredictable. She gave whatever she had; she said what was on her mind. Thoughts and feelings charging from her, rough and unadulterated, kinetic. It had been a month since Katie had consulted the *I Ching* and she was feeling a bit rusty. But Deb said that this was important, that her friend Sarah was lost and hurt, her life story buried deep, and hiding from her.

And then, as if summoned, there was Deb, a whirlwind, pulling Rachel with one hand, a second reassuring hand on Sarah's shoulder. Introducing them, then a moment later driving off, gone as quickly as she had come.

Sarah sat in the old armchair in the living room, trying without much success to figure out what this particular social situation required. Recalling the picture on the wall of Bea's parlor, the woman waiting to see the doctor, sitting worried in her chair. "Norman Rockwell," Bea had said, like that meant something. "Not the real painting, that's in the museum in Glendale. A family joke, from my daughter, which is why I kept it, who hated going to the doctor."

Katie sat opposite her on the aging red velveteen couch, pouring tea into the cups on the long coffee table between them. Katie had brought together under one roof the spoils of many years' worth of thrift shop and yard sale scavenging, tables and chairs of many styles and many colors that, more than anything else, were supremely comfortable.

Nervous now, Sarah decided to concentrate on the warmth of the woodstove, the occasional crackle of the seasoned hardwood as it caught fire, and the smell of wood smoke intertwined with the lingering scent of Katie's made-from-scratch fresh-baked muffins.

"My friend Natalie makes this tea. She calls it Really Relaxing Tea," Katie said as she handed a cup to Sarah, then one of her old-fashioned cloth napkins, moving the butter dish and muffins her way. Sarah spread the napkin across her knees, waiting for Katie to take her own cup. Then together they drank. And only after Katie had begun to spread butter on her muffin, did she take her own.

"Every person who comes to me, comes with a different problem, a special story," Katie began. "Often, neither of us knows what that story really is. Many times, beginning is like trying to drive through night fog; one moment everything's clear, then the fog descends and it's so thick you're driving blind. Ironically, if you're desperate for more light, and you switch on your brights, that extra light just comes bouncing back at you, making it harder to see.

"So, too, with consulting the *I Ching*. Many times we don't know where we are, but I've learned that with patience we can find ways to move through the fog."

Sarah put her cup down, looked straight into Katie's eyes, falling into them, lost for the moment, then managing to catch herself and look away. She began slowly, barely above a whisper: "Do I know how to drive? I don't know. Did I ever drive? I am lost, Katie. Everything I might have known is gone. All I know is that I am here. And that I feel a there, somewhere in back," her hand pointing behind, "but it's just so far back I can't see it. Bea says when I first arrived she thought I was badly hurt but I don't remember. I don't know where I came from or why I am here.

"Last night I was very scared and I think for the first time I cried because of the not-knowing. In my dream, seeing someone coming toward me, to hurt me." Sarah stopped. As if afraid that by talking about it, she'd slip back into last night's nightmare.

Katie reached out to squeeze her hand. Sarah sighed, offered a weak smile, then slowly picked up her tea and drank. Katie lifted her well-worn yellow copy of the *I Ching* and held it up for Sarah.

"Sarah, Deb told me a little bit about your situation. I'd like us to consult this book, the *I Ching*. To help us take the first steps through the fog. It's collection of stories, a guidebook written more than two thousand years ago in China. I'm hoping the stories will help us find out who you are, to find out if you can drive, and where you've been and what's happened to you.

"Now like pretty much everything else in life, there are several ways to consult the oracle, and different ways to interpret its wisdom. I trained with Dr. Chau in New York City but, as Deb probably warned you, I'm a quirky, often eccentric person and many times I just don't follow the rules, Dr. Chau's rules, or anybody else's. It might be annoying to some experts but I interpret the stories in my own way. Based on how the coins land, many practitioners concentrate on some lines more than others, but I use just about anything in the stories that makes sense to me, wherever it is. To help me help you, to help you to see, and to find answers. So I believe that the *I Ching* and I can help. Deb told me that you've been reading the newspaper. So I have a copy of the *I*

Ching for you to take with you later. Hopefully, you can do some exploring when you have time. But right now, I'd like us to give this a try."

Katie placed the three Peruvian coins in Sarah's right palm then gently closed Sarah's fingers around them: "I want you to relax and breathe slowly for a minute."

Sarah closed her eyes.

"Good, thank you, Sarah. Now I want you to breathe in through your nose, hold it for a moment or two, then let the breath out through your mouth. Feeling the breath. Letting go of the tension. Again and again."

As Sarah relaxed, her right thumb slowly and gently caressed the raised outlines of the embossed llamas on Katie's coins.

"We start with a question, Sarah. I'm pretty sure there's a question or two you've been thinking about, an important question that can't be answered with a simple yes or no. Take a moment, Sarah, and try to clear your mind. Let it come to you. When you have it, open your eyes and tell me."

Sarah sighed, and the sound of the wood fire gradually filled the space. Sarah took another deep breath and opened her eyes. And now without hesitation, she asked: "Why am I here?"

Katie smiled: "Perfect ... Now while you're thinking of your question, toss the three coins on the table."

Sarah cupped both hands together, cradling the coins with great care. She shook her hands several times, then gently let the coins fall to the table: two tails and a head.

"This may sound confusing at first, but it gets easier each time you throw the coins. Tails count as two and heads, the llamas, count as three. So that's a two + two + three," Katie counted, "which totals seven, and makes it an odd number and a straight line. Odd number lines, seven and nine, are straight lines; while even number lines, six and eight, are broken lines.

"We build our hexagrams from the bottom," and Sarah watched as Katie drew a straight line on the yellow pad, "with the energy rising up." Then Katie drew a straight line a few inches over, "and then we build a second hexagram, which as you'll see can sometimes be different.

"Now you get to throw the coins five more times. Each time, thinking about your question."

Sarah concentrated, then threw the coins with the same result:

two tails and a head. And she watched as Katie added another straight line directly above the bottom line of both hexagrams. Sarah nodded, then tried again: three tails.

"Two + two + two," then Katie explained: "Whenever you throw three of a kind, Sarah, we call it a changing line, and turn it into its opposite on our second hexagram. So three tails, a six, turns from a broken line here for the first hexagram," and Katie added a broken line above the two straight lines, "into a straight line on the second hexagram.

"Later, when we consult the book, you'll see how this second hexagram can add new insight to your question."

Sarah took the coins and threw again: three tails. She smiled as Katie drew another broken line on the original hexagram, and the changing straight line on the second.

"You're doing great, Sarah. Two more throws." Sarah closed her eyes to focus once more on her question, then gently threw the coins to the center of the table. Two tails and a head, a seven, and Katie drew straight lines on both hexagrams.

"This is it," Katie said and watched as Sarah threw three tails again. "Two + two + two, that's six, even, and your last changing line. So this is what we have," pointing to the two complete hexagrams she had drawn.

"Now we look up the hexagrams to see what stories you've come up with," as she thumbed through the book. "The first hexagram is called 'Chieh' or 'Limitation.' The second is 'Chien.'

"And as we move through 'Chieh,' I'm going to read aloud some of the words and phrases that might provide possible answers to 'Why am I here?' Remember, there's no pressure; no right or wrong. There are so many ways to understand these stories, but when all is said and done, this is your story. And I'm sure you'll find clues that I miss entirely. So please let me know if anything stands out for you:

A lake occupies a limited space. When more water
comes into it, it overflows. Therefore limits must
be set for the water. This image shows water
below and water above, with the firmament
between them as a limit ...

"So," Katie began, "here's our first hint: a lake and the land.
Every lake contains a certain amount of water. Any more, and the
lake overflows its banks, flooding the nearby land: the limits of the
lake. And the notion of limits applies, as well, to human behavior:

... it means the fixed limits that the superior man
sets upon his actions – the limits of loyalty and
disinterestedness.

"The lake and land may be important landmarks, the geography
of your life. But the *I Ching* is also asking us to consider how you,
or someone around you, has been acting. Like the water, there's
just enough and then too much. Money, perhaps, or pleasure,
power. Some of what we do in life is motivated by loyalty,
generosity, and the desire to do good, while other things we do are
prompted by the desire to gain a personal advantage."

Sarah looked at the first hexagram, trying to gather her energy,
all of it directed down and to the lines.

Until, unable to maintain her focus, one line melted into
another. Then slowly and sadly Sarah looked up and into Katie's
eyes: "I'm sorry. I don't know about a lake or too much water. I
don't see it. I don't remember. It doesn't mean anything at all to
me," she offered, then fell silent.

"That's all right, Sarah," and Katie waited a bit. "I understand.
This is just the beginning. We need to be patient. I'm going to
continue to read. You never know what word or phrase might
spark a memory. Hopefully, sooner than later, some of this will

make more sense:

> THE JUDGMENT
> LIMITATION. Success.
> Galling limitation must not be persevered in.

> ... If a man should seek to impose galling
> limitations upon his own nature, it would be
> injurious. And if he should go too far in imposing
> limitations on others, they would rebel.

As Katie paused to catch her breath, she saw Sarah close her eyes, her brow knit with worry. "Was there something in that last section?"

Sarah hesitated, then asked: "That word ... what is that 'galling' word?"

"All of us forget things in small ways, Sarah, words we've used before, the name of someone we've known for years, what we're supposed to be shopping for in the supermarket, but it must be so very hard for that to happen with almost everything. 'Gall' is a kind of outrageous behavior, a form of audacity, and 'galling' means frustrating, infuriating, even humiliating."

Katie watched as Sarah considered all this, nodding more out of unconscious habit, it seemed, than conviction. Katie continued on, moving deeper into 'Chieh,' glad that once again the *I Ching* was coming alive for her:

"I see two possibilities here: the first, that someone has held back, limiting his or her potential, and his ability to accomplish something.

"Then there's the other possibility: that one person has tried to prevent another person from taking action, restricting his or her ability to move about, to come and go, what the *I Ching* refers to as 'the galling limitation' imposed by one person upon another. And, given those circumstances, the *I Ching* suggests that:

> Not going out of the door and the courtyard
> Is without blame.

Often a man who would like to undertake something finds himself confronted by insurmountable limitations. Then he must know where to stop. If he rightly understands this ... he accumulates an energy that enables him, when the proper time comes, to act with great force ...

"Here," Katie continued, "those 'galling limitations' have become 'insurmountable limitations.' So it's important to recognize this situation, to acknowledge that it's time to stop, to take stock. Then resting, recovering, growing stronger, and hopefully knowing when the time has come. The time to act."

Sarah sat there silently, letting the words wash over her, as she often stood in Bea's shower, as the water fell, many drops, pitter-pattering off her head, cascading down her neck, her shoulders, breasts, stomach to legs, smacking the porcelain tub, a tiny lake for just a moment, then swirling down the drain. Thinking the hot water helped. Growing stronger, she wondered? Well, yes, a bit. A little bit.

Katie continued on, aware that Sarah had been distracted and was just now slowly returning: "That door could be a real door, the way out of a place you no longer want to be. Out to the courtyard and beyond. A symbol of freedom. Choice. Change. Your mind, your job, your life. Leaving home, ending a relationship. And always when it comes to making changes, it is important to wait for the right moment."

Sarah heard Katie's "change ... your job ... your life," but there were no pictures to go along with the words. She felt empty and sad.

The door, the courtyard seemed so familiar to Katie. Had someone recently thrown "Chieh?" She didn't think so. Trying to flip back in time, but then remembering her dream. When she had been the one before the door, stuck there, not going out. Days before meeting Sarah. Was there some deeper unconscious connection at work here?

Katie paused, taking a bite of her corn muffin, a sip of tea, then continuing: "Confucius, the great Chinese philosopher, consulted the *I Ching* so often that he decided to add his own comments. About 'Chieh,' Confucius wrote:

> Where disorder develops, words are the first steps.
> If the prince is not discreet he loses his servant. If
> the servant is not discreet, he loses his life …

Sarah's right hand came up to massage her forehead, her four fingers pressing in then across, as if the rubbing could erase her headache, several times back and forth, softly repeating: "the servant loses his life," as much a question as a statement, trying her best to make sense of this, to put these pieces together with the lake and limits, the door and courtyard, but it wasn't easy.

"I hope I'm not overwhelming you, Sarah. Or scaring you. But these are obviously very strong words. And what's especially troubling is the implication that these are matters of life and death! You asked: 'Why am I here?' And a possible answer is that you're here because back there things went from difficult to intolerable.

"Perhaps there were words. A warning. A disagreement. Indiscretion. Maybe someone, maybe you, did something stupid. Or inappropriate. Bringing disorder. Threatening the way things were. When, according to 'Chieh,' conditions became dangerous enough to warrant this advice:

> Not going out of the gate and the courtyard
> Brings misfortune.

> … Once the obstacles to action have been
> removed, anxious hesitation is a mistake that is
> bound to bring disaster, because one misses one's
> opportunity.

"Clearly, when things get to this point, words aren't enough. Your dream. Maybe back there you experienced this kind of anxious hesitation."

Katie paused, looking over to Sarah, who was sitting there so very still, partly dazed. Katie was worried she had overwhelmed her with information. Ironically, filling Sarah's lake with too much water.

Katie took several more sips of tea, spreading jam on what was left of her muffin, hoping to give Sarah more time to process some of this. She looked more closely into Sarah's eyes, a unique mix of blue and green. As tired as the rest of Sarah seemed, her eyes were very much alive. If not quite comprehending it all, still dynamic, still reacting.

Sarah could sense Katie's concern, and wanted to make sure that Katie knew she was trying. And so even though she didn't quite know what to say, she offered a slight smile.

Katie heard Rabbit's paws smacking the front door. "Excuse me, Sarah, my dog Rabbit is back. I'm going to let him in. Why don't you rest a minute or two and Rabbit and I will rejoin you in a bit." Sarah nodded ever so slowly.

Rabbit had traveled about ten miles on his way back from an overnight at Margaret Dennard's, stopping to visit with some dog friends, and checking bones he had buried along the way.

Katie opened the door with a simple "welcome back." As if his day-long absence was any other dog's two-minute trip to a nearby tree.

Rabbit, as always, was glad to see Katie again. He stopped in the kitchen for some water, then sensed Sarah in the next room, felt her sadness and confusion, and silently made his way to say hello.

Katie watched as Rabbit quietly nestled against Sarah's legs, trying not to startle her, and as Sarah gently moved her left hand to pet him. Katie gave them a minute or two.

"We're almost done, Sarah, and while this might seem completely mystifying at first, I'm hoping this will spark some memories. So I just want to finish up with this passage:

> Sweet limitation brings good fortune.
> Going brings esteem.

Katie paused: "Putting some of these pieces together, I see a story about a journey from a place inside out to another world. Inside that door, there's danger. We're told it's possible the servant might lose his life. Maybe that's you; maybe it's someone you know. Or, more broadly, perhaps the *I Ching* is reminding us that we're all servants in one way or another. At risk every day, always faced with choices, stuck behind doors, in social situations that don't work for us, and confronted with new opportunities. Maybe death is literally death, but maybe it's about taking the easy way out in life, making the safe choices, giving in to 'anxious hesitation,' doing someone else's bidding, not living up to who we could be.

"But the truth is, I get the feeling that your choice is or was more extreme than our usual choices. If so, the moment must be seized. No hesitation; it's time to go."

The words hung there. Rabbit stretched, then stood up and moved to Katie's side, nuzzling against her leg. She paused to scratch his head, then began again: "That closed door accurately illustrates your present predicament: you're without access to your past life, to what has happened to you. So together we have to find the right way and right time to open that door."

Sarah tried to see the door. She wanted so much to see the door. To remember opening the door, but couldn't.

Katie could see how tired Sarah was. She moved to the bookshelf, and grabbed a new copy of the *I Ching*. She spoke slowly while she found and bookmarked the two hexagrams:

"Let's hold off on looking at 'Chien / The Creative,' the second hexagram, until next time. Please take this copy. Hopefully you can look at 'Chieh' with fresh eyes and instincts. I'll ask Deb to bring you back in a week, and we'll see what we make of this. I know there's a lot more for us to discover."

TWELVE

According to Donnie's always grateful coke client at the phone company, she hadn't made any cell phone calls that afternoon or evening to any of the airlines or hotels, or anywhere out of the country. She must have ditched the phone, Donnie figured, because there were no new calls at all.

And, checking online, Peter could see there were no recent credit card transactions charged to any of their accounts.

Luckily, because the vacation story had worked so well, Peter hadn't had to deal with any cops. Now, with Arthur's card game out of the question, he had too much time on his hands, time to rethink and relive it all from the very beginning.

Remembering how once he found the lake house and its owners, he had begun to see article after article about the family in the local newspaper, putting faces to the names, then the picture of her graduating from The Academy at Little Pointe. Beaming, so beautiful, so confident. Reading about how happy she was to be moving on to the University of Michigan at Ann Arbor. Remembering the moment he decided she would be the way to make him pay.

With his great grades and phenomenal College Boards, it wasn't hard to get in, to get a scholarship. And all these years later he could vividly recall how he had stood at the top of the large lecture hall scanning the room for her that first day of "Contemporary American Literature." Having followed her a few times around the campus, she was easy to find. And he headed down to take the empty seat beside her.

He was the first to take the opening day challenge. "I've been doing this quite a while," Professor Adamson began. "And I suspect many of you may have taken this particular course because you secretly hope you can finally write that term paper on 'The Social Significance of MC Hammer.' Well, I'm here to remind you that before there was twentieth century American literature, and, by the way, pop songwriting scarcely qualifies as literature, there was the American literature of the nineteenth century.

"I always like to see what my students are bringing to this class, to examine whether they truly appreciate what the past has provided the present. So please take a moment to reflect and remember, and share with us the names of the most important books written in the ten years preceding the Civil War?"

Adamson began what he proudly called "the wait." He reveled in the awkward silence that set the tone for the term to come. He loved to establish the power balance he needed to keep these young, often unruly minds at bay. Adamson had barely looked from the right side of the room to the center when Peter began to speak without having been called on.

"I'd have to say, Professor Adamson," as he slowly rose to his feet mid-sentence "that in the decade beginning in 1850 some extraordinary work was published. There was Hawthorne's 'The Scarlet Letter' in 1850, followed the next year by his 'House of the Seven Gables.' Melville wrote his 'Moby Dick' that same year, and in 1855, Whitman's epic 'The Leaves of Grass' was published."

Peter sat down to a stunned silence, and it took Adamson more than a minute to regain his stride. "Thank you," he managed to add, "Mr. ... " waiting for a name. Peter left him hanging a beat, then provided: "Bishop, Peter Bishop." He stole a glance to his left: she was only one of the many who began to breathe again.

Adamson compensated for his shaky beginning with a long and uninterrupted monologue detailing everything he expected from them during the course, from respectful class participation to thoughtful yet innovative term papers. And Peter seemed content to join the growing sleepiness. As class came to a close, he offered his right hand and leaned over to whisper to her, "Peter Bishop." She smiled, aware that her smile was his second victory of the morning.

In many ways, that introduction shaped the trajectory of their relationship. Peter never seemed to hesitate. His impressive brainpower was matched by an inexhaustible confidence. And so he wanted her phone number, a first date, a fifth, then to live with her off-campus, and very soon after, wanted her for life.

She had often been sought, but never pursued with that kind of single-mindedness of purpose and unrelenting enthusiasm. She had always assumed she was attractive. She had done very well in school and, unlike many of her girlfriends, hadn't had much trouble recognizing and appreciating her intelligence. Along the way she had had her flock of boyfriends but the sons of her father's friends, and the country club boys never quite cut it, seemingly more devoted to image than substance. It wasn't surprising that she so often found herself bored by their self-absorption. In contrast, Peter always cared about what she was thinking and feeling.

When they studied together he not only inhaled information, but seemed never to forget it. It was as if learning was a competitive sport for him, a contest he was determined to conquer. That first year, he was one of the few students who didn't live in Ann Arbor, commuting the more than forty miles from Detroit. Even then gambling thirty hours a week. And so his class time and study time seemed almost precious to him.

He almost effortlessly got an A plus from Adamson while she, putting as much energy into the relationship as she did to studying, worked mightily for her A minus. Perhaps it was the unpredictability, the unlikelihood of Peter that made all the difference for her. She found his never wavering attention intoxicating. And Peter was the very first guy she had dated who thought and talked about money with ease, as if money was toothpaste. The country club boys were so dreadfully self-conscious about wealth. Money, for Peter, while something you might want, even need, was never worth obsessing about.

It was exhilarating to finally acknowledge, then dispense with the subject: for in so many ways her family's wealth had marked her life. All of them, she included, had lived lives circumscribed by the walls of wealth, protected, yet marginalized, by privilege. Their social circle, sense of the world, and expectations all revolved around their near constant desire to maintain and protect the life they had become used to. Her father seemed to hardly care about his work. And like her mother before her, immersed in money, spoiled by money, she had no great calling and never found anything to fully capture her imagination, except for her attraction to flowers and plants.

Because Peter seemed so unimpressed by her finances, always so self-possessed and uninterested, so sure he could have however much money he wanted or needed all on his own, she was able to relax for the first time. This relationship, she was convinced, had nothing to do with where she came from, her grandfathers, and great-great grandfathers, the family bank, their investment firm, her mother's money, or her father's money, or her trust fund.

Peter proved it over and over again. His success at school was matched by his ability to make money. And he seemed to have an uncanny ability to honor the sensibility about money that ruled her family life. The more they had, the less they talked about it.

Peter always had a stack of crisp new bills, carefully folded one atop the other, held in perfect place by an extraordinarily artful silver and turquoise money clip. And he was the only one of her boyfriends to insist on paying for dinner when they dined with her parents at Chez Nous, her mother's favorite restaurant.

Even with her, and she never prompted him, Peter would only say that he had friends and private clients who invested in the national and international markets, and that as a consultant, he was able to use his quick mind and analytical instincts to make them and himself a very good living. They relied upon his discretion, of course, and he made a point of keeping business separate from the rest of his life. And he knew that she, of all people, could understand and appreciate that.

On the day after they married, as they packed for a honeymoon on St. Barts, paid for by her father, Peter surprised her with the checkbook for their new joint account stocked with a hundred thousand dollars. The two and a half carat Tiffany Setting engagement ring had momentarily derailed her father but at that moment, checkbook in hand, the near constant echo of his voice, "just be careful he isn't with you for the money," faded forever.

She was now completely immune to any of her father's insinuations. And somehow, without really being aware of it, she settled into a life that was mostly about her marriage to him. If she had once upon a time expressed a desire for an independent existence, that need slowly faded away. Like her mother before her, trust fund secure, she began her work with several local charities.

Peter made sure she never knew anything about the world he really came from. He had told her and her parents that his folks had died several years before, and that he was alone in the world. But the truth was that before there was Peter Bishop and Ann Arbor and American Literature, there was Petey Kean.

Looking back on it, the University of Michigan was a snap compared to the street. His father, John James Kean, was a petty thief who, in an alcoholic haze, made the mistake of trying to rip off the wrong guys. John James had exceptionally quick fingers and could take a card off the bottom without almost anyone seeing. Unfortunately, his dad didn't realize that Tommy Dappolita had been carefully monitoring the nightly game at Castronova's from behind the peephole in the backroom.

By the time his dad figured out that he had been made, Tommy was whispering in Steve Castronova's ear. Steve smiled and fifteen minutes later they let John James leave the table with the grand he won. But he never made it out of the alley alive, and Petey's mom, Irene, never saw a penny of that grand. But because Steve had the hots for Irene, he had Tommy Dappolita move the body to the outdoor basketball court by the elementary school so she could at least find and quickly bury what was left of him.

Nothing was ever the same for his family. The loss of their father, the even more dreadful poverty, and the brave-faced despair of their mom affected the sons differently. Petey was humiliated, then committed to transform that humiliation into a steely determination: he would craft a life so very different than the one he had been given that he would be unrecognizable. Donnie, on the other hand, could only express his bewilderment with a simmering, sometimes explosive rage. If Irene wasn't so physically and emotionally exhausted, she might have noticed the turning point in her boys. But the changes went unmarked, and never spoken of.

Irene, increasingly desperate, started to tend bar for Steve, then provide favors for Steve's male friends, which paid a lot better than mixing drinks. Until one day a very rich associate of Steve's, and a man who too often lost at cards and football and the ponies, offered to employ her exclusively for a few months, then transferred her to an even richer, and far more private business associate of his.

Petey never again challenged his mom's authority: he was too busy with his newfound ambition. In some ways, he began to supplement her waning influence with Donnie, part brother, part father. But it was very hard. Donnie had little interest in Petey's surprising agenda: homework and study and the daily trips to the public library a couple of blocks away. And so many times, when Petey lost himself in learning, Donnie would slip away to his friends, to smoke dope, drink beer, and pop whatever pills they had managed to scrounge. If they were lucky, they'd come up with some coke or speed. Then Donnie learned how to pick locks and increased his options.

The time Donnie and Petey shared most fully was the half-hour every afternoon they met up at Eddie's garage to lift the weights Eddie's father had bought off the TV shopping station, the weights he used for two weeks, then abandoned. Petey soon got bored but Donnie, over time, added hours every day to his routine.

In the years following Irene's death, his increased strength, coupled with his growing lack of restraint, earned him many opportunities to make some extra cash in the neighborhood. In Donnie's case, "muscle" was an apt description. And his talents soon included debt collection, body-guarding, dealing, and the occasional assault.

For Petey, it was always about mind not muscle. Having mastered the library's card catalogue and inter-branch lending, he turned his attention to the world of computers and the internet. He quickly realized that a savvy researcher could, with patience and determination, learn something important about almost everything.

Petey began to look at the world as if it were a school assignment, to look at human behavior as something that could be deciphered. He toyed with the idea of majoring in zoology, of heading to the Antarctic to study penguins. But he knew that leaving would never redress the deep hurt. And it certainly wouldn't be fair to the penguins.

He began to notice how few people were fully committed to who they were, or what they did, or what they dreamed of. There was an innate laziness at work, or an abiding fear of taking the risks necessary to excel, to completely become. In the midst of the journey himself, it was hard to respect those who held back.

And later at Ann Arbor, it only took the first student-faculty conference with Adamson to see his hollowness. There was the book-lined office that Adamson had filled with the paperback books he obviously relied upon, no precious leather-bounds for him. He wanted you to appreciate he was no dilettante but rather a working reader. His books had makeshift bookmarks popping up every few pages. And in the very center of the shelf, the three of his own: "The Existential Emerson," followed by "Hawthorne's Use of Grey: The Incongruity of Color," and, in his mind, the most hip, most recent: "Norman Mailer's War with Himself."

Adamson tried to make up for the paltry sales of his last book by assigning Mailer's "The Naked and the Dead" to every advanced lit class he taught, and by successfully arguing it belonged on the sophomore seminar: "Understanding Our America." Hoping that the more Mailer, the more Adamson.

What bothered Peter the most was how Adamson hid behind

his authors. Starting with the implicit warning Adamson offered toward the end of their conference: "You've clearly got potential, Mr. Bishop, but never forget how illusive it all is. What was Emerson's summation, after all? 'Good bye, proud world! I'm going home; Thou art not my friend; I am not thine.'"

Peter smiled and nodded encouragingly, all the while thinking how weak that was. He wanted his A so he refrained from reminding Adamson that his time was just beginning, or from offering a far more appropriate Emersonian counterpunch: "In skating over thin ice our safety is our speed."

Instead, he reminded Adamson that this class was the class he most valued; that even though others had many times warned him how much Adamson expected, and how hard you had to work for your grade, he had discovered early on you could learn more than you would ever imagine about American Literature. Then he smiled, and looked Adamson in the eye, adding: "And isn't that exactly what college should be about, Professor Adamson?"

In fact, he had paid a guy in the Registrar's Office a hundred bucks to see what courses she had signed up for, and another hundred to add his name to Adamson's class.

THIRTEEN

Little Francis knew it could have been worse. What were the odds there'd be three different guys named Francis in his class? It didn't take long for Mike Quinn, the class bully, to re-name them all. Besides him, there was Fat Francis and Francis Flunky. It never seemed to matter that he grew up to be two hundred and seventy pounds and six foot five inches, or that he could break Mike Quinn in half if he wanted to waste the energy. He would die Little Francis. All because he was a little shrimp in the first grade of their neighborhood parochial school.

Only Petey called him Francis. It drove Mike Quinn bat-shit. One day when Sister Margaret left their third grade classroom for a minute, Mike grabbed Petey and pulled him close like in the movies, trying to scare him. Always years ahead of the others, Petey kept smiling then leaned in close to whisper in Mike's ear: "You're a moron, Mike. You take your hands off me, and keep them off me and my little brother, and I promise I won't make your life miserable by proving to the other kids every single day all through junior high how stupid you really are."

It took Mike Quinn's stage IV pancreatic cancer for him to tell that story. Little Francis had come to the hospital with some silly balloons and Mike started laughing like crazy: "Give me some of that brandy you've always got stashed and I'll tell you why I let Petey call you Francis."

It's probably why he always cut Petey and Donnie some slack. Of course, no one in the city would ever have suspected Little Francis had even the smallest of soft spots. He was notoriously thorough in his efforts for Arthur. There were at least a half dozen men who'd never see the light of day thanks to what Arthur thought of as his interventions.

The name certainly didn't help Fat Francis because he ended up overweight and gay, quite a handicap in their deeply Catholic neighborhood. Not that it mattered to Little Francis, because Fat Francis was a standup guy. Who after school would make them all English muffin pizza and later opened a ritzy restaurant downtown.

Francis Flunky hightailed it out of town once he turned sixteen. He owned a fairly successful Pack and Ship store in Phoenix, Arizona until he took a couple of rounds in the chest. Some stupid

Mexican gang dispute he unknowingly got caught up in when a customer decided to pack and ship fifty pounds of someone else's weed out of his store.

And, for reasons he'd never quite get, meek Arthur Flynn magically turned into "Don't Fuck With Arthur Flynn!" Little Francis had been working for Arthur for years now. Ever since he aced sniper training but got bounced from the Army for almost strangling an officer.

When the Flynn clan disappeared most of the Castronovas and annexed their territory, Arthur found himself at the very center of his family's ruthless gambling and drug-dealing operation. Arthur, though, never looked the part. Instead, he most closely resembled one of those dusty neighborhood accountants who wore the boring brown shoes and brown pants and slightly crumpled, once-white shirt. That guy working out of the one-room office, busy only during tax time.

There was something off with Arthur's eyes and from the time he was five he was stuck with thick glasses. He never made it past five foot six, and unfortunately had lost a large swatch of hair by twenty-five. While his large hooded sweatshirts failed to mask his extra pounds, the puffy cheeks, and clumsy loud laugh hid the fact that he had become a sneaky, cold-hearted, and calculating bastard.

Arthur, for the moment, didn't want to kill Petey. And Little Francis wasn't yet ready for Arthur to ask him to intervene. They were both still superstitious: Sister Margaret hadn't gone a day without reminding them that if they kept sinning, especially against their fellow Catholics and fellow classmates, but mostly against her, everlasting hell with its life of perpetual pain would be right there waiting for them.

And the truth was everybody from the neighborhood was rooting for Petey. They had never let on, but all of them except Fat Francis had had the hots for Petey's mom, and early on, pretty much everybody figured out how she was supporting the boys. It didn't take much in the sympathy department to know that if their moms had been as hot as Petey's, they wouldn't have wanted to be on the receiving end of what could easily have come their way. So all of them, without ever really talking about it, decided to give Petey and Donnie a pass.

Arthur was always wanting to be absolutely sure about things. Always wanting to know not only the story he was told, but the story behind that story. Whenever anyone would say "trust me," Arthur would smile and say "sure thing." And then, after the guy was gone, he'd turn to Little Francis and tell him, "I'd rather know than trust." Then Little Francis would find out every last bit of whatever was really going on, and whenever there was a problem, a really big problem, he would take the appropriate steps.

Arthur, of course, knew from the very beginning all about the phony ID. Even as a teenager he had tracked every step of Petey's transformation to Peter, and so knew all about his studying, his time at Ann Arbor, then Little Pointe and the fabulously rich new family.

All those years, he had a pretty good deal going with Petey. He'd provide the place and the poker players and charge a fee for services: the liquor, the pills, pot, the coke, and the sex. And, of course, there was always a mark or two amongst them. In exchange for the free ride, Petey would kick him back five percent of his winnings. And Petey would win a hell of a lot more than he'd lose. Most times.

But the drag was the possibility that this time around Petey would turn out to be just a slightly smarter version of his father, and even with the rich wife wouldn't be able to make good on his debt. And have to be dealt with.

So when Arthur called him into the office, Little Francis was once more hoping that day hadn't come.

Arthur had one of those wooden chairs that could rock back and forth a bit, and roll about the floor. He had always wanted to be able to stick his legs up on his really big wooden desk, but never quite got the balancing act together. It looked so cool in the movies. But a couple of times he leaned back too fast and too far and flipped the chair over, banging his head on the wall.

Arthur paid others to do his paperwork, so mostly he sat behind the desk and read the sports pages, racing forms, or People magazine. Little Francis thought it was ridiculous but knew his boss wanted to feel like other bosses, bosses with real offices and real memos and all that other stuff. So a while ago he went to Staples and bought Arthur a stapler, a paper clip dispenser, some note pads, and a bunch of pens and pencils. But they were so rarely used, they had made their way into the desk drawers.

Arthur looked up at Little Francis: "So where is Donnie now?"

"Betsy said because of the missing wife, he was going to

Cleveland to check out a cousin, this dentist's wife. So one of our Cleveland friends found him and followed him to the bus terminal. Where some bag lady told Donnie she might have gone to Des Moines. Our guy gave her a fifty and says that even though the bag lady's a bit loony, the info could be legit."

"What's that numb-nuts going to do, check every fucking bus terminal in America? That's got to be a day's driving, right? Cleveland to Des Moines goddamn Iowa."

"Six hundred and sixty miles, boss."

"What's the clock on Petey?"

"You gave him another two weeks."

"Why the fuck did I do that?"

"You were feeling sentimental. Because of Donnie, boss."

"Well, that's when Donnie was still here and still working for me. Not driving all over the country looking for that rich bitch."

"What do you want me to do, boss?"

"You tell him I want him back. Tell him I have a job for him."

"What kind of job?"

"My friend from Vegas is coming back into town again and I need someone with him. Just in case."

"I'll tell him."

"And the Petey problem ..."

"Yeah?"

"Remember our talk about smelling?"

"Smelling?"

"I told you years ago that what I liked about you was that you could smell fear ... Do you remember what I said I could smell?"

Little Francis nodded. But he knew that nodding wasn't enough because Arthur was wanting to make a point, to hear it out loud: "Money, Boss ... you said you could smell money."

"Petey, no matter what he said about needing some time, I can smell the money. He's got some. Probably not as much as what he owes. But it's pissing me off big time that he's holding out on me. Just come to me with the dough and say: 'Arthur, this is just a part of what I'm into you for, but it's all I got.' If he did that, I'd feel a lot better than I do. Anyway, I'm sticking to my word. I said two weeks, but I'm telling you not a day more."

*   *   *

This was so complicated it hurt Donnie's brain. Could it be that she really was the "Burger lady; nice lady?" And of the three D's, had the "Burger lady" actually picked Des Moines?

Petey knew all about odds. Petey would know what to do, and he was getting ready to call when his phone rang. Thinking it was cool how Petey called just when he was thinking about him, he answered: "Hey, Petey …"

"It's Little Francis. Arthur needs you. He's got a job for you. He says forget about Cleveland. And forget the buses. It's important. Get your ass back here."

Donnie didn't have a chance to say anything. Little Francis hung up.

Donnie called Petey, who answered on the third ring. "So listen, Petey. The Museum here in Cleveland didn't pan out and I also checked out the cousin's house. Nothing. Then I figured I'd check the Greyhound station. A crazy lady recognized her from the picture but said her hair was black. Called her "Burger lady; nice lady." Said she could've gone to Dubuque or maybe Des Moines or maybe Denver. All D's. Then after I gave her the second burger and another fifteen bucks, she said Des Moines.

"You want I should go to Des Moines, Petey? Or maybe Dubuque? Denver? Shit, I could do all three. But also I just got a call from Little Francis. Arthur's got a job for me. Wants me back now."

"I was just going to call you, Donnie. I've got interest from some money people in Chicago. You did great going to Cleveland. But it doesn't make a lot of sense to have you driving all over the country without better information. Plus, we've got to keep Arthur happy. So I could really use you back here in case there's news. Who knows, what if she's in a hospital somewhere in a coma and wakes up and they call? Do me a favor and tell Little Francis you'll do the job for Arthur and get here as soon as you can."

"Sure, Petey."

And it wasn't until Donnie was on the road and fifty miles closer to Detroit that he realized that Little Francis and Arthur had known somehow that he was in Cleveland. Not just Cleveland but the Greyhound station in Cleveland, thinking they were good, really good. Scary good. So good he wouldn't mention it to Petey. No point worrying him.

FOURTEEN

She read "Chieh" several times, the *I Ching* the first book she had read in … well, who knows? Sometimes the letters were blinking, sometimes melting, then gone, but she kept going back to the beginning of the passage, to try again and again. Everything was jumbled up in her mind. Katie's words colliding with her own thoughts: master, servant, water over lake, limitations, and then more limitations, and the door and the courtyard. Sometimes one shouldn't go out the door, but then other times not leaving brought misfortune. Sarah wasn't sure what this misfortune was, but she was guessing it wasn't good.

That night, at the dinner table, it was harder than usual for Sarah to follow the conversation. She could see Bea Foster's lips moving but she was still thinking about the *I Ching*. Until Bea Foster gave up words for waving, and Sarah finally saw Bea's hand traveling back and forth in front of her.

"Dessert, Sarah? I made some apple pie. Mr. Foster's favorite. He loved his apple pie."

The old man grunted: "That was his mom's fault, made him a pie twice a week. I said, 'you're spoiling the boy!' Never had pie when I was a kid."

Sarah shook her head. No pie. Not tonight.

Then hours later, lying there in the dark on the bed, the black lines of the hexagrams passing beneath the lids of her closed eyes. And then the dream: moving sleepily and slowly through white. She looked down to her toes, sinking deep into soft clouds as she walked. So very comfortable until, in the very back of her mind hearing that word "misfortune," then feeling it, a kind of dread seeping in, supplanting the soft comfort. Somehow she felt she ought to be getting out of there. Then another voice, so hard to hear at first, from far off: "not who we thought." A familiar voice, maybe. Feeling she should move but move towards what, she wondered? To the door, the gate, the courtyard?

She looked up and almost immediately she was blinded by a sparkling bright sun, the light piercing through the fog of her mind. And, for the slightest moment, she saw a man in black. But the light hurt, and she averted her eyes, hoping to find the soft comfort once more. Trying to hide, to blend back into the clouds. But all too quickly she saw the shadow moving toward her, and woke before the approaching collision.

Sarah was drenched in sweat, her heart racing. The clock said three-twenty. It took a while to figure out where she was, in the bed, at Bea's, and to feel her legs. She swung herself out of bed and walked slowly to the small bathroom. She found the cold-water faucet and cupped her hands, then splashed her face. Back in bed, even as the nightmare began to fade, she knew it wouldn't be easy to sleep.

FIFTEEN

The round-trip drive to Cleveland had taken its toll but Donnie tried to hide it. Peter saw that familiar look on Donnie's face: the dreadfully eager need to please, his desire to do whatever it took to make things right, to be back in his brother's good graces.

Which was convenient because there was work to be done. And once again Peter needed Donnie to do it.

But Peter knew down deep that it was he, not Donnie, who had made the biggest mistake of all. He had waited too long.

He would always remember that day. The morning, picking the old asshole up at what they called his country place, the place Peter coveted. Peter knew all too well, even if she didn't, why for years he religiously spent parts of Tuesday and Thursday and the occasional weekend night there.

Then taking him once again to the all too predictable Sunday brunch at the Club. Thankfully, the second even more serious heart attack had taken enough out of him to put an end to the interminable small talk. And all she really wanted was to read her Sunday New York Times in silence. So by default he was allowed his Sudoku puzzles.

It was during the next phase of their Sunday, while out on the boat, energized by the breeze, the speed, that he was overcome by the sense that he might actually be able to salvage this dream of his, the land, the houses, and simultaneously dispense with his debt to Arthur.

The sun was particularly bright. There was hardly a cloud in sight. Looking out from the bridge at his ever more fragile father-in-law, he imagined one of those cheap egg timers with the white sand dripping down. These days, the S.O.B. couldn't go anywhere without his oxygen.

As much as he hated the guy, he knew how attached she was to him. Just watching the two of them there on the deck, whispering to each other, it was hard to imagine what she'd do once he was gone. She always seemed so content when her father was around. If you erased the oxygen tank, you were seeing a picture you could have seen last year and the year before that and the year before that.

Peter had made reservations for dinner at Luigi's. They always enjoyed Luigi's. She loved the manicotti. A couple of glasses of red wine would help. He had prepared his plans for the development in a spiffy packet, and thought just before dessert, he'd show her what he wanted to do.

Later that evening, as she was finishing up her dinner, he began: "I'm not sure I've mentioned the new consortium I've been working with. They're an eclectic group of entrepreneurs from Abu Dhabi and Qatar, along with representatives of some serious Swiss investment funds. I've been talking to them about a state of the art development with several high end units and a private dock and beach. Everything's green, from using non-toxic construction materials, radiant heat, solar panels, extensive common grounds and organic gardens.

"I don't mean to be morbid, dear, but your dad isn't going to be with us much longer. And I thought, well why not dedicate all this to him: he's always been a bit of a visionary. We're combining luxurious living with a twentieth-first century approach to sustainability. The way I figure it, the Potter Road property would be absolutely perfect."

Ever so slowly he could see that look seeping into her eyes. That was the problem with playing cards for a living. You paid an awful lot of attention to people's faces. In this case, it was the look she got when she knew she was going to disappoint. He hated that look because he so rarely saw it. And he had learned that because she so reluctantly found herself willing to say no, there was virtually no chance you could change her mind when she did.

She hesitated, picking at her profiteroles. "I'm sorry, but Daddy just spoke to me about the land. This afternoon, in fact, out on the boat. He asked me to promise to give it all to the Land Conservancy, in memory of Mother. It's obviously very, very important to him … I told him I would. So, unfortunately, you are going to have to find some other land."

Luckily, he controlled his anger and smiled. "Well, of course, dear. That's a very lovely gesture on your dad's part. And I'm sure, with some additional work, I can find somewhere else to put the project," thinking that the fucking asshole is going to screw me one last time before he croaks, and as his smile faded, he turned his attention to his cheesecake.

She was relieved he took it so well. And she could see him thinking of alternatives. That was one of the things she most admired about Peter, his adaptability and resourcefulness.

*   *   *

He could have asked Donnie to kill the son-of-a-bitch anytime after his heart problems. Make it look natural and avoid all this crap. His problems with Arthur, needing to kill her, Donnie's stupid trip to Cleveland. If only the old man had died before he laid this eff-ing guilt-trip on her, involving her in this bullshit legacy. Hoping that leaving the land to the birds and bees would somehow undo all the shame he had brought to his marriage.

So it was very painful to admit how badly he had miscalculated; how he had missed his moment. Knowing that more than ever, he needed Donnie to fix this. So very ironic considering how from the day his mother died, he had thought of Donnie as someone to carry and to care for, younger, dumber, and ill-equipped.

Looking back, there were moments on the road from Petey to Peter, from Detroit to Little Pointe, that stood out like markers. Like when he discovered that the smart people, the rich people who mattered and could make things happen, that they had their own way of speaking. Why say "hate" when you could sound so much more refined by using "abhor?" With the added bonus that whoever you were talking to might not even realize that you despised them.

There was no denying that when he finally understood he could successfully pass, he knew Donnie couldn't come with him. There was no way Donnie could even walk the prim and proper streets of Little Pointe without sticking out, let alone be satisfactorily explained as a brother at the Country Club.

And it was only because Donnie was so deeply loyal that he allowed all this to happen with regret, not fury. It was only because Donnie loved him more than he loved Donnie.

And now, ironically, the occasion called for Petey more than Peter. Or, much better yet, for Donnie. Now Peter needed Donnie as much as or more than Donnie had needed Petey all those years ago.

SIXTEEN

"As I looked back at your reading," Katie began, "I was struck again by the changing circumstances of 'Chieh.' Most of us, at different times, have been either a master or a servant, with more or less power. Parent; child. Owner; employee. In control of a situation, or not. What stood out for me was the critical need to carefully navigate that uncertain universe. The need to exercise caution, refrain from hasty action, then as circumstances change quickly respond with courage; to know when to stay and when to go."

Sarah cried out: "I couldn't ... I just couldn't."

"What do you mean?"

"I couldn't see a door. The way out. Last night and before, and before that. In my dream, inside with white clouds. I'm looking down at more white. Maybe there's a door like in 'Chieh' but I don't see it. I couldn't get to it. I look up and there's bright light blinding me, and someone, I think a large man, is coming toward me. Then the white turns to black."

"I'm so sorry you're having such frightening nightmares. This place you're describing, Sarah, is it big or small? A home? An office? A store?"

"I'm not sure, a place that maybe I know, that maybe I live in. But I don't, do I? I live at the Fosters. In my dream, he is moving toward me, and I am afraid. I'm sweating. My heart is beating too fast. My body shakes."

"Sarah, you asked: 'Why am I here?' The dream is a possible answer. If disaster was waiting for you behind that door, no wonder you felt compelled to leave.

"Before I met you, Sarah, and before you threw 'Chieh,' I had a dream. I was in what might have been a home, but a home very different from this. It was a big and grand space, like a place my parents took me to as a girl in Manhattan. I felt there was someone else there, but couldn't see anyone. The door led to a courtyard, a beautiful garden. But I couldn't open the door. I couldn't get out. I don't know why. It was very confusing. Maybe I was experiencing some of that 'anxious hesitation,' but fortunately I didn't feel any of the great fear you did ...

"In 'Chieh' there's the suggestion that not only the servant, but the master is in danger:

> If an individual is bent only on pleasure and enjoyment ... If he gives himself over to extravagance, he will have to suffer the consequences, with accompanying regret.

"We're talking here about a life centered on pleasure. Is that you, Sarah? Were you living an extravagant life? And if so, was your money earned honestly? Are you a successful businesswoman? An heiress? A rock star?

"In recent years, we've seen such great extremes: multi-million dollar bonuses to executives while jobs are shipped overseas and homes foreclosed. With so many millions of us living beyond our means, it's not hard to imagine being so burdened by debt, so desperate, that one chooses to engage in criminal behavior ...

"I'm sounding a bit too much like my parents, and I don't mean to rant ... But sometimes rather than deal directly with the loss of a home, the bankruptcy of a business, rather than face the shame of dealing with friends and family, people run from those they might have disappointed, from those who know them, love them, from everything they know."

Sarah remembered the crisp bills she had brought with her. She hadn't told Katie about the money. Why, she wondered? Was this what Katie was talking about? Was she ashamed of something she had done?

Katie sat through the silence.

Sarah tried hard to remember. She had spent so little of the money.

"I've had breakfast and lunch at Dom's, sometimes coffee and tea. And Deb took me back to MagicMart, no kids this time, and we bought a pair of new sneakers, these sneakers," pointing down "and a couple of pairs of jeans and underwear to go with what Bea and I had gotten. That doesn't seem extravagant, does it?" Sarah paused, "But back there and then ... I don't remember."

"Well, Sarah, you could be the master, but considering your dream, you're just as likely to be the servant in this story. And I'd like to believe that both literally and figuratively, you have made it safely out the door. Here, Sarah, alive and free, not there."

Rabbit, having moved from nap to awake, journeyed from the

kitchen to the living room, briefly checked on Katie, then walked toward Sarah. Rabbit stared at Sarah for a moment, then licked the left hand which clutched her left knee. Startled for only a moment, she brought her right hand to his head and gently scratched behind his ear. Rabbit smiled, then Sarah smiled.

Katie poured some more tea: "If the first hexagram is about what's behind the door, the second hexagram could be about life for you beyond the door:

Ch'ien / The Creative

These unbroken lines stand for the primal power, which is light-giving, active, strong, and of the spirit ...

When an individual draws this oracle, it means that success will come to him from the primal depths of the universe and that everything depends upon his seeking his happiness and that of others in one way only; that is, by perseverance in what is right.

... and the process is represented by an image from nature: "The clouds pass and the rain does its work, and all individual beings flow into their forms."

Sarah repeated slowly: "The clouds pass ... " Katie smiled and slowly Sarah smiled back. After a moment or two, Katie continued:

"This is so very positive and powerful. But I want us to read a few more selections:

Hidden dragon. Do not act.

... The dragon is a symbol of the electrically charged, dynamic, arousing force that manifests itself in the thunderstorm ...

"And then, Sarah, the *I Ching* reminds us about what's at stake when ambition and arrogance challenge one's commitment to living 'right.'

... danger lurks here at the place of transition from lowliness to the heights ...

"And warning us about the 'titanic aspirations that exceed one's power:'

Arrogant dragon will have cause to repent.

A precipitous fall would follow.

"We have only known each other a very short time, Sarah, but according to the reading, you may have been, or perhaps still are, in the midst of a critical battle about the right way to live. It could be about money or power. It could be a battle within, or a battle with others. It's possible the figure coming up the stairs is symbolic, that part of you that is ambitious, arrogant, dark and dangerous to yourself and others. Or he could be real ...

"I'd prefer to believe that despite whatever it is that has brought you here, that despite the clouds, the thunderstorm, the precipitous fall, well, that there's success at the end of this struggle. That you are indeed a manifestation of the creative, and that there is great light in you."

SEVENTEEN

Frank Falco parked his taxicab a block away from Dr. Silver's office on West End Avenue. He wasn't as pissed off as he was last Friday, but he certainly wasn't happy. His rehabilitation had started with the Department's mandated therapy: standard operating procedure for an Officer Related Shooting. But after several months, Frank still didn't feel right. The Department shrink had suggested Dr. Silver and he had reluctantly agreed to see her.

Sitting in the waiting room, he had the same feeling he had had before each session: he had nothing new to say, thinking he'd be better off taking a long walk in the city.

At three sharp, Dr. Adrienne Silver appeared at the door to her office and said hello. Her hair more white than gray, he figured her to be in her late sixties or early seventies, reading glasses hanging around her neck from a delicate silver chain. Probably no taller than five-four but radiating a power and confidence that made her seem far larger. While there were many small creases spreading out from the corners of both eyes, her eyes were youthfully intense. Several shades of gray, they matched both the gray pants and hand knit gray sweater she was wearing. Frank followed her into the office and moved to the comfortable chair a bit to her left, about eight feet across from her, with a view over her shoulder to the aquarium behind and the colorful fish who called it home.

She smiled, then without any preface quickly asked: "So Detective Falco, tell me again what happened that night?"

Frank couldn't keep the annoyance from his voice: "What happened to your notes? Didn't we go through this last session?"

Dr. Silver let her eyes do the smiling this time: "I have my notes, Detective, and I've read them. But what I know, and you might not, is that each time you tell me the story, you tell it differently. You remember different things. Now I know you're familiar with this phenomenon because that's what happens when you question people. But at those times, you're doing the asking, not the answering. Controlling the conversation. Let me assure you, it's appreciably different."

Frank didn't say anything, thought about it, and reluctantly found himself agreeing. "I guess you're right ... So, yeah, I'll take you through it again. Gloria and I had just had dinner at Havana

Moon, one of those inexpensive Chinese Cuban restaurants on Broadway, on the west side of the street, and we decided to take a walk uptown, maybe find some ice cream before going back to her place. We were talking about whether or not to pick up a movie. I was angling for that new caper movie with Denzel Washington when two guys come out of the delivery alley that leads to the back of the grocery. One grabs Gloria from behind; the other, the really big one, comes after me.

"The thin, wiry one who has Gloria says something like, 'Give up your money, your watch, jewelry, and you and this lady live to walk away.'"

"I must have laughed or sneered or something like that. Gloria thought I said something like: 'You must be kidding!' Anyway, whatever it was exactly, my tone just set them off. And that's when things turned cruel. All of a sudden, the thin one dragged Gloria with him, taking a step towards me. That was the first time I saw his knife. When I looked toward him and Gloria for just a split second, the big guy lands a punch to my head. And I go down.

"The big guy comes over to kick me in the stomach. I'll never forget that. The contempt. It wasn't so much the breath being slammed out of me, and the pain in the gut, but the look on his face like I was some kind of bug he could step on, or smash. The enjoyment in his eyes seeing me hurt. Then he was coming towards me on the ground.

"I think that's when I heard Gloria's scream. She might have been screaming before but that was the first time the sound penetrated. It was like time was stretching, sort of like that super-slow motion you see on television for football games, and it was like hearing everything with those big clunky headphones on. I managed to roll. I still can't remember exactly how. Now I'm seeing the big one coming for my wallet, and I can see his knife. In his right hand. The fury's rising in his face as he's realizing, because I'm moving now, he's not going to be getting the wallet so easily. And I can see the knife moving closer and closer.

"Somehow I reached out and got to the ankle holster and pulled my Ruger. Gloria said I shouted, 'Drop it, Police!' I can remember a shout, then some sort of a plea like 'Don't ... don't, I'm a cop!' But the big one seemed so filled with contempt, as if the gun wasn't there, didn't matter, could be overcome by sheer will and hate ... I'm hoping he comes to his senses. I'm pretty sure I said 'don't' again. Gloria swore the knife was almost at my throat before I fired. And that's the last thing I really remember."

"When did you learn who they were?"

"They took us to the same hospital. They said I passed out from the blow to my head. I think maybe his forearm hit me. They said my head probably hit the pavement. He died on the operating table. The bullet nicked the heart.

"I think I heard one of the nurses say he was just fifteen. Later they picked up the other one, his older cousin, twenty-one."

"Thank you, Detective. Now, can you tell me what's new about how you told the story this time?"

Frank was surprised by the question. And tried to think back to what he had just said. After a few moments of silence, "No. Not really."

"This was the first time you remembered that they both had knives, and acknowledged that you understood at the time that both you and Gloria could have died. You also clearly remembered that you repeatedly warned them and refrained from firing your weapon until the young man's knife was perilously close to your throat. Not only that, but you acknowledged that you and Gloria saw and experienced pretty much the same thing."

Frank nodded slowly.

"You know, Detective, there have been several studies involving Officer Related Shootings, and they've discovered some interesting things. A very large percentage of officers found they were responding to the threat as if they were on automatic pilot. They couldn't remember many of the details, but remembered that time seemed to have slowed down for them, and that sounds seemed muffled. About forty percent of them experienced some variety of 'disassociation,' a fancy way of saying that they were feeling detached, or as if what was happening wasn't really happening to them."

Frank found himself slipping back in time. Recalling how everyone in the department tried to make him feel better. Telling him things like the kid was as big as a linebacker. Nobody could have known he was fifteen. It was you or the kid, someone said. He would have killed you. Then they would have killed Gloria.

He got it. It all made sense. And so here he was with Dr. Silver. Of course, it didn't help matters that he had inherited his parents' distrust of therapy. But the best thing about Dr. Silver was that she pressed him at a time when even his closest friends fell victim to an almost fatal politeness. She was sometimes relentless. It resembled, in many ways, a highly skilled interrogation.

The problem was that after all this talk, he still couldn't change the fact that he had shot and killed a 15-year-old boy. Not deliberately, or with malice aforethought. Not even, the Internal Affairs report reluctantly confirmed, with negligence. But however you sliced it, the kid was dead and killed with his gun.

"Where are you, Detective?"

"Sorry, Doc' ... Fell back into it there for a bit."

"And how does that feel, Detective?"

"Feel?"

"Yes, feel ... we're getting a clearer idea of what you did. What you know. Now let's get a better idea about how you feel."

"Pissed ... Tired ... Really pissed ... I don't know. I want this done with. I don't want to dream about it, think about it, remember it, or talk about it. How's that?"

"That's a beginning, Detective. So who are you pissed at? Me, for asking these questions?"

"Sure, why not? I can think of a lot of things I'd rather be doing besides having this conversation. And yeah I know it's my choice to be here ... but you asked! I'm pissed at those assholes for trying to kill me and Gloria. I'm pissed at the kid for forcing me to kill him. I'm pissed at myself for letting it all get to me. I'm pissed at Gloria for leaving me, even though I know I pushed her away. Which means I'm pissed at everything and everyone. So, yeah, that definitely includes you."

"What about your parents? You haven't mentioned them? Are you pissed at them?"

"What do my parents have to do with any of this? They're dead!"

"I'm asking you, Detective."

"Why do I think 'nothing' isn't going to work for you?"

"Is that because it wouldn't work for you, if we switched seats?"

Frank laughed. "Good answer."

"Well, if it's really that good, how about you just answer the question. Are you pissed at your parents?"

"My parents were leftists. I'm a cop. They fought the cops ... well that's not really fair. Not them personally. They were always very peaceful. But when I was a kid, we all went to rallies about

Central America and globalization and abortion rights, and the emphasis was always on the victims. And I appreciate that. Of course, now that I've been on both sides of a demonstration, I know a lot of us on the job are probably just as freaked out as the demonstrators. Granted, we have the nightsticks, the shields, the tear-gas, the horses, and, yeah, the guns.

"But we have the responsibility to preserve public safety. And our orders. And, of course, my folks and their friends and the thousands of other demonstrators were always on the other side of the barricades. People are screaming at you. Some of them just inches away. Some of them spitting. Pushing and shoving. Then there are the assholes throwing rocks, maybe bottles, usually at the back of the demonstration. It gets crazy. Sometimes it feels like you're just protecting yourself and before you know it you're called a pig and someone's yelling, 'Police Brutality!' And yeah, I know the Bill of Rights is important and I acknowledge that some cops lose it. And then all of sudden one of us is clubbing someone and using the pepper spray. But it's like a war out there."

Frank stopped, a little uncomfortable about how loud he had gotten, wondering if maybe he seemed a bit out of control. "Sorry … I probably didn't really answer your question." Dr. Silver didn't say anything and after a moment, Frank began again:

"My dad was away much of the time. Where exactly was always a big secret. After he died, my mom talked a little bit about what he had been doing and where, but not with a lot of detail, because she was still involved in the work and didn't want to endanger anyone.

"But I heard a steady stream of talk about social justice, equal rights, and fighting oppression … The need to help peasants and workers, create farm cooperatives, build day care centers, I'm sure you get the idea. In Nicaragua, El Salvador, Venezuela, Bolivia, Chile … "

"You sound slightly dismissive, Detective. Are you suggesting that what they were doing was a waste of time?"

"No … well maybe … I don't really know. I know I hardly had parents; Katie hardly had parents."

"Is that why you changed your name, Detective? Because you felt your father wasn't really a father …"

"How do you know about the names?"

"Not from the FBI, or the Department, Detective. I'm not one of those therapists who pretend not to have a life. I'm not a neutral presence. They may have been your parents but a lot of people who cared, who care about human rights, knew and respected them. I'm one of them. I met your parents and heard both of them speak on occasion. And in one of those great New York City coincidences I was at your father's Memorial to pay my respects.

"So, Detective, I presume you were born Frank Greenberg and that somewhere along the way, you decided to become Frank Falco, taking your mother's last name. I'd salute you as a feminist, only I suspect you made the choice out of anger."

Frank thought about asking her to say more about when she had met Carl and Theresa, but was overcome with his own memories:

"Carl seemed to have patience for just about everyone in the entire world but me. He wanted me to be smarter than I was, more compassionate than I was, more responsible. He was brilliant. I don't know if you know this, but his father died when he was eight, and they had no money. He started to work in his uncle's hardware store after school. Somehow he graduated high school, but never made it to college. Still he managed to read at least one book a day. Arguing with my dad was a waste of time. He could always quote some brilliant British historian or Balzac, a poet from Trinidad, a novelist from Nigeria, or Karl Marx or Ché Guevara, for that matter.

"He'd insist on reviewing my homework and each time a bunch of what I wrote would be crossed out in red. There would be rewritten sentences in the margins, and arrows that led to the other side of the paper with even more corrections. He always made it better, but ..." Frank trailed off, then looked over to Dr. Silver, who was quiet.

After a minute or so, Frank continued: "So I always figured he wouldn't have been particularly happy with my choices. Especially my decision to go into the Police Academy. And as I began to make a life for myself as an officer, I always imagined I had let him down somehow."

"So Detective, I'll take that as an acknowledgment that you were, and still are, pissed about your father. I'm going to make a slight leap here. After you finish being angry with me, I want you to think about what I'm saying in much the same way you'd think about a case you're working on. I think part of the problem here is that the shooting has brought the long-standing dispute you've had with your parents, and probably more with your father than your mother, back to the surface.

"The reality that we're dealing with here is that you didn't shoot a ruthless Mafioso, and you didn't shoot Timothy McVeigh or Osama bin Laden. You shot a poor black kid. You're very aware he was fifteen, but I notice you never mention his race. Of course, you were justified. Of course, you had to shoot. To protect yourself; to protect Gloria; and to protect every other person on that street. You were only doing your job, doing what you trained to do, and exactly what un-armed, innocent people like me need you to do at times like that.

"But, and this is a significant but, your parents spent their lives trying to understand why young people like your assailants would turn to violence, why hatred so often replaces mutual respect. They spent their lives fighting for equal education, good housing, jobs for young people of all colors. So, in some ways, your shooting that kid, in your mind, in your subconscious being, might have been a failure not only for you, but for them as well. For all of us really, for our schools, our neighborhoods, our families, but that may be broadening it all too much for us right now, and I really want you to narrow your focus here.

"I think you've been dealing with a deep layer of added guilt. You've taken on what I'm guessing is your imagined, probably exaggerated version of both your responsibility and their disappointment. So in your mind you've not only failed yourself but even more importantly you've failed your parents. If you could really hear how you speak about your father, you'd see how affected you still are by what you believe is his disapproval. It's something you're convinced of; and it's profoundly powerful.

"It would be presumptuous of me to dispute your judgment, and your portrayal of your father. Obviously I wasn't present. But I do know from a lifetime of work that it's one of the great and recurring tragedies of life that parents and children communicate so poorly.

"With greater understanding, you and your father might have come to realize that you made similar choices, albeit in very different ways. Of course, there are all kinds of police. And I've worked with quite a few in my practice. From polite and patient to sadistic and psychotic. But having gotten to know you a bit, I think I'm safe in saying that, like your father, you've been trying to use your talents to help bring some kind of justice to human interactions. You may not get this, and, unfortunately, we can't really check with your father, but in your separate and different ways, you both were trying to help the weak resist those who prey upon them. There are many police officers motivated more by an urge to control than a desire to protect. And there are political reformers more motivated by ego than inequity.

"But I'm bringing some rationality to this, some distance, looking at it from the outside, and you still seem to be trapped within. Anyway, let's change the subject for a second. When was the last time you went out for a drink or dinner with any of your buddies on the force? The last time you went out on a date? The last time you had a conversation with a friend or your sister?"

Frank sat there. He didn't actually know the answer to any of those questions. "A while," he offered.

"That's what I thought. You need to talk to someone beside me. I could tell you to go out with friends but I don't think you will for a while. So I'm invoking my Therapeutic Prerogative here. Think of it as part of the process … a transitional opportunity. I'll be right back."

Dr. Silver was back in a minute, carrying a large cage. By the time Frank could get up to help, she had put the cage down on the coffee table before him.

"Detective Falco, I'll like you to meet Danger. Danger, this is Detective Frank Falco. I want you guys to hang out for a bit, to get to know each other. I have a feeling this is a match made in heaven. If not, I'll be glad to re-think it."

Danger, green and a bit of blue, was a Quaker parrot about six inches tall. With his claws gripping its thin bars, Danger tried to poke his head out of his cage. He let loose a series of squawks, and looking directly at Frank, he declared: "Good boy! Good boy!"

Dr. Silver smiled: "You are, Danger. Such a good boy! And I want you to be a good boy for Detective Falco."

She looked from Danger to Frank:

"You've become obsessed with death and loss, Detective Falco. You killed a young man. You lost Gloria. You've lost your parents. You're not in touch with your sister. You've given up going to the precinct or drinking with your buddies. It's time now to introduce at least one living thing into your routine. I would have suggested a houseplant but I have a feeling, because it's non-verbal, you'd forget it was there. I thought about a dog, but then I had a much better idea. A bird! But not just any bird, an extraordinarily smart bird, and a bird I can vouch for, Danger!"

"It just so happens that Danger isn't getting along with my two other birds or my husband. Danger's a lot like you: obstinate and feisty, and if you violate his sense of space and security or he doesn't trust you, he's apt to bite you. The bite won't kill you but it will hurt.

"It'll be a toss-up as to who's really in charge. He's physically challenged because of a bad leg, but has perfectly adapted to his circumstances. Even though he hobbles, he gets where he needs to get. Perhaps you can learn something from Danger. In any event, think of this as a necessary therapeutic intervention. And, of course, if you can't handle him, or he decides you're not trustworthy, I'll find him another home.

"Here's a book about Quaker parrots, some food, some treats, a list of what you shouldn't feed him, and extra toys ... Let Danger into your life and think about what we've talked about. Time is up. We'll talk some more next time."

EIGHTEEN

Sarah hesitated, then asked the new question: "What was my life like back there?"

Katie could see that the coins felt more familiar to Sarah. She watched as Sarah moved from observer to participant.

Sarah shook the coins, then tossed two tails and a head. She picked up the pencil, looked at Katie, paused, and said: "two + two + three. That's a seven: an odd number and a straight line, right?"

Katie watched as Sarah drew a straight line at the bottom of the first hexagram, then hesitated a moment. "Another straight line at the bottom of the second, Sarah. Only three heads or three tails is a changing line."

Sarah drew another straight line at the base of the second hexagram, then picked up the coins, shook and threw again. Three tails. "Let's see, that's two + two + two, a six, a broken line. And changing." She added a broken line above the first line and a straight line to the second hexagram.

Each of her last four throws came up the same: two tails and a head, and she added four more straight lines to both hexagrams:

"The first hexagram is different, but your second hexagram is the same as last time," Katie reminded her. It took Sarah a few moments to find "T'ung Jên / Fellowship with Men." She handed the book back to Katie, who began to scan the chapter.

"I'll start with a few things that stand out for me:

> ... It is not the private interests of the individual that create lasting fellowship among men, but rather the goals of humanity ... If unity of this kind prevails, even difficult tasks like crossing the great water, can be accomplished ...

Katie paused, then read some more:

> The beginning of union among people should take place before the door ... The basic principles of any kind of union must be equally accessible to all concerned. Secret agreements bring misfortune ...

> There is danger here of formation of a separate faction on the basis of personal and egotistic interests. Such factions ... originate from low motives and therefore lead in the course of time to humiliation.

"In our dreams, we have both been before a door, and neither felt fellowship, peace or unity. And you were threatened. Sooner rather than later, I hope we'll learn something about the relationships you had back there. What they might tell us about personal, egotistical interests vs. fellowship, selfishness vs. a concern for others. To discover what secrets might have been kept from you. Or the secrets you might have kept."

Sarah was quiet for a while. "Unfortunately, if I had a secret, it is still a secret ... As for the low motives, the humiliation, I really don't know ... "

Katie had the distinct feeling there was something Sarah wasn't saying. Then reminding herself to be patient: "Sometimes things happen that so shock us, our system shuts down. It's a way to protect ourselves, to allow us time enough to heal. It's a way to ensure that we're strong enough to face what has happened. For me, that event is the death of my father and I'm probably still not totally ready to face it ...

"But, as the *I Ching* suggests, not knowing could also be the result of not being told, of being excluded, of not belonging to the group or union that has made the secret agreement. Or of being lied to."

Sarah closed her eyes.

Katie began again: "This is both important and disturbing:

> He hides weapons in the thicket ...

> Here fellowship has changed about to mistrust.

103

Each man distrusts the other, plans a secret
ambush ... We are dealing with an obstinate
opponent ...

"Speaking of things you may not want to remember: here are
former friends becoming enemies. This could be a family dispute,
an affair, a marriage, a friendship, or business venture that's broken
down. And the dark figure of your dream, well, he could be the
manifestation of the secret ambush the *I Ching* describes. Symbolic
or literal."

Sarah opened her eyes and reached for her tea. She tried to
imagine family, marriage, a business venture. She could, of course,
conjure up Bea's at dinnertime, Dom's, and Jack's gas station. And
family could be Deb and the kids. But that was here, not there. She
put the tea cup down and shook her head.

Katie slowly began again: "In 'Fellowship with Men,' the *I
Ching* offers two different visions of a union: the first relationship,
while marked by differences in status and sustained struggle, offers
in the end a measure of happiness:

> Two people are outwardly separated, but in their
> hearts they are united. They are kept apart by their
> positions in life. Many difficulties and obstructions
> arise between them, and although it costs them a
> severe struggle to overcome the obstacles, they
> will succeed. When they come together their
> sadness will change to joy.

"Then there's the other, far less happy possibility:

> The warm attachment that springs from the heart
> is lacking here.

"The reading reminds us that while we can transcend our
differences, holding different beliefs, coming from diverse
backgrounds, or wanting different things in life can just as easily
undermine the bonds between people.

"It's happened to me with my brother, with boyfriends, and
bosses. It can be very painful sometimes. I don't mean to minimize
your condition, but there are many forms of amnesia: the most

pronounced, the traumatic loss of our memory, but what about the ways we lose our sense of connection to the world, or forget how to love and be loved."

Sarah could feel her back tighten, imagining the warmth of that warm attachment slowly leaking from her, feeling her body grow cold.

"You asked 'What was my life like back there?' and again you've come up with 'Ch'ien / the Creative' as your second hexagram. So let's think about the combination of 'Fellowship with Men' and 'the Creative.'

Sarah was still silent as Katie continued: "We're reminded that success comes only by persevering in what is right. There are many who live with darkness, or require darkness to do what they do. More and more it feels as if there was a dispute back there about how to live life. And while we still don't know what happened, at least we know the dragons came:

> There appears a flight of dragons without heads.
> Good fortunes.

Sarah pressed down on the muscles of her neck, hoping to rub away some of the growing tension. She knew she needed some time away from the words, the too many words. When, perhaps later, with some perspective, she might see Katie's dragon. She closed her eyes for several moments, sighed, then opened them and said sadly: "Like your dragon, I seem to have lost my head. And somehow I am here, not back there. Bea tells me I took the bus, but perhaps your book is right, and I took a dragon."

NINETEEN

Donnie was dreaming about it again. Thinking it was probably stupid of him, but he felt he just wasn't dressed right. The jeans he hadn't washed in days, the work boots. Considering how eff-ing fancy the house was. Real stupid. Knowing that if he was going to mug and kill anybody else in the whole world, he wouldn't be worrying about any of this stuff.

Thinking he would have felt a whole lot more comfortable if Petey had just once invited him to the house to visit. Because he was completely put off by how eff-ing big that room was. It was mostly gigantic open space, all that marble, and only a few dinky end tables. And that weird white couch he was afraid he'd get dirty and that glass table with the magazines about fancy houses. No comfortable chairs to take a load off. Like one of those really big rooms in the movies where rich people in the old days danced all dressed up.

His mind blown by that curving marble staircase. And considering all the coke, plus the ecstasy he did, the nagging thought that he wasn't on his game.

Taking a couple of toots waiting for her to come home, well maybe a lot more than just a couple. Watching her enter, still wearing her workout clothes, then quickly moving upstairs to shower and change. Thinking it was nuts to kill such a beautiful lady. Another toot or two before trying to get the ski mask on his face, and spacing out a bit figuring the best way to hold the gun with his gloves, safety on, butt out. Should have gotten those really thin football gloves, not the thick winter ones. Lame ass way to do this.

The mask was Petey's idea, to make it look and feel like a robbery gone bad. Making Donnie pretend like he was an actual robber. Because it would help to make it what he called more authentic. Well, the mask was maybe a good way to look like a thief and hide his face, but then when he saw her, it made it a complete drag trying to make it up those curvy stairs without tripping. Hardly seeing anything. Then the sweat falling into his eyes, the stinging making it even worse. Even stoned he knew that this was dumb.

The thing about Petey was that anything, actually everything he said always sounded so eff-ing convincing. And hitting her, like one of those home-invasion things. Making sure to take her ring. Which felt pretty creepy. Thinking it would be so much easier just to shoot her. Two shots to the heart.

She was coming down the stairs when the phone rang. Thinking what a stupid thing it was to keep his phone on. But after a couple of rings, and looking in all his pockets for the goddamn phone, he rolled over and found himself in his own bed, still mostly asleep, the dream gone. It was morning and answering it, Little Francis was yelling, telling him to get up and get his ass over to check in with Arthur. It was time to go to work.

The job was to protect Bobby V. A safe trip home to Detroit, a gift from Arthur who always stayed with Bobby V. on his trips to Vegas. Unfortunately, as Little Francis always reminded him, Bobby V. had made a lot of enemies during his Detroit days. So just stay alert and keep him safe, was all.

But pretty much everybody in Detroit who knew Bobby V. knew that he had a regular routine, beginning first with Antoinetta's, and his usual order of pasta fagioli, stuffed mushrooms, veal parmesan, rigatoni with red sauce, some extra garlic bread, then a pair of cannoli helped along by a couple of espressos.

After dinner, it was a trip to Bella's, the exclusive, high-class version of Big Pink, and Bella's very special room, and a fifteen-year-old or more likely an eighteen-year-old girl who could pass for fifteen. Then on to Maguire's Pool Hall.

So nobody, especially Donnie, was particularly shocked when this big guy came out from between some cars on the street in front of Bella's screaming that Bobby V. had screwed his daughter. But screaming wasn't all he had in mind.

Donnie saw the guy reach for his gun and moved quickly to his left to shield Bobby V. Which is why the bullet landed in the fleshy part of Donnie's upper left arm instead of ruining Bobby V.'s vacation. Donnie was sufficiently pissed off to fire first one, then two, then three shots into the guy's chest. Then, despite his own wound, managed to drag the guy out of sight and into a dark alley.

It only took a quick phone call, and within moments Arthur's guys were there to clean things up. Little Francis took Bobby V. on to Maguire's and Donnie was taken to be sewed up by some surgeon who, because he loved the horses, and the wrong horses way too much, owed Arthur a bunch of favors. Then, Arthur gave

Donnie an extra two grand for taking one and saving his friend's life.

Donnie knew he hadn't wanted to kill the guy; he hadn't even wanted to hurt him. Because if he had a daughter he might have done the same thing. But he really couldn't stand it when people shot him.

Some people liked the feel of a gun in their hand. Liked feeling they had an advantage. But Donnie wasn't crazy about guns. He knew and understood fists and feet and street fighting. Guns made everybody stupid and careless. People who wouldn't think twice about going up against him one on one wouldn't hesitate to pull a gun. Like the guy who just died because he had a gun, and decided to use it on Bobby V. If he had just taken a punch at Bobby V. he'd still be walking the streets, with a limp maybe but walking.

TWENTY

Katie had worked for Anne at "Books, Books, & More Books" for five years. For Katie, there was something comforting about the smell of used books, the faint musky scent of those who had held and read these books in years gone by.

Old books were in her blood. Carl had had the odd idea, the delusion actually, that dragging first Frank, and then both his kids, each and every Saturday from one used bookstore to another counted as family time. Carl would park Katie in front of the old-fashioned Howard Pyle books with their rich illustrations of knights and pirates and Robin Hood, or if she were particularly cranky, Audubon. Frank was left with sports.

Frank felt he was being scammed, pissed that this was somehow considered a worthy father-son activity, but Katie learned early on it was best not to fight it. Instead, she surrendered to the lush worlds of the Round Table or Sherwood Forest. Each week it was pretty much the same, an hour or so at each of two or three or sometimes four Manhattan bookstores.

The thing about Carl, unlike most buyers of books, was that he read all the books he bought. Every room, even the hallways in their small apartment in the Bronx, was lined with books. They overflowed their shelves in the living room, were stacked on every flat surface. There were books in the kitchen, books in the bedrooms, books in the bathroom.

Katie had worked several jobs in the Berkshires before she went to work for Anne. She had made coffee, mixed drinks, and taught as a third grade substitute teacher. These jobs all required her to be nice: too nice to too many. When she went to her interview with Anne, she was very clear that this time she was ready to devote herself exclusively to inanimate objects, to the books but not the book-buyers. Which was fine with Anne at first, because she had ten years' worth of books still waiting in the two storage barns out back, several small mountains of boxes of books she could hardly remember buying. Books destined, she hoped, once they were inventoried, to be bought and read all over again.

And, in fact, Anne did far more business with virtual customers, the legions of world-wide-web people she would never see or meet or chat with, than with old-fashioned flesh-and-blood buyers of books. Because the reality was that "Books, Books, & More Books" was located off an obscure country road, more than an hour from any city of substance and far from easy to find.

Not only was the scent and spirit of former readers present, but Katie could often feel Carl hovering as she opened a used book for the first time. She remembered his half-hearted attempts to bring order to his books. No sooner had he brought the alphabet to bear on one bookcase, than he added stacks more. There was almost no room to put them, let alone put them in their proper place.

Without realizing it, Anne had offered Katie another chance to confront the perpetual disorder of her childhood. This time, space was not the problem. What was required now was the strong will and determination and organizational dexterity necessary to bring discipline to Anne's disarray. With Anne's blessing, Katie began in the storage barns, moving books from their original boxes to clearly marked new boxes.

As she did this work she couldn't help but marvel at how profoundly the world of books had changed. Carl truly loved his books: each was a small treasure. But now as older readers died and their television-bred, Kindle-loving children sold off their belongings, so were these same books bought by used booksellers by the box-load rather than by title. It was as if the notion of the separate, hopefully unique work of art was on its way out. It was becoming ever so clear that these books were now commodities, and hardly valued commodities at that. Sold by the pound like fish.

Katie began with blue-labeled boxes for fiction, a series of red-labeled non-fiction boxes, then boxes for children and boxes for young adults. There was an incredible sense of peace to the process. Katie soon discovered that "Books, Books, and More Books" existed in its own time zone, outside the constraints of real-life commerce.

Several months in, Katie had become concerned by the slow pace of progress, wondering whether she shouldn't have created more boxes. Maybe an A, B, C on through Z for fiction, and more subcategories for the ever-expanding self-helpers. It was then that Anne confessed she had been born a Ferber and shared in the proceeds from every tube of Sunshine Shampoo sold throughout the known universe. When she turned eighteen, she married and then ten years later divorced Hamilton Faber, the first-born prince of the Coffee King franchise. As a recipient of large chunks of both the Ferber and Faber fortunes, Anne never had to worry about "Books." So there was really no need for Katie to sweat it. And she had, in fact, far exceeded Anne's expectations.

As it happened, by the end of year one, the old boxes had been replaced by the new, and the books began their migration from the storage barns. Some months into year two, Anne gently moved her into the main building, where she was sometimes coaxed from shelving the new books to share her love and knowledge of them with the occasional real-life customer. All of which pleased Anne no end.

Before year three came to a close, there was an entire section entitled: "Katie's Favorites," and Anne had her in front of the old Underwood typing out short and snappy praises.

"I want to expand 'Katie's Favorites,' a whole section I'm adding to the website," Anne announced that morning, "so you are going to have to do more reading. As of today, I'm instituting Rule 76 Part B: which stipulates that if there are no customers requiring handholding or with real money they're ready to hand over, and if there's no need for emergency shipping, then you're supposed to read a book of ours you've never read."

"How come I've never seen Rules 1 to 76 Part A?"

"They're on a strict need-to-know basis; either that or I've completely forgotten them!"

It was Rule 76 Part B that allowed Katie to take the time to roam without guilt from Mythology to Reference to read about dragons. And it didn't take long to discover that dragons were everywhere in the human imagination.

The Catholic Church had made it pretty clear that there were only two types of dragons: bad dragons and really bad dragons, and thanks to God, a few very blessed dragon-slayers. In one of the best known dragon encounters, the hapless citizens of Silene had tried in a variety of ways to placate their fire-snorting beast. First, they sacrificed their sheep. Then they sacrificed their kids, until eventually, even the King's daughter was offered. Fortunately for the royal family, Mr. George, having found and been favored by Christ, arrived in the nick of time. He dispatched the dragon, saved the day, and earned himself a sainthood.

There were different versions of the dragon tale: most that ended in death for the dragon, but a few where the dragon wisely chose conversion. Generally speaking, though, most of the dragons of the middle ages were plunderers and pillagers.

But Katie soon discovered that the Chinese, having given the world the compass, chopsticks, and the *I Ching*, had another view. And long experience with the very best of the dragon breed. Much like the Greeks, the Chinese proffered a beast of benevolence, a sometimes magical, wise, and spiritual creature. And, even today, the Chinese consider it auspicious to have been born in the Year of the Dragon.

So, after a morning of reading, Katie, for the moment at least, was hopeful that Sarah's dragons were of Chinese descent and a portent of positive things to come.

*   *   *

At about the same time Katie was working on Rule 76 Part B, Sarah was sitting at a table at Dom's, scrunched up against the wall, looking out the window, nursing a cup of coffee and eggs over easy. Every half hour or so, Deb was able to sneak a break and join her. Sarah told her she had been thinking about dragons.

Deb smiled: "Did I ever tell you about my friend, Toni. She takes photographs and loves to dance and write and sail and really loves the water," Deb explained. "And because we don't have an ocean, Toni doesn't live here anymore. But one day before she moved to Maine, she was baby-sitting for Rachel and Jack, Jr. She made up a story about two sad children, and a magic butterfly, and wrote this short poem:

> Would you believe me
> if I told you
> there was a butterfly
> living in the ear
> of a dragon

"So I taped it on the refrigerator. And ever since, I have good feelings about dragons and the positive influence butterflies have on them. The kids won't let me take it down."

*   *   *

Katie was filling web orders, finding, packing and weighing the books, then calculating the postage. But all the while, she was thinking back to Sarah's hexagram, 'Ch'ien.' She remembered one of Dr. Chau's earliest teachings: "You see one thing when you first look at the answer; you see something entirely different when you take a single small step to the left or to the right." He had often reminded her to look at a passage many times, in the throes of many moods.

She thought about dragons without heads. Because for now, Sarah was all about losing her head, or at least the majority of its contents. The past was still the most profound mystery for Sarah, and whatever had happened back there was reflected in the deep sense of regret you could see in her eyes.

She had taken flight, changing where she was and whom she was with. Katie, unfortunately, still didn't know enough about her to know if she had changed her ways.

TWENTY-ONE

When you picked somebody up at the airport you never knew where your taxi was going to end up. You hoped, of course, for Manhattan and some happy-to-be-home wealthy tippers. But tonight, after an eight-hour shift, Frank found himself in the North Bronx. Not a good sign for a Saturday night. He could easily end up trapped in the borough for hours, moving from one measly fare to another. So rather than ferry some late bar-hoppers back home from the Grand Concourse to god-knows-where in the East Bronx, he lit the off-duty sign, and began the drive back to the garage.

Frank had been driving a cab for almost four months now. He jokingly called the cab his real therapy. And, during these sessions, at least the dough was coming in rather than going out. Not that Dr. Silver hadn't done her best, but he was growing impatient with the hour he spent with her three mornings a week, and the spare time he spent aimlessly walking the city.

After all the talk, all the thinking, he was beginning to accept Dr. Silver's suggestion that what continued to cripple him resided in a place other than where he was rational. And for the time being, the last thing he wanted to do was to go back out on the street with his badge and revolver feeling so distracted.

Dr. Silver's parrot seemed to have some of the best ears in the city. Danger was able to filter out the sound of Frank's footsteps from the ambulance sirens, car alarms, door slams, and noisy neighbors. As his key hit the lock and he opened the door to his apartment, Frank was met with a symphony of screeches.

The apartment on Amsterdam Avenue was as messy as his mind: books and magazines scattered everywhere, coffee cups and used silverware buried beneath mail, opened and unopened. Somehow he had moved enough of the mess to make room for Danger and his cage on the kitchen table.

Carl, at least, always had Theresa to restore order to his perpetual tangle, but unless Danger was ready for cleanup duty, he and Frank would continue to live in chaos. And these days Frank hardly saw the clutter. His indoor life pretty much began and ended with the wide screen TV and its constant companion, his digital video recorder.

He leaned in toward the cage: "Good evening, Danger. Yes, it's good to see you, too, but don't forget that the neighbors get up early! How about we talk, swap stories, rather than squawk?"

Danger moved along his perch to get closer. "Now you might be wondering how my night went ... Well, it wasn't the best shift, and certainly wasn't the worst. Made about seventy-five bucks in tips. And you? A productive evening?"

Danger pressed his face against the bars, pretty annoyed he had been left alone all night, and convinced that Frank owed him. "Cracker," he suggested.

"Good idea ... The problem is I spaced out on the crackers."

Danger tried again, a bit more loudly: "Cracker!"

"I was going to stop at the all-night bodega but ..."

Danger did a full one hundred eighty degree pivot on the perch, turning his back to Frank. Frank tried to muffle his laugh.

It was becoming painfully obvious to Danger that Frank just didn't get basic Quaker commands and wasn't much good with following orders. He clearly had his work cut out for him. So he turned around and came back to try again, more slowly this time: "Cracker ... Danger ... Good boy ... Cracker ... One ... two ... three ... four ... five!"

"I know. And I appreciate that a measly cracker is not too much to ask for." Then Frank went to look through his kitchen cabinets but all he found were two bags of Cheetos. He always had Cheetos.

Danger tried again: "One ... two ..."

Frank was trying to remember whether or not Cheetos had made it onto the official Danger Do Not Eat list Dr. Silver had prepared for him, the list that had somehow disappeared along with last month's unpaid phone bill. He remembered avocadoes and chocolate and Teflon cookware and electric cords ... thinking he probably would have noticed if one of his favorite snacks had the potential to kill his therapist's bird. So Frank broke off a small piece and slipped it between the bars. In a split second, it was in Danger's beak, then gone.

"Cracker," Danger pronounced, immediately granting official cracker status to this odd and airy orange thing. And still hungry, Danger wanted more: "Cracker!"

Frank dumped some more Cheetos into Danger's dish. "Good boy," Danger offered. Keeping to himself the "it's about time!"

As Frank went to put the bag back in the cupboard, he could

see the blinking red light of his answering machine, mostly hidden beneath the growing stack of mail that covered most of the far corner of the kitchen counter.

He hated those nagging numbers. And liked it less and less as the number morphed over time from one to two to three on up.

Once, when the messages made it to nine, he lost his cool completely. He threw the machine into the wall. Unfortunately, it didn't take long for his shift supervisor to complain that he couldn't leave a message, and Frank reluctantly had to replace it. What with therapy and Dr. Silver, and his recent efforts to address his occasional lack of anger management skills, the new machine was safe for now, if most often ignored.

Tonight it was flashing "3." Answer me. Answer me. Answer me. But he wasn't ready yet to surrender. Remembering that while he had fed Danger, he hadn't fed himself. He opened the refrigerator, hoping for something he was pretty sure was no longer there: half a roast beef sandwich or a couple of slices of leftover pepperoni pizza. He was moving the mayonnaise jar to check the deeper recesses when the phone rang. He knew if he waited through the first three rings, the machine would kick in. It was late but he knew that somewhere there was always someone who wanted to power-wash his nonexistent siding or lower his credit card interest rates or knew where he should send his money to conquer heart disease.

"Frankie! Pick up, for God's sake. I haven't heard from you in ages! I miss my brother. My very stubborn brother."

For several moments he was stuck there, the mayonnaise jar in one hand, the dead cheddar in the other, when he heard her hang up. Katie hadn't called in months. It didn't take a rocket scientist to figure out it was his fault, beginning the night she mentioned his spiritual crisis.

As he moved toward the phone to call her back, he realized he hadn't called her in so long, he'd forgotten her number. Last time, he had written her number on the back of an electric bill. Which was now who knew where. And, of course, cheapskate that he was, he had refused to spring for the extra five bucks a month Verizon wanted for Caller ID.

He was about to start searching through the paper pile when he heard Danger struggling to unlock the little front gate of his cage. Using his beak to grab ahold of the top loop of the long metal rod that kept him a prisoner, lifting it about an inch, then watching forlornly as it fell back down with a maddening clang. Only to try again.

"I spaced out, Danger. I'm sorry. Too many hours of no flying, no talk, no TV, and no cracker. Sorry." By the time Frank made it to the cage, Danger had attached himself to the inside of the door, ready to swing his way to freedom. He was out before the door was halfway open.

Having long ago mastered his disability, Danger could get anywhere he needed by using his strong left foot to secure himself, while his damaged right foot extended up and out into the air. As he climbed the outside of his cage, his beak functioned like an extra arm or foot and he moved with speed and agility. A short flight from the cage and he was standing on top of the refrigerator looking down at Frank with his bright, deep dark piercing eyes, his razor sharp pinkish brown pointy beak reminding Frank it paid to be diplomatic.

Frank was learning new things about Danger every day. Though Dr. Silver had cautioned him that his cage was his sanctuary, Danger seemed already to have expanded his territory to the kitchen and living room. And it was pretty obvious that Dr. Silver hadn't allowed him to watch anywhere near enough television, because these last few days Danger was enthusiastically making up for lost time. At first, there was the fight for the remote control: Frank needing it to change channels; Danger wanting to devour its bite-size buttons.

Once Frank learned to hide it out of sight beneath the cushions of the couch, they had come to a new understanding. Every night Danger would perch on Frank's knee, where he seemed to enjoy just about everything Frank watched. Except for the gunshots, or the high-pitched screams, which sent him swooping back to his cage with an indignant screech, only to return after he had had a few moments to regroup.

Deciding to pass on SportsCenter and still buzzing from his night of driving, Frank decided that this might be the perfect time to put Dr. Silver's theory to the test. To see whether Danger was indeed the willing and openhearted listener Dr. Silver believed him to be. And to test himself. To see whether he was more willing now after this bit of therapy to share his inner self. And so mostly because Danger was a bird and not a guy, and even better, not a fellow cop, Frank began:

"While you were so cruelly incarcerated in your cage, I was cruising down the FDR Drive. I kept hearing Dr. Silver tell me that my being stuck has something to do with my left-wing parents. And a lot to do with my unconscious ambivalence about being a cop."

Danger was already shaking his little parrot head.

"Give me a break, Danger. I just started. And I know disapproval when I see it. So what are you trying to say: family's a sore subject? I'm a trained detective. So where exactly did Dr. Silver find you? A pet shop? Did she rescue you from some dotty old guy living in a two-room apartment with a half-dozen other birds?"

Danger thought about asking for another cracker but the human clearly wasn't done.

"Maybe you're thinking: 'what is he bitching about? At least his folks were there for him. Mine gave me up before I could even fly.' O.K., my folks might have done a piss-poor job with me, but they probably did a hell of a lot better than yours. So I'll try to be sensitive about the subject. And, just in case I haven't told you lately, any friend of Dr. Silver is a friend of mine."

"Dr. Silver ... Good morning. How can I help you?"

Danger sounded exactly like Dr. Silver sounded whenever she answered the phone, and Frank burst out laughing.

And it took Danger only a few seconds to mimic Frank's laugh, matching him perfectly, which made Frank laugh even louder, and the slightly lunatic laughter of the two of them ricocheted throughout the apartment. Until, after a few minutes, Frank grew self-conscious, his laugh slowing, as he wondered whether sharing his late night with a small bird was more a sign of approaching madness than the progress Dr. Silver hoped for.

TWENTY-TWO

Thanks to Deb, Sarah had mastered the laundromat. First collecting quarters during the week then buying the Arm & Hammer liquid detergent, buy one, get one free from the Big Y supermarket. Most usually she went around ten or eleven on Monday morning when it was several single moms, and on their one day off, the many Mexicans who kept the local restaurants running. Always amazed at how expertly they rode their bicycles, no matter the weather, balancing their big laundry bags on the handlebars.

Wash N Wait was all about getting your wash in at about the time the other folks were five or ten minutes into their drying cycle. That way you could seamlessly move your wet clothes into the soon-to-be available dryers.

It was there from the faded old magazines that Sarah learned that George Clooney had a night out with the boys in San Juan, that not only Guy and Madonna but Téa Leoni and David Duchovny were calling it quits, and about the five tips to look and feel like a star!

There was something so very satisfying about folding and piling the clean laundry back into the blue recycling container that Deb had given her to use as a laundry basket. And putting the now-fresh clothes back into their proper places in the bureau in her room at Bea's.

Later that evening, for the first time, sitting at the dinner table, Sarah began to sense that things were off. Even though this was the regular and reliable Monday night meatloaf, mashed potato dinner she had become used to, she had the vague feeling that she ought to be elsewhere, in some other dining room, eating some other meal, with dinner mates other than Bea and the men.

That night, as she lay upstairs in a state of mostly sleep, she could feel her body tighten. Suddenly, it seemed there wasn't enough space for her. Bea's place, with its small dining room, her modest upstairs bedroom, had from the very beginning offered a sense of safety, sanctuary. Tonight, she felt crowded. The walls were too close. The ceiling was too low. Why, she wondered, hadn't she noticed it before? Why was it bothering her now? Why did she feel out-of-place?

It wasn't quite two in the morning but she got out of bed and quickly slipped on her new robe. Hurrying, almost fleeing, down the stairs and out the front door. Standing in the dark on the porch, feeling with the fresh air a palpable sense of relief.

She looked out to the lawn, to the two lights pointing up to illuminate Bea's sign. What was she doing at Bea Foster's Bed and Breakfast? Then, as if for the very first time, noticing the houses everywhere around her. They seemed to press against Bea's house, to press against her. She felt short of breath, and even though there was a chill in the air, she began to feel hot. She thought of the coins, and the book. Limited space. Galling limitations made real.

She sat on the top step and tried to relax. She imagined herself back with Katie, drinking tea. Closing her eyes, slowing her breath. Ten minutes later, when she felt a bit better, she moved back upstairs and to bed.

*   *   *

Sarah woke with a newfound sense of urgency. She washed, got dressed, made sure to take her copy of the *I Ching*, and then went walking. She made her way up Main to the park bench by Grove Street.

She sat and after a minute or two, opened the book to "Fellowship with Men." Remembering her question: "What was my life like back there?" And now without Katie, to see, to hear for herself the answer. And as she read aloud, several phrases stood out: the danger and the personal and egotistic interests. She felt cold, buttoning the top two buttons of her sweater. It felt as if the hexagrams were coming to life. Faint at first, she could see a "secret ambush," a dark figure coming up the stairs, coming closer. So what had she had done back there?

She closed her eyes to short circuit the growing fear, breathing in and out, one minute, two, three, as gradually the tension seemed to recede. And ever so slowly the stairs and the man on the stairs began to fade away. While just as slowly, another image took its place. A woman standing before a window. In a very large wood-paneled room, looking out a many-paned window upon a spacious meadow. But then all too quickly it was gone again.

She opened her eyes to Brett, and thought of Deb who the other day had asked Sarah to go with her and the kids to check out the sales at the Holyoke Mall. They had stopped for gas. Sarah remembered the affection she had seen in Jack's eyes as he watched his wife at the pump. She thought this might be true fellowship, then as the memory faded, shivering, cold again, feeling that for the moment this kind of connection was missing for her.

She returned to the *I Ching*, which spoke of a coming together in spite of problems:

> They are kept apart by their positions in life …
> But, remaining true to each other, they allow
> nothing to separate them …

Why, she wondered, didn't she feel this way? And continuing on:

> The warm attachment that springs from the heart
> is lacking here. We are by this time actually outside
> of fellowship with others …

Why did this feel closer to the truth? Was there no true fellowship for her back there?

The second bookmark was for "Ch'ien." Another way, perhaps a second chance:

> When an individual draws this oracle, it means
> that success will come to him from the primal
> depths of the universe …
>
> … it is wise for the man who consults the oracle
> and draws this line to wait in the calm strength of
> patience.

She had, hadn't she, at Katie's urging, with Katie's help, been patient? And now she had seen, even for a brief moment, a glimpse of the window and the field. And so she wondered: with continued patience, would she see more?

She knew her next question: "Where is the meadow, my previous life?"

TWENTY-THREE

"So I opened up, Dr. Silver. I tried talking to Danger about my parents, even about what you called my ambivalence. But between you and me, he wasn't very sympathetic. I obviously don't know his story, but I'm guessing he's still bitter about his own childhood. And it probably didn't help that I gave him Cheetos instead of a legitimate cracker-cracker.

"Anyway, I missed a call from Katie. I told you, didn't I, that I hadn't heard from her since she said I was having a spiritual crisis.

"I was going to call her back but couldn't find her number. It's unlisted. First thing the next morning I looked for twenty minutes but still couldn't find it.

"As I'm searching, Danger comes out with a loud 'Hello' and then another 'Hello,' one every few moments. Like he's telling me to get it together already and call Katie. Maybe mocking me. But I was trying, I really was.

"Maybe I was over-reacting but Danger was looking more and more disgusted. Then, looking down at me from the top of the refrigerator, he announces: 'With a quack-quack here … and a quack-quack there!' I'm guessing that's the ultimate parrot put-down.

"Anyway I'm getting the strong sense that he's not a particularly patient bird. And it's becoming pretty clear to me that if I really want to explore some of this deeper stuff, I should be talking more to you and less to your slightly bitter parrot."

"Thank you for that strong vote of confidence. But in Danger's defense, you did get the point. You need to call her back. He's a big believer in the telephone. And just so you know, Danger spent far too many hours listening to Burl Ives sing about Old MacDonald and his farm. Unfortunately, my husband used that record to send our grandson, Isaac, off to sleep when he came to visit. So maybe Danger was telling you it was time for you to get your ducks in a row?"

"Pretty good, Dr. Silver. Though in my very messy apartment I'd be lucky to find a single solitary duck, let alone a row of them."

"Well, in the meantime, Detective Falco, how about you tell me about your relationship with Katie?"

"Katie? … Well, all the usual older brother/younger sister stuff might have worked after Carl's death when she was a kid, but later when Katie turned down a full scholarship to grad school, I might have gone a bit overboard. I was afraid she was throwing away an incredible opportunity, and might have told her she was a major league moron. And that I was thinking about dragging her ass up to school. Not surprisingly, she told me I was a condescending jerk.

"And I know it's hard for me to take her advice. I was complaining after the shooting how the department-mandated shrink didn't understand me. Katie said: 'That's a lame excuse. You're being lazy. It's time to do the hard work. And you can do it. It's time to find your center!'

"I was pissed … and I'm pretty sure I told her to take her center and shove it. She hung up. And we haven't spoken since.

"You know, the truth is if we switched places, I probably would have told her the same thing: to stop whining! It's just hard having her so far away. I was always able to meet her for a quick dinner in Chinatown or Little Italy. To check in, sometimes to apologize. A lot of times to apologize. I'm not like Danger: I don't do well with phones. I wouldn't be surprised if Katie moved to the country mainly to get away from me and Theresa. Now it's just me she's getting away from."

"So what's the real reason you haven't called her back?"

"I was going to, but it took me an entire day just to find her number. Then … well, do you remember what you said about how a needle sometimes gets stuck on a scratched record, and plays the same note over and over again … I got to thinking about how all of a sudden I go out for a walk with my girlfriend and I kill someone and boom I discover I don't know up from down, and have to accept the fact that my life is more than half gone.

"I've been a cop for more than two decades, a detective for fifteen years. If you're right, Dr. Silver, on the job for all those ambivalent years. A bad marriage, several relationships that started off with promise then went over the cliffs, and a German Shepherd named Sam who went stir-crazy in my Manhattan apartment and ended up with my ex-wife Stephanie and her new husband Phil and their big yard in Great Neck.

"What if Gloria and I had picked another restaurant, a few blocks south or a few blocks north or, even better, if we ordered in? What would have become of us? Would my ex-girlfriend Gloria still be my girlfriend? That's probably not an answer to your question. For all of my life I tried to take care of Katie, but right now I can barely take care of myself. And so I sure as hell wasn't confident I could offer Katie anything worth having. The fact is I didn't know what to say.

"Thank you for the answer. And I'd like to come back to Katie in a bit, but in the meantime could you tell me more about Gloria."

"Gloria is a high school teacher. She has an incredible smile, and almost always looks on the bright side. She teaches English to these inner city kids, gets them writing some amazing poetry, reading books no one thought they would read, James Baldwin, Edith Wharton, James Joyce. I don't know what she was thinking about trying to be with me. I'm as cynical as she is optimistic.

"Gloria left several months ago. It might have been all the publicity after the shooting, those articles in the New York Post and the Daily News, the TV news coverage, the sudden exposure and invasion of privacy. More likely it was my deep and unrelenting depression, and my occasional meanness. She told me that even though the sex was great, I'd be gone a few minutes later. She said she had too much to do, thought too much of herself, and that our friendship was too new for her to put up with my disappearing act. She told me to call when I got better. There were days I was pissed off at her. Thinking that I had saved her life. But the truth is, I could do both: first save her life, then make it miserable. I miss her, but I haven't called. I know I'm not better."

"By the way, Detective Falco, you're right about Danger's childhood. I got him when he was two from a friend who rescues parrots. Danger didn't say a word to me the first year. And he bit my husband every time he could. So, yes, he was angry. But, over time, he's mellowed. He's more social. Which brings me back to you. Appreciating how you've always seen yourself as Katie's caretaker, a surrogate father rather than brother, friend, or equal, well you're probably better able to really communicate with Katie now than you've ever been before."

TWENTY-FOUR

Peter dreamt he was in Vegas. Unstoppable at the Texas Hold'em table, pulling sets and straights and boats, until he could bluff his way to victory with an unsuited ten-nine. This was his best Vegas dream ever. He pocketed a quarter of a mil. Usually he'd walk past the slots, a sucker's bet. But this time, feeling invincible, he headed to the high roller slots. He fed a hundred into a corner machine. Hitting the button, while just moments later, the lights flashing, the loud bing-bing-bing, his winnings multiplying until, unfortunately, his eyes opened in the now much too big bed of home.

Ordinarily, he wasn't superstitious, but this time he took the dream as a sign. He could easily take some of his stash and slip out of town tonight without Arthur knowing. He'd win back what he owed over a glorious Vegas weekend. An hour later, he told Donnie he had to meet some real estate developers in Oklahoma City, and got him to agree to stay at the house and man the phones once more, just in case she surfaced.

In truth, Donnie was tired and not all that psyched about going back to the house. What with the long trip to Cleveland, and having to kill that guy who came after Bobby V., well it was too much traveling and too much of what his mom had called "drama." Not enough time to rest, to hang out at Big Pink.

But he took Arthur's bonus money and called Will the Weasel and got himself a quarter ounce of Arthur's mostly uncut stuff, the best coke in the Motor City, Will assured him.

Then he waited through the last of Betsy's shows. Two hours into a series of trips to the men's room for tooting, he had pretty much left this world. At which point, Petey's instructions had been transformed in his mind from "don't let anyone come over" to "I trust you. Just be careful who you bring." And, of course, when he was coked out of his mind, he really, truly trusted Betsy.

He wasn't thrilled to see the marble staircase again. At least he knew he never, ever meant to hurt anyone unless he absolutely had to. Reminding himself that what he did was never about inflicting unnecessary pain like some of those other guys who collected money. Guys who seemed happy to be hurting folks. For Donnie, it was never, ever personal. He was pretty sure you could ask just about anybody in the neighborhood and they'd tell you that deep down Donnie was a really nice guy.

Betsy had long ago learned that Donnie was as good as they came. He was generous with his coke and tried his best in bed. Even though she was as close to him as any man, she never had the heart to tell him she much preferred women. Or how pleased she was with the sweet, slow joy she shared with Dora.

The house was pretty incredible. The gates, the beautiful gardens, the driveway. More rooms than anyone needed. Marble everywhere, and that big wide circular staircase. She had only seen one wing, but shit, the master bedroom was as big as her entire crummy apartment. And even the smaller guest bedroom, which Donnie had taken, was twice the size of her living room.

The bed must have been a king-and-a-half because every once and a while, after a bottle of some very fine wine, when Donnie moved off to the end table on his side of the bed to prepare some more toot, it felt as if she actually lost sight of him. But she could hear him, never more focused than he was with the razor blade, up and down, chopping the big clumps of coke into the tiny little pieces you could easily snort. Like a manic woodpecker: tap, tap, tap, blade to plate, blade to plate, blade to plate.

Then another two big lines vacuumed into his nose, the rest rubbed into his gums, completely stoned out of his mind, Donnie started talking in a mad coke rush:

"Can you believe this fucking house? My dead mother would die all over again if she found out Petey ended up in this place. After my father got whacked, we lived in a car for a while. Never really spent time with my brother's wife. Makes sense, right? I don't fit. Like at the eff-ing fancy dinners they do here.

"She was in the papers all the time and I got curious. Petey doesn't know but for a while I followed her. Most people never check their mirrors so if you stay back a little, you're golden. Just to see what her life was like. I kinda like her, actually. You can tell a lot about someone by the way they treat others.

"Like her cousin in Cleveland, she goes to these outdoor places in town where you sit out on the sidewalk and eat. Never got why you'd want to be breathing the exhaust but they seem to think it's cool. I could see her smiling at the waiters and waitresses, and with the binoculars I could see she's a big tipper. I think she'd like me if she got the chance. I bet she wouldn't care so much like Petey does about my dirty mouth, the 'fucking' this or that or the 'son-of-a-bitch' that might slip out."

Like Donnie, Betsy's great weakness was her love of coke. Luckily, she had disciplined herself not to use her own money on it. And she was much better about money these days, banking as much as she could, thinking about the day she'd find something new to do with the rest of her life. Maybe nursing or the social worker kind of thing. But when someone else was providing it, well it was just plain silly to say no. So between all the coke and the wine, she was barely holding on. She could see Donnie's mouth moving, and by the look on his face could see he meant what he was saying. But even though Little Francis would be disappointed, it was asking a bit much for her to figure out right now exactly what Donnie meant. And Donnie almost always took her silence as interest.

TWENTY-FIVE

"Looking out that window, it felt like I was looking out at my life. So my question is: 'where is that meadow? Where is my life?'"

Sarah closed her eyes to concentrate, shaking then letting the coins go. Three heads. Then two heads and a tail, a broken eight. Two tails and a head, a solid seven. Then two eights in a row, and the final toss, two tails and a head, the solid seven on top.

Sarah searched through the index of the hexagrams until she found "Pi / Grace," then her second hexagram, "Kên / Keeping Still, Mountain."

Sarah handed the book to Katie who began: "Let's start with this note from Confucius:

> If good does not accumulate, it is not enough to make a name for a man. If evil does not accumulate, it is not strong enough to destroy a man. Therefore the inferior man thinks to himself, 'Goodness in small things has no value,' and so neglects it. He thinks, 'Small sins do no harm' and so he does not give them up. Thus his sins accumulate until they can no longer be covered up, and his guilt becomes so great that it can no longer be wiped out.

"Remember 'Chieh' and the lake? Again, Sarah, it feels like your answer is less about geography than something more spiritual. It seems this is a place where small sins accumulate, and goodness is neglected. So let's think about what might have happened there."

Sarah was silent, taking this in.

"The *I Ching* offers a clue:

A beginner in a subordinate place must take upon himself the labor of advancing. There might be an opportunity of surreptitiously easing the way – symbolized by the carriage – but a self-contained man scorns help gained in a dubious fashion. He thinks it more graceful to go on foot than to drive in a carriage under false pretenses.

Katie could see that Sarah was concentrating. "How does one get ahead in life? With honor and hard work, or with shortcuts and scams? Is there a man or woman of false pretenses in your life? Or a self-contained, graceful man? Or are we talking about you, Sarah?"

Sarah, eyes still closed: "I don't know. I just don't know."

"That's OK, Sarah, let's look at the second hexagram." Katie turned to "Kên" on page 200:

... a man who serves a master stronger than himself ... is swept along, and even though he may himself halt on the path of wrongdoing, he can no longer check the other in his powerful movement.

Both Katie and Sarah were silent, allowing the words to sit. The silence was broken by Rabbit's deep and prolonged yawn. Katie got up and walked with him to the door, letting him out for a bit. Talking as she returned: "Perhaps you got caught up in something beyond your control, Sarah? Unable to be stopped. Or maybe you couldn't stop someone in your life from doing wrong."

Sarah had no answer, took a sip of tea, then reached for the book. She turned back to read some of "Pi," the first hexagram. Then, after a long pause she said: "'Pi' speaks about grace, and ornament, and a charming life.

"It says:

Grace can adorn, but it can also swamp us.

"Then 'Pi' asks:

> Grace or simplicity? … Which is better - to pursue
> the grace of external brilliance or return to
> simplicity?

"So if the *I Ching* is speaking about me, and if the meadow is mine, have I lived that life of wealth, of grace, an ornamental life?

"I wonder because the other night at Bea's I felt like the parlor shrank, and suddenly my room seemed too small. I had the strong feeling that in my life back there I was used to lots of space."

Sarah paused: "I haven't told you something … Maybe because it really confused me, scared me even. Or maybe because I wasn't sure about you, not sure I trusted you … but now I think it might help. I'm beginning to feel that I don't belong here …

"I'm not saying it right … The important thing is to tell you about the money, lots of money, stacks of crisp one hundred dollar bills that I had with me … Money that fits with the magnificence and luxury of 'Pi' and that very big meadow outside the window … I hope I'm not insulting you but it's the kind of meadow that wouldn't belong to Deb or Bea Foster or probably you, Katie. And seeing that figure at the window, I felt at home, of belonging before that meadow, stretching as far as my eye could see."

Katie took a few moments to sip her tea: "I understand your reluctance to talk about the money. You had no reason to trust me. You didn't know me. And it's possible as more of your past returns to you, you'll discover that this new life just doesn't fit you. That Brett and Bea's and your friendship with Deb is an improbable chapter, and that this is a place you've come to only because of your amnesia, a rest stop. An unconscious, not a conscious choice.

"So it could be that as your old life returns to you, you'll realize that this is a life that's too small for you, with not enough space for you to move around in, make your mark in, with not enough room to breathe. Maybe life at Bea's no longer seems to fit."

Katie found and read from 'Chieh.'

> If an individual is bent only on pleasure and
> enjoyment it is easy for him to lose his sense of
> the limits that are necessary. If he gives himself
> over to extravagance, he will have to suffer the
> consequences, with accompanying regret.

"'Chieh' and now 'Pi.' Necessity versus excess. What is enough for one person isn't enough for another. A three-room apartment or a gigantic house. But it's important to remember that you've been dreaming, and while the meadow and the house may feel like yours, it's possible that you're connected to them in another way. You could have been the interior decorator or the housekeeper. You could have been the cook. You could have walked past this land a number of times and dreamt of owning it.

"As for the cash, it could be yours, and you took it simply because you needed it. You could have taken it because you didn't want others to take it. You could have stolen it. We don't know the truth yet. And let's not forget the other people in this story. Especially, the obstinate opponent!"

Sarah closed her eyes. Almost instantly she could see the meadow, and to the left a landscaped garden, and flowers of a dozen glorious colors. But there was no one there.

"I don't see anyone else ..." The image faded and Sarah, discouraged, opened her eyes. "You know, when you mentioned 'sins accumulating' and 'false pretenses,' I was frightened. Vaguely remembering a voice, a warning ... Perhaps I'm only imagining this, and don't want to accept the fact that these passages accurately describe my own sins."

Katie sat there in silence. There was so much she didn't know. And she had no idea what this new secret, the money, might mean. Slowly she returned to "Pi," her index finger scanning the text. Quickly finding some grounds for hope:

"But there are other possibilities, Sarah. 'Pi' suggests that things can work out:

> However, it is not the material gifts that count,
> but sincerity of feeling, and so all goes well in the
> end.

Sarah paused and closed her eyes for a few moments: "I don't think I would be here and sitting with you if everything had gone well."

TWENTY-SIX

Peter definitely wasn't reliving his Vegas dream.

For the longest time he got one shitty hand after another. At least the smarter card sharks had moved on to other tables. He was at the point where he couldn't stand to see another four, when he got the pocket pair of them. Stubbornly staying in, he drew a third four on the River, but got beaten by a drunken dry cleaner from Green Bay, Wisconsin who shouldn't even have been playing at that point, but used that same four of clubs to make his flush to the nine. Down a grand on that hand.

The problem was too much money and much too much television. Everybody and his grandmother was a poker player these days. A really good poker game was like a well-choreographed dance. Everyone knew the odds, and there were conventions, strategies the best players followed. But now it was like everyone was deciding to dance his own dance. The chaos was killing him. Peter was playing with a bunch of completely undisciplined and unpredictable players. Emitting way too much contradictory information and playing one improbable hunch after another.

They all had watched too much "Poker Time" on TV, and almost all of them were sporting shades or wearing ridiculous baseball caps to hide their eyes. Maintaining an incessant, extremely lame chatter while pretending they were learning something useful about their opponents.

Somewhere between hours five and six, he parlayed the Ace, Queen of Diamonds into a boat and made back ten of the twelve grand he was down. By then, he had a splitting headache, and was wishing coronaries on half of his fellow players.

Peter cashed out, feeling far less confident in the predictive powers of his extraordinary dream. But thought he might as well see it all the way through to the slots.

You had slightly better odds with the corner machines. More traffic, better visibility. The casino thinking you'd be more likely to stuff your machine if you saw some conspicuous winners amongst your neighbors. And you had to hand it to them: the whole notion of slots was such a clever idea. No dealers, no wages, no benefits to pay and a small army of players occasionally winning but mostly losing. A steady and reliable return of five to ten percent.

You had to work to win at poker and blackjack and the other table games. Paying attention. Thinking. But all the slots asked of you was some dough and a dream.

Peter took a short stroll through the machines, trying his best to blot out the pain of his throbbing head. He was just about to settle on a Double Gold hundred dollar machine when he felt a hand clamp down on his left shoulder.

"How's about you and I have a talk?"

Peter turned to see a guy a foot wider than he was. And before he knew exactly what was happening he was being gently steered away from the slots and toward the exit.

"This is your lucky day, Petey. Lucky because I found out you were here before our mutual friend in Detroit. Now usually where one of my close friends has a strong personal interest, well, he'd be the first person I'd be talking to. Especially because I know you're into him for so much money.

"But it happens your brother just took a bullet for me. So this trip never happened, right? I had my friend at the front desk check you out of the hotel. The bill's on me. Your suitcase is in the car outside waiting to take you to the airport.

"As soon as you and Arthur are cool, come back and see me. And bring your crazy ass brother. In the meantime, tell Donnie that Bobby V. just took one for him."

And before he knew it, he was sitting in the back of a stretch limo, driving from the Strip back to McCarran International Airport.

*   *   *

Donnie was glad Betsy had left sometime during the night. No way Petey, unexpectedly coming home early, would have been nice to her.

He and Betsy had gone through all the coke and considering everything they had done, the guest bedroom didn't look all that bad. He was glad he had managed, or more likely it was Betsy, to put the garbage in the trash.

Even so he figured Petey would freak out. But he hadn't. And wasn't freaking now. Which was weird and Donnie wasn't sure this was good. In fact, Petey, looked pale and a bit shaky.

"How did your meeting go?' Donnie asked.

"Meeting?" then slowly remembering what he had told Donnie. "Not great." Trying to wrench his brain back from his close call in Vegas to imagine a meeting in OKC. Thinking that like the best athletes he had slipped into a slump. His timing was off. His judgment, too. In Vegas, he had clearly lost his focus.

He didn't want to think about how easily Bobby V. could have ratted him out to Arthur, or worse. He wanted to thank Donnie, but knew it was a bad idea. The last thing he wanted was Donnie letting it slip to Little Francis or Arthur that he had been gambling in Vegas with money Arthur could easily imagine was his. Or that, because of Donnie, Bobby V. had let him off scot-free.

Donnie couldn't remember a time when Petey had been this unsure of himself. All of a sudden he wanted to get the hell out of there. And Petey could see the doubt in Donnie's eyes.

"I've got to find some money people to come in on this deal, Donnie. I may need you back here again, buddy?"

"Sure, Petey ... Get some rest. You look tired. I'm headed out to Arthur's ... Call me!"

TWENTY-SEVEN

Sarah woke up afraid. It was still dark. Wondering whether the man in her dream was the one unchecked in his powerful movement?

She was quickly overcome by the other thought that gnawed at her: whose money had she brought with her? Had she stolen it? Was this the evidence of her own wrongdoing?

Exhausted still, she slipped back down under the covers and into a series of small nightmares: often frightened, waiting for the worst. She woke several times during the night, tight and tossing. But when the morning finally came, she knew something important about her life back there, more about the where. She had dreamt of two separate homes.

Sometimes she was back in the big, cold, stone house. And she knew now that the white clouds she had seen surrounding her were the painted white walls beside her and the plush white rug beneath her feet. She knew the bright blinding light was a crystal chandelier. There was no modesty to this house: its ornate circular stairs, ostentatious marble floor, and its extensive gardens.

And the man appeared each time. Ski-masked. Coming up the stairs. She could tell he was strong: climbing the stairs with purpose. She grew increasingly afraid. She wanted to scream but didn't think she could.

Luckily, she awoke before he got to her. Aware that the house of these nightmares was not the house of the meadow. That house was big as well, but there was a rustic feel to it, and it more closely exemplified the sense of grace, if not simplicity, the *I Ching* talked about.

The first time she dreamt the dream, it felt as if she was outside looking in. As if what was happening was happening to someone else. This time, she was in the midst of it, aware how important these dreams were. A sign she was right to feel fear. For better or worse, with Katie's help, she was regaining form, substance, retrieving bits and pieces of herself.

When she finally fell back asleep, she found herself outside the meadow house, standing off to the side in a small grove of tall trees. The leaves rustling in the breeze. She felt as if she had known this land, this house for many years. And she was very sad and very angry.

Overhearing a bit of conversation so soft that at first Sarah could barely make out "not who we thought he was," and as she turned from the meadow to her left, she saw water between the trees, and a boat moving slowly along the shore. And she felt she knew that water well.

She had asked where the meadow was, and now she was there. Uneasy, maybe; afraid even. But she felt sure she wasn't the housekeeper. This house was hers. The meadow was hers. And so, was it here where the sins were accumulating? And whose sins, she wondered?

*   *   *

Tiny fragments of these dreams lingered as Sarah showered, the details fading while she dressed. She left the house and began to walk, thinking she'd treat herself to bacon and eggs at Dom's, and maybe some time with Deb. But halfway there, her favorite bench was empty.

Sarah sat. Leaning back, arms extended, grasping the back of the bench, stretching her very tense shoulders. Her eyes closed. Breathing softly. Slowly the sounds of town faded. She could sense the meadow house behind her; she could smell the new mown grass, and she knew that when she turned to the left she would see the water. And then from behind the grove of trees, moving right to left, a boat. Concentrating, she could hear the slap of the water, and gradually the sounds of the people on deck rippled about her.

There on the bow, she could make out the words: *The Sarah*. And she knew she knew this boat well and with this certainty, the memory of a story. About naming this boat. Remembering an older woman. Sadly, Sarah couldn't see her face, but there was a bible, a beautiful dining room table, a lot of wine, and the woman's laughter, intense and brittle, announcing while inebriated: "This time we will celebrate a woman!" And the challenge: "Who cares what your cronies at the Boat Club will say, your silly Admirals and Commodores." Then more, slightly manic laughter. All of this slowly fading as Sarah found herself back in Brett, confused and hungry. Reluctantly ready to continue on to Dom's.

Sarah found a seat at the far end of the counter. It was amazing how quickly and competently Deb could move, one hand placing the ketchup, salt, and pepper back in their proper places, the other hand sponging off the counter. Taking one order then totaling another. Zipping from the counter to the kitchen and back again. Sarah found herself wondering whether in her previous life she had noticed how hard good waitresses worked.

Then a few minutes later, sharing Deb's short break behind Dom's, Deb's time to sneak a smoke, a cigarette so secret she swore Sarah to silence. "I thought it was a truck that gave me back my name Sarah, but it was really a boat," she blurted out to Deb.

"What do you mean?"

"I thought I remembered my name because I saw the Pastries and Pies truck. But with Katie this last time I asked about my life back there, and then dreamt I saw the meadow, and there on the left was the water, and on the water, the boat named *The Sarah*."

"And you think this is your boat? You know I've always wanted to know someone with a real boat ... Really, your boat? ... You've got to forgive me, Sarah, but Jack Jr. woke me at four and I couldn't go back to sleep. I've had three cups of coffee already and it's not yet nine. I'm wired. So I guess the important question is: when can we go sailing? ... And do you even call it sailing if you don't have sails? Actually, you never said if the boat had sails. Or whether it's big, and how big is big?"

Sarah was laughing: "Only three cups of coffee? ... It's a 55-foot Viking ..." Sarah stopped dead. "Oh my God, I didn't know I knew that, and I'm pretty sure I don't know exactly what that means ..."

Deb started to laugh. "That's a pretty big Viking. I've had lots of men, but never a 55-foot Viking. Don't they come from up north, Greenland or Iceland, maybe Lapland? Do you think we should call Katie ... Hey, wait a minute, I have another idea. Richard is probably still at table four. He's a computer whiz. Before we bother Katie, let's get him to check out Viking boats on the internet."

Deb and Sarah headed back in and over to see Richard. Richard was one of those way too smart throwback kids. No contact lenses for Richard; instead he depended on a pair of faux tortoise shell eyeglasses his dad got online at that discount website, eyeglassesforeveryone.com. His dad saved a bundle but they never quite managed to sit properly on the bridge of Richard's bumpy nose. He was always adjusting them up or down or sideways.

With his father's hand-me-down clothes, Richard was the only kid in town who even had, let alone dared to wear corduroy pants. He invariably matched them with a pair of scuffed black leather shoes, not even noticing the snazzy Nikes all the other boys sported. He insisted on wearing an old navy blue woolen watch cap which, depending on how his frizzy brown hair was clumping that day, pitched precariously to one side or the other of his head.

And yet Richard was somehow blissfully unconcerned with the putdowns his uniqueness provoked. He not only stumbled to the beat of a different drummer, he was that drummer. Using pencils and pens and tables and chairs, he was perpetually searching for, but most often missing the beat. But more than any of his friends, and here's where any stereotype crumbled, he was supremely happy with himself. Deb couldn't ever remember hearing him complain.

Deb had only to ask and within moments Richard had his laptop out, typing away. Richard's best friend was Google and he loved looking things up. It took him just a couple of minutes to find three different 55-foot Viking yachts for sale.

"There's a twin diesel convertible in Hampton, Virginia saying it's 'rigged with the best of everything,' going for 1.275 million dollars," Richard offered.

Deb's eyes widened. "Holy shit, Sarah. I think my neighbor Ken Martino bought his rowboat for a hundred bucks." Realizing she just cursed, "Sorry Richard ... Forgive my language. Two cups too many."

Richard smiled but it was clear he hadn't even noticed. "Check this out. There's a Viking in Wilmington, North Carolina. Whoops, it just sold for just a bit under 2 mil. And here's an article about the Quincy Jackson Company in Michigan. They do custom carpentry and restoration work exclusively on yachts, and there are some photos of the work they did for $100,000, using 'mahogany and several other exotic hardwoods' on a Viking that was purchased several years ago for a mere 1.1 mil.

"And according to Mr. Quincy Jackson himself, the boat is 'Viking's most popular convertible,' which they work on all the time. It's your basic 55-footer with, let's see, an orthopedic mattress, an HD TV, teak dinette, and central vacuum system. It's got a Simrad-Robertson AP22 Autopilot with RPU 80 Drive Unit (J300X), whatever that is. Sounds pretty impressive, right?

"And, let's see, here's one in Miami Beach, Florida. I've always wanted to see Florida. It's $839,000 but doesn't have an engine. If we can get it into one of the repair bays, I bet Jack can put in an engine. I'll check later to see what a decent engine goes for."

"Thanks, Richard," Deb laughed. "But unless they're willing to put it on my credit card, I think we'll pass on both the boat and the engine for now."

Richard laughed: "Remember, this is just the first page of Google results. There are Vikings everywhere. I'll keep checking."

"Well, in the meantime, Richard, if you want some more coffee, it's on me."

Deb steered Sarah back to her corner seat: "Now that I know your Viking's got a teak dinette, I definitely want that ride."

Sarah smiled, "Well, considering you taught me about Wash N Wait, that's the least I can do."

Deb laughed. "So where is your Viking?"

"I don't know. Except that my dream boat is in the water near a beautiful meadow by this really lovely wooden house. With Katie's help, I hope we find it and I can give you that ride."

*   *   *

Deb took the kids and Sarah to Brett's lake after her morning shift. Sarah smiled because the lake of her dreams seemed so much bigger. But they had the small beach all to themselves and there were only a few solitary fishermen out in motorboats on the lake. They spent a relaxing hour watching the kids try to skip stones on the water.

A little bit later, Sarah sat on the steps to Bea's porch wondering whether it was possible she had two homes and a million dollar boat?

If she concentrated, she could filter out the sounds of town, the cars and kids, the barking dog. Then, eyes closed, she could hear the gulls, wave after wave slapping against the hull. Feel the boat moving gracefully beneath her, feel the cushion she was sitting on, her right arm extended out along the railing, the breeze rippling between her outstretched fingers, the power of the wind pushing her fingers back.

She could sense someone sitting on her left beside her on the boat. She could hear him wheezing. A man she seemed not to fear; someone she felt comfortable with. Feeling a sense of peace, of having been cared for.

Sarah imagined Katie: "Look around. What else do you see?" She turned her head. The sun was bouncing off the glass windows of the bridge. She could see the dark outline of a man; this, too, seemed familiar. As if he was often at the wheel.

She turned back, looking down. She could see a canister of oxygen set in a small cart. She tried to look up and around but before she could she heard the insistent beep of a garbage truck backing up to the cans across the street, and Brett had returned and the boat was gone.

Progress. Katie had been right, and that with patience, she could and would retrieve parts of her story, her life. Acknowledging how lucky she had been to come to Brett. To have found Bea and Deb and Katie; and to have moved from that completely blank and terrifying unknowing, from the paralyzing fear of not belonging, to a growing sense of connection.

She looked more closely at the small world she found herself in, Bea's front lawn, her quaint garden. And for the first time, Sarah found names for some of the flowers she had just recently taken for granted: the purple and white and pink coneflowers, the Stella D'Oro daylilies, and the intensely blue Geranium Rozannes. Somewhere back there, she had known flowers.

Staring intently at the darker blue tendrils of the Rozannes, the white center, the blue petals, she lost herself in shades of blue. And ever so slowly the flowers faded, her eyes closed and she was softly rocking, surrounded by blue sky, blue sea.

"Listen, darling," she barely heard, his voice pale and labored. "I've been meaning to talk to you about this for awhile, and we both know time is running out ..."

She closed her eyes more tightly, and moved a bit closer to better hear his voice: "You have absolutely nothing to worry about. There's a trust I've set up for you. I know you're attached to the Potter property and appreciate that your mother left it to the both of us, but I've figured out a way for us to donate it to the Land Conservancy in your mother's name. Please do this for me. I know she would approve. Believe me when I say it is the least I can do to compensate her for my numerous failures ... And there should be some fairly substantial tax benefits for you!"

Sarah heard herself laugh. Then the voice continued: "I've found something out about your husband that is very, very troubling so I've also put aside a fair amount of cash. Maybe I'm just nostalgic for simpler times but do you remember that special place at Potter we had when you were little, where I left you notes? Well, when the time comes, they'll be an envelope for you from me."

The wheezing began in earnest. Sarah struggled to hold on to the voice, the boat, the rocking, but they were fading fast. And as Sarah slowly opened her eyes, the blue of the water had turned into the many blues of the geraniums.

TWENTY-EIGHT

Katie was amazed at the change in Sarah, her eyes bright, the energy and enthusiasm, the fragments bursting from her: the two houses, the large body of water, Deb and Richard and Google and the Viking, Bea's Geranium Rozannes.

Sarah needed to know more about that day on the boat, the two men. Katie smiled as Sarah took charge, the coins already in her hand, asking: "What can you tell me about *The Sarah*?"

She took a deep breath and with eyes closed tossed the coins. She opened her eyes to three heads: "That's nine," she announced proudly, "a changing line." Drawing a straight line for the first hexagram, and a broken line at the bottom of the second. The second toss was two tails and a head. The third: two heads and a tail. The fourth was the same: two heads and a tail. The next to last toss was two tails and a head. And her last: two heads and a tail. She drew the final lines of her hexagrams: "Chieh" and "K'an."

Sarah compared the lines she had drawn to the hexagrams in the Index. It took a moment to find "Chieh / Limitation," the same hexagram she had thrown on their first session.

Sarah smiled: "I guess the *I Ching* decided I wasn't paying attention the first time. So here's 'Chieh' again.

"I've been doing some reading at night at Bea's. There are two trigrams in every hexagram, right? In this case, "Chieh," the three lines at the top, which is 'The Abysmal, Water' and the three lines below, 'The Joyous Lake.' Maybe sending a mixed message about *The Sarah*. I seem to remember that 'abysmal' means pretty terrible, so we've got bad yet joyous. Then there's 'the limits of loyalty and disinterestedness.'"

"I think you're right, Sarah: we're going to learn something new from 'Chieh.'"

Sarah continued: "Now this is spooky:

... economy, by setting fixed limits upon expenditures, acts to preserve property and prevent injury to the people.

"I was looking at Bea's geraniums and daydreaming when I found myself back on the boat. The man with the oxygen tank whispered something about Peter ... no, no, Potter ... Potter Road or Potter Street, about a conservancy and preserving the land ... It was pretty noisy out there on the boat, with the water slapping, the wind. He could hardly breathe, wheezing, asking me to do this for my mother."

"You know, Sarah, we have a land trust right here in Ripton. To help us preserve farmland and open space. So this could be an example of acting within the 'moral sphere,' a different way to utilize wealth, and the very opposite of extravagance."

"Do you remember, Katie, what you told me about driving through fog? He asked me to do this for my mother ... But there's still so much fog. I have no idea what my mother looks like, or looked like. Because now, according to this man on the boat, my mother is dead. I have no idea what kind of person she was. I don't know what's real and what's imagined? It drives me mad that I don't remember whether or not my own mother is still alive."

"I'm so sorry, Sarah ... But believe me, you're making major progress. You asked about *The Sarah*. Well, now you've seen yourself on the boat. And there are two people with you, one older and ill, the other behind the wheel and seemingly in control. You've been asked to preserve the land.

"And because of the work you've done, there's more to discover. Who are these two men? How do they know each other? It's possible the older man is your father, but he could be an uncle, your mother's friend, or a family advisor. And why is he asking you to do this? Does he, do they have your best interests at heart?"

Sarah was silent, letting these questions wash over her.

But Katie wasn't done. She knew there was still so much to figure out. Inspired by what Sarah was discovering, and energized by the challenge, Katie reached for the book, then read aloud:

He who knows no limitation
Will have cause to lament ...

If he gives himself over to extravagance, he will
have to suffer the consequences ...

Katie couldn't help herself, and again the questions spilled out:
"Who, I wonder, has given himself over to extravagance? Either or
both of these men, or all three of you? And while it's unlikely the
older man on oxygen is the dark figure coming up the stairs to hurt
you, what about the other man?"

Katie paused just long enough to take a breath: "Which brings
us back to the last lines of 'Chieh:'

> Galling limitation.
> Perseverance brings misfortune.
> Remorse disappears.

"Whose remorse?" Katie asked. "And without remorse, isn't
there apt to be even more misfortune?"

The word "misfortune" lingered in the silence. A minute
passed. "Forgive me, Katie," Sarah offered, "questions, and more
questions. So many questions. Not enough answers ... Do you
mind if I take a break? If I go outside to walk with Rabbit?"

"I'm so sorry, Sarah ... You're right, let me make some tea.
And I'll be here when you get back."

*   *   *

Sarah returned ready to try again. She turned to "K'an / The
Abysmal (Water)," her second hexagram, and slowly began to read:

> As an image, it represents water ... giving rise to
> all life on earth.
>
> In man's world, K'an represents the heart, the soul
> locked up within the body, the principle of light
> inclosed in the dark ... The name of the
> hexagram, because the hexagram is doubled, has
> the additional meaning, 'repetition of danger.'

... the hexagram is intended to designate an objective situation to which one must become accustomed ... In danger all that counts is really carrying out all that has to be done – thoroughness – and going forward, in order not to perish through tarrying in the danger.

Sarah looked up from the book to Katie: "So danger times two. Maybe I've been in danger, and maybe I still am? Is the *I Ching* telling me this is a real danger, and not just the danger of dreams? And so if it's a real danger, I need to go forward, to figure things out, and somehow survive ..."

"That sounds right, Sarah. But, as we've seen, it is not always easy to discover exactly what needs to be done, or to make that happen."

Katie reached over for the book and continued to read:

By growing used to what is dangerous, a man can easily allow it to become part of him. He is familiar with it and grows used to evil. With this he has lost the right way, and misfortune is the natural result.

Here every step, forward or backward, leads into danger. Escape is out of the question ... disagreeable as it may be to remain in such a situation, we must wait until a way out shows itself ...

"You asked about *The Sarah* and the answer is once again 'danger.'"

Sarah reached out to take Katie's hand, gently holding on for a minute, then letting go. She slowly closed her eyes and, after a short pause, Katie began to read again:

In times of danger ... What matters most is sincerity ... Still another idea is suggested. The window is the place through which light enters the room.

... we must begin with that which is itself lucid
and proceed quite simply from that point on ...

Sarah opened her eyes and nodded: "Well I was there, standing
at the window, looking out at that land. And the more I looked, the
more I saw."

"It sometimes feels to me as if we're in a race ..." Katie
offered, "with a puzzle to solve, your puzzle, and the stakes are
high. And so this next passage really scares me:

Danger comes because one is too ambitious ...

A man who in the extremity of danger has lost the
right way and is irremediably entangled in his sins
has no prospect of escape. He is like a criminal
who sits shackled behind thorn-hedged prison
walls.

Neither of them spoke. Rabbit stood and moved close to Katie,
then placed his head on her knee. He, too, seemed worried.

TWENTY-NINE

Sarah was looking out the window but wasn't really seeing anything. She was still stuck in the session, sitting silently as Deb drove the back roads to Brett, slowly moving them off the mountain to the Tottingham Valley.

She wasn't sure whether she was overwhelmed by what she had learned so far, or overcome by how much more she needed to discover.

When they hit Tottingham, Deb tried to cheer her up, suggesting an impromptu trip to the Outlet Village. But Sarah, deep in thought, told Deb she thought she'd just hang out at Bea's, or maybe walk a bit in Brett.

*　　　　*　　　　*

Exhausted by her session with Sarah, Katie, fully-clothed, lay on the bed. She thought it would be hard to nap this early in the day but barely made it to ninety as she counted backwards from one hundred.

And very quickly the dreamlets came: the firescape and the cantor on an autumn Saturday morning, his Hebrew song wafting like a breeze across the alleyway that separated their apartment building from the synagogue, Katie feeling sad that in the years they lived there, she had never once gone to services. Then helping her mother with the lasagna, breaking apart the meatballs and sweet sausage that had spent hours floating over a low flame in the big pot of red sauce.

She wished she could have spent more time with Theresa but the kitchen faded, and the noise of the Bronx slowly dissolved into the strange sounds of Guatemala: insects, birds, barking dogs, and Spanish screams. The heavily armed soldiers were dressed as civilians. Some inside, others outside the jungle church. Like summertime firecrackers in the city, a seemingly never-ending pop-pop-pop-pop-pop. As families fled, the soldiers fired. A teenaged girl jumped from an open window and began to run. The soldier not much older took aim. She looked back at him, to face her death. His rifle sighted, he hesitated. Perhaps she looked like his sister, his girlfriend. His rifle stuck there on his shoulder. She turned away and ran into the jungle, safe and out of sight. As the soldier turned back, his Captain shot him in the chest.

When Katie woke she was shaking. To the bathroom, furiously splashing cold water on her face, determined to dispel both her dream and Sarah's reading.

Katie knew that whether she could see them or not, Carl and Theresa were there with her. Today. Always. Theirs was a bond that transcended most every parent-child difficulty: disappointment, occasional despair, even death. Perhaps it was one of the benefits of having to call them Carl and Theresa for all those years, but Katie early on understood their limitations. She knew them as flawed fellow mortals, and never felt the need to judge them.

And yet, as a consequence of their unrelenting social activism, they had terribly little tolerance for what they considered trivial or a distraction from what really mattered, for egocentrism, self-absorption, and all the other things they considered "flakey." And the one and only time Theresa humored Katie by throwing the coins, she had asked: "Why should I consult the *I Ching*?"

Theresa threw "Ch'ien / The Creative," and when Katie found the hexagram for her, Theresa read this aloud:

> When an individual draws this oracle, it means
> that success will come to him from the primal
> depths of the universe …

She stopped mid-sentence, closed the book, and announced dramatically that the *I Ching* had quite rightly recognized her extraordinary powers. She laughed for a bit, and proclaimed any further consultation with the oracle unnecessary. Then she told Katie she'd rather read Chekhov. And that was it for Theresa and the *I Ching*.

And had he lived, Katie knew she could never even have tempted Carl to try, and today, could easily imagine the disdain of his spirit: "As much as I love you, Katie dear, I'm so very glad I died before you descended into mysticism."

The last time she had tried to talk about what she did with the only other living Falco-Greenberg, Frank had scoffed at it all, trying his best to shame her with recollections of a hodge-podge of sketchy gurus, like the Reverend Stephen Goodheart of 'blest,' or

Swami This and Swami That, as he called them. Reminding her about the diaper regression guy who had hung out with The Purple Heart rock-band, and all the tabloid astrologers. Then when she still wouldn't buckle, listing some of the faux-gypsy scam artists he had dealt with as a cop. Saving for last the sleaziest of them all, Madame Donka. Donka Schmonka, as he called her, had managed to cheat one of the starlets of "As The World Turns" out of a hundred grand. Pretending over the course of eighteen months to communicate with the girl's dead mom, who tragically succumbed to leukemia when the girl was eleven.

Katie insisted many times over that she really, truly hoped that Madame Donka had not only made full restitution, but suffered accordingly. Then unsuccessfully tried to assure Frank that none of this had anything at all to do with what she did with the *I Ching*.

Which was why Katie was certain that wherever Carl, Theresa, and Frank were at this moment, they were unanimously scoffing as she prepared the sage. But her recent dream and Sarah's last reading had deeply affected her. She was frightened because, in reading after reading, danger was always present.

Over the years, Katie had come to believe in evil: the Star Warsian dark side, if not the biblical devil. Carl and Theresa had seen it in Latin American death squads and the racial hatred of segregation here at home and with apartheid in South Africa, but Katie's experience was based more on what people in her own community could do to their lovers, employees, elderly parents, or to their children.

In the time since word of her work had spread beyond the narrow confines of Ripton, Katie had seen her share of troubled souls. Several cases still remained with her. There was the deeply wounded young woman who, without fully understanding why, had become the lover of her manipulative therapist. She had helped an older man uncover the several layers of denial that had kept him from acknowledging his abuse by a counselor at a Vermont summer camp. She worked with a wife whose husband slept with the babysitter and spent their savings on meth.

There were a myriad of run-of-the-mill and forgivable human failings, many unintentional manifestations of selfishness, but also large numbers of other acts of significant, well-planned cruelty. So Katie knew first-hand there was often a need for spiritual cleansing, and that both she and her house could do with an occasional fresh start.

Maybe it wasn't the actual smudging that helped as much as having to slow down, to gather the sage, the careful lighting, then watching as it ever so slowly burned, the smoke rising. She could feel herself moving step by step away from Sarah's reading, away from the boat, the land, the danger, to the smell of the sage, to the home she adored, and back to her self.

Some people said the scent of the sage reminded them of marijuana, but for Katie it was closer to the smell of burning leaves. Reminding her of the lower middle class neighborhoods of the Bronx, and the autumn ritual as homeowners lit the fallen leaves of their few trees in trash cans, the smoke spreading to the street where the kids played touch football in between the traffic.

As Katie smudged the second floor with the smoldering sage, the remnants of Sarah's reading had successfully moved to the back of her brain, not gone, but no longer debilitating.

Then, somehow, all of a sudden she was back sitting on the front stoop of their apartment building. It was a Sunday and Sundays always made her sad because they inevitably turned into Monday and school. Carl, of course, was away somewhere and Theresa had a waitressing job for a catered wedding and Frank was playing some street game or other, and even though she had been people watching and pigeon counting she felt so very alone.

A few minutes later, Frank, still sweating, took a break to come check on her. Because no matter what was happening, he always came to see how she was. He took one look at her face, held out his hand, and took her across the street to the candy store for a strawberry ice cream cone.

And she knew that this time she wouldn't just be calling Frank to say hello but asking him for help.

THIRTY

Sarah walked from Bea's to the bench where she sat quietly, eyes closed, hoping she could shed the image of the shackled criminal. The sounds of the nearby traffic gradually faded. Her breathing slowed. She could feel the tension melt from her shoulders and neck. One minute became two; two became three, and ever so slowly, the sights of Brett receded.

Until she was back at the wood house, once more looking out the open second floor window. She heard birds. She smelled the new grass of spring. The sun lit the green field. She could see it all so much more sharply now. It was an incredibly beautiful scene: a rolling meadow that stretched acres to the faraway tree line. She felt freer now, able to take a step back away from the window. As she turned, she could see how artfully the room had been furnished, with beautiful built-in oak bookshelves, an antique roll-top desk, several divans, and lush Persian rugs.

She knew this room. She knew these books. She could remember running her index finger along their spines, eventually settling on one and pulling it out to read. She could see the antique stuffed armchair beside a lovely end table, lit by a Tiffany, a luscious Pansy, the stained-glass lamp bathing that corner of the room in a gorgeous pool of peach, yellow, rose, blue and green. She could recall a young girl sitting there, a bit stiff and overly conscious of her arms, and the fragile lamp she had been told so many times was worth a small fortune and would someday be hers: all the more reason to watch your elbows, she had been taught.

Then, in the briefest of moments, the girl was older, a woman, moving about the room as if in a haze, grief-stricken, heading towards the chair, sitting, her left hand slipping into the space between the cushion and left armrest, carefully lifting the sealed envelope.

As she stared down at the single P written on the front of the envelope, she heard the sound of footsteps coming up the stairs. When, without thinking, she surrendered to the strong urge to stuff the envelope in her purse.

Then, Sarah flinched as she felt something smack against her leg. And, as she opened her eyes in a panic, she saw two ten-year-old Brett boys standing sheepishly before her, hoping to retrieve their bright green tennis ball from beneath her feet. The taller one pushed his buddy, "Sorry, lady ... he's such a dork!"

Sarah nodded, her heart still racing, unsure whether to be happy or sad that the spell had been broken, to find herself back in Brett. As strange as it seemed, she was pretty sure she was both the girl and the older woman in the upstairs study.

Each answer brought new questions, wasn't that what Katie said? So why had she taken the envelope with a P written on it? Was this the package the sick man on the boat had referred to? Then, why had she so quickly hidden it in her purse? Was she afraid; in danger? And, if so, who was coming up those stairs?

She still didn't know why, but whatever the sick man had said that day on the boat seemed to have changed things for her.

And as the boys ran off, Sarah realized how tired she was. She got up and slowly began to make her way back to Bea's.

*   *   *

Again, the multicolored pools of light, of rose and peach, yellow and blue, and she was young, feet dangling above the rug below, sunk so deeply in the comfortable chair, the book open in her lap. A favorite place, it felt like.

She was trying hard to lose herself in the colors of the lamp, to keep the arguing voices at bay. But they kept bursting through.

"Abigail, how many times do I have to assure you that this has never, ever been about love? I may wear a three piece suit to work, dear, but underneath it all I'm just a man, a fairly primitive man ... and men, well, you know."

"Please, Courtney, don't make it even worse by patronizing me. You've promised me time and again ..."

"You know how discreet I've been. I've taken every precaution. I know I'm weak ... but, you know, we've always had different ideas about it ... and such very different needs ..."

"Courtney, not that again. I have no interest in being punished or in punishing you in bed, although, believe me, to teach you a lesson you will finally understand, I may very well have to do it in court. I've long ago come to terms with your twisted taste. But you promised me I would never have to see any of them ever again in my house."

"How was I to know you'd decide to come to the Lake House

at ten o'clock at night during the work week? How many times have you've told me that you don't even like it here!"

"I came to check the library. Because your daughter had to write a paper about the Civil War. Are you saying that your whores are more welcome in one of our homes than I am?"

"You know that's not what I mean ... just that you caught me by surprise!"

This fight was not going to end quickly, she realized, as she brought her hands to cover both ears, pressing them to find the silence. Was this her fault? She shifted to face the lamp, so that her vision was enveloped by the soft colors slowly melting together.

She jolted from sleep. The clock to her left read two-thirty. She was back at Bea's. She could hear the rain loudly smack the window.

Sarah lay in the dark and willed herself to remember Courtney and Abigail, thinking once more about the limits of loyalty.

THIRTY-ONE

Frank loved his morning coffee. Savoring every sip. When the phone rang. Once … twice …

This time Frank was close enough to answer, and this time, thanks to Dr. Silver, he was actually hoping it was Katie.

"Hello … Hello." But all he heard was a dial tone, adding a "What the hell!" as he hung up.

Danger cocked his head and made the sound of a ringing phone once more. One ring … two rings … then, for effect, a pitch-perfect Frank: "Hello … Hello."

Frank smiled: "Very impressive …"

Then, remembering that there were messages waiting for him, he went over to press the rewind button. The first message was a loud hang up, shocking Danger, who quickly climbed down from the top of his cage and back inside through the open door. The second message was a simple "Frankie, call me!"

The third message went on at length: "Frank/Frank, brother mine. Listen, my dear, all is forgiven, at least for the moment. I'm working with a woman who doesn't know who she is. Not like you. She's not just confused. Everything's gone. She can't remember a thing. It puts everything in perspective. And I think for the first time in my life, I could use a detective. God, that's a scary thought. You think maybe Carl is writhing in his grave?

"And lucky for you, Frankie, you are my one and only favorite copper. I need you. So get back to me. Pretty please." Then the hang up.

THIRTY-TWO

Nobody besides Donnie knew that Little Francis went to St. Anthony's two or three times a week to pray. And Donnie knew only by a crazy accident, the wrong place at the wrong time, working for Arthur, shaking down the fruit and vegetable guy across the street from the church when Little Francis just happened to come out after a late morning mass.

Little Francis waited till Donnie had pocketed the pay-off, then walked over to put a thick hand around Donnie's right bicep, squeezing like one of those blood pressure cuffs. Donnie was amazed once more by how gigantic his hands were, and by how much his arm was hurting. This was as serious as Donnie had ever seen Little Francis, looking him dead in the eye and announcing: "Donnie, you never saw me here! You understand? Never!" And Donnie never told anyone he had seen Little Francis go to church.

Little Francis knew he couldn't return to St. Mary's without everyone in the neighborhood knowing about it. But he thought he'd be safe across town at St. Anthony's. He always found a spot in the last pew where he could sit quietly. And wait for a time when he could make his way to the confessional without any fuss. He and Father Patrick had long ago arrived at an arrangement that worked for them. Father Patrick would take his confession without comment, or the slightest hint of judgment. And there was much to judge. In return, Little Francis would never mention the fact that Father Patrick consistently raided the collection box to help pay for his extremely private and very expensive sessions with Margery-Mark, the twenty-five year old transvestite at Bella's.

The last time he made it to St. Anthony's, Little Francis had found himself praying for Petey and Donnie, afraid the dark cloud he was sensing was indeed headed their way. And even Donnie seemed worried enough about Petey to come to Little Francis a few days later to ask for some help. Donnie had never asked for anything except to buy some coke before they stepped on it too much, so Little Francis thought the least he could do was to listen.

It turned out Donnie wasn't looking for Little Francis, or Arthur, for that matter, to change the rules or make an exception for Petey and his debt. He was just hoping they knew of some money people who might be willing to come in on Petey's real estate deal.

Little Francis sent Donnie out to pick up some payoffs, then went in to see Arthur, standing there for just a second to gauge his mood. But Arthur could always tell when Little Francis wanted a favor. It was absolutely the only time he saw even the slightest bit of doubt in Francis's eyes. And he didn't like it.

"Spit it out, Francis! For God Sake!"

"Donnie came to ask if I, if you, knew anyone who might want to invest in Petey's scheme. He's beginning to realize his brother is losing it."

"Francis ... I don't have to worry about Donnie, do I?"

"He wasn't asking for any special favors. Just some money people Petey could make a pitch to."

"Francis, you understand that Donnie and Petey don't fully appreciate how much we know about Petey's project, and about Donnie looking for the missing wife. Whatever happened, wherever she is, it's going to be real hard to find someone to sign on to Petey's deal. Because the first thing any smart person is going to want to make sure about is the deed to the property. It's all about the deed, Francis."

"Boss, I don't need to tell you that you can always find folks to take any side of a bet. Suppose you bet on Petey, and you bet on the land, and her body is found floating in the lake. Like maybe she killed herself or drowned. Then the deed's not such a big deal, right? I'm not saying it's gonna happen but if it did, and you took the bet, you'd be one happy guy."

"Francis, I'm going to call some friends in California. But no bullshit. I'll tell them straight up what I think about the odds. At least give Petey another shot. His last shot, Francis. I mean it. His last shot.

"And please make sure all our friends, especially Dan Shine and Will and Betsy, understand how much we appreciate their keeping track of the Kean boys."

*   *   *

A couple of hours after Petey got the call from California, he was at the airport, and on the phone with Donnie. "They're thinking my real estate development might work for them," not knowing it was Donnie's talk with Little Francis that had helped make this happen.

Then the next day he called Donnie as he unpacked in his Los Angeles hotel room: "I'll try and keep you posted each night but it seems like they're looking to launder some serious dough."

Donnie, back in the house for the third time in a month, didn't know about Petey's incredibly close call in Vegas, or Petey's growing appreciation that time was running out on him, but he felt that with every passing day his brother sounded more stressed. It wasn't enough that he had left detailed written instructions, but he kept repeating himself. Like there was enough food for a week. When Donnie wasn't working for Arthur, he should stay in and stay away from the windows. There's Caller ID so you can see who's calling, and except for his calls from California, he shouldn't answer the phone. That the speaker on the answering machine was cranked up so Donnie could just listen to the messages. And if there were any important developments, he should call Petey immediately.

Adding that whatever Donnie did, he shouldn't invite over anybody he knew from the old neighborhood. Especially Little Francis or Arthur, or anyone who knew them. Considering how much he owed Arthur, Petey didn't want anyone knowing about the artwork, her jewelry, or the cash he had stashed. So no strippers. No card games.

Luckily, Petey had all the sports packages on the satellite and there was soft-core porn on several stations. But by the second day, Donnie was going a bit stir crazy. He had already snorted what was left of his coke. So he asked Betsy to score some more and spend the night.

On the fourth night Donnie managed to make it to the phone before Petey hung up. Petey was trying to sound upbeat but it didn't seem too good in California. And Donnie could always tell when Petey was bullshitting, himself or other folks.

THIRTY-THREE

Frank took the bus to Kennedy Airport, yet another confirmation that despite the name change he really was Carl's flesh and blood. Theresa disliked money, and never had much. But she had become expert in living without, living a good life with just a little. Extraordinarily generous, she joyfully spent whatever she had. Carl, on the other hand, held on tight to every nickel, convinced that once it left his pocket it might never come his way again.

Frank's $80,000 salary was considerably more than what Carl or Theresa had ever made in a year. And yet, the Carl impulse not to spend money you didn't have to spend was strong within him, and Frank knew he could save some serious bucks renting his Ford at the airport, rather than midtown.

He stopped at the apartment to pick up Danger. Frank made sure Danger's seatbelt was secure, then covered his cage with a thick blanket. And the enforced darkness seemed to do the trick because Danger chose to stay silent rather than criticize his driving.

Katie sent him up the West Side Highway to the Saw Mill to Route 684 to Route 22. The drive up to Brewster had been bumper to bumper, the intricate, slightly insane dance of lethal metal machines weaving in and out, searching for the slightest advantage, barely conscious of the insufficient room between them for safe braking, each embracing the odd delusion that last-minute acceleration would save the day.

As a special treat, she suggested back roads from South Amenia to Sharon, Connecticut where there was no one in front of him; no one tailgating.

Frank, a city boy, had come to terms with urban annoyances like the everywhere roaches and the occasional rat. But the country was something else. It began when Carl and Theresa decided to do the kids a favor and send them to Camp King Philip, a "progressive" summer camp. King Philip had a little lake with leeches, loads of angry fire ants, and where there wasn't poison ivy, there was poison oak. There was mandatory archery in the morning, lanyard-making at lunch, and a campfire at night with Pete Seeger impersonators, and as much as Katie loved the compulsory multi-culturalism, it completely creeped Frank out.

Even so, in spite of his antipathy for the rural, Frank could feel the tension of the city slowly draining from him as he moved through small farm country, and its big green pastures.

Frank wasn't sure what it would be like to see Katie on her own turf, on her own terms. He knew from their phone call that there was Rabbit the dog, a sometime boyfriend, a spare room, and someone for him to help. Thanks to Dr. Silver, at least he knew how nervous he was. He probably wouldn't have acknowledged the nerves before the shooting, the doubt, and the three times a week.

Through Salisbury, Connecticut, Route 41, then into Sheffield and the Berkshires of Massachusetts. He was beginning to understand why she might not want to come back to the city. There was green everywhere, a large sky, and hills that sparkled. Turkeys that seemed to fly, and cows. And no apartment buildings.

Twenty minutes later he pulled into the parking lot of Guido's, a fair-sized food store on the outskirts of Great Barrington, thinking that considering his many months of rudeness, the least he could do was bring gifts. But as he wandered the aisles looking to add some food to the coffee he had scored in the city, he was embarrassed to discover that he had almost no idea what the new, more spiritual Katie loved to eat. He jumped back in time, remembering how they would journey by subway to Manhattan. Exploring until they got stuck at Zabar's on 80th and Broadway, dreaming they could eat everything they saw. He took a chance and bought tuna salad and pasta salad, sliced turkey breast, salmon cakes, brie and cheddar, guacamole, fresh olive bread, and homemade pastry.

From the small neighborhood feel of Great Barrington back into the country. Where it took only ten minutes to travel to Ripton, and only a few seconds to move past Ripton's downtown, the post office and general store on the right, the church on the left, and up another little hill past the library. Katie had told him to turn right past the gas station that was no longer a gas station, then right again after a quarter of a mile. At which point Frank had to slam on the brakes. Discovering Ripton still had dirt roads and, even more surprising, a pack of people nonchalantly riding horses like the dirt road was theirs. And causing said riders to shake their heads sadly as they barely survived yet another encounter with a clueless out-of-towner driving much too fast, and unfortunately wrenching Danger back to life with a series of shrill squawks.

Katie's house was on the left, her funky white Volvo parked as promised in the driveway. Frank grabbed the groceries with his left hand and Danger's cage with his right. Before he got to the door, Katie was out and hugging him. She took Danger's cage from him and led them into her large combined kitchen/dining room.

"First things first. Let's get Danger settled. I figure he'd like to be where the action is and I spend a lot of my time in here, cooking, sitting, sipping tea. So I cleared some space in the corner for his cage," lifting the cage up to the counter. And gently moving the blanket off. "Hello, Danger ... I'm Katie, Frank's sister ... I have a feeling you've already heard him complain about me."

Danger had a slightly dazed look in his eyes, swiveling his head back and forth trying to figure out where the hell he was this time, and why these crazy humans kept moving him from place to place.

Katie smiled at him. "This is the country by the way. So you'll be hearing a whole bunch of new sounds: country birds and insects and coyotes and you might even see some mice running across the floor. No more garbage trucks or car alarms, I hope!

"Let me introduce you to Rabbit, my beautiful and brilliant husky. He lives here, too, although he likes to travel a lot." Then with a two-tone whistle, and a simple call, "Rabbit ... we're in here!"

Frank was impressed by how quietly and gracefully Rabbit moved toward him. His deep, dark black fur on the top of his head highlighting the white of his face, ears up, eyes alert. There was something so very compelling about Rabbit. He stopped for a smell or two, then walked over to Katie. Katie gently moved the cage down so that Rabbit and Danger could look each other over. As Rabbit approached to check out the visitor, Danger took a quick step back on his perch.

"That's quite a beak you've got there, Danger. You could do some serious damage to Rabbit's snout. And Rabbit, Danger is Uncle Frank's friend. He's not a free-range chicken, and not available for lunch, you got that?"

Frank could sense Danger was more than a bit disappointed that he hadn't exactly shared with him the new challenges this trip would present. Hoping to minimize the damage, Frank quickly rummaged through Danger's bag and pulled out a Nutri-Berry treat. Announcing: "Cracker, Danger! Cracker ..." as he lifted the little side window up an inch to drop the treat in his food dish. But Danger immediately turned his back and walked to the end of his perch. One measly treat just wasn't going to cut it this time.

Frank looked over to Katie, hoping she hadn't noticed his latest failure as a foster-parrot-parent, but she was busy unpacking the bags from Guido's, moving the food into the refrigerator.

"You've outdone yourself, Frank ... we'll be feasting for days. And I've got some fresh grapes and blueberries I think Danger will appreciate. It's the least I can do considering how I've dragged him away from home."

Katie washed a handful of fruit in the sink and then diced it all into small bite-size pieces. "Danger, I'm sorry, sorry, sorry that you had to travel so far. And I appreciate your coming, because I really need Frank's help. I hope you'll like this treat."

Danger was clearly interested in this Katie being, a possible new friend, an ally, offering such interesting gifts. He moved to the dish and took a bite of grape. "Do you want a cracker?" he asked her, a gesture of Quaker reciprocity, hoping Frank might learn something from this generous being. "Cracker?" again, just in case they hadn't heard, then leaning in for another bite.

"Maybe later, Danger, but thanks for asking. Frank, is it OK if we talk now?"

Frank smiled: "Sure, let me grab some bread and cheese and you can fill me in."

Katie waited a moment for Frank to get settled then plunged in: "So this all began when my friend Deb brought Sarah over to see me, hoping I might be able to help her. We think Sarah arrived here in the Berkshires by bus with no luggage, not knowing who she is or where she came from. Arriving, I subsequently learned, with an awful lot of money in every pocket and her purse. Afraid or unwilling to go to the police.

"I know you think that what I do is wacky but with the help of the *I Ching*," and Katie reached out to hand Frank her copy, "Sarah and I have been figuring out some things, and in small ways her amnesia is beginning to lift." Katie paused to see how Frank was doing.

Frank smiled. "Don't worry. I'll let you know when you've lost me."

"Sounds good. So, for example, Sarah's been dreaming about a wooden house with a very large meadow that borders the water, and another larger house with marble floors, and a circular stairway. She repeatedly dreams about standing on the stairs in the marble house as a dark figure is coming towards her, an arm raised as if to strike her. My guess is something violent happened to her there and that's what triggered the memory loss.

"And, let's see, she daydreamed about a boat called 'The Sarah,' which might explain why she thought her name was Sarah. But more recently she dreamt about a letter in an envelope with a P, and now she's wondering whether Sarah is really her name. Oh yeah, the water is a very big lake. By the wood house, which she thinks is off a street named Potter. And, let's see, she mentioned that the boat is a 55-foot Viking."

"What did you do with my little sister? You sound like you're a cop working a case."

"Wait, there's more. First, she said she saw the boat from the shore, but then dreamt about being on it. Sitting beside an older guy, who's sick and on oxygen, with someone she couldn't see steering it. Then the older guy mentioned a Land Conservancy. I know this is all a jumble but that's often how things reveal themselves when you're doing a series of readings over the course of weeks.

"Most of all, I think she's in big trouble. You might call it a coincidence but the *I Ching* continually mentions 'danger.' I want you to meet her. Deb's going to drop Sarah off tomorrow morning for another appointment. And this might be pushing it a bit, but I'd like you to join us for the session to see how I work."

Frank picked up the book and found the bookmark for page 116. He took a moment to check out "K'an/The Abysmal" and began to read aloud:

> The abyss is dangerous.
> One should strive to attain small things only.
>
> When we are in danger we ought not to attempt
> to get out of it immediately; regardless of
> circumstances; at first we must content ourselves
> with not being overcome by it ...

Frank put the book down. "OK, so if we're attaining small things here, let me try something ... It seems like we're talking about the kind of 'danger' that happens not to be a bird ..."

Katie smiled: "Absolutely: in Sarah's readings there's plenty of danger but not one parrot."

"Well I promise to read some more of this later ..."

"Thanks so much for coming, Frank. It means the world to me."

"Hey, Sis', there's no way in hell I'm ever going to understand this Ching thing, and probably you too, if I don't put the time in."

"And Frank, I'm really sorry for not appreciating what you've been going through since the shooting. From the very beginning, everything was just a bit too much for me with Carl and Theresa and you, the turmoil and stress, all so charged and dramatic, and it was just easier to go inside, to escape. And I was just so used to you being there for me. But you never really had anyone taking care of you, did you?

"Because you were older and they needed your help. I needed your help. Losing Carl was so terrible, and so shocking, and then when you went into the Academy, I felt I was losing you. And maybe at first I felt like you had abandoned me, had crossed over. Of course, that wasn't true but I was young and stupid ...

"And Mom and Dad ... yeah I really enjoy calling them that now that they're gone and can't correct me. They were just under so much pressure doing the absolutely frightening work they were doing, then trying to make ends meet, well they just didn't have the time or ability to make things easy for us.

"I'm not sure Theresa ever got it together to tell you, but in those last years ... actually I remember once sitting next to her during one of her chemo sessions when she told me that if she ever needed a cop, she'd hope with every fiber in her body it would be you. That she would trust you with her life. I'm just so sorry we all waited too long to tell you."

Frank's eyes were wet. He stood there silently, then slowly moved to hug her. At which point Danger unexpectedly joined in, perfectly mimicking Katie's "sorry ... sorry ... sorry ..." Which immediately got them laughing.

THIRTY-FOUR

For the first time in a long time, Frank didn't dream about the knife. Instead, his dreams were an ever-changing kaleidoscope of pieces of the past. He and Carl at a baseball game, so far up in the upper deck of the old Yankee Stadium that he was afraid they would fall out of their seats; a march on Washington with a sea of signs, the family walking with a group of Chilean and Salvadoran and Argentine exiles, their chants echoing through the streets: "¡El pueblo unido jamás será vencido!" Then moving back through the marchers to hear the same chant in English: "The people united will never be defeated!" Seeing the smiles on Theresa and Carl's faces, Katie riding on Carl's shoulders.

Or leaving the 20th Precinct on West 82nd with his partner Ken after the dayshift. Tired after checking out a string of violent robberies, then investigating a murder on Columbus Avenue. When Ken stumbles, knocking him against a woman just standing there. Apologizing several times for his clumsiness, and in the midst of his confusion, seeing the sparkle in her eyes. When Ken chimes in: "Least you can do is buy the lady a drink!" Only learning later that night that this delightful Gloria was Ken's cousin, and that Ken, of course, knew it would take extraordinary measures to get Frank out on a date.

Frank woke up to a mishmosh of bird sounds, none of them coming from Danger, and the scent of chicory-flavored coffee wafting its way up the stairs. He decided to put off shaving in favor of caffeine.

Frank came down to find Danger happily perched on Katie's shoulder, a cup of coffee and some olive bread toast waiting for him.

"Katie, dear ... The coffee smells great. I guess I was inspired by those mornings right after Carl came back from New Orleans ... I think he had been meeting with those radical priests from Latin America. Remember how he had a shopping bag full of French Market coffee cans, and, of course, telling us how lucky we were to be drinking the best coffee in the world?"

"Frank, you called it 'The Year of the Chicory.' I can still see Carl sitting at the kitchen table, never more happy than when he was taking his first sip of coffee in the morning. He kept saying, 'it's all about the chicory.' Then when his supply ran out, all of a sudden it was 'The Year of Bustello,' that thick dark Puerto Rican blend he quickly decided was even better than French Market. And now that I think of it, I was probably the only ten year old on the block drinking coffee every morning.

"So thanks for bringing chicory back into my life, Frank. Although these days I'm partial to green tea. And by the way, I never had the chance to say how sorry I am about Gloria ... And sad I didn't get to meet her. I really enjoyed talking to her ..."

"You spoke to Gloria? I never knew. She never mentioned it."

"I called looking for you one night. She was at your apartment waiting but you were late getting home and she answered thinking it might be you. So we talked about you, which, shockingly, is what we women do about the men in our lives."

"I'm sure you did a better job talking to her than I did. Everything came crashing down on me. I told myself I was fine. That I did only what I was trained to do. Just protecting Gloria. Telling myself it was self-defense and I shouldn't sweat it. But all the while, I felt like I was sinking into quicksand. I had nothing to hold onto.

"But thanks to Dr. Silver, I know a lot more now. I know that I never really dealt with losing Carl, then Theresa. I know that the shooting was one death more than I could handle. And the one death that was squarely on me. Then I was fighting with you and feeling even more alone."

"Frank, I've seen you in some very challenging situations, during very difficult times. Remember that time Carl and Theresa were arrested in Washington? Then Aunt Edith came down with pneumonia and couldn't come over to watch us. It was just you and me in the apartment. Do you remember how you made me dinner every night, then picked out my school clothes, made and packed my lunch and walked me to school? Day after day until they got out of jail. The other girls were jealous: one day you had me wearing a purple blouse, a green dress, and red sneakers. And how you read to me every night?

"I went with whatever was at the top of the pile of clean clothes. I remember I was just so pissed that Carl and Theresa hadn't given me any warning ..."

"Frank, I hope you've figured out by now that they probably didn't think they'd be arrested. They were peacefully picketing the

Salvadoran Embassy to protest U.S. aid to the death squads. Didn't some crazy person or provocateur throw something at the police? Anyway, they were gone for more than a week, and you were there, always rock-solid. So I bet that when you realized Gloria was in danger, you did exactly what you had to do.

"And it's why I asked you to come, Frank, because like Theresa, if I had to trust Sarah's well-being to anyone, it would be you."

"Uh, thanks, Katie, but how about you tell me what you and Gloria talked about?"

"Sorry, brother-dear, but that is clearly covered by my *I Ching* Practitioner Privilege!"

"So there's doctor-patient, attorney-client, and a privilege for priests, but how exactly did you qualify?"

"When Gloria asked me to do a reading ... right after we talked about how you became withdrawn after the shooting, withholding, and stopped making love to her!"

"Holy shit! I'm not sure I'm comfortable with all this."

"It's a bit late for that ... Maybe after we figure things out for Sarah, I'll do a reading for you."

"Well whatever you and your *Ching* told Gloria, it certainly worked out swell for me. I may just have to pass on that offer."

"We'll see about that ... But the fact is once again I really do need your help."

THIRTY-FIVE

Frank didn't have a chance to respond because they heard two loud knocks. Then Sarah calling out: "Hi Katie, I hope I'm not too early. Deb has to take the kids to the doctor for shots."

Katie held out her right hand for Danger to step onto, and slowly moved him back to his cage. Danger hopped in and quickly reminded her he deserved a treat for complying so quickly: "Cracker!"

Katie turned to Frank: "Can you give Danger something while I go get Sarah settled. Why don't you move his cage to the living room so he's not alone? And then I'm going to ask Sarah how she feels about you joining us." Frank dropped a treat in Danger's dish, moved the cage, then headed back upstairs to shave while Katie went to greet Sarah.

"I hope you don't mind, Sarah, but I've asked my brother Frank to help us. He's on leave from the New York City Police Department ... The last readings have frightened me. Some of what we're discovering has convinced me that you're at risk, and there is no one I trust more than my brother."

Rabbit lay down beside Sarah as she settled herself. Sarah could just barely make out the Spanish-sounding voice she heard in the deepest recess of her consciousness, "No police."

"If you're willing, Sarah, I'd like him to be here with us this morning."

Katie could see the doubt in Sarah, the hesitation, then watched as she slowly decided to take the chance.

Sarah nodded, and Katie began again: "Just to warn you, he's pretty skeptical. The idea that a Chinese book written so long ago can actually help us figure out what's happening today is a bit much for him. I'm hoping he'll learn as much from us as we'll learn from him. Oh, and appropriately enough," pointing to the cage, "Frank's parrot, Danger."

"Really? Danger? Do you think the *I Ching* sent us a parrot because we're still not getting the message?"

Katie laughed: "I think we're making progress. We're beginning to rediscover your sense of humor."

"Well, it is pretty funny and if you believe your brother and his parrot can help, that's good enough for me."

"Thanks, let me get him," and Katie moved to the stairwell and called up: "Frank, if you're ready, I'd love to have you meet Sarah." They heard the stairs creak as Frank made his way downstairs and into the living room. Sarah stood and Frank extended his hand to shake. Sarah took his hand, then shook it. Several seconds passed before Frank realized he was still holding on. When he reluctantly released her hand and began a bit awkwardly:

"Uh ... hi, I'm Frank Falco and, as I'm sure Katie has warned you, I'm her non-believing brother. It's good to meet you."

Sarah smiled: "Thank you for coming, Frank ... But I think you've got it backwards. Katie should have warned you about me. First, I named myself 'Sarah' after a bakery truck, then I discovered that I had borrowed the name from a boat. Now it turns out my name might actually begin with a P. Which is a pretty good indication I could use some help. Maybe even from a parrot ... But I've gotten used to 'Sarah,' so why don't we stick with it."

Katie was amazed. She had never seen Sarah so alive and enthusiastic. And as she watched Frank watching Sarah, she realized he was completely distracted. He seemed to have fallen into her blue green eyes. Katie finally broke the spell: "Well, I'm sure we'd both like to hear about this P. Does that make sense to you, Frank?"

"Uh ... yeah, sure ... I think I'll just watch and listen for a bit."

"I've been doing some of those meditation techniques you showed me, Katie, and every day I've either been remembering more or dreaming more. I was back in the lake house ..."

Sarah turned to Frank to explain: "There's a beautiful old house with an enormous meadow, beside a very big body of water. It's the lake I first saw *The Sarah* on ... so wide that wherever I am, either standing on the shore or out on the boat, I can't see the other side." She stopped for a moment. "Of course, that's in dreamland. I don't really know what's real. Have I completely confused you?"

Frank smiled: "Nope, not yet. Katie briefed me. You've dreamt about two different houses, a lot of land, a lot more water, the aforementioned boat named *The Sarah*, and there's now a P, which you haven't explained yet ... But I'm still with you."

Eyes sparkling, she continued: "Good, because it gets weirder. In several dreams, I'm in a room on the second floor of this lake house. As a younger version of me, and then a more me-like me.

Actually I still don't remember how old I am. One time I'm in this very comfortable chair with an envelope, with the famous P written on the outside. It feels as if the letter has been waiting for me, because somehow I know that it's there between the armrest and the seat cushion.

"Then, in another dream, I'm back in that same chair in an earlier time, a girl, overhearing an argument probably between my parents, about my father's infidelity. Oh, and I forgot to mention the conversation on the boat about the Land Conservancy."

"Thanks, Sarah," Katie offered. Frank began to rub his forehead. Katie had seen Frank make that motion many times before, a sure sign he was already at work trying to figure things out. Frank turned toward Sarah:

"The young you-girl and the more you-like-you, well it reminds me of the story Carl once told me about a speech he made at York University up in Toronto, Canada.

"Carl was our dad. After talking for an hour or so about Jesus and social justice and caring for the poor, he was incredibly thirsty. Someone passed him a container of orange juice, and he took a swig. No one, unfortunately, told him it was laced with LSD. Next thing he knows, he's on this little island in the city talking to a duck. The way Carl told it, he and the duck spoke for quite a while and, for those particular moments in the space-time continuum, he was absolutely convinced he understood everything that duck said. Which is my way of saying that for the first time in my life I'm thinking I could use some of that orange juice, because I really don't speak duck."

"For better or worse I think I understood that ..." Sarah offered, "and, at the risk of undoing all the progress we've made, one time I dreamt I was looking at the younger me: she's maybe ten, reading in the comfortable chair beside the Tiffany lamp. I looked away for just a moment and when I looked back, she or she/me was much older. I'm not sure I know anything about drugs. Or even taken them. Does LSD melt time and space?"

"I'm an Officer of the Law. I wouldn't know."

Katie smiled: "Well, if anyone could speak duck it was Carl ... You know, Sarah, I don't think we talked about this before, but what did it feel like when you were in that room in that house by the lake?"

Sarah closed her eyes for a moment or two, opened them and

slowly began to remember: "Well, each time it was different. When I was a young girl, the chair I sat in felt familiar, the lamp, the bookcase. I felt secure, safe. Until I heard the argument. The man, maybe my father, well, there was a kind of pathetic self-justification to his voice, as if he couldn't just come out and admit he was a selfish bastard. And there was an almost clinical nastiness to, well I'm guessing it was my mother's voice, as if she enjoyed skewering him. There was no true warmth or real affection in either of them."

Sarah paused, "You know, Katie. I really hadn't thought about how I felt about any of this until you asked. I'm amazed that I noticed so much. I obviously don't know what or how I felt about any of this when I was a girl and it was happening to me, if it was really happening, but recalling it as an adult, experiencing it now, or just dreaming it, I felt disgusted.

"Then seeing myself as an older woman, there was still that coldness to the room, as if the house itself in some ways had been spoiled. As if the chill from that argument and probably others like it had infected everything.

"And finally when she/me had the envelope with the P, well before she had a chance to open it, she heard footsteps coming up the stairs. She seemed concerned, maybe afraid, and quickly stuffed the envelope in her purse."

As Sarah paused, Frank reached over to take one of Katie's yellow pads and began to take notes.

"Frank, you know I always take extensive notes after all of my sessions, and I'd love it if you could review them at some point."

"Sure, Katie ... but I'm just going to jot down some of what I'm hearing and thinking right now. Helps me to put the pieces together ..."

"Pieces ... that's what I'm dealing with. I feel like I'm regaining tiny little pieces of my life every day and I am very grateful to you, Katie, and, of course, the *I Ching* ... but it is also so very slow. I guess the question for me now is what's next, what's the best thing I can do to completely reclaim myself ..."

Katie smiled. "That makes perfect sense, Sarah, and it won't surprise you if I suggest throwing the coins one more time with that question in mind. We can hear what the *I Ching* has to say and then as Frank has some time to consider all this, we can get his advice about what he thinks needs to be done.

"OK, Frank, we've got Sarah, her question, three coins, and

some ancient Chinese wisdom."

"Katie, my dear, I'm just glad to be here," then looking over to Sarah, "and to help in any way I can."

Sarah asked: "What's next for me?" The coins spilled onto the table: two heads and one tail. Frank watched as Sarah drew a broken line then another broken line alongside it. Sarah then tossed two sevens, followed by an eight, then a seven, and a final eight. Her two hexagrams were identical:

Sarah located "Ching / The Well" in the index, then flipped through the pages to find the chapter. She gave the book to Katie, who read aloud:

> Ching / The Well
> … The well from which water is drawn conveys
> the further idea of an inexhaustible dispensing of
> nourishment …

Katie looked up to check on Frank who offered a nervous laugh: "If it's OK, I'm going to hold off writing until you get to something I understand …"

Katie laughed: "Sounds like a plan to me," then continued:

> … the foundations of human nature are the same
> in everyone …

> If a man wanders around in swampy lowlands, his
> life is submerged in mud …

> This describes the situation of a person, who
> possesses good qualities but neglects them … As a
> result he deteriorates in mind. He associates with
> inferior men and can no longer accomplish
> anything worthwhile.

Katie paused, smiled at Frank, then continued to read:

> An able man is available. He is like a purified well whose water is drinkable. But no use is made of him. This is the sorrow of those who know him
> ...

Katie turned back toward Frank: "Hmm ... So how long has it been since you last worked for the Department?" Then, without waiting for an answer, quickly looked back down to read some more:

> ... there are times when a man must put himself in order. During such a time he can do nothing for others, but his work is nonetheless valuable, because by enhancing his powers and abilities through inner development, he can accomplish all the more later on.

Katie laughed: "Whoops! So much for assuming you've been wasting your talents. The *I Ching* tells me you've been busy enhancing your powers, brother Frank. Just in time to help us."

"And I thought I was driving a cab and therapizing ... Am I missing something? I don't remember throwing the coins? So how did this reading somehow become about me and not Sarah?"

Katie smiled, "The *I Ching* works in mysterious ways. Sarah asked: "what's next?" And here you are. So maybe you're what's next. And these words might actually be true for the both of you:

> A well that is fed by a spring of living water is a good well. A man who has virtues like a well of this sort is born to be a leader and savior of men, for he has the water of life ...

> The well is there for all. No one is forbidden to take water from it. No matter how many come, all find what they need, for the well is dependable ...

> Supreme good fortune.

Katie closed the book. Then Sarah started to laugh. And Katie began to laugh. Frank looked from one to the other, his brow furrowing, completely confused. Which only prompted more laughter from Katie and Sarah and then, joining in, Danger.

In between breaths, Katie managed: "You know, Sarah, today I've not only heard you tell a joke but it's the first time I've heard you laugh."

Sarah did her best to stop. "You know, Katie, I think I can say the same thing. That's the great thing about not remembering. You get a second chance at everything." Sarah paused, then looked to Frank:

"I'm sorry, Frank, we're not laughing at you. I've been doing these readings with your sister, and I've been asking questions, and throwing these coins and looking up answers in the book, and what has come back to me has been about darkness and dragons and danger and more danger, and I don't mean your bird."

Sarah reached for the *I Ching*. "And let's not forget the hidden weapons and the obstinate opponent!" She quickly found "T'ung Jên / Fellowship with Men" and read out loud:

> He hides weapons in the thicket ...

> Here fellowship has changed about to mistrust.
> Each man distrusts the other, plans a secret
> ambush ... We are dealing with an obstinate
> opponent ...

"And now all of a sudden you're here. And even though there's still some swampy mud and inferior men, we're told an able man has appeared and the well is full and the water is drinkable. And now, thank goodness, some supreme good fortune. Considering all that, the least I can do is laugh."

Frank fidgeted in his chair, blushing: "Uh, I ... Just so you know, I buy my water of life in plastic bottles from the corner store. And I probably pay too much for them. But you're welcome to whatever water I have.

"I get my answers from people, not books. Although, thanks to a certain reversal of fortune, I've recently been on the answering end of the questions. Anyway, I wasn't bad at the job, but I'm not about to promise anyone, even a beautiful amnesiac, anything close to supreme good fortune."

It was Sarah's turn to blush.

Katie turned back to the *I Ching*: "Frank, do you remember that odd expression Dad used: 'If the shoe fits, wear it!' Which I always took to mean: if something applies to you, don't fight it. Just accept it and deal with it.

"So here's the shoe: it's pretty clear to us you're the able man who is available. Granted, the 'savior of men' stuff is a bit much. As for 'no use is made of him,' let's just say there may be some important work for you to be doing right now in addition to driving a cab. As for 'this is the sorrow of those who know him,' that would be me and my sorrow. So Frank, what's next?"

Frank thought about the last year, about the knife, about Dr. Silver and the work he had done with her.

"Well, I guess," he began, and looked to Sarah, "if I'm going to be of any help, I'm going to have to ask you a bunch of questions. Questions you may know the answers to; some, considering your amnesia, you probably don't. There may be questions you may not want to know the answers to. I may be discovering answers that help and answers that hurt. And, of course, if you do know, you just may not want to tell me a whole lot about it. All of this gets to be pretty personal. I don't have a badge here or any authority.

"So to break the ice, I'll start first. What the *Ching* book and my sister might be referring to here is the fact that a while ago I shot and killed a young man, a man-child really. I was off-duty. It was self-defense, but he's dead. It's a bit true that I spent some time putting myself in order, but it's also true that I spent a lot of time feeling like a miserable failure, or as Carl might have put it, 'wallowing in self-pity.' 'Wallowing' was one of his favorite words. And I'm sure I was miserable to others, especially my former girlfriend. So it's probably true that I caused sorrow in others. I certainly wasn't here for Katie.

"As for inner development, now I've got a therapist and a bird. I'm not sure who has helped more."

Sarah laughed: "Maybe I need to get a bird? Or maybe I can borrow yours?"

"It might be too late. Danger seems to like Katie a heck of a lot more than me."

"I'm sure Danger is just flirting with me," Katie added. "But there's more, Frank. This may sound overblown, but just as our folks tried to make life better for some poor people in Central America, you, too, have tried to bring some justice to the streets of New York. You found out how difficult that can be, and discovered the personal price you pay for such work. But that doesn't mean the work doesn't have to be done. So forget the *I Ching* for a minute. How about bringing a real with all your human flaws kind of experience?

"According to 'T'ung Jên,' a well of living water provides for all. Don't you think Carl and Theresa would love this image:

> No one is forbidden to take water from it. No matter how many come, all find what they need, for the well is dependable.

Sarah paused: "That sounds very much like The Apostles: 'Distribution was made unto every man according as he had need.'" Then she stopped, amazed. "Wow, I don't know where that came from."

Frank laughed: "Maybe in your other life you consulted the Bible? Who knows, maybe you're a minister? No disrespect intended, Reverend Sarah, but knowing Carl and Theresa, they might be more comfortable with the Karl Marx version: 'From each according to his ability, to each according to his need.'"

Frank's smile faded as he looked from Katie to Sarah, then back to Katie: "OK, now just to be crystal clear, my leadership and detecting skills are pretty stale at the moment. So how about we lower everyone's expectations …

"Not to mention that it might take some time for me to get used to listening to, and consulting with a bunch of very old, actually very dead Chinese fortune-tellers. Folks I've never even met … So with these reservations, Sarah, I have a few observations for you to think about and react to."

Sarah nodded and Frank plunged in:

"I'm guessing you're a well-educated, bright woman who has had some money. Now Katie mentioned you had a whole bunch of cash when you came. But I mean money you've grown up with or maybe married into, money you've become used to over time. You may not remember, but the odds are you have a husband or long-term boyfriend out there. Depending on how much money it is, you may or may not have a job. The reason you're here probably has something to do with that husband or boyfriend or maybe girlfriend."

Sarah turned to Katie: "Is it possible your brother is Chinese and nobody told him?"

Katie smiled: "I wouldn't put it past Carl and Theresa not to mention a sperm donor from Shanghai."

"How did you come up with all this, Frank?" Sarah asked.

"First, the way you talk ... I'm betting you've been to college. You're a reader. You're a thinker. There's an ease to the way you talk and think. What was that expression you used: 'clinical nastiness?' That's something only a very smart person would say. Even though you're confused, you've got an air about you. Cultured people call it 'poise.'

"Class is a dirty word in the world we live in, but rich people speak and think, even sit and stand differently than poor people. Rich people are supremely comfortable in the real world. And because of that there's a way rich people look at you, behave towards you. They know, in a very practical way, that this is their world, not yours. I'm sure our folks would have added the proviso, or the slightly demented dream, 'for now, at least.'

"That's the money part. Then there's the husband part. Now, this is one of those exaggerations with a whole lot of truth to it. Maybe I've spent too much time with my male compatriots, but, with apologies to Rabbit and the several exceptions I've met, many men are dogs. You're an intelligent, beautiful and probably fairly well-to-do woman. There's almost no chance in hell that men would have left you to yourself.

"Many men want, desperately need women, need to seduce them, win them. Wealthy women especially, because that's like winning the lottery. Add beauty to the package and, if for some strange reason, one man, one boyfriend, one husband blows it, there's guaranteed to be a very long line of men just waiting in the wings. Women may not be conscious of this, but they are always there: the guy's best friend, the next-door neighbor, your best girlfriend's husband or boyfriend, your boss, on and on.

"I'm sure love is there for some, but for many men we're talking about the hormonal imperative. Then there's the male ego and the contradictory impulses to control yet be taken care of ... Add the extra money stuff, well, you get the idea ...

"Now as Katie will gladly confirm, I'm a cynical guy. Worse, I'm a cop. And I've also never spent any time in the ladies' locker room, where the talk about men may or may not be any more pleasant, but I can't imagine it ever being as crass as the men's locker room at the Academy. Not much talk about love. Anyway, I don't want to get on one of my rants, but the fact is I've been that guy once or twice. So what was that about the shoe fitting?"

Katie smiled: "I hate to disappoint you Frank, now that you've taken up our cause, but of the nine members who've come through my women's group in the last few years, four of them have had or are still having an affair that their male or female mates know nothing about. And there's no one as cruel as a woman jealous of one of her women friends."

Sarah laughed: "Wow, so much for romance. This might be even more disturbing if I knew who I was, or who this supposed husband or boyfriend was … "

"Since my sister is giving you the benefit of the doubt, I will too. I sometimes talk to young recruits at the Academy so I hope this doesn't sound like a lecture. Let's start with the reality that about ninety percent of violent crimes are committed by men. And more than twenty percent of crimes are committed by men against women. In the mid nineteen seventies, there were give or take five male murderers for every one female killer. But it's gotten worse and by nineteen ninety-nine, it was about nine to one.

"In 2008, the FBI found that 92% of female murder victims were killed by someone close to them. And that twelve times as many women were killed by a man they knew, rather than a male stranger. More than 20% were murdered by their husband.

"I know a lot less about this case than all these Chinese detectives you've already got working for you, but based on experience, I'm betting that the danger you're in is coming from someone very close to you.

"Now when I'm trying to figure out who committed a crime, I go out and talk to a lot of people. I check out the scene, interview potential witnesses, friends and family of the victim, people who might have had a motive to hurt or kill the victim. I've never dealt with someone who's got amnesia. Plus you and Katie and the book have been going at this in a way I don't quite understand … "

"I'm really happy you're here, Frank," Katie began. "Let me explain. What we're doing begins with the appreciation that there's a dimension in life very different from your statistics, than what we can hold in our hands or measure. The spirit is about thoughts, dreams, intuitions and inspiration. The unconscious. Probably not so different from the therapy you're doing. And I use the *I Ching* as a way to access that part of life with those who come to me.

"Something happens when you admit to yourself you have a question that needs answering. With the question in mind, you throw the coins. The coins lead to the hexagrams, to the stories, myths or lessons. But really, it's about the interaction you've created by opening up your concerns to exploration and examination. For instance, the *I Ching* offers a possible answer to your question. So what does this story mean to you? Does any of this ring true? And many times a 'no' can be as revealing as a 'yes.'"

"Doing this with Katie," Sarah added, "removed a good deal of the pressure I felt about not remembering. I was actually doing something. I was able to find parts of my life at my own pace, sometimes sideways rather than head on, something I couldn't do by myself. Katie also taught me how to relax my mind, and the stories helped me to dream. Sometimes they were nightmares; sometimes they were daydreams. Maybe I've fooled myself and all I've done is invent memories that never happened … I don't think so but if you are willing to help, perhaps you'll let me know what's real and what's not."

Frank nodded but Katie could see he was fading fast. And after they said goodbye to Sarah, she put a couple of homemade apple muffins in the toaster oven.

THIRTY-SIX

Katie went to bed at ten and Frank decided to use the time alone to review her notes. In a large black bound sketchbook, Katie had charted Sarah's questions, the hexagrams she had thrown, some quotes, and her observations.

First, Sarah had asked: 'Why am I here?' and thrown "Chieh." Katie had underlined the word "lake," and had written "Confucius." Frank found the appropriate *I Ching* bookmark and read what Confucius had to say:

> It is a good thing to hesitate so long as the time for action has not come, but no longer. Once the obstacles to action have been removed, anxious hesitation is a mistake that is bound to bring disaster, because one misses one's opportunity.

Katie had written: "It is hard to know whether to stay or go."

Considering how easily Katie had included him in Sarah's story, there was obviously some latitude to this *I Ching* business. Art more than science. And he, probably a lot more recently than Confucius, had experienced anxious hesitation first hand. So while it was obvious that Sarah had left wherever she had been before to come here, wasn't there was another way to interpret the passage? What if these words described not Sarah, or her hesitations, but was referring instead to the one who tried to hurt her, who tried to prevent her leaving? Who, by hesitating or making some other mistake, had allowed Sarah to get away.

Katie had copied this from "Ch'ien / The Creative," Sarah's second hexagram:

> Arrogant dragon will have cause to repent.

Arrogant dragon? So many years on the force, so many despicable creeps, and never once had he come across a dragon.

Then, all of a sudden, laughing as he remembered that day when out of the blue, declaring a mental health day, Theresa made them skip school, driving them to the Bronx Zoo. And how Katie spent months drawing animals they had actually seen and others she had made up, like the long pink and purple lizard.

So it wasn't hard to imagine Katie's poster: "The Dragon. Wanted for Questioning. Seven feet five inches tall, twelve feet long, pale green, big fangs, and breathes fire. Armed and extremely hot." Smiling at his own bad joke ... then back to the *I Ching:*

> When a man seeks to climb so high that he loses touch with the rest of mankind, he becomes isolated, and this necessarily leads to failure. This line warns against titanic aspirations that exceed one's power. A precipitous fall would follow.

Katie had drawn stars beside "titanic aspirations" and "precipitous fall" and quoted Sarah's responses: "I would love to recall even a single everyday, normal aspiration, let alone a really big one." And "Does this mean I took a fall?" A smart woman, Frank reminded himself, very smart. But this passage, too, could just as easily be describing the other person. He had caught so many men whose arrogance and ambition and self-absorption had transformed them for the worse.

When Sarah asked about her life back there, she threw "T'ung Jên / Fellowship with Men." Katie had made a short list of phrases she thought important: "secret agreements, separate factions, more danger, weapons in the thicket, and a secret ambush."

Frank found "T'ung Jên" and began to read:

> The beginning of union among people should take place before the door ... The basic principles of any kind of union must be equally accessible to all concerned. Secret agreements bring misfortune ...

> There is danger here of formation of a separate faction on the basis of personal and egotistic interests. Such factions ... originate from low motives and therefore lead in the course of time to humiliation.

He knew a hell of a lot more about low motives than he did about dragons. And a lot more about how easily those unions, partnerships, relationships, or maybe just agreements between people disintegrated over time, made worse by mistrust. How easily one thief could turn on another. And yes, in the end, bring misfortune to them all.

The *Ching* called them personal, egotistic interests but in his experience, you could trace most disputes, including domestics, back to one or two or all three of these: love, money, and power.

Then there was Sarah's dream and the guy coming up the stairs. The secret ambush, the likely work of a bent and twisted human.

Sarah asked about the meadow and Katie copied this excerpt:

> ... a man who serves a master stronger than himself ... is swept along, and even though he may himself halt on the path of wrongdoing, he can no longer check the other in his powerful movement ...

Frank smiled. He might be getting the hang of this. The creep trying to smash her. Or if the *Ching* had gotten it right, two of them. Leader and follower.

There was Sarah's money, a lot of money. The most common of motives. And so this could easily be the work of a small gang.

Sarah had said: "One of most terrifying aspects of amnesia is not remembering whether you are kind, honest, and caring, or just some dreadful creep or criminal."

And Frank was surprised to find himself rooting for her, hoping the money belonged to her.

Katie continued: "Sarah on boat again, a man beside her, another in the flybridge. Sarah remembering 'flybridge' as if for the first time. Man is ill, oxygen tank, asking Sarah to donate property in the name of her mother." Quoting Sarah: "A mother I still can't see in my head" and "The man, an apology, putting money aside for me."

Then Sarah had asked about the boat and threw "Chieh / Limitation," and "K'an / The Abysmal (Water)." Frank found "K'an" and read:

> The name of the hexagram, because the hexagram is doubled, has the additional meaning, 'repetition of danger.' Thus the hexagram is intended to

designate an objective situation in which one must become accustomed, not a subjective attitude …

Katie had written "danger twice over" and copied this:

Here every step, forward or backward, leads into danger. Escape is out of the question … we must wait until a way out shows itself …

A man who in the extremity of danger has lost the right way and is irremediably entangled in his sins has no prospect of escape. He is like a criminal who sits shackled behind thorn-hedged prison walls.

Beneath them she had written: "Call Frank."

Frank closed Katie's notebook. Then he closed the *I Ching*. It was after eleven and he was exhausted.

THIRTY-SEVEN

There was no street or knife or shoe or even a Gloria in his dreams, not a trace of New York City, only a disjointed patchwork: a boat, a large field, a Tiffany lamp, an old man dying, and a man dressed in black climbing marble stairs much too quickly for comfort. All of it tinged with a pervasive sense of dread.

Frank woke at three in the morning unsure of where he was. The calming sound of muffled traffic was gone, replaced by an eerily omnipresent silence.

He lay in bed for a few minutes more, but there was no point pretending. Somehow he had taken on Sarah's problems in his sleep. His brain was buzzing. He slipped on his jeans and went downstairs. Thinking if he was up he might as well be really up, he headed to the fridge to fetch some iced coffee.

His and Katie's notes were where he had left them next to the book and the coins. Rabbit came silently from wherever he had been to see what was happening. Satisfied that everyone was safe, he lay down beside Frank's chair.

Danger, sensing he had rare early morning company, quickly woke and began to pace back and forth in his cage: "Do you want to come here?" he suggested from beneath his cover. Frank couldn't help but laugh. Which only encouraged Danger to ask: "Cracker?" Frank shook his head, then added: "Cracker, you've got to be kidding. It's three in the morning. Go back to sleep!"

Luckily he was alone, because if he had to explain what he was preparing to do, especially to Katie, he probably wouldn't be doing it. But the book was before him and he held the coins in his hand. And the question had wormed its way through sleep to the surface: "What can I do to help?"

His first throw was nine, three heads, a straight and changing line. The second throw was eight, two heads and a tail, a broken line. The third and fourth throws were identical: sevens, one head and two tails. The fifth throw was another nine, three heads, and his second changing line. The last throw was another seven, one head and two tails.

With some effort, he found the two hexagrams, "T'ung Jên" and "Lü."

He knew this wasn't going to be easy without Katie. But at least he'd be able to see for himself whether any of this made the slightest sense.

The first hexagram was called "Fellowship of Men." He began to read:

> ... clarity is within and strength without.

Which reminded him of Dr. Silver, though he wasn't quite sure what it meant. Then:

> It furthers one to cross the great water. The perseverance of the superior man furthers.

Maybe that large lake Sarah talked about? But again with the superior man stuff ...

> It is not the private interests of the individual that create lasting fellowship among men, but rather the goals of humanity ... But in order to bring about this sort of fellowship, a persevering and enlightened leader is needed ...

The goals of humanity: more of Katie's 'if the shoe fits' stuff, and much more Carl and Theresa's territory. If only he had paid more attention. But they had kept to themselves the details of what they were doing, how and where and with whom, wanting to protect him.

Fellowship? He had spent the last many months without fellowship. Dr. Silver kept him tethered to the real world, while the passengers in his taxi reminded him on a daily basis of the best and worst of humanity. But, for the most part, he was alone and aloof and nursing his wounds. Not quite creating fellowship.

> The beginning of union among people should take place before the door. All are equally close to one another. No divergent aims have yet arisen, and one makes no mistakes ...

He read some more. Wasn't this the same reading Sarah had gotten? The secret agreements and separate factions bringing danger. Taking the other by surprise. Somehow, again, their stories met.

> The warm attachment that springs from the heart is lacking here ...

True these many months for him. Until perhaps now, he thought, with Katie, with maybe something important to do. "What can I do to help?" he had asked. Realizing he hadn't been specific, and so maybe this answer was more about his own life than Sarah's. And about helping himself as much or more than helping her.

In "Lü / The Wanderer," the second hexagram, there was a lot of stuff about shooting pheasants, a burning bird's nest and a cow, all of which he decided to leave for another day. Or maybe never. But, still, there was some of "Lü" that made sense:

> When a man is a wanderer and a stranger, he should not be gruff nor overbearing ... He must be cautious and reserved, in this way he protects himself from evil. If he is obliging to others, he wins success ...

> Thus the superior man
> Is clear-minded and cautious
> In imposing penalties,
> And protracts no lawsuits.

Cautious was pretty much standard operating procedure when checking out suspects and crime scenes, because so many times you were a strange element in someone else's community. But this last bit completely blew his mind. Who, he wondered, had told the

Ching? He hadn't even told Katie about the lawsuit that was hanging over his head. Only his lawyer and Dr. Silver knew the boy's family had recently decided to sue him. Claiming he'd been negligent and caused their son's death. Like there were other ways to deal with that knife coming toward his neck. A kind word. A compelling argument. A call for compassion.

Given the circumstances, facing knives, he had been pretty clear-minded, cautious even. So, it was easy enough to agree with the book on this one: the last thing he had needed was this first civil suit, let alone to provoke another. But the *I Ching* wasn't done:

> When grass on a mountain takes fire, there is bright light. However, the fire does not linger in one place, but travels on to a new fuel. It is a phenomenon of short duration. This is what penalties and lawsuits should be like. They should be a quickly passing matter, and must not be dragged out indefinitely. Prisons ought to be places where people are lodged only temporarily, as guests are. They must not become dwelling places.

Well, he could certainly go along with the quickly passing lawsuits, but based on his real-life experience on the streets, you could forget about this temporary prison bullshit. When it came to some of the lowlife scum he had put away, it was hard not to want to keep them in jail for at least several lifetimes. Maybe before these Chinese folks put out a revised edition, they could hang out at Attica, the supermax state prison, have lunch with some hard-core inmates. Guests, my ass.

Frank stretched his shoulders and neck then read some more:

> The Wanderer here described is modest and reserved ... Moreover, he wins the allegiance of a faithful and trustworthy servant – a thing of inestimable value to a wanderer ...

> If he knows how to meet the situation and how to introduce himself in the right way, he may find a circle of friends and a sphere of activity even in a strange country.

So the *I Ching* seemed to be saying that to help he might have to hit the road. Travel to that strange country. And while he wasn't quite sure of modest and reserved, he could manage polite. And he could and would remain on guard, and do his best to protect Katie and Sarah.

But there was still one more thing that continued to nag at him. Sarah used big words in amazing ways and seemed so damned smart. He remembered Carl taking him to see some old black and white movies when he was a kid, a few with characters who had amnesia. And they always seemed as if they were in an incredible fog. Maybe even slightly stupid. Could Sarah be faking? Could she have made all this up? Was this some elaborate Donka Schmonka-like scam that Katie, and now he, had wandered into?

THIRTY-EIGHT

For three hundred bucks and a couple of grams of coke Betsy had absolutely no problem telling Little Francis everything that happened when she was with Donnie. Unfortunately for Little Francis, she was almost always stoned when she was with Donnie and much of what she remembered was a jumble. And so he wasn't always sure about what had actually taken place.

Nevertheless, Little Francis passed on Betsy's version of the latest: Donnie was getting seriously worried about Petey, and worried about what Petey might do if his land deal fell through.

Arthur quickly checked with his colleagues in California, who acknowledged that while Petey had put together a pretty impressive plan for the development, he had zip for leverage. Of course, they'd be more than willing to pony up the money and take care of the problem. Thinking they could find the living wife, or provide a substitute dead one and a willing coroner, but if they did, they sure as hell wanted control of the project and almost all of the return. Minus, of course, what Arthur was due.

But so far, they told Arthur, Petey was being real stubborn, which meant that it didn't look like anyone with any brains would front him the dough. Which, Arthur knew, meant he wasn't getting paid anytime soon.

Which meant time was running out for Petey.

THIRTY-NINE

Deb didn't want to admit it, but every once in a big while, it was too much for her. She loved them all, and her new and unexpected life, but sometimes the Deb with crazy dreams and purple streaks could be seen lurking in the far distance. The Deb with too many boyfriends. The Deb who spent a winter in New York City following the Blonde Redheads, then hitchhiking across the country that next summer. The Deb who was convinced Cosmetology would take her to Hollywood.

Somehow her life had become predictable. Dragging the kids here, there, and back home again; making meals at home for everyone, then serving even more meals at Dom's.

It might explain why she cherished her relationship with Sarah. Everything with Sarah was happening for the first time, fresh and new and never boring. Sarah was always so thankful, but really it was Deb who was most grateful for the friendship.

Meanwhile, the kids were campaigning in the back of the car, demanding to see Daddy. Knowing the odds were pretty good that if they made it to the garage their dad would give them candy money. Deb tried to put them off, worried about the long list of things she had to do. There was buying food for the next couple of days at Price Chopper, then on to the Outlet Village to return the new pants that Jack-Junior decided he hated even more than broccoli. Then some ink cartridges for Jack's printer at work, and then to the hardware store for the off-white paint she needed to cover up Rachel's most recent attempt to finger-paint a tiger, a lion, and bear on the downstairs bathroom wall. Excruciatingly aware that she might not be able to accomplish most of this if the kids mutinied.

So to the sound of their celebratory cheers, she turned the car around and headed to the station. Rachel and Jack-Junior knew enough not to run through the repair bays but somehow managed to make more noise than the air compressor and summon Jack to the cash register. Then Deb saw Richard's Subaru on the lift and knew what she needed to do.

For a while now, Deb had been feeling that she hadn't done enough for Sarah. Thanks to Katie, they had found Tippy in less than a week. And she really appreciated that Katie had taken

Sarah on, and knew how devoted Katie was to helping her. But it was very hard for her to see Sarah, day after day at Dom's, still stuck without knowing who she was.

It was difficult to imagine but in this very short time Sarah had become a part of the family. Even Rachel and Jack-Junior, who couldn't be bothered with any adults other than their dad and mom, seemed to like her. And Sarah, unlike most adults, never talked to the kids like they were morons or puppies.

So now Deb wanted to give Sarah the gift of knowing love, the gift of home. To give to someone else what she had been given in life. And she knew how to do it.

She waited till Jack had bribed the kids to take him aside. "I need a favor. Actually it's more a favor for Sarah. I want to trade the work you're doing on Richard's car in return for him doing some investigating on the computer. He's a whiz with searching out stuff. What do you say? I'll cook you a steak and sauté some mushrooms and onions and be real nice to you tonight."

Jack smiled, because without telling Deb, he'd been giving Richard a break for years and, in return, Richard was always fixing the station's computer.

"I'd love a steak. And I especially love it when you're nice to me. Tell Richard the brakes and exhaust system are on us."

That night, after she put the kids to bed, Deb made a list of all the things Sarah had shared with her these last few weeks.

Deb headed straight for Richard when he came in for lunch the next day. Even with his usual discount from Jack, Richard had already been stressing about the four or five hundred bucks he'd need. So he was thrilled he could wipe his bill away with computer work he loved.

Deb told him about the amnesia. She was real clear: find out who Sarah is and where she lives and how they could contact her family. She started him off with a list of some of what Sarah had dreamt about: the big Viking; her quarreling possible parents, Courtney and Abigail; and the two houses, one on Potter Road. Richard tried to explain that while the assignment might sound simple, it might take some time. Then, thinking about a new exhaust system, he promised to do his very best.

FORTY

There was a dog barking a few houses away, and the sound slowly roused Sarah from sleep. A little before four in the morning. She remembered she had liked Frank. It was a relief. There were only a few people she felt comfortable with. Not knowing put you at a great disadvantage. Even the most routine conversations could lead to deep and dreadful black holes, enormous awkwardness. Frank had his own disabilities, and was willing to admit and poke fun at his own failings.

She had seen the effort Frank was making. Watching the skepticism in his eyes as the coins hit the table and the lines were drawn, she could see his affection for Katie overcome the doubt. She was feeling less alone. She no longer heard the dog. She was slipping back to sleep, to dreaming.

She had put the "P" letter in her purse. She heard the door open and felt him approach. No longer at ease, she was aware that this feeling was something new and very sad. But he seemed not to notice the shift in her. Which only added to her confusion. She did her best not to flinch when his hand found its way to her lower back, signaling it was time to go, and guiding her from the room.

He drove her from the wood house to the marble house. The gate closed behind them and they pulled up onto the driveway. She could hear crunch after crunch. And it felt as if the car was settling downward into a quicksand sea of a million small white stones. Sinking down. Further and further.

But they made it to the front door. She could tell she had never liked the house. She remembered a time when someone, it might have been her mother, insisted they take it, a wedding gift. Reminding her that it had been in the family for years, and ought to stay with us.

Then he had added: "Think of how much we'll save, dear. In a few years, we'll use the savings for our own house, smaller, more charming." But the house had always felt cold. Like her family. And she somehow sensed that smaller house had never happened.

Inside, standing there, she knew she should have replaced the second-floor carpeting, that the deep white fleece only added to the sterility of the place. But she must have decided early on that she could never make this place her own, realizing at that moment that it was only one of many battles from which she had withdrawn. There was a stack of magazines on the table. She picked up the latest Architectural Digest but put it back down a moment later.

He was going to talk to some of his investment partners about reconfiguring the development deal. They'd be looking at some land out on Route 3 and he wouldn't be back until after she had gone to bed. He kissed her forehead. Soon after she heard the sound of the tires pressing down on those very small stones. When she opened her eyes she was in bed at Bea's. It was a few minutes after five in the morning. The dream was gone.

FORTY-ONE

Richard had a mission. And thanks to his parents, a sound-proofed space in their basement where he could sit blissfully before his powerful PC, his dual monitors, and snazzy speakers.

Richard had read science fiction books since he was a small boy, watched science fiction on TV, and went to see every science fiction film that played within a hundred miles. He loved science fiction and more often than not dreamt about robots and rocket ships.

He also adored his computers: the desktop at home and the MacBook Pro for away. He now spent more of his time on the internet than interacting with human beings, and when he needed money he made websites for local merchants. Sometimes Richard imagined Google as his own private starship, so proud that he had learned over the years to cleverly caress ever more speed and accuracy out of the search engine, asking a question in a variety of new ways, taking each and every permutation of a query and trying it again. Then turning those answers into additional questions.

Each search became Richard's version of an interstellar exploration, with his own private wormholes, and gutsy jumps into the unknown. And befitting such adventures, Richard had created his own musical soundscapes to accompany these quests, the loud electronics of Ratatat or the otherworldly trances of Black Moth Super Rainbow guiding, encouraging his choices.

Richard liked to say that each internet journey began with a first Google. And, anxious to begin, he had set his alarm for six in the morning. Just a few minutes later, he began the search for Sarah, opting to start with Potter Road. He found his first Potter Road in West Palm Beach, Florida, and with a click, saw palm trees lining both sides of a wide street that led to the water. But that was the Atlantic Ocean, not some big lake. He found Potter Roads much closer to home in Framingham and Rowe, Massachusetts, but far from any significant water; then some in Wilmington, North Carolina; and in Des Plaines and Park Ridge, Illinois.

There was another Potter Road in Chico, California, a rural farm community; a Potter Road in Troupsburg, New York, with a population of about twelve hundred people and very few big boats; and a Potter Road near Lake St. Clair in Little Pointe, Michigan. There was a West Potter Road in Milwaukee, Wisconsin, not all that far from Lake Michigan. Maybe Sarah had left out the "West" in her dream. Both of these last two Potter Roads looked promising.

Most exciting of all was the Potter Road in Leongatha, Australia. He had always wanted to hang with kangaroos. But sadly, Sarah didn't sound anything like those "G'day" Aussies in the Outback Steakhouse commercials he loved so much. So he probably wouldn't be making it Down Under on this assignment.

Richard boosted the volume, then quickly found a South Potter Road in Lancaster, South Carolina, but that, too, was nowhere near a large lake.

He continued on, making a list of every Potter Road he could find, a list he would later compare with his Viking list and the Courtney and Abigail list.

FORTY-TWO

She was afraid. It took a while but she finally slipped a finger in under the flap of the letter and ripped across the top. Familiar handwriting, shaky but still legible:

> Penelope:
> Your mother and I early on decided to spare you knowledge of the great failures of our marriage. She told me, even so, that you knew what was happening, but I always preferred to think otherwise. I told myself she secretly hoped you knew so you would take her side. Perhaps it was too disturbing to imagine you were always aware of the terrible job we did as parents.
>
> In any event, you are reading this and now both your mother and I are gone, our battles over with and insignificant.
>
> If there was one thing that your mother and I agreed upon it is that we both wished you a much happier marriage than we ever managed for ourselves.
>
> We did our best to hide our disappointment about Peter. At that point, you certainly weren't going to pick someone we approved of.
>
> There are a few things you should know. Michigan is an "equitable distribution" state, wherein the marital property shall be divided in a divorce in an equitable fashion. But understand, equitable does not necessarily mean equal, but rather what is fair. You certainly brought more to this union than he did. Should the parties fail to reach a settlement on property and debt issues, the court will declare the property award.

I'm sorry if I have shocked you by talking about divorce but this is probably the least of the shocks I'll be presenting you with. Things become clearer as one faces one's impending demise.

What I have done recently was to use my failing energies to do what I should have done long ago, and that is to investigate how I could best secure your future. I was shocked to discover what Peter was up to, and even more appalled to discover that Peter isn't really the person he represented himself to be. He is Peter Kean, not Peter Bishop and, from what I've discovered, it is unlikely that he was ever within a hundred yards of a real bishop. He assumed the identity of a Peter Bishop who died as a child.

I mention divorce law because I sincerely hope you will contact Michael Barton at Barton, Crumley, and Crumley. He has worked his way up from his time at the Little Pointe office to Senior Partner in Detroit. You went to school with his daughter, Cecilia. I have retained Michael and made sure he will take good care of you.

Truth be told, I haven't always lived the exemplary life, and I have had, and still have, some unsavory acquaintances. And I have only just learned that Peter is an inveterate gambler. He owes more than a half a million dollars in poker debts to an unscrupulous drug dealer.

You have to hand it to him: the man has gall. I imagine Peter will do anything he can to get you to use your assets to resolve that problem; most likely pressure you to turn over the Potter Road property. So as we discussed, I have had Michael ensure that something socially useful comes of the Potter Road property. He'll need your signature.

Be assured that my need to make this land conservancy happen is far less admirable than will be attributed to me. I caused your Mother unforgivable pain at Potter Road and this is the least I can do.

I hope this newfound information about Peter dissuades you from helping him. Of course, by the time you're reading this *The Sarah* should be in your name as well, so I can only urge you not to sell it to support his bad choices.

More importantly, I have secured some irrefutable evidence of Peter's dubious activities for Michael to utilize should you decide upon divorce.

I also spoke to Donald at the bank. In the event that you feel you need an extended vacation to clear your head I have provided more than enough funds for you in safety deposit box #423. Here is the key.

I'm sorry, Penelope. Despite my failures, I love you very much.
Father.

She woke from the dream. It was six-twenty. She had been asleep for less than two hours. The dream so real. There was so much to remember. She grabbed the pen and pad on the nightstand but the letter, and her memory of it, faded so very quickly. Then she slept until nine.

Later that morning, Frank and Katie met her for a short chat at the bench in Brett. Frank told her he was going to help any way he could.

Sarah smiled then took out the paper she had torn from the pad.

"It was very early in the morning. I wrote down 'poker' ... and 'Potter' ... and 'check with the lawyer' ... I'm sorry but I can't remember his name anymore. I think my father said I knew his daughter ..."

Frank asked: "Sarah, exactly what do you mean when you say 'your father said?' Did you get a phone call? Did you remember a conversation?"

"I'm mixing it all together. I was asleep, dreaming. My father had died. It was that letter I found in the study, in the chair in the lake house. The envelope with the P ...

"And you were probably right, Frank. In my dream it felt as if I was with a husband. Then we were back in the marble house. He had to leave. Then after he left, I took out the letter. In my dream I could hear my father's voice as I read it. It must have been very important because I grabbed a pen and tried to write down what I remembered but I was so very exhausted I fell back asleep. I'm so sorry ... I've obviously lost so much of it."

Frank put a reassuring hand on her shoulder: "Everything helps, Sarah, and you never know, sometimes the smallest fragment can mean the most."

FORTY-THREE

Back at Katie's, Frank drank coffee and made grilled cheese and tomato sandwiches for lunch. Talking to Danger, a one-way conversation, as he changed the newspaper on the bottom of his cage, adding clean water, and filling the food dish. Then he borrowed Katie's cell phone and took a walk with Rabbit down the dirt road. They walked about a mile past the town dump, then back the way they had come, and up to the rise where Katie had said cell service was best.

When she had given Frank her card with her private cell phone number, Dr. Silver had told him to call if it was important. Not exactly sure what qualified as important to Dr. Silver, Frank decided to go with the notion that this was important to him.

It hadn't been hard for him to find out that she and her husband spent long weekends and part of the summer on Fire Island. It seemed to be the vacation spot for an entire flock of Upper West Side therapists. He was hoping he'd catch her at home rather than out and about with a lot of people around.

She picked up on the fourth ring. "Good morning, Detective Falco."

"Uh ... good morning, Dr. Silver, how did you know it was me?"

"You're not the only detective in this therapeutic relationship. You've told me your sister lives in the Berkshires and I know that the area code up there is 413. And I assume Katherine is her given name. My daughter went to summer camp a few miles from Ripton and I know it well."

"Pretty impressive, Doc' ... There's something I think you can help me with. I've told you about this semi-psychic stuff Katie does. Well, she's been working with a woman who can't remember who she is, although bits and pieces are coming back in her dreams. I'll explain more when I see you in the city but this woman, Sarah, throws the *I Ching* with Katie.

"The point is this lady is smart as a whip and uses words in ways that are, well, incredibly clear and impressive. I'm deciding how best to help her. But just a little while ago, I started to wonder about this whole amnesia thing, and whether Sarah could be faking it. So I thought you'd probably know more than anyone I know about this kind of thing."

"Well, thank you. I've never actually treated anyone with amnesia, but I have read a lot about the subject. It's very complicated and even now there is so much we don't understand about it. There's retrograde amnesia and anterograde amnesia and, to complicate matters, they can sometimes both happen to the same person at the same time.

"Some traumatic event, it could be a stroke, a severe fall, or a blow to the head, causes injury to the brain. We're not exactly sure why, there's often nerve damage, and the axons or nerve fibers can be damaged. With retrograde amnesia, the person loses memory of past events, sometimes of the most recent memories before the traumatic event itself. What can be confusing to friends and loved ones is the person can sometimes recall events from long ago, and yet have no access to what has happened to them in the recent past.

"With anterograde amnesia, short term memories of events following the brain injury are affected, and there is, in layman's terms, a kind of re-forgetting, an inability because of the accident to create new memories. I don't know if you have ever been around someone with serious cancer of the brain, but there is often increasing short-term memory loss, even to the point where the patient will not remember that he or she took a pill just minutes before.

"But again, much about the brain is a mystery to us. So yes, this woman can have amnesia and still have access to many other parts of her brain. She could have retained her ability to choose words and express complex thoughts and feelings, yet not be able to recall much or even any of what might have happened to her, especially something traumatic."

"Thanks Dr. Silver, this helps a lot. Danger is doing the best he can to help me with this, but his medical knowledge is limited."

"Well, he might surprise you."

"I appreciate your time … I'll put a check in the mail for you."

"I'm on vacation, Detective … keep your money. And just so you know, I'm glad you're with Katie, and I'm glad you're helping. Please be careful, both Danger and I have gotten used to you ... And, as the *I Ching* reminds us, 'perseverance furthers.'"

"Very impressive, Doc' ... and have fun at the beach."

"How do you know I'm at the beach?"

"You're not the only detective in this therapeutic relationship."

Frank, feeling relieved, walked back down with Rabbit to Katie's house.

Katie had a fresh pot of French Market coffee waiting for him. Frank had that pleased look on his face, the look she had seen so often when they were younger and Frank had figured something out: a math problem, or some slightly confusing passage in the book he was reading, or his next move in chess. Even though they were out of practice, she had a fairly good idea he would be telling her sooner than later.

"So I got a little suspicious this morning," he began, "wondering how come Sarah is so good with words, so smart like Carl, and yet can't remember basic things that happened to her. So I called my therapist, Dr. Silver and ..."

At which point Katie smiled and raised her hand.

"Uh ... you're not going to let me finish, are you, Sis'?"

"Not unless I'm completely wrong, which I'm pretty sure I'm not, because you found out about retrograde amnesia and that it's possible to have nerve damage, and loss of cognitive functions in one area of the brain, controlling some aspects of memory, while other areas continue to function."

Katie could see the conflicted signs of disappointment yet pride flick across Frank's face.

"Frank, it was the first thing I checked after I met her."

He smiled, then added: "Good work! I'm ready to help."

FORTY-FOUR

Richard began his second day of online sleuthing with the Viking. Like most of those who spent time imagining far distant galaxies, wishing for the day he could beam aboard a Starship Enterprise of his own, he was a big believer in signs and signals. And he knew by Sarah's reaction that they had stumbled onto something really significant with the boat. His favorite authors were always imagining the future, and their characters could sometimes conjure up complete plans for a revolutionary hyperdrive in their dreams, down to the last screw, or retrieve in their sleep some critical revelation about the Ancestors that enabled them to safely guide their starship home.

In that spirit, he typed in "55 foot Viking boats for sale." Richard knew rationally that for every boat for sale there were probably hundreds more happily being used. And there was no reason to believe that someone was selling Sarah's. But he was following signs here, confident that even a seemingly useless link would eventually lead him somewhere useful.

The first time he had searched, he had found boats in North Carolina, Michigan, Florida, and New York. But he knew that search hadn't been thorough enough. This time he found additional locations in Hampton, Virginia; Warwick, Rhode Island; Georgian Bay, Ontario; Cawley's Island, South Carolina; Jakarta, Indonesia; and Athens, Greece.

He went back to check his first list. Both Wilmington, North Carolina and Little Pointe, Michigan had Vikings for sale and a Potter Road. He quickly found the official website for Wilmington. There were just under one hundred thousand people living there. The city was close to the Cape Fear Coast in the Atlantic, and home to a branch of the University of North Carolina. They had a performing arts center and fancy restaurants and movie and television studios. Richard thought Sarah was certainly pretty enough to be cast as the Chief Medical Officer on any television starship, and it didn't take much to imagine her living and working there.

If the Atlantic Ocean had been a lake, Richard might have spent more time surfing websites in Wilmington. But he was certain he was on a major intuitive roll here and decided to take the Little Pointe plunge.

Little Pointe, Michigan had a population of just under six thousand. There were farms and country estates and mansions and the town was a simple commute from Detroit. It was a small place: several miles of land and much of that was waterfront on Lake St. Clair. The lake, twenty-six miles from north to south, and twenty-four miles from east to west, connected Michigan with Ontario, Canada. In comparison, Peck's Pond in Brett wasn't even a mile long.

So his next Goggle was "Viking yachts and Little Pointe." Richard clicked his way through a series of sites until he found a complete list of all boat registrations for the town. Alphabetically, beginning with *A Lively Day*, to *Beautiful*, *Northern Star* to *The Sarah*. Bingo! Cue the music. As he read from the list: *The Sarah*, Registered to Penelope Davis, Viking Yacht Co., 2002, Recreational."

Richard was so happy he decided to celebrate with a trip to Goldie's Miniature Golf.

*   *   *

On the third day, Richard went looking for Penelope Davis, and to see what, if any, relationship she might have with Sarah. Mother, daughter, cousin, aunt, grandmother, friend, or maybe Sarah had worked for Penelope Davis. Because you never knew: just maybe she had hit her head, and with the amnesia, began to fantasize that she was rich; deluding herself that the boat was hers. If he hit his head, Richard suspected he'd probably imagine himself Luke Skywalker. Or the young Captain Kirk.

The next step was to run a people search. Richard started with the free search sites. According to Babasearch, there were 97 different incarnations of Penelope Davis spread all across the country. Peekaboo found only 17. Amerisearch found 50. Whitepages, 68. Richard added some paper to the printer and started printing the lists.

It was time to spend some money, no expense spared for the new muffler. So he signed up for a year's worth of Virtualsearch, the site used by serious searchers. And quickly discovered that if the Penelope Davis he was looking for was the Penelope C. Davis of *The Sarah* then she was the daughter of Courtney Davis and Abigail Curtis Davis. And, if the information was still accurate, she lived at 101 Lakeview Road, Little Pointe, Michigan. She was forty-one years old and married to a Peter Bishop.

His brain jumping from Sarah to Penelope back to Sarah, the next step was to search for pictures of Penelope the boat owner, hoping he would find Sarah somewhere in the background of one of them. When all of a sudden he flashed on *The Talented Mr. Ripley*, that creepy Matt Damon movie he had seen several years ago at the Plattsford Cineplex. Should have been called *The Completely Terrifying Mr. Ripley*. Scared the shit out of him. And now his mind was spinning. A lot of times things weren't what they seemed. Like those really old *Twilight Zones* his dad still had on VHS. You thought one thing was happening but really it was something else entirely. Like the gourmet restaurant serving the parts of dead people for dinner.

What if Sarah was a Mrs. Ripley, a stone cold psycho-killer who murdered the real Penelope Davis then stole her identity? Maybe killed her on the boat. Then dumped her body in the middle of that big lake. And maybe just a little bit later she hits her head on something and forgets all about the murder. Which is why she seems so innocent.

Or if she's sneaky like Matt Damon, well she's just pretending she forgot. A really convincing liar. And thinking she's gotten away with it. That is, until now when he and Deb stumble onto what she's done. Which could mean only one thing: now she's got to get rid of them, too.

His loud "whoa" somehow made it from his brain out of his mouth … Shivering, momentarily stuck in this bad movie of his own making, still with a whole bunch of things left to do in life and not in any way ready for an early death, Richard headed for his half-size refrigerator, popping it open, then quickly slugging some Pepsi, the sugar and caffeine stimulating the rest of his brain, short-circuiting the paranoia. Slowly realizing there might be other less bloody, easier to swallow scenarios. Like Sarah had really truly forgotten who she was; like maybe she was best friends with Penelope Davis. Or maybe Peter Bishop's sister. Downing the rest of the Pepsi, and thinking he needed to get out of the basement and into the daylight. Maybe score one of Chicken City's Chicken Double Bacon Cheddar sandwiches and some large fries.

*　　　　*　　　　*

The next morning, after checking up on his beloved Boston Red Sox, Richard searched for "newspapers and Little Pointe, Michigan." Google sent him to *The Little Pointe News*. Like many small town papers, while light on national and international coverage, *The Little Pointe News* had on-line sections devoted to Community Events, Features, even Local Announcements. There were photos of two country clubs, marinas, mansions for sale, and a beautiful ballpark. It didn't take long, using their Site Search, to find multiple listings for the Davis family.

According to Ginger Shipley, author of the "What's the Pointe?" column, Penelope had once again successfully chaired the December Fundraising Dinner for the LPYP, the Little Pointe Youth Project. Richard smiled as he read that the program was designed to create mentoring opportunities for Little Pointe's teenagers-at-risk. He and his friends were always at risk and many of them couldn't manage anything better than a part-time job at Magic Mart. You'd think those Michigan rich kids with their boats and Little Pointe Junior Boat Club, their tennis courts and golf course wouldn't need a Youth Project.

Ginger wrote that they had raised $50,000 at the previous year's dinner, and according to Penelope, were close to $65,000 this year. "There is no issue more important to our community," Ms. Davis told Ginger, "than to ensure the safety of our young people and to provide them every opportunity to succeed." And right there was a picture of Penelope at last years' dinner.

"Holy shit," he muttered. All dressed up, she was drop-dead gorgeous. Sarah was Penelope. Ginger wrote that she was wearing Valentino, with matching pearl earrings and necklace. She stood there, with a supportive arm around her father, who seemed frail. As if it was hard for him to stand.

Her hair was blond and much longer, her eyes seemed to sparkle and she was smiling. Looking like she owned the place. The more Richard looked through the archives of *The Little Pointe News*, the more he found. Most of the time Ginger called her Penelope, though once in a while it was Penny. There was Penelope Davis and Courtney Davis at a Chamber of Commerce meeting; Courtney and Penelope at a fancy dinner at the Yacht Club; Penelope holding up a check for $25,000 for the Red Cross; and Penelope and husband Peter Bishop at a charity ball held at the Museum of Contemporary Art in Detroit, although Peter seemed to have turned his head to the side so that you couldn't clearly see his face.

Celebrating, Richard turned the music up as he proudly printed the pages with her picture, article after article about where Sarah/Penelope had been and what she had been doing. He called Deb and they arranged to meet at Dom's.

Deb was thrilled with all of it, but it was definitely going to take some time to get used to the new Sarah. The more she looked over the printouts, the more she saw how radiant and self-assured Sarah seemed. Penelope, Penelope, Penelope. And the more she learned, the more she knew she had been right to try to give her back her real life. It seemed so glamorous.

"Listen, Richard," she asked, "I need you to find a phone number for her family. I want to make absolutely sure that we've got this right before I tell her. Positively, perfectly right. It might really set her back if she gets all excited and it turns out we've somehow made a mistake. These photos and this info have pretty much convinced me, but I need to take that next step and make sure. Do you understand? So I need to swear you to secrecy. Not a word to anyone until we're totally convinced."

FORTY-FIVE

Donnie didn't remember too much about the last three days, but he was glad there was still some coke left to help him wake up. Remembering that maybe a day or so ago, he had given money to Betsy to get some more. The phone hadn't rung much, and when it had, it was someone looking to raise money for the kids of the marching dimes or to help those polar bears stuck on the melting ice.

Petey called a couple of times, and even through the haze of coke, Donnie could tell he seemed less confident.

And then last night Little Francis called his cell to say that the Quincy Brothers were a week late on their payment and he should stay ready.

Which is why when the phone by the bed rang the next morning and he saw "Dom's" on the Caller ID, he answered right away. Because even though Arthur let his lame ass brother-in-law Dominic Kelly put his name on it, and even pretend he was running the seedy bar a few blocks from Big Pink, everyone knew who really owned Dom's. And if Arthur somehow knew he was at Petey's and he was calling, well both he and Petey needed to know what he wanted.

But it was pretty confusing to be talking to a lady, not Arthur or Little Francis. Who said she worked at Dom's and went on and on about a Sarah who came there and didn't know who she was. That this Sarah probably fell on her head or something, and would sit there without hardly saying anything at first, but was now drinking coffee, eating eggs over easy, and reading the paper, which shows how much better she is.

This sounded just like one of those phone tricks Arthur sometimes played when he was drunk or just pissed off, waking Donnie up really early in the morning or late at night pretending to be the Dog Officer calling about a lost schnauzer or congratulating him for winning the free cruise to Pago Pago. Because Arthur always liked to poke fun at him, laughing his ass off, and telling everybody all the time how dumb Donnie was to be falling for this crap.

And this seemed extra fishy because the last time he was there Dom's only had those creepy sandwiches in cellophane that you took straight from the refrigerator into the microwave or for a couple of bucks some potato chips that were weeks old, and the coffee tasted like mud. So unless Arthur had completely changed the menu, no one who could taste things would even think about eating at Dom's, except if you were so completely blotto that you needed something to soak up some of the liquor before you drove home.

And so Donnie kept saying "uh huh," imagining himself on the speaker phone with Arthur, with maybe Little Francis trying to keep from laughing in the background.

Then the lady, calling herself Deb, was talking about a friend using "googles" on the computer, and wanting to be "verifying" something. When it seemed to Donnie that out of nowhere, this Sarah person had turned into Penelope. And the Deb lady was asking what could Donnie tell her about Penelope and her boat?

Which pissed him off big time because this was the boat he had never been on, the boat he would love to go on. Remembering how Petey kept saying it was just too dangerous for him to go on board, even though he was sure there were times when nobody would have seen him. Thinking that Petey could pretend that Donnie was checking out something mechanical or maybe was a carpenter.

This was definitely confusing because Donnie didn't think Arthur even knew about the boat. Certainly never mentioned it. And all the while he was getting real pissed because this Deb was talking and talking and talking and what he needed the most to deal with all this confusing crap was another snort or two. And if it wasn't for not wanting to mess things up for Petey, he would have screamed something like "would you just shut the fuck up and hand the phone over to Arthur or Little Francis already."

But still she talked: "I haven't told Penelope I found you all yet. I was really hoping to surprise her." Saying she wanted Penelope to be "reunited with her family!"

And there was no way he could get to the coke without putting the phone down.

"I'm Donnie," he said, "my brother Petey's not here right now." But then quickly remembering that Petey had reminded him that for the rest of the world he wasn't really Petey anymore. And so he had to back up: "Peter, really ... I forget sometimes but he hates Petey. And just so you know I haven't even been on the boat." Then stopping for a second, thinking that that may have sounded a bit stupid. What kind of brother wouldn't be allowed on a boat? "Seasick," he tried.

He could hear her shuffling some papers and Donnie was thinking any minute Arthur would jump in to call him a fucking moron. Saying how they've known for a while about the boat. Or Little Francis bragging how they got him one more time. But it didn't happen.

Then she started on about something she had just read about the Youth Project. And her picture. Which made no sense at all. Thinking what the fuck does Arthur care about a Youth Project? Wondering if maybe Arthur had gotten bored and wasn't even listening anymore? Which meant that now was probably the best time to put the phone down on the bed and roll over and get the rest of the coke.

Which, thank God, he had already chopped. So he picked up the straw and did a quick line for each nostril. And then back to the phone again, not quite hearing her all that clearly right away, preoccupied with the coke's first surge. Stopping to think for a moment: was it possible that Penelope had somehow made it to Dom's? That after he had smashed her and split from the house, Penelope had somehow gotten up, and gotten herself together enough to drive. Stashed the car at the airport to fake them all out, then took a cab back downtown. Like Sister Margaret had talked about, with those fishes and the loaves, or Jesus rising from the dead even with all those nails, an eff-ing miracle. Which even if people like him couldn't understand, it did happen if you really believed and prayed all the time.

Could it be that Dan Shine and everyone looking for her had messed up? Which maybe meant the Weasel had been holding out on him. That, maybe never even leaving town, or taking a bus, Penelope had wandered into Dom's where this Deb person took care of her.

This was all too confusing. Penelope calling herself Sarah. At Dom's. Of all the places in the world. And did this mean that Penelope knew the truth about Petey and him and Arthur and Little Francis and the old neighborhood? About what Petey owed Arthur?

Could it be that somewhere along the way Petey had told her the real story? And forgot to tell him? Isn't that what married people did? Share secrets.

So maybe this Deb lady knew a lot more than she was letting on? Like knowing it was him who had tried to kill Penelope. Wishing now he hadn't taken these last big snorts. Because sometimes the coke was just too much for your brain, and you went from being sharp to completely crazy. Seeing things that weren't there and thinking things that weren't real. Wondering if any of this would make more sense if he wasn't so stoned?

His brain just wouldn't shut up. Maybe Petey had told Arthur that this whole thing was his fault, botching the job, not killing her when he had the chance? Which, because Donnie messed up, was the main reason he was having trouble coming up with the money he owed.

And now Arthur, probably sleeping with this Deb, which is what he always did with the ladies who worked for the Weasel and his brother-in-law, was sitting there at Dom's, laughing about how, after everything Donnie did wrong, Penelope was still alive.

Problem was there were just too many possibilities for his coked-up brain to deal with. And still, as he faded back in, this Deb lady continued to talk and talk some more:

"You understand, don't you, that I don't want to disappoint Penelope, or raise her hopes unnecessarily? So I need to make sure you're Penelope's family. I'm hoping you can help me with this. We don't really know much about her, except that she appeared in Brett, and didn't know who she was."

There was silence for a moment. Then not getting a response, she continued on: "So if you don't mind, I've got a couple more quick questions. Like when was it you first knew she was missing? And do you have any idea what happened to her? Bea thought she might have banged her head."

Donnie realized that maybe he was just over-thinking all of this: "Uhh … listen lady. I'm not sure what's going on here. Can we go back to the beginning? What exactly is it that you do for Arthur at Dom's?"

"Excuse me?"

"Truth is I don't really remember where this Brett Street is, and where she's staying? So like how close is this Brett to Big Pink? And how far is it from Dom's?"

Now Deb was getting annoyed: "Why in the world are you

talking about Big Pink? My husband has that CD. It's by those guys who played with Bob Dylan, right? Dom's is on Main Street, right next to the mill. Is that why Sarah came here? Has Sarah vacationed here in the summer? Maybe she's been to Dom's before? Or to Tanglewood?"

"Who's this Sarah person again?"

"Maybe I haven't made myself clear … Sarah is Penelope and the information I have is that Penelope Davis is married to Peter Bishop … And as I told you before I'm calling from Brett, Massachusetts. Are you sure you're really related to Peter Bishop? I don't remember seeing a brother in any of the pictures."

Shit, he thought, what does Arthur have going in Massachusetts? This was sounding more and more like a set-up. Thinking now that Petey was going to be major league pissed off that he even answered the phone. Then he remembered India. He should have mentioned India. If he could just get a word in, she talked so much. Getting real annoyed again.

"Of course … Peter is my big brother. I've known him my whole life. He always took care of me. And who the hell are you? And what's Penny got to do with Massachusetts?"

"Listen, Mr. Bishop. My name is Deb Spencer. I work at Dom's Restaurant in Brett, Massachusetts. Penelope, who we called Sarah when she didn't know her real name, came to Dom's pretty soon after she got here … How about you give me your brother's cell phone number, and I'll call him directly. Quite frankly, you don't seem too concerned about your sister-in-law, or her amnesia, and I'm beginning to get worried."

"Sorry, lady … I got confused. Our friend Arthur has a place called Dom's and I saw Dom's name come up on the phone gizmo. So when you mentioned her I was thinking that maybe Penelope somehow was there with you and Arthur, which is very confusing because of India, which is where she is, or where she was, except now you say Massachusetts. Which really doesn't make sense. She was always going on and on about visiting India … and Peter bought her a ticket and those hotel reservations, which is why I figured India."

And then remembering her car, quickly adding: "Peter even had me go pick up her car at the airport, long-term parking. Because he had to work and she flew out of there for their dream vacation and they was going to meet later on a beach in India. Her BMW at the airport."

Thinking that was a really smart way to say it, when Donnie heard the click of the phone, yelling "shit!" as soon as he realized she had hung up on him. And then at least remembering to press the arrow of the phone's Caller ID so he could see and write down her number. Which he should have seen from the first was a 413 number, not 313.

FORTY-SIX

Deb quickly gathered the print-outs from the desk in the back office at Dom's. She knew she had messed up. The sweet return she had imagined for her new friend wasn't going to happen, at least not right away. Not if that Donnie guy really was Penelope's brother-in-law. Because there was something seriously wrong going on there.

It didn't seem like her family was worried about her. Donnie, or whoever he was, seemed to have no real concern for her. Let alone love. Plus all that suspicious stuff about that Arthur guy and Dom's. Not to mention how weird he got when she asked about the boat. He seemed so different than Penelope. It was hard to believe they were connected. He actually sounded a lot like the lame guys she had grown up with in Holyoke, Massachusetts. Guys with no dreams and a lot of attitude, always in trouble, always trouble for her.

In no way did this Donnie guy fit with the pictures and articles Richard had found. The money and grace Penelope seemed to have. The fabulous clothes. The fancy dinners. Probably a lot like how she wouldn't fit in with Penelope's life in Little Pointe, or feel comfortable hanging out on Penelope's boat. Maybe whatever friendship they had was only about Brett and her memory loss and wouldn't carry over.

Meanwhile, Deb was frightened, frightened for Penelope, and embarrassed. She had told Donnie about Dom's, about Brett, and about Penelope's amnesia. She rushed to the kitchen to tell Joe she had an emergency and had to split. And she began to drive much too quickly to Katie's.

*   *   *

Frank returned from his long walk with Rabbit to find Katie rifling through a bunch of computer printouts, her face compressed with concern. All through her childhood, Frank had seen Katie's mood reflected on her face: happy, sad, worried or in wonderment. And over the years he had grown especially sensitive to her moods. Almost immediately, he was as worried as she was.

"Damn it, Frank, everything has changed. I've told you about Deb, the waitress who first met Sarah at Dom's, the restaurant in Brett. Who brought Sarah to me. And is still very close to her. I'm so sorry I didn't get you and Deb together. You might have warned her.

"Deb's been learning about Sarah's story as we learned about it. Except that she was frustrated by how slow everything seemed to be going; although if you ask me, Sarah has actually been figuring things out at a pretty remarkable rate. Anyway, Deb decided to speed things up. With information about the name of the boat, and Potter Road, and some of Sarah's other memories we've recovered, she had a local kid do some surfing on the internet.

"He's obviously very, very good because he found all kinds of information about Sarah going back years: actually information about Penelope Davis, Sarah's real name it turns out, and Little Pointe, Michigan, where she lives, complete with pictures of her and her father and her husband, Peter Bishop, even a phone number. Deb just dropped this off and I've got it all here.

"Deb wanted to make sure the information was absolutely accurate before she told Sarah or me, so we wouldn't get our hopes up. And so she decided to call their home in Little Pointe from the restaurant during her break. She reached someone named Donnie, who claimed to be the brother-in-law. Now, she's completely freaked out because she got the strong impression that Sarah wasn't even missed. She's convinced something is terribly wrong out there.

"He came up with a whole series of disconnected stories, including the fact that she was on her way to India and he found her car parked at the airport.

"Deb feels miserable and afraid because without really thinking about it, she gave them her name, the phone number at Dom's, and alerted them to the fact that Sarah, I'm sorry, I mean Penelope, lost her memory, and has been coming to the restaurant. And by calling, she also revealed to them that Penelope's memory is slowly coming back."

Frank was silent for a few moments, then: "Shit, Katie … This is bad, really bad." Frank quickly flipped through the material, jotting down names and addresses, muttering and cursing to himself.

He ripped the top sheet from the pad, folded it, and put it in the back right pocket of his jeans. Then reaching for his wallet, and taking out a credit card: "Katie, I'm going to grab some clothes. I need you to find the nearest major airport to Little Pointe, Michigan, and make a reservation for me on the first early morning flight out of JFK tomorrow. Then, pick the best photo you can find of Penelope.

"Maybe she was on her way to India and had an accident or got mugged at the airport. Forgot what she was going to do. Though I'm not sure why she'd want to be flying to India with all that cash. Or why a mugger wouldn't have found and taken it all. It doesn't make a lot of sense. But whatever the truth is, it's likely all there in Little Pointe. Her home, her family. And it seems to me the first place to look is the airport, where her car was supposedly found. Then I'll check out this Donnie and her place in Little Pointe.

"I love you, Katie, more than you know." He gave her a hug and went to pack.

FORTY-SEVEN

Donnie was pissed that he had answered. That he had to tell Petey that he messed up again. There was no way this was going to be fun. He dialed and Petey picked up on the third ring, annoyed from the start: "Please, Donnie, make this quick … I don't know whether these guys are completely jerking me off or what? Now they're demanding 95% of everything. Trying to squeeze me. There's no way I'm going to relinquish what I worked years for. I'll give it another day or so to see if they come up with a more reasonable offer, but I may have to bag California."

Then the pause, and even though he wasn't sure where to begin, Donnie jumped in: "Listen, Petey, you got to believe me, when I saw Dom's on that little ID box you got for the phone, I really thought it was that dump that Arthur owns near Big Pink. You remember the place with the pickled eggs in the big bottle. I hate those eggs."

"Why would Arthur call from Dom's, he's hardly ever there?"

"That's what confused me. But I thought Arthur might have a job for me. Except it wasn't Arthur, it was this lady who works at Dom's. I thought maybe she and Arthur were playing one of those jokes on me, like the time a couple of months ago when Pizza Hut delivered ten ham and pineapple pizzas for me at eleven at night, large pizzas and the wings. Cost me a fortune. But she went on and on about, wait a second, I wrote some of this down, 'verifying' and 'reuniting,' and about how this Sarah lady came into the restaurant, which was the confusing part because it was called Dom's.

"Then she started talking about Brett. I haven't been to Dom's in years. The closest I get is Big Pink, and I don't know any Brett that's anywhere near Big Pink and told her so. Which is when she got all annoyed and said Brett, Massachusetts. And that, oh yeah, I forgot, and that this Sarah didn't know who she was. But this Deb lady after a bunch of checking on the computer, she was thinking there was a chance this Sarah lady might be your Penelope, mentioning your name, and started asking about the boat. Which, you know, I don't know nothing about this boat, which we don't have to talk about right now."

He stopped, waiting for Petey to explode.

"Hang on a second, Donnie ... This might make sense. It could be that smack to the head didn't kill her but completely messed up her memory. Amnesia is what they call it."

"Yeah, she might have said amnesia too ...

"Give me a moment to think about this ..."

Donnie sat there, some of the tension fading, but still not sure why Petey wasn't yelling at him.

Then Petey was back: "So if all this is true, then somehow Penny managed to make it all the way to Massachusetts. Maybe it really was her in that bus station. Pretty impressive. But now, thanks to the woman who just called, we can find her. This woman just told us Penny comes to a place called Dom's, in Brett, Massachusetts. And that one way or another, she's figured out who Penny is and where Penny comes from ... Amazing.

"So the question is: how much time do we have before this all explodes in our faces? Did she tell you whether Penny's memory has completely come back? Has Penny remembered what happened to her? And did she say whether Penny's figured out who tried to kill her?"

"I don't think so. I think that's the verify part, like she didn't want to say anything yet to Penelope about where and who and what she discovered without verifying you were her family. And I didn't do any verifying. And just so you know, she never mentioned the cops or anything like that."

"You didn't happen to get her name or phone number: you know, there's the ..."

"Yeah, Petey, first thing I did after she hung up. I got it right here for Dom's in Brett. And I wrote down the name she gave me too, Deb Spencer. Oh yeah, I tried to tell her about India, but I don't think she cared."

"You did great, Donnie. But we don't have a lot of time. Hang on a second, and let me check my laptop. Let's see ... Brett, Massachusetts ... Give me another minute ... Uh, yeah, here it is ... it's in the part of Massachusetts that's near New York State, not Boston, west not east ... Let me blow this up. We can get to it three ways: there are airports in Boston, Hartford/Springfield or Albany, New York.

"In the basement, Donnie, next to the workbench, there's a big metal cabinet for tools. In the bottom drawer, under the wrenches, there's a compartment where you'll find a bunch of cash. I want you to fly out as soon as you can. I want you on the first flight that arrives at any of those airports. Rent a car and scope out Dom's. Now I'm talking about Dom's in Brett, not Arthur's dive, got that. And you know you can't take a gun on the plane."

"C'mon Petey."

"I'm joking, Donnie. If she's taken care of this time for real, without us being caught, and there's a body to be found, well then I can get the land. Make the deal. And make Arthur happy. We're going to make this happen right this time, OK? For Mom, and for us."

"OK, Petey, for Mom and for us."

"Find this Deb and she'll lead you straight to Penny. Call me when you get to Brett, and when you find a motel to stay in. I'll try to wrap things up here and get there as soon as I can. Then we'll figure out a plan that works. And Donnie, you did great. I mean it."

FORTY-EIGHT

Flying from Detroit to Washington then into Bradley Airport in Connecticut, Donnie was thinking how almost his entire life he was running to catch up to Petey. Always behind, because he never really understood Petey's plans. And it didn't help that somewhere along the way Petey had decided it was pretty much a waste of time explaining them to him. Even though it was Donnie's job to make things happen.

Donnie knew a guy in Springfield, Massachusetts who used to work for Arthur's uncle and still came back home to Detroit to visit his sick mother. A pawnbroker, he was just a few blocks off the highway, and if he knew who you were, he was perfectly glad to exchange clean pieces for clean cash. And for some more cash to throw in a bit of coke.

Donnie loved driving on coke, reenergized, the early afternoon crystal clear, everyone driving eighty on the Turnpike. Happy until he remembered again how much that Deb lady had ticked him off. Just hearing about the boat pissing him off big time.

It was obvious Petey didn't even know how big a deal the boat was for him. Probably didn't even remember the day Mom had given him, not Petey, the little toy tugboat. Blue and red with a yellow stripe. He loved that tiny tugboat. Sometimes he would skip school and head down to the Public Dock and Terminal where he would watch real boats, but for every other day, he could at least stare at his little toy tugboat and dream.

Of course, he never told a soul. They would have laughed; maybe punched him, all in fun to begin with, but he wasn't about to let anyone mess with his dream to live on the water. So he never showed it to anyone. Never admitted that he had it with him every day. In his pocket even now, the paint fading, all these years later. And Petey now with a real boat available, not even liking it all that much, not appreciating the water, and as smart a guy that he is, never figuring out a way to get his little brother on board.

Donnie knew his chance for joining the Coast Guard was pretty much out the window by fourteen when he was skipping school and breaking into houses and boosting the occasional car.

Petey's fancy big house he didn't give a shit about. He knew even if Petey had invited him, he would feel funny with his scuffed work boots and jeans, not knowing where or how to sit, or what to say. But Penelope, that bothered him too. When he saw her in the papers, and he saw her smile and friendly eyes, and then when he decided to follow her, he thought that maybe they could be friends, that maybe once she knew about his toy tugboat, she would just say straight up, "Please, Donnie, call me Penny. And please come take a ride with us on the boat. I'm sure you'll love it." Of course, that changed when he tried to kill her.

All because Petey had been completely obsessed with getting back at that family. It drove Petey nuts. It spoiled Petey. It spoiled everything.

He loved Petey. There was no one else once Mom died. When they had no home, Petey had kept them out of foster homes, out of juvey. The places he found to squat. All the book learning. Finding Sammy the Scratcher, and stealing and saving enough to buy a new name, IDs, a driver's license a year before he knew how to drive.

Donnie always said and always believed he'd do whatever it took to take care of Petey. Leaving the fancy house, he was pretty sure he had killed Penny. Then thinking that she had collapsed and died somewhere nearby. But now after the conversation with the Deb lady, he knew he really hadn't. Now, with the new gun under the driver's seat, he was ready to kill her all over again.

Petey might pretend he was coming to help, but they both knew Petey didn't have it in him, never had it in him. Think it or do it. Donnie was the doer.

"It's a crazy world," his mom would always say, mostly to herself, resigned to her dying, saying it was just her time. So maybe the last time just wasn't Penelope's time. But now for Petey's sake he had to make sure this time it was.

In the meantime, the coke was wearing off, and he realized he was starving. How in the hell did those airline companies get away with not feeding you? Charging more than six hundred bucks to fly and a simple sandwich was too much to ask.

So he was thrilled to see the Burger King on the Massachusetts Turnpike. He once had to punch a guy out who just wouldn't believe him when he said how much better the flame-broiled Whopper was than a Big Mac. With cheese and large fries and soda. There were a couple of state troopers eating a few tables away. The gun was still in the car but he had forgotten about the vial of coke he had stuffed in the front pocket of his jeans.

So he had to remind himself that they didn't know him here. They had no reason to think about him. Had no idea what was in his pocket. No idea he was here to kill her.

But in this strange place he didn't know, with the troopers so close, he realized he needed to do the job quick, so he could get back home where he was most comfortable. And with Petey in California maybe for a few more days, it was time to take some initiative. It was pretty obvious what he needed to do. Get to Brett, find the Deb lady, follow her to find Penny, kill Penny. Head home. The sooner the better.

Preoccupied with planning, he got up with his tray without looking, banging into the chair beside him. One of the troopers briefly looked his way. Donnie offered a stupid smile and, trying hard to keep his cool, made it to the trash bin. Then, a little too quickly, to the exit. But the troopers were once again focused on their fries.

Back on the turnpike, the exit to Brett came quickly, a long set of sweeping curves to the tollbooth. A few minutes later, Donnie pulled into a Motel 6 a couple of blocks down Main Street, paying with cash for five days, hoping it would be two at the most. Buying a map of the county at the check-in counter. Then, in the phone book in his room he found J. and D. Spencer, 42 Princeton Street, Brett, Massachusetts, less than a mile on the map from where he was.

Hers was the fifth house on the left, distinguishable from the other pre-fab homes only by all the toys and the slide and swing set on the lawn. Lucky kids, he thought. He and Petey never had a lawn, never had these kinds of toys. In his neighborhood, playgrounds were set in cement. With broken metal backboards for basketball and metal swings. If someone snuck up behind you and pushed your swing with all his might, you could easily be flying off the seat, pretty much guaranteeing scraped knees and bloody palms when you hit the concrete.

A mini-van was parked in the driveway, so Donnie decided to drive past, parking beneath a big tree. Slumping down in the seat, waiting. It was three-thirty with lots of daylight left, thinking if this was his front yard, he'd be climbing that ladder and zipping down the slide till it was so dark out you couldn't see a thing.

A half-hour of slouching paid off when the kids finally came out to play and a lady he assumed was Deb followed, parking herself in a nearby white plastic chair with a People magazine. She was hard to miss with that wavy jet-black hair. She had sounded shorter on the phone, and a bit dumpy. But she probably worked out because he couldn't see an extra ounce of fat on her. Or else picking those kids up had kept her in great shape. There wasn't anything soft about her. He could have plunked her down in his Motor City neighborhood and she would have fit right in without a problem. Actually she was pretty hot. When the kids started to fight, he could see she was intense, up in a flash, moving with no hesitation to separate them. Probably smart, remembering that when she called, how quick she got suspicious and figured out there was something wrong.

At least now he knew what she looked like. Smiling, thinking, good job Donnie. Then deciding to take a chance, he drove off and found a sporting goods store, some coffee and a bathroom at the outlet mall. After a good night's sleep at the motel, he'd be back before dawn.

*   *   *

Arthur never liked the fact that Donnie combined dealing his coke with doing it. Unlike Little Francis, who would do anything and everything Arthur asked with efficiency and restraint, Donnie always had control issues.

And so Arthur wasn't at all happy when Little Francis told him that Donnie once again had left town without word.

Then he heard from Springfield Lou about the gun and the coke. Petey and Donnie were royal pains in the ass. He had a mind to send Little Francis all the way to Massachusetts to drag Donnie back, but it was Petey and his money that was most important right now. As much as he appreciated Donnie's talents, he was getting pretty close to cutting Donnie loose.

FORTY-NINE

The closest airport was the Coleman Young in Detroit, eight miles from Little Pointe. While waiting at JFK, Frank bought a cheap cell phone. And at the business conference center, he copied the best picture Katie had given him, then made some simple cards with his name and new number.

He slept through most of the flight and before he knew it, he was at the Detroit airport. If Penelope had driven there, she could have interacted with several people. Frank's recent stint with the cab taught him that no one knew more about comings and goings than those who made their living dealing with those who came and went.

Security guards and the men and women who sold tickets were the most overwhelmed, processing people as quickly as possible, then sending them somewhere else. Assembly line work, shuttling people like frozen chickens. But the porters survived on tips, by making human connections, however brief.

And so he quickly went to work, speaking to those stationed at the drop-off zone for the departing airlines. They were some of the poorest people working in the airport, white and black and Latino working class men and women who might have squeezed out a high school education, or immigrants with few options. Probably made between sixteen and twenty thousand bucks a year.

It was harder work than you might imagine, lifting and lugging and pushing the overstuffed suitcases of hundreds of impatient and demanding travelers, their stressed out mates and spoiled children.

Frank hoped someone might recognize her from the picture, or unconsciously betray the slightest shock of recognition. A few had the semi-hooded look that comes from being on the wrong end of more than a few sessions with cops or Immigration. And about eight or nine of the porters reluctantly took his card, probably hoping to short-circuit the interaction.

But of all the guys he spoke to, one stood out: José Castillo, according to his name tag. Short, compact, a bit of Mayan mixed with Mexican, you could see the years of hard work in his body, muscles tight and taut. He had a razor-sharp wariness, and as soon as he had seen the photo, he began studying Frank as intently as Frank was studying him. So he was pretty sure Castillo knew something. He decided to grab a bite at the snack bar, hoping Castillo might be more talkative after his shift.

As Frank worked on his second cup of coffee and what passed for ham and cheese, he acknowledged he was out of practice. Talking to a shrink, shooting the shit with an odd grab-bag of passengers, and going back and forth a couple of hours a day with a parrot, however feisty, well it just wasn't the same as working the street. Trying to figure out who was lying to you, and why, when the stakes were life and death.

Here, without a badge, their hesitation to talk could simply be because they felt he was hassling them. Who knew how many of these guys had phony papers, or just a backlog of bitterness when it came to answering questions? And, in those cases, it probably wouldn't have helped if he had flashed a badge. But it wasn't hard to see that he hadn't been a working detective in a while.

Frank headed back outside to the curbside where the porters were working, making sure to stay out of the way. Castillo, probably on a break, was nowhere to be seen. There was definitely an ebb and flow to the traffic; and in between takeoffs, he'd been able to show her picture a few more times. He was pretty sure none of them had seen her.

But he grew increasingly uneasy. Deb's phone call. That indefinable sense you develop about a growing threat. He called Katie.

"Listen, Katie, I'm getting a really bad feeling about all this. I want, I actually mean I need you to keep Penelope away from that restaurant, and for someone to pick her up and get her to your place for the time being. We have no idea what's driving this Donnie guy and Penelope's husband, or whoever else may be involved. If your book is right about the danger, and I'm not being paranoid, they know she's in Brett and she could be in serious danger. I'm assuming Deb would have told you if she mentioned you to Donnie. So please do me a favor, and get your boyfriend to stay over with the two of you.

"There's a guy here at the airport who I think knows something, and I want to talk to him before I head off to her house in Little Pointe. I'll try and get back to you as soon as I can. In the meantime, please get whatshisname ... Ralph, please get Ralph to help." He waited for Katie's reluctant yes, then hung up.

Frank made his way around to the back of the terminal as the shift ended and a small, ragged army of porters, baggage handlers, food service workers, and cleaners shuffled out in a semi-daze after an exhausting eight and a half hours. José Castillo saw Frank coming, then walked right up to him.

"Cómo puedo ayudarle, señor?"

Frank's Spanish was pretty dreadful but he tried: "Bueñas noches, señor." José Castillo smiled and decided to do him a favor: "Maybe we try some inglés too. I am not so good with it, but maybe better than you with español? I asked: 'So, for how can I help you?'"

Frank retrieved the photo of Penelope: "I am looking for this woman."

"Where is your ... How do you say?"

"Badge?"

"Sí señor ... Are you Policía? Policeman? Immigration?"

"No badge this time ... My name is Frank Falco ... Mi nombre Frank Falco." Frank put out his hand to shake ... José Castillo smiled but kept his hand at his side.

"Where I come from ... men with questions ..."

"I understand, Señor Castillo ... But I am trying to help this woman ... I used to be policía in New York City but not right now, now I am only trying to help ... Does that makes sense ... Comprendo?"

José Castillo fought the impulse to tell the nosy cop "Comprendo" meant "I understand" not "Do you understand?" but softened a bit as he remembered his own battle with pronouns and tenses. "This woman ... who is this woman ... Her name?"

Frank took out the sheet of paper with Penelope's information from his back pocket: "Penelope Davis. That is why I am here. ... ¿Cómo se dice ... How do you say, amnesia?"

"Spanish, the same, amnesia ... Why me, señor?"

"I don't know, exactly ... hunch or a feeling that you can help me help her."

"OK ... But nothing ... No sé nada." Pointing to himself: "Nothing ... I know nothing of this lady."

"Something, señor ... Very important ..." and Frank handed him his card.

José Castillo nodded, then moved past Frank.

"¡Hasta la vista, Señor Castillo ... Muy importante."

"¡Adiós ..." and José looked down at Frank's card, "Señor Falco."

Frank watched as José Castillo hurried to the bus stop, thinking he had seen another flicker when he had mentioned Penelope's name. Frank went to get his car.

José waited impatiently for the bus, checking occasionally to see whether Frank Falco was still there, watching for him. The bus came a few minutes later. He was glad to get on board. He hadn't told Frank Falco that he had been studying English for four years. Wondering how much trouble this gringo would make for him? Wondering who he was? How did they say that, a cop undercover? Someone the husband had hired? Did the husband know he had helped her?

He hadn't told Frank Falco that the last time he saw her, she was still shaking, so badly beaten, the bruises covered with make-up, so confused ... Amnesia, it made sense ... She didn't understand many things he had said to her.

José called his brother Juan and asked him to meet him at the restaurant. Then quickly warned him about this Falco: about six feet, thick and strong, with dark hair, dark searching eyes, eyes not used to believing people. There was a chance that he might actually be here to help Señora Davis, but there was no way to know. But if Señor Falco was any good at his job, he would probably find Juan and Juan should be ready.

*   *   *

Frank stayed back five or six car lengths then slowly and methodically moved up. By the time José got out of the bus, he was only one car back. He quickly took the next right and parked.

As he walked back to the corner, Frank saw José check his watch, then head into Enrique's, the corner restaurant across the street. A few moments later, he watched as a slightly younger man, looking a lot like José, walked towards the restaurant, then in. As he jogged across the street, Frank was thinking that just maybe something might come of this.

José saw Frank enter, then did a quick scan to see if there was any way he and Juan could make it out the back door before he got to them. But there were two customers in the aisle, plus Maria, the waitress, with a tray full of dishes to deliver.

Frank saw José sigh and shake his head.

"I know" Frank offered, as he stood before them, "I haven't done or said anything to give you any reason to trust me. But I'm a pretty good detective and I already know several things: you don't like cops, and you may have very good reasons not to like us. I know somehow or other, you know this woman," taking Penelope's picture out and placing it in the middle of the table so the both of them could see.

Frank registered the slight flicker of recognition in the face of José's friend. "I also know" looking directly at José "that you understand English much better than you let on. And much better than I understand Spanish."

"This woman is Penelope Davis. She lives at 101 Lakeview Drive in Little Pointe with her husband, Peter Bishop. Peter Bishop may or may not have a brother named Donnie. I have a very strong feeling that Penelope is in danger. She is a friend of my sister, and my sister is helping her in Massachusetts. So if Penelope is in danger, so is my sister. And I love my sister. And I will do anything to protect her.

"I just met Penelope and I like her, too. Someone who knows my sister and knows Penelope just told this Donnie where she is staying now. So what do you think, José? From everything you know and everything I've told you today about her amnesia, do you think Penelope has a problem? And my sister?"

José's friend looked at Frank, then pointed to José then back to himself: "Señor, por favor ... Please, just a minute." Frank nodded, then moved to grab a chair from the next table, giving them space and time to talk to each other. Frank's meager Spanish deserted him. They spoke in short rapid bursts, and though he understood none of it, they seemed in a matter of moments to have come to a decision. José's friend looked to Frank, nodded then pointed toward the seat next to José.

José turned to Frank. "This is my brother, Juan. He works at the house. He has seen this brother much in the last weeks. He was told Señora Davis was on vacation in India. Let me speak to your sister. Please."

Frank looked at José with added respect, took the phone from his pocket and started to dial.

"Is she a married woman or single?" José asked.

As he listened to the phone ring, Frank smiled: "I think she will always be a señorita in spirit."

"Her last name?"

"Greenberg, Katherine ... Katie."

"Katie, this is Frank ... I am sitting here with two gentlemen who might be able to help us. They obviously don't know me, and with good reason, don't trust me. Señor Castillo would like to talk to you. I am going to give him the phone." Frank passed the phone to José.

José took the phone and began to speak. "Señorita Greenberg, I am José Castillo. Thank you very much for speaking with me. My English is still needing improvement. But please tell me about this woman you and your brother are worried about."

"Thank you, Señor Castillo, for speaking with me. Please let me know if I am speaking too fast and if I say anything you do not understand. My brother is a good man even if he looks mean and angry sometimes."

José looked over to Frank and smiled, then said: "Sometimes, yes."

'Well, I asked him to help Penelope. A friend brought Penelope to me when she came to town. She thought her name was Sarah then. She had lost her memory. I think she must have hurt her head. I help people find their way, to find things they have lost.

"Slowly, she is finding herself, and with every piece of new information, Penelope is remembering more about her life. Many people do not understand but occasionally I see things, and feel things, and now I am feeling great danger."

"Señorita Greenberg, there is a woman in our village who saw the birth of my son, Pablo, four years before I found my wife and we had our baby. She told me he would be missing a toe. You do not have to explain these things to us."

"Thank you, José. Penelope dreamt of a fancy house, and marble stairs and a figure in black coming up the stairs towards her, we think to hurt her. And of another house near the water and land everywhere you can see. We feel like the land is in danger as well."

"Juan, my brother, works for her and he knows these houses and this land well, and I saw her, probably that same day she was hurt. She had been hit, I think you say beaten, and had fallen. Her face was very, very bad ... At the airport, I told her about the buses and took away her phone and cards for credit and cut them all up. So they would not know where to look for her. We told no one this story. I am sorry but we did not know who to trust. And they could send us back. I am glad she is safe with you. I will help your brother. I know that Juan would want you to say 'thank you' to her for her kindness. I will give the phone to your brother."

"Gracias, José ... thank you very much."

FIFTY

It was so unlike Katie to ask him for a favor. Calling him first thing in the morning to say her brother Frank insisted she needed help. Just in case someone wanted to hurt her and the lady. At first Ralph took it the wrong way: wondering if it was up to just Katie, would she even have asked him?

But Ralph was quickly humbled, having to acknowledge that he didn't really know what trouble she was talking about. And that as much as he told himself he loved her, he either hadn't paid enough attention to what she had been saying or she hadn't trusted him enough to share what was really going on. Like why someone might want to hurt them, and how it got to the point her brother the cop wanted him there.

All of which made him decide to do his very best to help her, to strengthen their connection.

The plan was to meet at Jack and Deb's at nine-thirty. A babysitter would watch the kids for the morning, and they'd take two vehicles to bring the woman to Katie's.

He knew how much Katie hated guns and knew Katie didn't want them in her house, but it was hard to square her feelings with the need to protect her. His dad had taught him to shoot when he turned thirteen, and so the farmer boy, deer hunter in him cleaned his shotgun. He'd stow it and some shells out of sight beneath the front seat of the pickup. And at least her brother would appreciate having it when he got there.

He and Jack Spencer went way back, including almost a decade's stint on the Brett Volunteer Fire Company Softball Team. The BVFC was always short a man or two, and even though Ralph was a Ripton boy the league made allowances.

Over the years, their conversations were pretty much confined to "Hey Jack!" with a quick "Hey RP!" back, or vice versa. Except for some occasional trash talk at the bowling alley or ballfield, or when Jack tried to claim his football New York Giants were as good as Ralph's New England Patriots.

Ralph drove past their house and swung the truck around, so he'd be facing the right way and ready to go. Jack and Deb were out with the woman at nine-thirty sharp. He and Jack exchanged quick looks and the three of them were in Deb's mini-van in a matter of moments.

Ralph had only gotten a quick glimpse of the woman but he had been surprised. Somehow, he had pictured her as an old, slightly dotty lady, imagining her memory loss as something like Alzheimer's. The truth was she was hot, or would be even more so, if she were dressed up. Not that he cared about that kind of stuff as much he once did, since Katie.

*   *   *

With two large lukewarm Dunkin' Donut coffees and three frosted donuts, Donnie was once more slouched down in the front seat. Glad he had scored the binoculars at the sporting goods store yesterday. Sitting in countless cars waiting for Arthur or his bigwig friends, he learned you needed some coffee to drink, some coke to snort, and something to piss in. With the binoculars he was able to park out of sight under a tree all the way at the end of the block. Then, a few minutes ago, he had watched as a really big lady in an old station wagon had dropped off a lady he thought might be Penelope. As soon as the lady was in the door, the car was off.

Five minutes later, a pickup made a swift U-turn and came to rest right before the driveway. Then he watched as the Deb lady, probably the hubby, and Penelope headed out and into the mini-van. Bingo! Definitely Penelope, definitely alive, walking fine, though her blond hair was shorter and she was dressed liked the Deb lady, long-sleeved t-shirt, sneakers, and jeans. Blending in. For the first time more normal than magazine special. Kind of weird that he liked her more this way, and now he was going to kill her. He called Petey but when it went to voicemail, he had just enough time to say he saw Penny and was going to follow her.

But knowing for sure he had found her mostly meant he could do this quickly, save Petey the trip from California. And get home sooner than later.

From his two short trips driving around, he knew this place was no way like the city. Hardly any cars, no buses, no cabs. Mostly a whole lot of pickups. So he was going to have to stay back a bit not to be noticed.

They got a head start down the street, the mini-van with the

Toyota pickup not far behind, maybe ten years old, with a bumper sticker you'd never see where he came from: "Support Your Local Farmer." Not much chance he'd lose that in traffic. They made a left, then a quick right onto Main. He was several hundred yards behind them, making sure he wasn't speeding. Past the library and town hall. He made sure the truck had a half block lead past the bank and Dunkin' Donuts, then moving to the right past Chicken City, Motel 6, and the other fast food joints.

A Honda, coming out of the Mobil Station, pulled in ahead of him, adding some additional cover, now a member of the convoy.

They drove beneath the ramp of the turnpike, slowed to check oncoming traffic then merged right onto Route 102. All three vehicles, and Donnie was wondering now if this Honda was somehow part of their plan. He decided to stay a little further back, and actually had a great view as they made a quick left off the highway onto Tottingham Road. Which was very quickly the real country, with lots of open space, thinking he was glad he still had the three donuts, because he might not see another donut shop for quite a while.

*   *   *

It was a beautiful crisp day and the drive from the dense, small-town streets of Brett to the vistas of Tottingham reminded Ralph why he couldn't imagine leaving the Berkshires, all these many years later inspired by seeing the forest, the open fields, and the hills.

Ralph had driven from the family farm to the center of Ripton thousands of times, but it had all changed with Katie. It was no longer the way to the General Store or to Doug Dennard's garage. It was now the way to Katie's, and there was an added tingle, an unaccustomed nervousness to a journey that had always been just about getting from here to there.

He was hoping to meet Frank, thinking when the time was right maybe her brother would have some guy advice he could offer up about Katie; that is, if Frank didn't think he was just a country bumpkin unworthy of his sister.

*   *   *

Katie was still having trouble dealing with the fact that she was about to be invaded. From the very beginning she had decided not to tell Frank she could feel, sometimes see the spirits of Carl and Theresa in the house with her: figuring there was enough going on for Frank right now, and the last thing either of them needed was to be getting into an argument about what she could or couldn't see. And so far she had done pretty well with Frank.

Probably, if she had to choose, she would pick Danger as a roommate over Frank. Danger was a lot less complicated. When Frank was in the room, he brought his own very different version of Carl and Theresa along with him, and it was sometimes hard for her to breathe, to move about the room without bumping into all of them.

For now, it was more than enough to deal with what Penelope could see, and what Frank could do to help her. And the truth was, she herself hadn't gotten to the point where, when she looked, she could see Penelope. She had begun the journey with Sarah and still saw Sarah. She had her own work to do.

The house worked perfectly for her and Rabbit. Letting Ralph in for one night a week was manageable enough, although each morning she could feel his longing, see it leaking out of him, hoping she'd ask him to return again that night, to claim some part of the place. Resisting the impulse to give in.

Sometimes she felt she had slowly and irretrievably slipped into a phobia of sorts. Imagining you weren't supposed to enjoy being alone as much as she did. She never doubted that Theresa had loved Carl, or that she was a steadfast partner and respected him deeply. But, even as a young girl, she had seen how much her mother relished the time Carl was out saving the world in places far enough away so that Theresa could have some time for herself. She remembered coming upon her by accident sitting alone on a bench in St. James Park. Katie had hid behind a nearby tree and watched Theresa, a soft smile on her face, cherishing a time and space all her own, dedicated to the crossword puzzle, no kids pulling at her, no questions from Carl about where he had left his keys or did she think there was enough ground beef for burgers?

She had grown very fond of Sarah/Penelope. The voyage with strangers through the *I Ching* provided a compelling challenge: each time committing herself to find the unique reality of the seeker, the truths of those particular moments in and for that singular life. But that didn't mean she was forming a bond that would live beyond the work. Because helping people find the answers to questions that needed answers was indeed difficult work; and she had learned you could help people, do the work, yet not want any other kind of connection.

But with Penelope, she could imagine a friendship, a continuing bond. She also knew that if she were right, that that might happen later. They were still in the midst of the work; and right now she needed to be her guide, more than her friend. And so she was worried that having Penelope in her home, that breaking those boundaries could be a problem for both of them. Not to mention she wasn't sure she was ready for Penelope to suffer her many idiosyncrasies, up close in all their lack of glory: the near constant talking to herself, but especially, the very messy bathroom.

*   *   *

Donnie remembered the trips with his mom and Petey to her cleaning job. The seven or eight miles from their dirty city street to Little Pointe was a journey from one universe to another, and he had mistakenly believed that Little Pointe was the country. But here, where you could drive without seeing a house for minutes at a time, he was growing uneasy. He was used to the man-made cover of alleyways, streets with broken streetlights, and the convincing invisibility of hiding behind big delivery trucks. He felt completely exposed out here.

They drove through this odd version of a town called Tottingham, past a tiny Post Office and one room schoolhouse, and then in a blink they were through it, and it was gone. No grocery, no gas station, or restaurant, hardware store, no nothing. Forget about a strip club or decent bar. What if the folks in Tottingham wanted a fried egg sandwich, ran out of gas or had a flat tire, or needed a wrench? It was creepy.

The Honda was still between him and the pickup. He had fallen back even more on the straight-aways, the binoculars on the passenger seat within reach. A few miles out of Tottingham, as he came to the rise of a little hill, he saw the mini-van slow and turn right, then the pickup. But the Honda sped forward on the Tottingham Road. So much for the convoy.

They were about two blocks ahead of him now as the road started to make its way up a pretty good-sized hill, and he was thinking he was glad it wasn't wintertime with ice and snow. Hoping, as he lost sight of them around the first curve, that if they were going to be turning into a driveway, they'd at least have to slow down or use their turn signals.

FIFTY-ONE

José wasn't due in at work until noon and that morning, as they drove to Lakeview Drive, he told Frank everything that had happened at the airport the day Penelope drove up.

"You might have saved her life, José. We don't know how, but probably because she listened to you, she somehow made it safely all the way to Massachusetts where she met my sister."

Then Juan told Frank of the many weeks he spent looking for work in Little Pointe, walking from one large home to another. He had always had a strong gift: he could grow anything and everything. His hands understood the earth, and he could coax and encourage the most reluctant of plants to reach upwards and higher toward the sun.

He had learned a crucial lesson at the first house, when they called the police on him, and he had to run. If you made it onto the property, you had to head to the rear of the house where there was a servants' entrance and hopefully a housekeeper or caretaker to speak to. The first week he had been told there was absolutely no work in twenty-five homes on both sides of Lakeview Road. The second week, twenty-three. Some of those who were lucky enough to be working in these houses would tell him that there were sometimes jobs washing dishes in the Little Pointe restaurants, or more likely cooking in the Mexican restaurants of Detroit. And he was slowly getting used to the idea of abandoning the earth for enchiladas.

Until he met the kind woman of 101. He had stopped, slightly stunned, looking in through the iron bars of the antique gate at the extraordinary array of colors. He hadn't seen her at first, in jeans on her knees, hands stained dark from working, the small droplets of sweat on her forehead, completely focused on weeding.

He moved along the fence staring at her gardens. There were many surprises. These were brave gardens he thought, not the extra careful, very predictable gardens he had seen so often in Little Pointe. As if there was one blueprint.

He wasn't aware that as he walked and stopped to stare that she had looked up to see him, smiling at his intensity. As he made his way back to where she was working, she got up and came to meet him. She looked at him closely, then pointed to a purplish pink flower. "Do you know about this flower?"

"My English is not so good but do you say 'cone, purple flower – Echinacea purpurea?'"

"Purple cone flower. Yes, you are absolutely right. I need help with my gardens. My name is Penny Davis. Would you like a job helping me with my plants and flowers and trees?"

"Yes, very much I need a job and I love your gardens ... My name is Juan Castillo. Yes, please ..."

Penny smiled, and slipped her hand through the gate. "My hand is very dirty ..."

Juan laughed as he met her hand with his and shook. "Estoy," catching himself, "I am ... very grateful."

They arrived at the front gate just as Juan was explaining how much he loved his job, loved those gardens, and that as much as Señora Penny disliked the house, she loved her flowers. And the other house by the lake.

They had all pretty much agreed that Penny was in enough trouble to justify checking the house. And because Juan had several times been assigned to bring in the mail when they were vacationing, he knew the alarm codes.

They rang the doorbell by the front gate several times but no one answered. Frank, ever vigilant, couldn't help but watch and laugh as Juan punched s-a-r-a-h into the keypad. "Do you know that all this time she's been away, Penelope couldn't remember her real name. She called herself 'Sarah.' Even now it is hard for my sister not to call her 'Sarah.'"

They drove up the stone driveway and parked in front.

It wasn't hard to see how accurately she had captured the emotional feel of the place. With its large heavy wooden door, he could see why going in and out had made such a big impression. How you could easily imagine that the door kept you in.

Juan punched in p-e-n-n-y and opened the front door. The entry way led to an elaborate and ornate, well, Frank was tempted to call it a living room, but he couldn't imagine being comfortable enough to actually live in it. There was space enough for a small circus. And he was having a hard time picturing the woman he had just met fitting in here.

Thirty feet in, you could see the winding marble stairs to the second floor. Where Penny was probably assaulted. For now, he wanted to see as much as he could, as quickly as he could. "I'm going to look upstairs. Be back in a couple of minutes." He took the stairs two at a time.

The master bedroom was enormous. He opened the his and her closets, both filled to the brim with clothes he couldn't in his wildest dreams afford. He laughed again, imagining how much he'd enjoy seeing the former and present Penny sitting at the same table for dinner. He quickly studied the photo of Penny and her husband, gorgeously gowned and handsomely tuxedoed, arms around each other's waist, a practiced smile for the camera.

If there was anything in this room that revealed anything important, besides the fact that her clothes were still here and she had obviously left in a hurry, he couldn't see it right now. The same with the bathroom, pausing for a moment to envy the Jacuzzi.

But the guest room was a mess: massive bed unmade, empty beer bottles, a full ashtray, an antique lacquered tray someone had used for coke, with a two inch stub of a drinking straw still sitting there beside the remains of a couple of lines. And there by the phone, a pad with a pen and pencil, the indentations clear. He took the pencil, rubbing it across the pad, and watched as Deb Spencer, Dom's phone number, Penny and Brett came to life once more. He tore the top sheet off and stuffed it in his back pocket.

This Donnie or whoever had been here had left in a big hurry and the empty beer bottles and coke only made it worse for Frank. The goddamn *I Ching* obviously knew trouble when it saw it, if you could call what this *I Ching* did "seeing." It was time to get his ass back to Katie.

FIFTY-TWO

It wasn't easy tailing them on these narrow country roads but Donnie was pretty sure he hadn't been spotted. Then he almost killed this fancy-ass bike rider, wearing ridiculous skin-tight bright blue shorts, a little white cap perched atop his head, weaving this way then that way, steering with one hand while swigging water with the other. Donnie had to swerve into the other lane to pass, just missing an old lady in an ancient Impala, then swerve back.

Seeing the bike rider in his rearview mirror give him the finger, it took every ounce of control not to slam on the brakes, get out, and royally kick his ass. But, as he reminded himself several times, he was keeping his focus on the job. Wishing that Petey, who still hadn't called him back, could see for himself the really good job he was doing.

He headed down the big hill, a decent distance from them, driving past a lake and small beach on the left. He watched as they slowed and braked for the stop sign up ahead. Then a left and a thousand yards later a quick right turn. Realizing he had no idea how many more roads he'd be driving.

When less than a minute later, they made a right onto Long Pine Road, a narrow dirt road with large overhanging trees on both sides. One big windstorm or blizzard and whoever lived here was in deep shit. He could see them up ahead, brake lights lit. He slowed and moved to the side of the road, waiting as they turned left into a driveway. He took a deep breath, then drove by, glancing only briefly at the mailbox, 146, then continuing on past the house.

*   *   *

Rabbit was waiting at the front door as Jack and Deb and Penelope drove in, followed by Ralph. Katie was busy in the kitchen with some last second tidying, putting on the kettle, starting the coffee maker.

Rabbit headed toward the vehicles. Penelope seemed more relaxed than the men, who both reeked of tension. Rabbit moved close to Jack, leaning into his upper thigh, prompting Jack to pause a moment and rub his head.

Katie was out the door and moving toward them. Ralph was looking at her, glad now that she had asked him for help, when he heard a car drive by, and turned back at the last moment to see the rear end of a new Chevy moving on past.

* * *

Frank dropped Juan off in the city then José came with him to the airport. "Thank you for helping Señora Davis, Frank. Now it's my turn. I think I can help you get home maybe sooner," José said, then headed to the ticket counter, moving from one station to another till he saw his friend, Louise. José moved to the right, waiting until she handed the boarding pass to her customer, then leaned in to whisper to her. He handed her Frank's return ticket and driver's license. She took a look down at his picture and started to check the computer. There was an open flight in forty minutes and Seat 4B was empty. Louise smiled as she offered Frank an upgrade.

Frank found himself blushing as he remembered his *I Ching* reading, and the circle of friends he might meet as he wandered. Then José went to check in for work.

Frank knew he had to speak to Katie and Katie's friend, Ralph.

* * *

Arthur wasn't surprised to hear from his California friends. He hadn't actually thought Petey would pull it off, but at least he could tell Little Francis that he tried.

Dealing with people you knew, his father had told him, was the most difficult part of the business. His father had feelings, and his father knew Arthur had feelings. So he tried to make it simple for his son: "Fuck feelings. Especially fuck family. And fuck-ups. A stupid cousin, a deadbeat friend will only drag you down."

He had already ignored his father's advice with the bar and Dominic, his waste-of-time brother-in-law. Which made it all the more important to honor his father's other hard and fast rule: "A debt is a debt is a debt. Meaning, Arthur, it must be paid; no gifts, no second-chances. There is nothing to be forgiven. A man gambles because he wants to win. There isn't a gambler anywhere on the earth who won't take your money with a smile when he wins. You ever hear of a gambler telling his bookie: 'Hey Sammy, we're friends. How about you keep the fifty grand I just won from you on the Lions' game!'"

This was more than your usual debt. This was half a million bucks. According to Jerry the Jew in California, there was still no way in hell Petey could guarantee the deal would go through. Even so, they were now willing to compromise: down from 95% to 90% of the eventual take. Which given the circumstances, Jerry thought was pretty damn fair. Considering all the work it would take to produce the body, or otherwise provide a lookalike substitute, bribe some cops, find a greedy medical examiner, and some DNA.

But Petey turned them down again, convincing Jerry that there was something else at work here beside making the deal and making good on his debt. Something deeper and more personal going on for Petey, and, because of that, there was no way they could trust him. "If you ask me, Arthur, and you should, this isn't about dough. The guy is completely unreliable. Get as much out of him as you can, and get rid of him! He's on the overnight flight from L.A. coming back to you."

Which is why Little Francis had driven to Little Pointe. And was waiting for Petey. The way Arthur figured it, considering how much Petey had won over the years, there was a very good chance he had stashed some serious cash. It was time to grab him and get that dough. Every little bit of it. And so Little Francis sat in his car and waited, and tried to forget that he knew Petey from the time they were five.

*   *   *

Having driven past the driveway, Donnie drove more slowly now, looking carefully on both sides of the road for a place to hide the car. There was a dirt driveway on the right, the grass overgrown. He decided to try it. It looked as if nobody had been down there in a while, weeds coming up in the center, ruts on both sides. Leading to a clearing and a half-burnt barn. He'd have to take his chances and hope no one cared about the place, at least not today or tonight.

He took a moment to toot some coke, finish a coffee, devour a donut, and take a piss. He took his gun, but left the phone in the glove compartment. After that spooky dream on the marble staircase, he definitely didn't want it distracting him at the wrong time.

Donnie wasn't great with trees and bushes or directions, and didn't have a clue about north or south or east and west. But remembering that Penny and the lady had turned into a driveway on the other side of the road, he headed back in the direction he had come from. And rather than walk where he could be seen, he crossed the road and headed into the woods.

First thing he noticed was the new smells: the dirt even was alive, the trees, and the flowers. A lot different than the dead and dying smells of the city: the dust, the stink of oil and gas, the everywhere exhaust, and the rotting garbage he was so used to. Soon there were the tiny black flies, quiet compared to the annoying high-pitched whine of the mosquitoes which came next, like hard to see miniature aircraft looking for some skin to land on.

It wasn't easy working his way to the house. The coke magnifying every difficulty. Feet, arms tangled by vines, baby trees trying to trip him. Beginning to take it personally, to sweat, the bugs in his eyes. Figuring out that the easiest way to kill the mosquitoes was to give them time to settle. Then, when they got comfortable, over-confident, ready to feed, lowering the needle, bam, you could smash them.

He came through the forest into a tidy backyard. There was a net set up in the middle of a big patch of lawn, and a bunch of small, oval-shaped rackets sitting on top of a large picnic table, with a couple of those little feather things. He had seen them play on TV. They called it "bad mitten" which didn't make much sense. But it was crazy how those Koreans or whatever they were could zip these little suckers at amazing speeds across the net, sending them high up in the air, kicking ass. The Olympics maybe.

There didn't seem to be anyone home. He thought about trying it but that was just the kind of thing to get Petey completely pissed off. Just his luck to end up in the slammer for losing someone's thingy.

Then through more trees, more brush, cursing as he swatted away a million more bugs. He was still pretty much hidden at the edge of the woods, but had a good view of what he was pretty sure was the clearing for the right house. And it wasn't long before he saw the Deb lady and her husband shut the front door, get back into their mini-van and head off. Which meant Penny was still there, and there was one less guy to worry about.

FIFTY-THREE

Katie handed the phone to Ralph. Frank spoke quickly without giving Ralph the chance for chitchat: "Listen Ralph, we don't know each other and there are probably better ways to do this, but I don't have a lot of time. I love Katie. She's in trouble. A helluva lot more trouble than she might appreciate. And what complicates this is the fact that Katie likes, needs to take care of herself. She's got this thing about asking anybody for help. Especially from guys. Especially from me. Especially if she thinks you are trying to rescue her. So do me a favor and try to be really cool about all this and keep it between us. By the way, I stink at keeping things from her, so I know it's not easy ...

"Katie's obviously reached out to you and I assume you really care about her if you're there. I don't know what she's told you but I just left Penelope's house in Michigan and someone there knows about Deb, about Dom's in Brett, and knows Penelope's alive and living somewhere nearby you guys. Thanks to Katie, her memory's coming back. And now her husband, his brother, or whoever these guys are also know that. From what I've learned here, I think they tried to hurt her real bad, maybe kill her.

"Looks like someone here left in a hurry. So I'm thinking one or more of them are headed your way. They might want to finish what they started, which means Deb and Katie and you are all going to be in their way.

"I need you to be thinking about worst-case scenarios here. Try the local cops if you think they'll help. I kind of doubt there's enough evidence for them to take this threat seriously enough right now to provide some manpower. But you know them better than I so if something suspicious happens, anything, please call them as quickly as you can.

"I have a pretty good idea Katie has let you know how strongly she feels about guns and violence, and I wish there was some way to respect that. Now I don't want to completely screw your relationship up, but this is probably not the time for the kind of creative non-violence my folks believed in.

"Katie tells me you're a farmer so I'm hoping maybe you've got a rifle or shotgun in your pickup or can easily get ahold of one. And I'm assuming you've bagged a deer or two along the way, or had to take care of some coyotes or wolves or whatever you have out there.

"I know it's a hell of a lot different seeing a person at the end of the barrel instead of Bambi, but if I'm right and this guy is intent on taking Penny out you may not have much of a choice. I could be totally off here, but I don't think I am … I'm about to board a plane right now, Ralph, and I just need you to keep everyone safe till I get back there … Do what you need to do and I'll take the heat and deal with Katie later."

"Uh, I'll do my best, Frank …"

"Thanks, Ralph … I'll see you soon."

Before Ralph had a chance to say goodbye, Frank was gone. It was time to get that shotgun.

*   *   *

As much as Frank was just plain weird, talking way too much, with all those Frank pauses, expecting to hear back some bird wisdom, Danger definitely missed him. He could tell something was off. The people seemed more nervous than usual, and the dog was moving restlessly from room to room.

Penelope was sitting at the kitchen table across from Katie, sharing some homemade bread and butter, trying hard to think of this room, this house as a safe haven.

Sometimes she'd see little moments flash before her eyes, like some wacky, out-of-order slide show: the hundred dollar bills on the bed; Bea's meatloaf with ketchup; sitting beside the Tiffany lamp; the boat moving across the horizon; and the oxygen tank.

She sipped Katie's relaxation tea but the guilt was growing: they were here, all of them vulnerable, Frank traipsing around the country, people she probably hadn't even known before. And still some of the most important pieces of the puzzle eluded her. Why? What had she done? Was there something she could have done differently?

*   *   *

Donnie was watching as the farm guy headed back to his pickup, thinking how great it would be if he left too, leaving just

Penny and the red-haired lady. But rather than just starting the sucker, the guy seemed to be digging around for something. A minute later, he was standing there with a shotgun, looking nervously back at the house.

Donnie knew double or triple aught buckshot was a drag. One shell could have like six or eight large pellets, each of which could take a big chunk out of you. So Donnie thought about taking him out right then and there but just wasn't sure he could get close enough, soon enough, to get off an effective shot. In the meantime, he'd be out in the open and sure to be spotted. Plus, the noise would let everyone know he was there. But now, at least, he knew that he was definitely going to have to take out this support your local farmer guy before getting to Penny.

The farmer walked quickly from his truck around the side of the house to the back door.

Donnie heard the door open and close, then headed over to get a better view.

*   *   *

He tried Donnie's phone one more time. Straight to voicemail. Calling for the fifth time as he drove home from the airport to tell Donnie to stay put until he got there. Cursing his brother, cursing his lousy luck, cursing his dead father-in-law, cursing Penny who just once could have said no to her asshole father. Smart beautiful Penny who, if she had just been someone else's daughter, he could have loved. Could have shared a life with, really shared, not just the exhausting act he had performed so well.

Cursing the assholes in L.A. who had wasted his precious time. Cursing the cards, and his fucking father who had died with such absolute stupidity, whose death had sent him and his mother and Donnie into this spiral of misery.

He guessed he still had somewhere between seventy-five and eighty-five grand in his hidden safe in the garage. From those nights when he had played to perfection, calculating and exploiting the smallest of advantages, while suppressing the impulse to guess. The nights he walked out of Arthur's on top. Plus, her jewelry, the diamond ring he could probably unload for half of what he paid, a quick twenty grand.

With everything unraveling, it was time for contingencies. Thinking he'd stash the cash at the airport, then give twenty-five thou to Donnie when they got back. Use some to get himself to India or Thailand, maybe Bali, the casinos in Macao. Then have Donnie bring Arthur the remaining cash. A goodwill gesture. Making clear he intended to take care of his debt as soon as he could. Hoping it might buy him some more time. At least keep Arthur from sending Little Francis out after him right away.

He was worried, though, that Donnie might do something stupid before he got there. Like buy some coke off a stranger, a narc. With the way things were going, nothing would surprise him.

As he pulled up to the gate he couldn't help but think about the alarm codes. He had asked her a dozen times to come up with something less obvious, but she kept insisting the last thing she wanted was to have to remember something complicated just to get into her own house. It was always a mistake to start down that road with her because she'd ever so quickly remind him that not only did she hate passwords, but she hated the gate and she hated the house.

Little Francis waited until Petey parked the car and went into the house, then made a U-turn and positioned himself a car length from the gate. He called Arthur to report in and settled in to wait.

Petey was out of the house twenty minutes later, moving quickly, carrying an overnight bag and an attaché case.

Little Francis watched through the fence as he got into his car and headed back down the driveway to the gate. He reached out the driver's side window to punch in the code. The gate slowly swung open and he eased out onto the street. Until Little Francis gunned his engine and swerved to block his car. He was surprisingly fast for such a big man, out of his car and to Petey's in seconds.

Petey watched almost in slow motion as Little Francis reached in through the open window, found the door latch, and yanked open his door. Still stunned, Petey saw Little Francis snatch the case with one hand and grab his throat with the other. Petey somehow managed to raise his hands in surrender. Little Francis slowly released his grip and said quietly: "Arthur wants to see you. I promised him you'd come alive not dead. For old times. That sound fair to you, Petey?" releasing his grip so Petey could answer.

Gagging, then able to manage: "Yeah, that's fair, Francis. And I'm sure he's going to want the case."

"Good idea. So I'm going to need you to park the car and come with me."

FIFTY-FOUR

Donnie was going to lose his mind if he had to stay out here much longer. Waiting in the bushes, he had probably gotten a hundred mosquito bites.

Now with every step Donnie took toward the back door, he heard another crack. How come these fucking little twigs made so much noise? You couldn't sneak up on anyone in the country. He wanted so much to get back to sidewalks, streets, Big Pink, anything besides these creepy bugs.

And what was Penny doing here in the sticks, when she could have gone anywhere in the world? All those fancy-ass dinners she would go to. With the snazzy dresses and high-heel shoes. None of this made any sense to him, reminding him again that like Petey was always saying, he just didn't get it, just didn't see the big picture.

The truth was, from where he always seemed to be standing, there wasn't any big picture to be seen. That's why he liked coke so much. It made the little things he did see seem so much more exciting. With coke, he could get completely involved in anything, almost every little thing he was doing. Working out with weights, a night with Betsy, watching Arthur's back. He knew the coke made him concentrate better. But, of course, Petey would put him down. Saying the coke made him jumpy. Made him act without thinking. Adding something snotty like "even more than usual."

Fuck it. He reached into his side pocket, unscrewed the cap of the little vial and dumped a bunch of white powder onto the fleshy space between his first knuckle and thumb of his left hand. Snorting into one nostril then the other, feeling the coke make its way into his system. Thinking any minute now ...

*   *   *

Ralph went into the kitchen to tell Katie about the shotgun. Figuring he'd deal with her anger now rather than add deception to the deal. So he told them briefly what Frank had said. And waited. While Katie recalled that very first reading with Sarah, remembering: "anxious hesitation is a mistake that is bound to

249

bring disaster ..."

Katie nodded, "OK, Ralph, this might shock Frank but I trust him ... and if he's right, we may not have a lot of time. Let me move to the other side of the table and, just in case, why don't you show us how your shotgun works."

Ralph, surprised by how quickly she agreed, hesitated just a moment, then explained as he went to fetch the gun from the hallway by the back door: "Well, it would be best if we were outside with a target, but from what your brother was saying that's probably not the safest thing to do right now."

Returning, Ralph moved his chair to sit between them. And began by stressing that the safest way to handle a shotgun was to be sure the barrel was pointing down, and to never point it at a person. Then he showed them how to sight down the barrel, and explained about the kickback. Only then did he teach them how to load. And pull the trigger.

Ralph slowly slid the gun and two shells to his right, to Katie, when Danger started to squawk: a loud "Arrrr ... arrrr ... arrr!"

Rabbit heard the back door open and close above the racket. And he forcefully moved his snout several times against Katie's thigh. When that didn't work, Rabbit began his husky howl. But Katie, not wanting to be distracted while she so very carefully handled the shotgun, quickly shushed him. All her attention funneled downward, to safely load that first shell. And when Rabbit realized she just wasn't listening, he moved quietly toward the doorway.

Donnie was glad to be inside again. Still scratching his most recent bites, he fought the urge to swat what were now probably just imaginary coke-induced mosquitoes. It didn't take long for the noise to get to him, all the squawking and howling coming from the other room. But more than anything, he tried to imagine the plane ride home. Thinking of Betsy and Big Pink, and a quarter ounce, and just in case Betsy was busy, a few cold ones watching that hot new dancer, Sapphire.

Moving toward the kitchen, he saw the lady with the wild red hair load the shotgun. No sooner did his brain register what was happening than his "fuck!" slipped out, way too loud. The three of them looked up, and Katie without thinking, began to slide the gun to her left over to Ralph. Almost immediately, there was what seemed to them a small explosion coming from Donnie's gun. Ralph's chest recoiled, and he was propelled backwards against the high-backed chair, then slumped forward smashing into the table. Blood spurted everywhere.

For Katie, time and space shattered.

Only later, when Katie and Penelope were questioned by Chief Paul and the State Police, were they able to recall exactly what had happened next. Rabbit was in the air almost immediately as Donnie fired. His teeth clamped down on Donnie's right wrist, and the impact not only loosened Donnie's grip on his gun, but propelled his arm away from Katie and Penelope. Penelope had instinctively reached out to her right to gather and sight the shotgun, and fire. Donnie never got off a second shot. Her shot was low enough to miss Rabbit head-on, but got Donnie in the gut. Donnie fell first; Rabbit, finally releasing Donnie's arm, tumbled on top of him.

While Penelope was trembling, Katie called 911. Then returned to hold Ralph's body. She began to sob as she felt the life slipping from him. Hands still shaking, Penelope put the shotgun down, and moved to check on Donnie. His midsection was punctured multiple times; and he was bleeding profusely. And silent. She kicked away his gun then moved to gently stroke Rabbit; but he too said nothing.

FIFTY-FIVE

The troopers were gone but Chief Paul was still at the house when Frank arrived. Frank had spoken to Katie as soon as he had gotten off the plane, then drove too quickly from Kennedy Airport to the Berkshires, to Ripton, lucky not to be pulled over.

Penelope had been given a sedative by Dr. Amory, who had been called by the ambulance squad. The Medical Examiner had come and gone; and Katie, refusing medical treatment, had rushed to the vet with Rabbit. There was still blood on the table and on the floor beneath where Ralph had been sitting. And even more spatter moving out from where Donnie had been standing, and where he and Rabbit had fallen.

Someone had covered Danger's cage but Frank could hear him moving restlessly back and forth on his perch. Frank took the towel from the cage. Danger looked up and into Frank's eyes: "Sorry, sorry. Boom, boom … Do you want a cracker? Sorry …"

Frank managed to smile through his exhaustion: "No thank you, Danger, but let me get you a cracker. I'm sorry, too, about the boom." He found a couple of treats and slipped them through the bars to the food tray.

Chief Paul came up to him with an extended hand. "Listen, Detective, your sister's fine. She's in a bit of shock but insisted on going with her dog …"

"Chief, thanks, but you should know I'm on medical leave so at the moment I'm not technically a Detective …"

"Believe me, the minute I heard you were in my town I checked up on you. Your captain assured me you're a fine detective. That's good enough for me. I'm just sad this is the way we're meeting, and so very sorry about RP. I've known the Parkers my entire life. So why don't you and me have a little walk and talk and compare notes."

Outside, telling the Chief what he knew, Frank realized he still knew only a fraction of the story. He went over his trip to Michigan, meeting Juan and José, the sense he got from Juan about Penny's kindness, her husband Peter's coldness, and the odd brother Juan had seen a couple of times recently. The guy he assumed caused all this and who was now in the hospital.

He told the Chief about José's quick thinking at the airport. By getting rid of Penny's credit cards, her cell phone, and convincing her to take the bus, to avoid the hospitals, José had gotten her off the grid, bought her time, and probably saved her life.

He told Chief Paul the little he knew about Penny's amnesia and life as Sarah, and Katie's attempts to help her. He recounted the conversation he had with Katie about Deb's phone call to Little Pointe, and how Deb had inadvertently alerted Donnie and Peter.

"Listen, Chief, I had a really bad feeling about this whole thing when I was in Michigan, and I want to be completely straight with you. I put some serious pressure on my sister to get Ralph here to help, and then when I spoke to him I urged him to protect them. He did what I asked and he died and that's on me."

"This is a very small town. I watched Ralph grow up, Detective. Between you and me, he was a complete asshole when it came to women. Almost broke Sophie's heart, my brother's daughter. Somehow your sister turned him inside out and taught him to love. You and I both know this entire thing makes no sense. I served in Vietnam. I know about guns, and I know too much about death. This is all on the guy who shot him. Turns out Ralph saved two lives. So, as terrible as it sounds, and I'll never say this to anyone who hasn't been on the front lines, and I'll deny it if it gets out, but I have to think we're up one life here.

"You should know it's touch and go with this Donnie fella and the doctor thinks he's got at best a twenty percent chance of coming out of this. That shotgun did serious damage to his guts. I had a chance to talk to him for a second at the hospital in Great Barrington. Mumbling something like: 'Tell Petey I'm sorry. Second time I messed up. She's hard to kill.' Then he lost consciousness.

"According to his Michigan driver's license, he was born Donald Kean. A particularly chatty sergeant in Detroit told me his dad, John James Kean, was a petty thief and gambler who they think was killed by the Castronovas, a Detroit family that ran poker and prostitution and drugs. The mother, Irene Kean, was left broke with two kids. She, too, had a record, having been picked up a few times when she first started to turn tricks. Seems she found some wealthy sugar daddy in a nearby town, and because of his serious pull, someone decided to let her be. She died of cancer before she was fifty.

"Our Donnie has a pretty impressive sheet: juvie and adult, with multiple assaults. He's muscle for Arthur Flynn, a bookie and drug dealer whose family took over once they retired the Castronovas. Detroit PD's especially concerned because the last few years Flynn's been expanding his operations.

"Based on my short conversation with Donnie, there's now an APB out for his brother, Peter 'Petey' Kean. Detroit said that they have a Confidential Informant who has played poker with him at several of Flynn's on-going card games. It seems Petey Kean's been living in Little Pointe, Michigan under an assumed name, Peter Bishop, Penelope Davis' husband. Turns out the brothers grew up with Flynn.

"Detroit tells me Peter Bishop has no record. For now, at least. And that's about it, so far."

"Great job, Chief, and thanks … I'd like to go and see my sister if that's OK? Is it possible for you to keep me in the loop on this one?"

"No problem, Detective, and know that this is a very big deal for us here and either I or the staties will be keeping an eye on Penelope Davis until we sort all this out and know she's safe."

"Since you checked up on me, Chief, you know my story. From what Katie told me on the phone, even though Penny fired in self-defense, she's going to need someone to talk to. I know somebody in the city once she's up for it, and considering what I've been through, I have a feeling I can help. I'm guessing it really hasn't hit her yet that the guy she shot is her husband's brother. Then the last thing on my wish list is at some point, I'd like to get a chance to interrogate the son-of-a-bitch husband."

"Well, I'm sure the Michigan folks are on it. I'll call you when and if we learn anything more. And when and if they find the husband. I really hope your sister's dog is OK. From what they told me he's a real hero going after this Donnie guy. Many a time I thought about bringing him in for trespassing, but then he'd walk right up to me, look me dead in the eyes, and smile. Then he'd just trot off. And I'd stand there shaking my head."

FIFTY-SIX

"You and I both know, Petey, or should I say Peter, that you're probably the smartest guy to ever come out of the neighborhood. I wish I had half your smarts. I wish Little Francis had a tenth of your smarts. But that's not the way it works."

If Little Francis cared about Arthur's slight, he didn't show it. Gloves on so he wouldn't leave prints, he was much too busy tightening the straps that held Petey in the chair.

"Sometimes having smarts is a curse. As you know, Petey, I'm not that smart a man, but after several years in this business, that's my considered opinion. Stupid people lose at cards, or at the ponies, or get fucked by a field goal attempt that hits the goalpost, and then piss and moan and curse their fate, but they come back the next day and try again. It's the smart people you have to worry about. They're always trying to even the odds or worse yet, beat them. Causing trouble. They're the smart-ass brokers and bankers who shafted everyone with their crappy mortgages. And their smart-ass kids who've figured out how to steal stuff from the internet.

"I don't give a shit about mortgages or music. But when it comes to my business, I care. I hate the card counters and the guys like you who figure out ways to win. And the guys who work for me but behind my back step on my coke to skim something extra for themselves. I put up with you for years because of the neighborhood, Petey, even though you thought you were better than us, with your hidden away high-class wife, but it was really because you and I had a common interest. We both know there are suckers everywhere hoping to win and likely to lose. I liked what I took from your winnings, and you made a good living at my tables. You know it. And I know it.

"After all the winning you did, I still don't know why you went in with half a mil of my money? What was it: greed, stupidity, or that Greek word Sister Margaret always used just before she smacked us with the ruler, you remember, saying we were acting better than we were? You're the college guy ..."

"Hubris," Petey offered.

"Yeah, hubris. Beats me why you took that chance. You

know, all I ever asked from you, Petey, is that when you won, you did it graciously. I know some big words, Petey. I know from graciousness. And you were pretty good about that. But the other part, the really, really important part, is that when you lose, you pay. That's something I care deeply about. And for a lot of reasons, because your dumb-ass brother has done good for me, and because of Little Francis here, I gave you time, and then more time to make everything good between us."

Arthur then pointed to the attaché case: "I figured you were holding out on me, because gamblers always hold out. Serious gamblers always have hidden dough, just like serious drinkers have some bottles stashed.

"You should have brought me this case on day one, Petey. I would have respected that. I would have appreciated your sacrificing your stash. But you didn't, did you Petey?

"I helped to set up your L.A. meet even though I knew the chances were piss-poor you would pull the deal off. I did that for you, Petey." Arthur paused a moment to take a swig of his coffee, then continued on.

"My L.A. friends say they would have helped, but you wouldn't compromise. I would have gotten back my dough. So it turns out you screwed me big time. First, there's the considerable amount of money I'm not going to get. Then, there's my employee, my muscle, my dealer, your stupid brother who always worked hard for me. You got him shot and he's facing serious jail time."

Petey's head jerked up, and for the first time, it seemed like he was paying attention: "What are you talking about? What about Donnie?"

"Donnie is screwed, just like you, Petey. I happen to have a friend whose retirement fund I contribute to. He works out of Headquarters. Detroit PD got a call from some country bumpkin Police Chief in a town called Ripton, Mass. Any reason Donnie would be in Dipshit, Massachusetts, Petey, except because you sent him? Like you sent him to Cleveland.

"Seems he tried to kill a lady named Penelope Davis. Ring a bell, Petey? Instead he killed some local guy, maybe her new boyfriend. Anyway, your brother took a shotgun blast in the gut. And the state and local cops there are asking all kinds of questions about your brother, which, after their first call to

Detroit, got them asking about me, and what Donnie does for me.

"Wondering what reason I would have to send one of my men seven hundred miles to Massachusetts to off some local farmer? So my lawyer said they'll be knocking on my door pretty soon and I should expect some extended time downtown in a small room trying to explain all this. You know how much I'm going to love that, don't you, Petey? And soon, very soon, they'll be asking about you. So you see what I mean about smart guys?"

Petey's head and shoulders slumped. He closed his eyes.

"But I'm going to move things along. And make a little deal with you. The sooner they have you, and you tell them that whatever went down had absolutely zip to do with me, the sooner they'll leave me alone. So I'm going to have Little Francis deliver you to the cop shop in Little Pointe. It's a lot safer for Little Francis than taking you down to Central. A present waiting outside their door, with this note informing them that you're, what do they call it, 'a person of interest' and Donnie Kean's long lost brother, wanted in connection with a murder in Massachusetts. Arthur leaned over to tape the note to Petey's coat.

"And, as much as I'd like to beat out of you every stinking penny's worth of what you owe me, Petey, minus what's in this case and that ring Little Francis found in your pocket, I'm not going to do it. You keep me completely out of this, there's a good chance some of my friends, and the friends of my friends, soon to be your fellow roommates, can help you survive the slammer. And I'm going to put what you owe on account. Who knows, maybe you'll start earning big bucks inside. Otherwise, payable if and when you get out. Maybe I'll still be here, or maybe my kid will be. We'll leave that for another day … We're done!"

Arthur waved goodbye. Little Francis picked up the chair and carried Petey out to the alley, then up and into the back of the nondescript delivery van one of Arthur's guys had boosted just a couple of hours ago.

FIFTY-SEVEN

Somehow sitting there, worrying about Rabbit, had kept the overwhelming grief about Ralph at bay.

The surgery had taken a while. By some miracle the pellet he took in his left shoulder missed major blood vessels. Now they were just cleaning up and suturing.

By the time Frank got there, the big issue was whether or not Rabbit would, in time, be able to get around the way he used to.

Katie started to tell Frank all her Rabbit stories: from the day Rabbit picked her to the three months he dropped out of sight without warning to make a husky family of his own ten miles away in Mill River. There were the tales her friends had told her about Rabbit's calls of kindness, the visiting hours he had spent by their side, somehow picking up on their sadness, their need. And how quickly, once they were feeling better, Rabbit would head off without thanks or reward. How Rabbit had brought Ralph home to her.

She told him what happened in the kitchen: so thoroughly focused on learning how to use the shotgun, on learning how to load it, they missed the sound of the back door opening. So excruciatingly aware now that if she had paid more attention to Rabbit's warnings, or better understood Danger's several squawks of alarm, had seen what was really happening, Ralph might still be alive. Adding that if she hadn't asked him for help in the first place, he never would have died.

Frank knew better than anyone how inadequate words were at a time like this, but that didn't stop him. His desire to protect her, to help her, to somehow fix this unfixable thing took over. He told her there wasn't anything she could have done. Donnie was always going to take out the person he regarded as his strongest obstacle. If Ralph hadn't been there with his shotgun, she and Penny would both be dead. And really, if it was anybody's fault, it was his fault for pressuring her in the first place to ask Ralph for help, and then for pushing Ralph on the phone to protect her.

But Frank knew she couldn't hear him. Just as he couldn't hear Gloria, or hear her, those first weeks.

Then Katie began to talk about Ralph, about caring for him

but not loving him, well maybe loving him, but not in-love loving him, and about having been honest with him about all of it, but wondering was that really enough? Was any of that fair? And now, of course, none of it seemed fair at all.

Frank listened as she continued on, but couldn't help think again about what he had asked Ralph to do, knowing that to protect Katie and Penny, he would ask Ralph to do it all over again.

And, for the first time, Frank knew, truly knew in his bones, that he had had no real choice but to shoot that night in New York. That it had, in fact, been the two kids who had set everything in motion. That, as horrible as this year had been, it was the right thing that he had been out there on Broadway, the right thing that it was his gun against the kid's knife, the right thing that his instincts and training had taken over.

Because it so easily could have been innocent civilians on the other end of those knives, and it would have been, if he hadn't been on that street at that moment. That by firing that bullet, he had taken one life, but probably saved another life, or several lives. He might not be able to explain all that to Katie right now, might not be able to tell her that this was true for Ralph as well, but he would some day.

Then the vet came out to say that everything looked as good as it could and that he wanted to keep Rabbit for observation for another day or two.

*   *   *

Katie drove straight home while Frank stopped to buy enough Chinese food for several days, thinking the most anybody would be able to do for a while was to make coffee or tea. It wasn't easy but he convinced Katie to drink a bucketful of that Relaxing Tea she swore by, and then sent her to bed.

First, Frank tackled the table, the blood-stained coins and book, then on his hands and knees spraying Katie's self-proclaimed Earth-friendly cleaner everywhere he could, its lemon-grass odors slowly overtaking the rusty smell of the hours-old blood. Using all his anger to scrub death from her kitchen floor.

Frank had made it abundantly clear that he didn't need parrot help this time, so Danger, still a prisoner, turned his attention to the finely chopped lo mein noodles Frank had put in his food dish.

Taking a short break but still feeling guilty, Frank looked up: "I'm sorry, Danger. I'm very sorry you had to go through all this." Danger walked to the edge of his perch, looked down at him, offered an extended stare, but had nothing to add.

*   *   *

There were clouds everywhere in her dream. Knowing now she was Penelope, not Sarah. She could hardly see more than an inch or two ahead. And yet she ever so carefully walked on, trusting somehow that she wouldn't fall, her left hand trying to wave some of the whiteness away, as if the clouds were cobwebs.

Her left foot seemed to have reached the end of the landing. She could sense the stairs and her left hand moved to find the handrail.

Taking every step very slowly. And with each step, the clouds began to sweep past her. About two-thirds of the way down, she could see him. He had done a lousy job with his ski mask and it had clumped up on him, blocking his nostrils. He was moving it off his face as he came toward her. She wasn't sure but he looked so much like Peter's brother. She remembered that day Peter sat in the morning room reading the Detroit Free Press. He was completely engrossed in a story about two men arrested for allegedly beating up a man outside a strip club. She stood there for a minute or two, unnoticed, looking over his shoulder, silently staring at the photo. There was a close-up of one of them, Donnie Kean, who if you looked very carefully, seemed eerily like a younger, thicker version of Peter.

Peter almost jumped when she said: "You wouldn't know it at first but he looks amazingly like you, dear." He was about to turn the page, when something swept over him, looking up to her: "My brother ... the blackest of the black sheep. I haven't seen him in years, and won't see him ever again. That's why I told you I was alone in the world. Maybe someday I'll tell you more about him. But not now," getting up from the table, straightening his tie. "I'm already late for an important meeting." Kissing her as he moved toward the door.

As Donnie moved up another step, she remembered there had never been that someday. And that she had let Peter deflect the few attempts she made to talk about it, until she had given up. Her dream-mind trying to make sense of the masked brother-in-law she had never formally met.

It seemed as if the man on the stairs was talking more to himself than to her. Something about "sorry" like Frank's parrot. And Petey. The first time she had ever heard Peter called Petey. "Petey's idea … "

So shocked she couldn't remember screaming, didn't remember calling out.

And this time she could see him reach awkwardly with his gloved hand for the gun from behind his back. Could see him raise his right hand in an arc; could see his arm come crashing down against her forehead. Could feel herself crumpling to the stairs, the light turning dark. Barely making out his last words: "Wish I had gone out on the boat with you."

When she drifted back out of the blackness, she could feel waves of pain pounding inside her head. Warm, sticky blood leaking out of her. Feeling as if she had been nailed to the stairs.

And after a minute or two Penny the dreamer realizing Penny on the stairs was now able to move ever so slowly. And then, paradoxically remembering that moment when the not-remembering had begun to descend upon her, the not-knowing who she was.

When Penny the dreamer woke up in Katie's guest room, she knew more than she had known in a very long time. But then all too suddenly remembering not only the stairs and Donnie on the stairs, but Donnie in Katie's kitchen. And then she began to tremble and weep.

FIFTY-EIGHT

A good poker player tries to take maximum advantage of all the available information. Then, accessing past experience and anticipating future possibilities, act with appropriate intelligence. That he might find himself sitting duct-taped to a desk chair outside the Little Pointe Police Station was a possibility Petey had to admit he hadn't seen coming.

He knew, though, that no matter what happened next, no one could take from him how far he had traveled. Considering where he had started, and how hard he had worked to get to where he was, well, that seemed to provide him with more than enough pride to exempt him from any expected sense of humiliation. And so, as he sat there trussed up like a pork roast, he felt merely that he had bet and lost. And that regardless of what was waiting for him, he had accomplished a hell of a lot more than either his father or mother or the kids he grew up with.

FIFTY-NINE

Frank and Katie were having a quiet breakfast. Danger, still traumatized by the events of the last day and night, sat on Frank's shoulder, muttering to himself.

Katie spread some blueberry jam over her rye toast, and took another sip of tea, then began to speak softly: "I'm not going to go to the funeral. I know I'm supposed to. I know it's the proper thing to do. But I feel like the little ceremony we had for Carl and then that odd remembrance for Theresa with all those people sitting in circles, the stories they told, singing all those folk songs, that did it for me. I can't imagine talking about Ralph in the past tense right now. Or having to grieve in public. No more funerals for me.

"I'm also very sorry, Frank, for not driving down to the city, for not sitting-in like Carl and Theresa in front of your apartment till you opened up and talked to me about the shooting. I'm sorry."

Danger shifted on Frank's shoulder to look in Katie's direction, cocking his head to the right to get a better look at her. "Sorry," he said. "Sorry."

Frank laughed. "Thank you, Katie ... and thank you, Danger. But I really wouldn't have let you in."

Then Danger began to preen Frank's neck, and as Frank tried to yank his head away, Danger bit him.

"Shit," Frank yelled, restraining himself at the last moment from flailing his arms. While Danger, rebuffed but indignant nonetheless, offered a loud squawk as he quickly flew away from any possible retribution to the relative safety of the table.

"Cracker," he demanded, boldly convinced that the trauma of the last twenty-four hours had at least earned him extra treats. And despite the nip, still hoping to provoke Frank into providing something more exotic than the pathetic bread crumbs he had salvaged from Katie's plate.

Then the phone rang. Once, then twice.

"OK, Danger," Frank responded, "that's very impressive, but how about you cut it out. You made your point several times over. I'll get you a treat."

The phone rang again. Frank looked back to Danger: "You

263

don't do subtle, do you?"

Katie laughed. "That's the real phone, Frank," then answering it: "Oh, hi Chief Paul. Well, she's still upstairs sleeping … I'll tell her as soon as I see her … Yes, he's right here. Let me get the phone to him."

Frank picked up the phone: "Hi Chief … That's great news. I'll tell her. She might be up for traveling, for giving a statement in a day or two. Could you give me the number of the Chief in Little Pointe? I think I'll go out there with her, and I'd love the chance to talk to the husband … Hang on, let me get a pen …" reaching for the pen Katie was holding out to him. Then, writing the name and number on a paper napkin. "Thanks so much, Chief Paul, for everything you've done. I owe you big time … absolutely, as soon as I'm back in town," hanging up. Then to Katie: "Her husband's in custody."

Katie nodded as they heard Penny coming down the stairs.

Frank was up, pouring her a cup of coffee and putting two pieces of rye bread into the toaster. Everyone was silent as Penny took a seat at the table, quiet until Danger broke the spell. "Good morning," he offered, then looking back at Katie, with another "Good morning …"

She smiled: "Hello, Danger … Good morning, everyone."

Frank and Katie both smiled as Frank placed the coffee in front of Penny then headed back to monitor the toaster.

She took a long sip and sighed: "Well I wanted to tell you both that for the first time in my dreams I could see Donnie and the black ski mask he used to cover his face … I think he was sweating because he raised it to his forehead. I saw his face. It took me a moment or two, but I know now that I recognized him from the newspaper. And so when he raised the gun to smash me, I knew it was my brother-in-law, the brother-in-law I had never been introduced to, and in his guilt or stupidity, he told me it was Peter's idea to kill me. So I knew all that as he hit me with the gun. I could be wrong but I have a feeling he didn't really want to do it. I was helpless. He could easily have hit me several times more, shot me, killed me …" She faltered, paused to take another sip, then began again.

"I brought this all to Brett, to Bea Foster's and to Deb and to you, Katie … and Ralph." Katie got up without a word and slowly guided Penny out of the chair and into her arms.

SIXTY

Juan and José met them at the airport. Frank watched as Penny's face brightened and a smile spread from the lips and jaw that had been so tightly clamped their entire flight. Juan and José stood there, so very glad to see her, but bound by a certain formality. When Penny, without hesitation, moved to embrace Juan, then turned to José, smiling as she moved his outstretched hand aside to hug him.

Then stepping back, tears welling up: "It's slowly coming back to me. I remember, José, and I must have remembered you that day at the airport because somehow, without knowing why, I did exactly what you told me to do. No doctors," then with a smile to Frank, "no cops. I took the buses, I can't remember how many buses, and then just to be safe, took a couple more to a place I must have thought would keep me safe. And so I will never forget what you did for me." Turning back to Juan, "And I hope my flowers did better than me, Juan?" Then Penny began to laugh even as she cried.

Juan and José waited in the car while Penny and Frank went inside. Frank pushed open the heavy door, and as they moved across the marble floor, Penny reached for his arm to steady herself, gasping as she saw the stairs, flashing back to the moment she had come back to consciousness, her hand covered with the blood from her head wound. Remembering how she had somehow staggered to the downstairs bathroom, in a haze, yet showering, washing the blood from her body. She could remember standing there, using every ounce of strength she had, the towel pressed fiercely against her forehead, many, many minutes, almost fainting several times, two or three towels until the bleeding stopped. She could remember using more and more makeup to hide the bruises, amazed that in the midst of all that pain and confusion she somehow understood she needed to disappear as quickly and quietly as she could.

Still clutching Frank's arm, she moved them to the little study she used as the office for her charitable work. She moved to the built-in bookcase behind her desk. Then letting go of Frank's arm, she pulled the first five books from the second shelf, piling them on the desk. She removed several documents and several bundles of crisp hundreds. She pulled an envelope from the pile and handed it to Frank: "From my father." There was a large P on the front. "I hid it here with the money I had moved from the safety deposit box. Somehow I remembered to take the money. And began to run."

SIXTY-ONE

Chief Mackenzie of the Little Pointe Police Department had a lot to say. He, too, had checked with Captain Rasch in New York City. Frank smiled, imagining how much time his boss had wasted vouching for him.

The Chief wanted Frank to know that maybe by New York City standards they were a tiny operation, but they were still damn good cops.

He waited for Frank's "Yes, sir," then told Frank he had known Penelope's dad since he was fifteen. And while he had never done this for an outsider, given what Rasch said and considering that nobody else was having any luck with the suspect, who it turns out hadn't said a single word since they read him his rights, well he'd be willing to give Frank a shot. Just so long as everything was by the book and monitored by one of his detectives. And if Frank did anything, and he meant anything, that might jeopardize the case, he'd be out of there in a second.

After many nods, an "absolutely" and "positively" and a final "sure thing," they shook. Frank went to read what they had on Petey and the Chief took Penny into his office to take her statement.

Twenty minutes later, Frank went to the observation room to check on Petey. A documentary filmmaker had once told him that if you went out of your way to make people comfortable, sooner rather than later they would tell you and the camera things they never told anyone. The need to share their story so much stronger than caution. And Frank had learned with experience that most people during an interrogation, as much as they reminded themselves that they were being watched and recorded, couldn't help but lose track after a while. Perhaps it took too much energy and discipline for most people to maintain that split focus: to be there in the moment, yet constantly account for the observations of the observer, to tailor everything they did and said.

Petey sat there, folded in on himself, almost completely shut down. It was time to shake him up. Frank left the room and signaled to the officer in the corridor that he was about to begin the interview.

Frank knocked on the door, waited several seconds, and knocked again. Then walked in and took a seat.

Petey still hadn't looked up.

"My name is Frank. I think you and I have something in common. I was born Frank Greenberg. My dad was a political activist. He was hassled all the time. I got hassled. I also got really pissed at him along the way. I got tired of being Frank Greenberg. So I decided I'd be happier being Frank Falco, taking my mother's maiden name. It made sense at the time. Seeing you, thinking about you, well, it seems a bit sad. For both of us. You don't know me, so you probably don't know whether I'm doing better as Frank Falco or should've stuck with Greenberg.

"I know you shouldn't believe everything you read, but from what I've read from various police reports, your dad dealt from the bottom of the deck, and got killed because of it. My dad disappeared all the time to places he never told me he was going to: to help, it seemed to me at the time, just about everyone in the world except his own family. And well, I've always had the sense he, too, was killed because of what he did, but I was a kid then, not a cop, and certainly couldn't do squat about it. Don't get me wrong. I know that what my dad did was a lot more socially useful than what your dad did."

Frank saw a brief flash of contempt move across Petey's face. He continued on without acknowledging it.

"I've done this a few times and I'm pretty sure right about now you're thinking you don't give a shit about my story. Maybe later; maybe never. I'm telling you all this to demonstrate I'm interested in your story, and hopefully I'll pick up something useful along the way. The Chief tells me you've been read your Miranda rights and declined an attorney. I'm guessing there's a lot you haven't said yet.

"But the fact is I don't know you, and to be completely honest, don't know whether I'm sitting across the table from Petey Kean or Peter Bishop right now."

Frank waited but got no reaction.

"I've spent a little time with your wife ..." pausing, and he could see a slight twitch of the upper lip ... "not in that way. When I met her, she didn't remember you; she could hardly remember anything. So I'm relying on first impressions here. It seems to me that Peter Bishop's been fading a bit. I have a feeling I'm talking to Petey.

"I stopped to see Donnie in the hospital before I flew out here. Maybe if you ask me, I'll tell you about your brother. From what Penny recently told me, he's Petey's brother, not Peter's."

Petey looked up, his eyes flashing with anger. Then he looked down at the handcuffs and smiled. "How about we dispense with the bullshit bonding exercise and you tell me about Donnie, and I'll tell you my story. The only reason I'm talking to you now is because we both know I'm already done, thanks to a lousy kings boat and the impatience of my dear classmates, Arthur Flynn and Little Francis. So maybe the Chief and you should send Arthur a fruit basket and a thank you note. Oh yeah," and Petey paused for a moment to look up to where he imagined the video camera was "and this is for the official record: they had absolutely nothing to do with anything Donnie may have done in Massachusetts.

"And, by the way, my dearly-departed father-in-law and my wife have given a shitload of money to the local constabulary, and I've never seen you before."

"Detective Frank Falco on medical leave from the NYPD. I shot a fifteen-year-old kid so they've asked me to take some time off. I'm not sure but they might be worried. Wondering whether I'm psychologically prepared to take out the next killer I encounter ... But, really, the main reason I'm here is that in his attempt to kill your wife, your brother also tried to kill my sister."

"He never returned my calls ... Knowing my brother, I'm sure it wasn't personal or well-thought out. I'm guessing from your accent, Detective, and the way you dress, maybe you know a bit about not being rich. We were always broke. Even on his best days, my dad, when he wasn't dealing from the bottom, was a pretty lousy card player. I heard from someone that before they killed him, they broke his hands finger by finger. Says something about my neighborhood.

"Some years later I studied literature at Ann Arbor. I was an 'A' student. I'm telling you this just so you appreciate I'm reasonably intelligent. Could be, this sounds to you like a typical sad-ass, self-serving excuse. I don't mean it to be. No excuses: a bunch of things happened. Confronted with these things, you might have done one thing. I'll tell you what I did. You can read the transcript later and get back to me with your considered opinion.

"Early on, my mom, and her full name was Irene O'Connell Kean, well she supplemented my dad's sporadic income with bartending. It's hard for a kid to have a sexy mom, because it's impossible not to see the way men looked at her. Or the way they would bend over the bar to order drinks or hit her up or talked about her when she was walking down the street … Actually, the way even my best friends looked at her.

"Things were pretty tough the first few months after we put my dad in the ground. My mom never let on but it was obvious there just wasn't enough money. And there were serious debts she never mentioned. Then suddenly something changed. I found myself sitting in the car, waiting for her to finish cleaning. That's what we called it. She called herself the cleaning lady: her second job, when she wasn't tending bar. And Donnie and I were stuck there together a few hours at a time in that old broken down used Pontiac. Not having any family to park us with, she knew there were limits to the trouble we could get into confined to the car, rather than at home in the apartment or, worst of all, out on the street. So she always took us with her.

"She'd give us each some comic books and candy bars with the strict instruction: never, ever leave the car. There were empty milk containers for us to piss in if we couldn't keep it in. Those were the nights that taught me about that other world. Of course, I never quite understood exactly how it worked then, but these cleaning jobs were way out of town, on tree-lined streets I never knew existed, with their large lawns and incredibly big houses. No apartment buildings; no busted streetlights; no gangs.

"It was a month or two into this two or three night a week routine, each night a different street, that something shifted, and our car kept returning to this one dead-end street with a beautiful big old wooden house. There had to be fifteen, twenty rooms, set at the top of what seemed like a never-ending football field. It took everything in the world for me not to bolt from the car and start running on the grass.

"Anyway, I started to turn the mystery of my mom's work into a puzzle that demanded to be decoded. The desire to figure things out shaped my life. What my mom was doing? Did the guy sitting across the poker table actually have the nut flush? Could be your theory about the two of us isn't all that wrong.

Seems we both became detectives of sorts.

"I started to wonder how many times a week you had to clean a house? When I asked, my mom said that the people in the house entertained a lot and were always making a mess. And that rich people always hired other people to clean up after them and always needed people to admire what they had.

"My mom, like a lot of beautiful women, was a lot smarter than people gave her credit for. She told me that I should always remember that it was these messes that fed us, so how about I shut my trap and quit complaining. I can still see her shaking her head. 'Unfortunately,' she said, 'it will all make sense soon enough.'

"Luckily, keeping Donnie inside the car and as quiet as possible was a full-time job. He was a restless kid, always wanting to move and jump around. That made it hard for me to get into any trouble. By then I had started to study, to read a lot, beginning to appreciate I needed a way out. We were all managing OK until that night a year in, when Donnie fell asleep, and his constant snoring got to me. It was too noisy. I couldn't do my homework. I felt trapped in there. I couldn't help myself: I just had to get out.

"I had to wander up the meadow, had to check out the house, had to walk around to the back, and then, of course, I had to peek in the window, to see what this cleaning was all about. And so I had to see my mom completely naked on the rug with this tall gray-haired old guy with no clothes except for a cowboy hat sitting on top of her, smacking her thighs like she was a horse. I stopped dead, my mouth hanging open. I was completely freaked out, totally humiliated.

"I was able to get it together quickly enough to get out of there before they saw me. But then the rage overtook me. I'm not making any excuses: it's just what happened. And this rage took hold of the deepest part of me.

"And we kept coming back. I knew somehow she was only doing what she needed to do to feed us. I never left the car again. And I must have known telling her would only make things worse. But deep down I felt responsible. Because if I were older, smarter, wasn't at school, if I had a job, made money, helped more, this wouldn't be happening. Soon after she got sick.

"I kept the secret of what I had seen for a few years after she died. But, as smart as I was, it slipped out of me over much too much Jack Daniels and coke with Donnie, and it was the last time I did coke.

"I didn't need drugs. Rage was rocket fuel for me. I learned to control it, called upon it to move faster and farther: to get away from the old neighborhood, to read anything and everything that might be useful. I used it defy expectations, to achieve more than anyone from the neighborhood might have imagined. I used it to become someone new. That sound familiar to you?

"And, you Detective, because you're an honest, law-abiding guy, you probably went to court to change your name. I started to play poker. It helps when, even though you're still basically a kid, you're the only one in the neighborhood who keeps track of the cards. And I won enough after a few months to give Sammy the Scratcher, Arthur's older cousin, a couple of thousand bucks to find me a dead kid's ID: Peter Bishop, who never made it a month.

"I took a shortcut. Looking back, it was a serious mistake to use someone in Arthur Flynn's family for such a sensitive task. Sammy promised no one would ever know. But I was young then and never imagined how entangled my family and Arthur's would get. Or how unlikely it was that someone like Sammy would ever keep his word. On the way over here before he dropped me off, Little Francis told me that ever since we were kids in school Arthur needed to know everything I was doing.

"If there is anything that counts as a mitigating factor for Donnie, it's the reality that learning about Mom's tricks, and the unceasing anger it sparked in him, were devastating. And he was angry to begin with. You could easily make the case that the mix of shame and fury drove him nuts. As my Psych Professor might have put it: Donnie just couldn't adequately process and accept the ambiguities of Mom's, or more accurately, our dilemma. He never made it to the place where he could appreciate the sacrifices she made to provide for us. It was a balancing act he couldn't manage. You know, he's never had a proper girlfriend.

"How are you with balancing, Detective Falco? How did you do with your family? Anyway, Donnie decided he hated Mom. Then he hated himself for hating her. He hated everything and everybody except me. I, on the other hand, hated the men who whistled at my mom, and more than anyone else, I despised the gray-haired guy atop her. I imagine the mark of a good detective is persistence, doggedly pursuing leads, with a bit of creative thinking thrown in. Never stopping until the perpetrator is brought to justice. I can relate.

"When I was older I spent months taking trips out from the city to the surrounding suburbs and towns, trying to find that house again. One house here in Little Pointe is worth a city block where I came from.

"It's rather remarkable what a thrift store Italian suit and tie and several trips to the Assessors Office can accomplish. And I found it. It's just a couple of miles from here. Owned by ACD, Incorporated. Abigail and Courtney Davis, the parents of the smart and lovely Penelope.

"Jumping ahead a bit, do you know that there wasn't a day I saw Courtney that I didn't see him as he was that night, playing cowboy, pinning my mother to the floor. And over the years I often saw him in a tux at fancy dinners, chit-chatting with senators and congressmen, giving speeches to the Chamber of Commerce, on the yacht, on the golf course and at the dinner table: but to me he was always naked, always the object of my unadulterated hatred. So maybe, like Donnie, I can get some expert to testify at my trial that such sustained loathing is prima facie evidence of mental incompetence. That's the expression, right, for what's pretty damn obvious. I guess the question for the jury is for how long a time can you be considered temporarily insane? Two decades?

"Speaking of mitigating circumstances, pretty much of everything that's on Donnie is really on me. I left him behind. He never really understood what I was up to, and I knew I couldn't pull off my transformation with him in the picture. It has to have messed him up even more. Just another wretched secret. And he always looked up to me. While I got pretty good at using my brains, he got really good at using his fists. So he always did my dirty work.

"You know, Arthur knew more about what was going on with the two of us than we did. Our lives became his own private movie. I was playing cards four or five times a week at his place, sometimes during the day and other times at night, telling Penny

I was working on deals, while Donnie was peddling Arthur's coke, collecting his money, and occasionally breaking bones for him. Together we made a shitload of money for him ... Except, unfortunately, for that last half mil I lost ...

"But I digress, and by the way, don't think I don't appreciate what a good job you've done getting me to talk. I probably would have anyway, but I might have made the locals wait a while longer.

"Maybe it's as simple as he took my mother, I took his daughter. That sounds a bit crazy, doesn't it? But I wonder: is revenge a kind of justice or a form of evil? I suspect I'm going to have a lot of time to think about it. There's got to be a poker game in prison, right?

"I was about to say that it was easy to meet Penny, to get her to love me. But I don't think that's true. It doesn't account for the hours and hours I spent reading, the hours and hours learning how to speak college-speak, and how to navigate a fucking formal table. The street is a million miles from Little Pointe.

"Not to mention all the bullshit I had to listen to over the years from them all. About the right tailor, the best appetizer, what to say to the Governor and when to say it? Do you have any idea how much time wealthy people waste talking about stuff that doesn't matter? With almost no clue about what life is like for just about everyone else in the universe. My mom who never graduated high school knew more about real life than that entire family.

"Courtney, of course, would never have let me, the Petey me, anywhere near his precious pedigreed daughter, while Penny, on the other hand, seemed not to care about that stuff. I can remember how she blew my mind by hiring this Mexican kid to take care of the grounds. No references. Never checked a thing about him. She said she had 'a good feeling' about him. 'Good feeling,' you've got to be kidding me ...

"You play cards? Spades? You think that maybe hate trumps love? If I tried really hard to separate Penny out from her dad, I could love her. Only I couldn't sustain it ... And she didn't make it easy. She loved the S.O.B.

"Imagine my surprise when I discovered I wasn't the only one in that family doing such a tortured dance. It didn't take long for me to see the incredibly controlled contempt of my mother-in-law. Abigail was a master of the false smile. At public events, she would look at her husband with what appeared to be great appreciation, and when being watched, allowed all sorts of the small affectionate gestures happy couples share, only to turn completely cold when no one was there. To flick his hands away. Maybe she had walked in on the same kind of scene I had witnessed? Maybe, by then, she, too, could only see Courtney naked on top of someone else?

"So there were three accomplished liars, three betrayers, in this small family: three out of four. Courtney was perpetually cheating on Abigail. Abigail pretended she loved him and never told her daughter the truth about her father or their marriage. And I was cheating on them all. Only Penelope was sincere. Heartfelt but blind. In a way, I always felt the most sorry for her."

Petey paused, "Because, if I'm being honest, I despised her ability not to see, not to know, to be so oblivious ... Anyway, besides taking his daughter, I was going to take his land. I still feel like some of that land should have gone to my mom. Do you know she continued to lie there beneath him even as she wasted away? Do you think he even noticed? Even cared she had cancer?

"And, of course, she had no medical insurance. I'm not the first son or daughter to watch a parent suffer because they have shitty healthcare and I won't be the last. But the contrast between the money Courtney was sitting on, and the avoidable pain my mother endured only made things worse for me. Twisted me even more. And whenever I felt guilty or conflicted about what I was doing to Penny, I just had to look in Courtney's eyes and I could continue on ...

"Maybe things would have been different if the guy from Lehman Brothers hadn't pulled the aces boat on me. But that's also on me. I played like a mark. I lost a hand I couldn't afford to lose. And you don't want to lose playing with Arthur's money."

Petey shook his head sadly. "At least I knew I was not who I said I was. I always knew I was committing a fraud. At the university, they were all so sanctimonious and holier than thou charging for an education they knew was hardly worth the fortune it cost.

"I was lucky. I got a full scholarship. I feel bad for the suckers with their student loans. The professors peddling the power of words ... As if reading 'Moby Dick' was ever going to make those bullying frat boys who were constantly obsessed with proving themselves to their rich dads any less obsessed with 'success.' As if studying 'Hamlet' could make any young man more tolerant of his mother's decision to sleep with a pig ... Give me a break. As if there was anything I could say to Arthur that would have made a bit of difference ... "

Petey lost the thread of his argument. He looked down to the chains that bound him, then back up to Frank. "Where was I?"

Frank smiled: "You were just about to tell me why you tried to kill your wife."

"Funny, Detective ... Am I boring you?"

"Not at all ... I was just thinking that once you sell your story to the movies, they'll probably want to zip ahead to the part where Brad Pitt decides to get rid of Angelina Jolie."

"No 'Hamlet' for you, Detective, no prolonged agonizing over the meaning of it all ..."

"Don't they all pretty much die at the end of that play?"

"Point taken. So I'll tell the movie makers it was all about getting the bastard back. Taking what was important to him. When I say taking, I really wasn't thinking violence. I was going to do it using my brains. I had the daughter and, if I hadn't messed up with Arthur, I would have had the time to figure out how to get the land. You have any idea how much that land is worth?

"My plan was perfect. Take all that open space, put up a big beautiful gate, install a state-of-the-art security system. Build luxury homes with private docks and all that extra eco-green stuff to make them feel virtuous. Knowing they'll pay a fortune for the privilege of living far away from people like you and me.

"But that goddamn ace did me in. The one card that changed everything for me.

"All of a sudden the clock was ticking. For me, the long-term became the short-term. Unfortunately, as far as Arthur was concerned, there never was a long term: an extension, maybe two. And so I really, really needed the land.

"Maybe my poker mistake affected everything else. I lost my edge. I'd been waiting for the old guy to die for years. But I waited too long. The son-of-a-bitch decided he needed a final grand gesture: to preserve the land, my land. For the dead wife he betrayed there week after week. Turns out there's no hand better than a rich bastard's dying wish. So there it was: he was going to screw me one last time, just like he screwed my mom. And, as always, Penny was determined to respect his wishes.

"The truth is my instincts were shot. Toward the end, it felt as if something shifted in Penny. All of a sudden, she, too, was slipping away from me. I didn't have enough time to fix things with Penny. Not enough time to fix anything.

"Arthur hurts people. To be precise, Arthur has people hurt, the people who don't pay their debts. Then, if they still can't pay, he has them killed.

"Which meant I needed Penny gone. As for my desire to make this happen peacefully ... well, I wish that would have worked out ... Anyway, with Penny gone, even if I couldn't manage to pull off the land deal in time, I could at least give Arthur some of the life insurance money ... I could live another day."

"Why Donnie?"

"I'm not able to do what Donnie does. I never was. There are lots of ways to hurt people. But bashing them over the head, shooting them, constitutionally that's more Donnie's style and, from what you've told me, your style. I know it's not fair getting someone else to do your dirty work but we do it all the time. Isn't that what cops are for, the army? Donnie was my army of one," and Petey's voice trailed off.

Frank waited a few moments. "Well, considering Donnie's experience and predilection, that's a college word, right Petey, Donnie's predilection for violence, don't you think it's interesting that Penny somehow made it out of your house alive and managed to make it to Massachusetts?"

"Yes, I do think it's interesting. Maybe Penny was Donnie's ace: the moment that changed everything, when everything went wrong. Maybe when it came down to it, he wasn't able to look her in the eye and kill her."

"You know, Petey, you haven't really asked me about what happened with Donnie?"

"So tell me, Detective, tell me about Donnie ..."

"Well Petey, I'm assuming Donnie did almost everything you

asked him to do. He found Penelope's friend, Deb. And through Deb, he found Penelope. Unfortunately, Penelope had made her way to my sister's house in Ripton. Where my sister and her boyfriend were. I don't know whether Donnie was prepared to kill Penelope, and my sister, and Ralph, Ralph Parker, but Donnie only managed to kill Ralph.

"Somehow, before he died, Ralph managed to fire his shotgun. Donnie took it in the gut and so far he's managed to survive. Ralph is, was, a well-liked local. A farmer. What do I know: I'm from New York City. But it turns out farmers are like an endangered species out there. They love farmers and Ripton is a very small town. I wouldn't want to be Donnie facing a local jury and a judge who most likely went to school with Ralph's parents."

"Well, like I said, Detective, any juror who spends more than a minute listening to Donnie will clearly get that he's missing some brain cells. The least I can do is put it all in context. I should never have gone in with kings full."

"Context. The local constabulary will be glad to give you a pad and pencil. All you have to do is provide the context. The more context you give, the better off Donnie will be. Thanks for telling me the story, Petey. We're done here."

And with that Frank was up out of his seat and out the door. He walked into the hallway where Penny and the Chief were waiting: "I told two lies. I told him his brother is still alive, and I didn't tell him that Penny was the one to shoot him. I put it on my sister's boyfriend, Ralph, the guy Donnie killed. I'm pretty sure he's ready to write it all out. Thanks, Chief."

Penny walked up to him and threw her arms around him. The tears streamed down her face and he held tight as the spasms of grief rippled through her.

SIXTY-TWO

Katie hoped her heartfelt letter to the Parkers would help them understand why she skipped the memorial service, but you never knew. Small towns relentlessly enforced what they regarded as propriety. And most people would regard missing the funeral of your boyfriend as more than just a social misdemeanor.

Anne insisted Katie take some time off from "Books" and so she spent hours each day with Rabbit. He made the kitchen his new home, resting on the same floor he almost died on. When Katie couldn't be with him, Danger took over. Walking awkwardly along the floor or gently perching on Rabbit's bandaged shoulder. Offering an occasional "sorry" when Rabbit shifted to find a less painful position.

Katie missed Ralph and missing Ralph reminded her how much she missed Carl and Theresa.

She spoke to Frank and Penny by phone every evening after dinner. They both seemed stronger. Penny was discovering more and more of her past life as she dealt with her father's estate and the reality that her husband was in jail. She was, she told Katie, obscenely rich now. And Frank, she told Katie, had proven to be a reasonable facsimile of the superior man. It was probably a little too soon, but Katie could see them sleeping together.

It took Penny only a week to start divorce proceedings, and to put the Lakeview Drive house on the market. She asked Michael Barton, her new lawyer, to secure the conservation of the Potter Road property with the single condition that Juan Castillo be employed as the well-paid, live-in caretaker of the house and land as long as he wanted the job. She instructed Michael and her new-found bevy of financial advisors to spend whatever it took, and use whatever political influence they had to secure legal status for the Castillos, and to help bring José's wife and son up from Mexico. And she asked them to discreetly purchase two businesses: Dom's Restaurant in Brett, Massachusetts in the name of Deborah Spencer, and Enrique's in Detroit in trust for José Castillo. With ownership to revert to him when his legal status was resolved. Then she and Frank flew back to the Berkshires.

SIXTY-THREE

Danger moved up onto Frank's shoulder for a better view, while Rabbit stretched his legs and slowly moved to rest against Penny's leg. Katie poured tea for Penny and then herself. Frank had a mug of iced coffee in front of him. Katie looked at Penny: "After all that has happened, it's remarkable that we're here at my table again and you're back at Bea Foster's."

"It was hard," Penny began. "In Little Pointe, I had to face the fact that what I used to imagine as my life back there was so very disappointing. Do you remember telling me that there are different forms of amnesia? Pretty ironic. Once I was able to remember seeing Donnie on the steps, the memories came flooding back. I went from not remembering what had gone on to realizing that I hadn't really seen or appreciated so much of what was actually happening. And having to acknowledge that I had been living one life, while my husband and parents were living another. It's humiliating and humbling.

"By the time I saw Donnie on the stairs I had begun to accept that my husband, my marriage, my life wasn't what I imagined. But then, as the gun came toward me, maybe that was too much for me. I don't know enough about the mind. About what you do with the knowledge that your husband, the man you have loved all these years, now wants to kill you? Maybe I didn't want to know that, wasn't ready to accept that?

"Do you remember the first time I came here? I threw 'Chieh' and the coins asked me to think about the lake and the land, and of loyalty and disinterest. While I was away I went back to read it again.

"My father, my mother, my husband were loyal only to their own twisted interests. At first I was convinced 'Chieh' was about someone else. About someone I couldn't remember. Exceeding limits; about their extravagances. But the question I had asked was 'Why am I here?'

"I know from the dreams I was having at Bea's, that as a girl I could see what was happening. But I wasn't strong enough to do anything about it. And so, on some level, I must have decided not to notice. Why? Because ours was such an easy life, an extravagant life. As much as I'd like to blame my parents and blame Peter, I, too, without hesitation, accepted these limitations. And if I was going to stay within our world, accept the great privileges and advantages of our life, well then I wouldn't see.

"I wrote this down," taking a sheet of paper from the right hand pocket of her jeans. This is what 'Chieh' says:

> If he gives himself over to extravagance, he will suffer the consequences, with accompanying regret. He must not seek to lay the blame on others. Only when we realize that our mistakes are of our own making will such disagreeable experiences free us of errors.

"All of us found different ways to prolong and protect and exploit this privilege. My mother and father and I were born to it. Peter – and thanks to you and Frank I now know who 'the man of false pretenses' is – well, Peter spent an enormous amount of energy, used so much of his impressive mind to wrest some of it from my father.

"Is it possible that for all those years Peter could never really see me without seeing my father on top of his mother? And how could I have not known that, not seen that?

"And so now I have to wonder: what if my husband and Donnie hadn't finally forced me out that door? Would I ever have left on my own?

"Is there a better place to do that wondering, do that work than here? When I understood how hollow my life had been, it made me want to return to the place where who I was, or where I came from didn't seemed to matter. Peter picked me because I was my father's daughter; Deb couldn't have cared less about my father; and you helped me simply because you knew I needed help.

"Maybe it will take forgetting who I was to become who I want to be. For now, I'm close enough to New York to drive – and I do know how to drive – into the city once a week to work with the therapist Dr. Silver recommended, and to work with you. In time, I'd like to find an unpretentious and charming house like yours up here. I have no idea what's next for me. Except that I'd like whatever happens to happen here."

Danger looked over to Katie, and then to Frank, as if waiting for their reaction. He paused, then looked to Penny and asked: "What?"

Penny laughed, then looking into Danger's eyes: "Not bad, Danger. 'What?' That's the question. What, indeed? What's next?"

Danger mimicked Penny's laugh, then looked to Katie and asked: "What?" And then over to Frank with his last "What?"

"Well, Danger," Katie replied, "I've never done this before … but maybe you're right. 'What?' is the question for all three of us. Maybe for all four of us, Danger, if you're up for it?"

Frank laughed. "OK, so I leave my bird with you for a week and a half and now he's your enthusiastic *I Ching* accomplice? Are you suggesting that we all ask the same question?"

"Why not? We can take turns throwing the coins."

"Won't you get fined for violating the rules of the International Order of Working Wizards?"

"Not unless you drop a dime on me and tell them."

Penny smiled, then reached for the three coins, looking back to Danger: "What's next?" she asked as she threw the coins. Three tails, a broken line with the changing straight line. She handed the coins to Frank, and began to draw the hexagrams.

"What's next?" he asked, and tossed two heads and a tail, another broken line.

Katie looked first to Frank and then Penny, and while asking "What's next?" threw two tails and a head, a straight line.

Penny's second throw was two heads and a tail, another eight, another broken line.

Frank duplicated Penny's last throw and his first: two heads and a tail.

Katie looked to Danger, smiled, then asked the question for the last time: "What's next?" and threw the third eight in a row, two heads and a tail.

Penny passed the hexagrams she had drawn to Katie, who quickly found them in the index and began to read aloud:

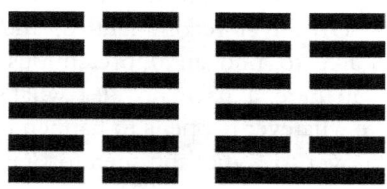

"The first hexagram is 'Ch'ien / Modesty,' and the second is 'Ming I /Darkening of the Light.'"

Frank shook his head: "Here we go again, Danger!"

Danger flew back to the top of his cage, then looked back to Frank: "Sorry!"

Frank laughed: "Me, too."

Rabbit moved over to lie beside Frank.

Katie started to read:

Ch'ien / Modesty.

THE JUDGMENT
MODESTY creates success.
The superior man carries things through.

Katie turned the page and skipped ahead:

... the superior man can carry out his work to the
end without boasting of what he has achieved ...
he imposes no demands or stipulations but settles
matters easily and quickly ...

No one spoke. Danger concentrated on cleaning his feathers. Frank was thinking about Katie, and her understated ability to slowly guide Penny from an almost complete paralysis to self-awareness. How in her own absolutely eccentric way she had taken Carl and Theresa's concern for others and made a simple yet completely sincere life for herself. And though he could see the deep and abiding grief she carried with her, there was no self-pity, only the desire to modestly carry on.

Penny felt waves of gratitude moving through her. For this brother and sister, so very different from each other on the surface, yet both willing to work on her behalf. She couldn't help but think about the people she had lived amongst: her mother and father, a marriage of accommodation, a continuing façade that masked dreadful grievances; her husband, so twisted by humiliation he would waste both their lives; and finally, her husband's brother, known to her now only because his older brother had asked him to kill her. The brother-in-law she had killed.

Penny knew that she had scarcely taken in all that had happened that afternoon. The act itself driven by instinct, fueled by adrenaline. She couldn't really remember the moment she had decided to fire the shotgun, if there had ever been a decision. Having gotten to know Frank a bit better, she could see that a killing never left you. For the moment, she had moved it away from the center of her consciousness. But she knew it was there, waiting for her.

Through the layers of guilt and pain, the loss of Ralph, her worry for Rabbit, Katie could see Penny, and Frank, more clearly than ever. For Penny had successfully grown to inhabit, then replace Sarah. And Katie was extraordinarily proud of Penny's unwavering willingness to dig deep to find herself.

She couldn't help but acknowledge the great energy she had wasted all these years in annoyance, in the misperceived belief that Frank didn't understand and love and respect her. Realizing now that what had been happening between them was merely their differences smacking up against each other, not in the most important way, the way they treated people, but in the ways they talked and walked about the world, the attitudes they had adopted to cope with their pain. They had merely chosen different ways to survive the darkness and despair that comes with living. Because, once again when it mattered most, Frank had proven he was right there for her.

Some of the exhaustion of the last days started to lift from her. Then she remembered there was still more the *I Ching* had to offer.

She began to turn the pages until she found "Ming I" and quietly began to read aloud:

Ming I, the Darkening of the Light.

In adversity
It furthers one to be persevering.

Here the Lord of Light is in a subordinate place and is wounded by the Lord of Darkness. But the injury is not fatal; it is only a hindrance. Rescue is still possible. The wounded man gives no thought to himself; he thinks only of saving the others who are also in danger ...

Almost in unison, the three of them looked to the top of the cage. And Danger, hearing his name, looked down on them, and asked once more: "What?"

Katie smiled, then continued:

> Therefore he tries with all his strength to save all that can be saved.

> This provides a teaching for those who cannot leave their posts in times of darkness. In order to escape danger, they need invincible perseverance of spirit and redoubled caution in their dealings with the world.

> The dark power ... in the end ... perishes of its own darkness, for evil must itself fall at the very moment when it has wholly overcome the good, and thus consumed the energy to which it owed its duration.

Tears formed in Penny's eyes: "Remember what you told me when I first met you, Katie, that every story was different? And that neither of us knows what the story is. Well, my story has plunged us all into the depths of darkness, you especially. You cared for me, you guided me, and you've paid an unimaginable price.

"While I had stumbled out the door in Little Pointe, I hadn't really gotten away from the darkness. I brought it with me. As for what's next, it's time for me to recreate some order in my life, to find some modest way to continue on. Or, as our *I Ching* puts it, somehow summon that 'invincible perseverance of spirit.' And because I have been so supremely naïve and unaware, to find that extra amount of caution as I move forward."

Katie hesitated, remembering back to those days when she first met Penny.

"I might have said something about chance and coincidence. Or something about how we would see where the coins and the story would take us. Well, this time your story in so many ways became my story and, in the end, my story yours. We were both in danger.

"Everything the *I Ching* has been telling us indicates this is part of a much larger story. A story that requires us to be brave at times, yet modest, willing to risk and persevere in risk. A story that reminds me of my parents, and a story that requires me to be more like Frank. And for helping me understand that, Penny, I'll be grateful forever. I might even see if I can get you a Certificate of Appreciation from the International Order of Working Wizards."

SIXTY-FOUR

The night before Frank decided to head home, his union lawyer called to say that the City of New York and the kid's family had settled out of court. The City's insurance company had agreed to pick up the tab and the family had signed a confidentiality agreement, so there was no chance that any more about the incident would become public. And it was likely, once the Departmental shrink signed off on it, that he could be back on the street within a month.

Katie made sure that he took a copy of the *I Ching* and a set of llama coins back with him to the city. He had thought about leaving Danger with Katie and Rabbit, but it didn't seem fair to make him adjust to yet another new custody arrangement. And the truth was, Frank wasn't yet prepared for a life without him. As crazy as Dr. Silver's scheme had seemed to him at first, it had worked. Danger was now a friend, now family.

As he drove home and the hills faded and the suburbs bloomed, Frank felt the sadness grow. There were decisions to be made. All of a sudden, a BMW swerved from the right lane directly in front of him. Frank hit the brakes and Danger's cage smacked into the dashboard. Danger squawked several times.

"Sorry, Danger. Sorry."

Danger cleared his throat, then announced: "Here a quack. There a quack."

Frank started to laugh. And from beneath the covered cage, mimicking in perfect pitch, a second Frank laugh, even louder. They laughed and laughed. Frank had his coins, his *I Ching*, and his bird.

THE END

ABOUT THE AUTHOR

Mickey Friedman is the author of *A Red Family: Junius, Gladys, and Barbara Scales,* the non-fiction oral history of a unique American Communist family, University of Illinois Press, 2009. You can learn more about it at aredfamily.com.

He has made documentary films about a wide range of subjects, including U.S./Nicaraguan relations, breast cancer, GE and its misuse of PCBs, and one soldier's year in Iraq.

The television adaptation of his play *Songs From The Heart: Edith Wharton* aired on BRAVO and PBS, and was nominated in 1988 for the Best Dramatic Special on Cable TV. A copy of *Songs* is in the Museum of Broadcasting. You can watch his films on YouTube and http://www.mickeyfriedman.com/?page_id=14.

He writes a newspaper column twice a month for The Berkshire Record. And is preparing a collection of these columns, *The Best Small Town in America.* In the meantime, many of them can be found at redcrownews.com.

He is hard at work on his second *I Ching* novel.